Stealing His Heart

P. A. DePaul

Northfair Publishing

Northfair Publishing

352 2ND Street Pike, 291, Southampton, PA 18966;

contact@northfairpublishing.com

STEALING HIS HEART

A Northfair Publishing Book/ published by arrangement with the author

PUBLISHING HISTORY

Northfair Publishing / 2024

eBook ISBN: 978-1-959324-06-5
Paperback ISBN: 978-1-959324-07-2

Dedication

This is for those who cherish love and loyalty.

Acknowledgments

Writing a book is hard. I'm not gonna lie. Some days are so rewarding I feel like I can accomplish anything. Other days, I wonder if I know how to tie my shoes. But, at the end of all the writing and editing (and more editing. Plus more editing), I have a story I'm proud of. This is one of those stories.

I am not smart enough or motivated enough to write a book all by myself. I need support, technical help, and sounding boards when I'm stuck. I'd like to thank the following people for providing their knowledge and feedback: Anne Angst, Amie Gledhill, Kate Forest, Michelle Grajkowski, and my dad (he came up with the ladder backpack. I love the way his mind works).

But above all, I thank you, my reader. You are the most important person to me. {{HUGS}}

Chapter 1

I should have thought through my position inside the aged wooden barrel a lot harder before I wiggled and curled my five-foot-two frame to fit within. Four hours ago.

In my long list of heists, this job won the award for Most Uncomfortable I Refuse To Do It Again, or Smuggling Position Never To Be Repeated, or whatever negative would fit on the certificate.

"I can't scratch my forehead," I whined under my breath. My thighs pressed against my breasts to the point I feared I permanently smashed my C-cups into Bs, but I still couldn't force my arm to slide from hugging my shins over my knees. "It's starting to sting."

"Holly," the raspy voice of my uncle Liam barked in the flesh-toned earpiece shoved deep in my ear, *"quiet. There's finally movement on the set again."*

We had been planning this gig for months, fine-tuning until we all knew our roles by rote. But none of us imagined the lead actor would be dumb enough to walk backwards while talking on a set full of pitfalls. Just as he started to turn, he smacked into some two-by-fours hauled on the shoulders of two crewmen. The director had to stop production for a medical assessment (no concussion) and makeup refresh.

Which left me in my current predicament. Stuck like an untrained contortionist, impatiently waiting with an unrelieved itch.

I tucked my chin, trying to rub my forehead against my knees. Dammit. I only managed to smash my eyes into my kneecaps, which meant my mascara probably smeared like a drunk girl partying too hard.

"Reggie," I whispered even softer, having complete faith in our tech. "When you meet me, bring something to wipe my face."

"Too late, Bells," Reggie answered through the earpiece right before two taps against the wooden cask thumped my back. *"I'm already here."*

Bells. From the first day Uncle Liam brought Reggie onto the team a year ago, he refused to call me anything else. Though, with a name like Holly Bell, my nickname could have been a lot worse.

Soft thunking invaded the complete darkness surrounding me, then suddenly light. I blinked rapidly as I lifted my head, focusing on the thirty-one-year-old, acne-scarred face peering down at me. "Scratch my forehead."

Reggie ignored my demand. Instead, he shoved his lanky arms inside and grasped my shoulders. "The hungover look doesn't exactly work for today's job."

I forced my blood-deprived legs to push, and with his help, we pried me out of the barrel.

"Ow. Ow. Ow." I crumpled to the grass beside an immaculately trimmed, tall hedge maze as blood rushed through my legs, making them tingle and burn. Precious sunlight caressed my skin, and I soaked it in as I chafed my spandex-clad calves and scraped my forehead against the grass for relief.

Reggie slapped the top back on the barrel, one in a grouping of four, and pounded it back in place with a mallet.

"I warned you I needed a wet wipe." Sitting up, I stretched my arms above my head and reveled in feeling my muscles moving fluidly again. Movie sets, whether on location or in a studio, had a ton of security measures to keep crazed fans, lurkers, and reporters out. Crew badges had to be displayed at all times, and the volunteer extras needed for background filming were militantly watched to make sure they didn't go anywhere they weren't supposed to be. Hence my fun time in the barrel. Security checkpoint averted. All I had to do was don my disguise and blend in with the paid actors, leaving me virtually invisible to the hired guards the insurance company demanded be on-site.

"Two guards coming your way," my uncle, the leader of our crew, snapped from overhead inside the cushy helicopter he had rented to oversee the entire layout.

I rolled and clapped my sports-bra-clad back against two of the barrels, resuming the tucked position I'd just escaped. Reggie shifted to stand in front of me, further hiding me from anyone walking by from the side. The crew badge dangling off the left edge of his sweaty navy T-shirt swung with his movements, smacking me in the head.

"Seriously?" I muttered, dropping my chin to keep from losing an eye while my knees protested returning to the tight position.

"Sorry," Reggie grunted, his legs knocking against mine as he shifted back.

As a twenty-eight-year-old, tragically single woman, my current arrangement could have been fun if it weren't for the fact that I had *zero* attraction to or chemistry with Reggie. Sigh. Good thing I got more of a rush from my job than sex.

"Everything okay here?" a gruff male voice asked just on the other side of the barrels.

"Yep." Reggie's badge bobbed as he motioned to the casks. "About to move these into place."

"Fine," the guard answered, then I heard a soft shuffling.

"Clear." Reggie jumped to the right.

I exhaled. That was too close.

"Two minutes," Uncle Liam announced through my earpiece. *"Get a move on, Holly, or you're not going to be in position."*

Reggie tore the top off another barrel and yanked out a black duffle, tossing it to the thick grass beside me.

I pulled out a peach dress, then cursed at the evil contraption lying on top of the cloak at the bottom. "I hate corsets. I can't breathe in them."

"Suck it up, Bells." Reggie turned his back and crossed his arms. If he wanted to act like a wall to shield me from passersby, he needed to gain at least fifty pounds to be effective. "This all rides on you playing your role."

Duh. Every single member of the four-person crew had a part to play, but I always had the hardest and most daring: the actual theft.

I jammed the corset around my ribs and sucked in a breath. Sometimes my uncle's restricted diet came in handy. Given how much time I spent forcing myself into the tightest spaces or into the evilest fashions for the job, he was right to limit my intake of fried food ...not that his rules stopped me from sneaking off to indulge.

Thankfully, the lengthy strings to secure the corset were designed so I could quickly fasten Satan's garment myself. Whipping my sports bra off, I wormed into the long-sleeved peach dress circa the early 1800s over my head, then jammed my feet into the ballet-style flats.

The fourth and final member of our crew, Gretchen, had all kinds of mad skills including sewing (she soared past my limitation of button replacement). She had designed and sewed everything into one piece, so I didn't have to fool with tunics, crinolines, or underskirts. I didn't need to be period accurate, I just needed the disguise to keep me from standing out. The high waistline gave me plenty of freedom to move my legs, but the corset already had me taking shallower breaths.

"The armored truck just pulled up with the sword," Gretchen announced through my earpiece.

Damn. I hoisted myself up.

Reggie swiped the flowing cloak out of the duffle and plopped it over my shoulders. I tied the leather cords together to keep it from falling off and raised the hood to hide my face and cover the shoulder-length black wig.

"It's too hot for this thing." The Georgia humidity had eased for October, but a line of sweat trickled between my poor, abused breasts.

"You have a better way to hide this and remain unnoticed?" Reggie dropped the empty duffle inside the barrel, lifting up the final item. A three-foot long claymore. An exact replica of the fifteenth-century sword. The pièce de résistance was the huge emerald (or, in our case, colored cubic zirconia) inside the round pommel and smaller "emeralds" along the scabbard.

I still couldn't believe the studio intended to use the real claymore in today's scene. It hadn't been seen in public for more than a hundred years, but when egos were involved, I guessed it wasn't that far of a stretch. The man who wrote the screenplay and forked over a hefty sum to fund the movie was also the oldest living member of the family who had the claymore in their possession. He had a whole marketing tour set up to pat himself on the back for infusing authenticity into the film—

"If you don't get your ass in gear, Holly," Uncle Liam growled, *"you're going to miss the window to make the swap without detection."*

I scowled. Easy for him to rule on high. He relaxed in leg-stretching comfort. I had only just gotten free after four hours of cramped boredom. I needed a bag of Skittles and a Coke, stat.

Tying the fake sword to the leather cords sewn into the cloak near my armpit, I tucked one arm inside to keep the claymore from giving away I was hiding something.

"No sign of your boyfriend yet, Holly," Gretchen chirped from her vantage point of the craft services trailer near the main thoroughfare that led to open space and the parking lot.

A jolt rippled through my parts that hadn't seen action in waaaaay too long. "He's not my boyfriend."

Didn't mean I didn't fantasize about FBI Agent Jackson Kendrick late at night or in the shower when I had the pulse setting on the showerhead pounding against my lady bits. No one needed to know either one of those sad facts.

Gretchen laughed, her girlish voice turning it into a giggle. *"Face it. A small part of you is hoping he'll figure out where we are and show up to foil our dastardly plot."*

For the past six months, the disturbingly gorgeous man had latched onto our tail and refused to let go. How did he do it? The question vexed me so much I fretted we had a mole in our midst, but that would mean Uncle Liam, Reggie, or Gretchen squealed, and I just refused to believe it.

The walkie-talkie clipped to Reggie's back pocket squealed. *"Need those barrels moved to Quadrant H now."*

Right. Showtime. I stepped around Reggie masquerading as a prop handler and crested the small but steep hill. The organized chaos of a nineteenth-century drama had come to life. The story had everything to do with the rightful ownership of the sword as told from only one side—not surprising with the source of the funding and the screenplay. The other family laying claim to the claymore (our client) didn't bother going to Hollywood or refuting the inaccurate history online—the court of social media was too fickle. Instead, they hired us to seize the sword and return it to them, the true heirs.

The chateau, thirty miles west of Macon, was adorned with so much foliage I could hardly see the fresh coat of paint gleaming beneath. Small gravel stones in the paths snaking across sections of the expansive back lawn bit into the bottoms of my thin, flat shoes, making me long for my beloved cross-trainers, but I kept going, promising my feet a spa day tomorrow.

My gaze landed on an athletic man in a security uniform complete with a black baseball cap pulled low. He jogged down the patio hardscaping's steps, holding the scabbarded sword in gloved hands.

The sun bounced off the massive emerald (real, unlike ours) in the pommel, sending my heart palpitating. I couldn't wait to wrap my hands around the piece of history.

From what Reggie could uncover, the guard would hand the claymore to the Props Master, who would give it to the actor at the right time.

Hustling toward the table set up on the outskirts of a tea party scene, I—

"Oh. Shit," I breathed, slowing my pace. "Change of plans." Pulling my hood forward to cover my face, I hissed, "It's Kendrick."

Chapter 2

"Goddamn it,"* Uncle Liam barked, causing my eardrums to vibrate with his vehemence. *"How the hell did he know we'd be going after the claymore?"*

Excellent question. I *really* needed to find out the answer.

"Everyone, abort," Uncle Liam commanded. *"Find your way to the warehouse—"*

"I'm not leaving." I edged closer to the second-tier actors and actresses having their faces touched up by makeup or sipping on bottled water.

"Holly, this is not negotiable," my uncle snarled. *"We'll step back. Replan—"*

"We can't," I whispered, bowing my head and sliding my free hand beneath the hood as if clutching a cellphone so I didn't draw any attention. "We've already analyzed every aspect of the sword's journey after today's filming. This is the most vulnerable point. We have to try."

My gaze flitted to Agent Kendrick now standing beside the props table, talking to the Props Master. By the fierce frown on the Props Master's face, he didn't appreciate Kendrick refusing to relinquish the sword.

Dammit. Of course the man would crap all over our preparations and strategies. "I'm going to Plan C."

"We don't have a Plan C," Reggie unhelpfully pointed out.

Keeping my movements relaxed, I turned to face the rest of the lawn. Reggie clutched a beat-up red hand truck with the last of the barrels strapped to it.

An idea sparked, and I straightened. "Reggie, do the other two barrels that came in with me still have your unique goodies inside?"

Reggie whipped his head toward me. *"Yeah...your Plan C need an explosive distraction?"*

"The biggest."

"Count me in."

"No," Uncle Liam snapped. *"It's too risky. Abort now."*

An old-timey school bell suddenly blasted, warning the cast to move into place.

"We don't have time to argue." I melded in with the other actors and actresses tromping onto the tea party set. Our client was counting on us to return their heirloom. "Gretchen, you do need to abort. Reggie, on my signal, light them up as close to Kendrick as safely possible, then hightail it. I'll meet everyone at the warehouse."

"We're going to talk about this insubordination, Holly," Uncle Liam growled from the still-circling helicopter.

Cramps gripped my gut, but I ignored them. Uncle Liam could talk all he wanted. As long as the team delivered the sword as promised, I wouldn't regret a thing.

Sticking close to a set of ladies standing near the tables featuring fine china and gossipy women, I surreptitiously kept my eye on the scabbarded sword. Kendrick passed it to the lead actor—the idiot who had almost knocked himself out—but didn't let go.

Idiot frowned and yanked, but Kendrick easily maintained his grip as he swiped his eagle-eyed gaze over the assemblage.

I ducked to hide behind a wall of actresses in voluminous dresses and winced at the corset biting into my ribs. *Stupid thing.*

"Places," the assistant director yelled just as another man quick-stepped in front of one of the cameras with a clapboard denoting the scene information.

Kendrick let go and crossed his arms over his too-well-defined chest. Polyester button-downs should *not* look that good on anyone. Neither should baseball hats show off perfectly defined cheekbones and an angular jaw.

Idiot strutted to his mark. The lead actress lifted her chin and fiddled with the enormous hat perched on her head, completely ignoring her counterpart.

"Quiet on the set," the assistant yelled.

"Action," the director commanded.

Actors and actresses sprang to life. Fake laughter and murmured conversations filled the background with the two leads' lines rising above. As unobtrusively as possible, I untied the fake sword from my cloak and mingled with a different set of men and women strolling toward Idiot who played the role of an earl.

The script called for a huge fight, and the volume rose as the leads traded cheeky insults. The attendees quieted and stopped milling to stare at the couple.

Damn. I paused, too, but I needed to get closer.

Earl Idiot thrusted the sword horizontally into the space between him and the "countess" while emphasizing some point or other. The leading actress latched onto the scabbard, trying to wrestle it from him.

Gasps and tittering rose as the guests crept forward, drawn into the drama of the scandalous fight.

Keep going, people. I wended through the throng, doing my best to stay on the outer edge so Kendrick couldn't lock on to me.

"Get ready, Reggie," I murmured, flitting to the next group who gossiped behind gloved hands.

"I'm good to go." Reggie patted the top edge of a barrel.

The countess shrieked and wrenched the sword free.

"Now." I leaped forward, racing to close the last five feet.

Kendrick dropped his arms—

BOOOOOOOOM!

The ground rocked as a fireball shot to the sky behind the props table.

I rammed into the lead actress as if I'd lost my balance and stripped her of the sword—at the same time dropping the fake one on the ground by her feet.

Genuine screams ripped through the cast as everyone goggled at the panel van parked behind the props table that was now in flames.

BA-BOOOOM!

Something inside the panel van exploded, sending everyone into a panic.

"Get out of here, Reggie." I lunged into the mass of running bodies, shoving the real sword inside my cloak.

"STOP!" a male voice bellowed.

I risked a peek over my shoulder and found Kendrick pushing through the throng. He dodged overturned tables and people running in every direction.

Damn. He should've been helping the downed cast members as part of his do-gooder badge. I'd banked on it. Once again, he'd crapped on a good plan.

Increasing my speed, I ran toward the chateau. My biceps quivered at the strain of trying to keep a three-foot claymore from destroying my shins.

Three studio-hired guards stumbled down the chateau's steps, effectively cutting off my planned escape route.

Veering left, I headed toward the abandoned craft services trailer.

"Guhg," I wheezed, suddenly jerked to a halt. Something had caught my cloak, and if I didn't get the damn thing off, I'd choke to death. Scrabbling at the leather cords at my throat, I tore at the knot.

Finally, I got the knot free and yanked the material, trying to pull it free but it wouldn't budge.

Shit. Shit. Shit.

It hid the sword perfectly.

Giving up, I dropped the fabric and started running again, hugging the sword to my front. The freaking corset limited my air, but I couldn't stop.

"Holly," Uncle Liam barked. *"We have enough room to land in the grass in front of the parking lot. Keep going straight. You'll make it."*

Relief surged, making me lightheaded. The sword cracked against my shins, grounding me. I winced with every step and realized somewhere along the way, I lost the useless flats.

"FLORENCE MANTLE!" Kendrick shouted way too close behind me.

He knew the alias I'd used to book my flight to Georgia.

"FREEZE! FBI!"

Shit! I zigzagged around the overzealous foliage. Did I try to shove the sword down my dress to hide it? I had no clue if Kendrick saw me switch the swords or only followed because he recognized my face.

Pulling my dress up, I jammed the sword under the fabric and promptly tripped over the end when the pummel caught in the tight seam beneath my breasts.

STUPID CORSET! STUPID ANCIENT FASHION! No wonder these dresses went out of style.

Yanking the sword free, I righted my body and plunged forward, holding the claymore with my left hand while using my right to keep my balance.

Whomp-whomp-whomp. The telltale echo of the helicopter rotors got closer, and I poured the last remaining bit of energy into my legs.

Uncle Liam threw the sliding door back and waved frantically for me to hurry.

I'm trying!

"HOLLY, DON'T DO IT!" Kendrick yelled, the helicopter blades whipping the words away.

I leaped for the opening.

Uncle Liam grabbed under my arms and screamed, "GO. GO. GO."

The helicopter rocketed up. My stomach dropped as Uncle Liam hauled me in and slammed the door shut.

I flopped on my back, sucking in air and hugging the sword tight. "Piece of cake."

Chapter 3

"*H*olly, don't do it."

I ran my forefinger absently around the edge of the burner phone resting on the seventeenth-century dining table gracing my open floor plan loft. I'd spent years converting the top floor of the old warehouse in the Meatpacking District in New York City into a home complete with a spiraling wrought iron staircase leading up to a massive master suite overlooking the living room.

"*Holly.*"

I hadn't worked up the nerve to share with the rest of the crew the alarming discovery that Agent Kendrick knew my first name...maybe my whole name. The acid in my empty stomach gurgled.

"I'm safe," I muttered to no one. No way could Kendrick trace the ownership of the warehouse to me. I'd buried it under so many layers of shell companies and false identities, a forensic accountant would pull his or her hair out trying.

Reggie would probably handle the news okay, Gretchen would become nervous and skittish, but Uncle Liam would lose his shit when he found out.

"*Holly, don't do it.*" The shouted command kept playing over and over.

For two weeks, I'd sat on this, waiting for the right opening—i.e. when Uncle Liam stopped launching into impromptu lectures about me ignoring his orders, jeopardizing the crew's reputation, and pulling reckless stunts. It didn't matter that I succeeded. Or that the family had paid us our two-million-dollar fee upon delivery. *Or* that we'd all stayed out of jail. I couldn't be trusted to own a brain.

Vivid rays of the setting sun beamed through the wall of industrial windows stretching from the ceiling to two feet from the new hardwood flooring. The Hudson River flowed five stories below, lazily hauling ships or gagging the wildlife brave enough to live within.

The old freight elevator roared to life, ripping me out of my thoughts. I jogged to the inner wall I added to section off the ginormous space—the money I saved on heating alone made the addition worth it—and opened the doors of an antique armoire. Multiple screens showed security camera views surrounding my building and inside every floor in full color. Inside the elevator, Reggie and Gretchen faced forward with blank expressions. The relief exhaling past my dry lips proved just how spooked Kendrick had me. Only the crew had access codes to my building.

Had I really imagined the FBI in the elevator to catch me? Stupid and dangerous thoughts. If I let Kendrick inside my head, I'd end up in a straitjacket—or worse, screwing up a job and causing my crew to get arrested.

Not gonna happen. To combat the guilt also making me antsy, I had to tell the others about Kendrick using my name. Today.

Leaning against the double-door frame, I waited for Reggie and Gretchen to cross the empty, undeveloped portion of the top floor.

"Why isn't Uncle Liam with you?" I let them in, closing the door behind us.

"You mean he's not already here?" Gretchen whirled, the crease deepening between her eyes.

Reggie jammed his hand through his unkempt hair and scratched his unshaven jaw. "It's been two days since he's contacted either of us."

Shuffling to the leather furniture in the living room, I plopped on the couch.

"I went by his place last night." The burner phone rested on my thigh, but it remained stubbornly silent. "Nothing looked out of the ordinary."

Gretchen paled. "You think he might have been abducted or something? Like, against his will?"

"I don't know what to think," I admitted honestly. "He's never disappeared like this before." Uncle Liam hadn't answered any of my calls or texts. "That's not all."

Reggie leaned forward on the angled loveseat. "What do you mean?"

"I...that is, during the..." I cleared my throat, searching for a way to break the news.

"Just spit it out," Reggie snapped.

"Agent Kendrick knows my first name." I clenched my jaw at the words ringing in the space between us.

Reggie jerked, and Gretchen blinked. A lot.

"He knows your *name*?" she asked in disbelief.

"I don't know if he knows my last name, but he said, 'Holly, don't do it,' right before I jumped into the helicopter."

Reggie lurched out of the seat and paced to the windows, then back. "This is bad."

Gretchen joined him, biting her thumbnail with every step. "Does the FBI know all our names?" She stopped and Reggie ran into her back. "Do you think the FBI arrested Liam?"

"No." *Yes. No. Hell if I know.* "No, I don't." That felt right, so I didn't question it.

They stared, waiting for me to justify my answer.

I waved my hand limply, searching for a way to explain my intuition. "It's just that Kendrick used *my* name. He'd come after me first. Right?" I stood, too restless to sit anymore. "Besides, if they did arrest Uncle Liam, we'd have heard about it in the news by now."

The sixty-inch TV mounted to a floating wall at the end of the seating arrangement broadcast a muted twenty-four-hour news station. Headlines scrolled along the bottom while talking heads debated something. They covered everything but an arrest of the leader of one of the most successful thief crews in the world.

So why wasn't he home or calling me back?

I chafed my arms. I *needed* to hear from my uncle. He was the only family I had. My birth certificate didn't list a father, and my mother died when I was five. When Uncle Liam took me in and raised me, he made me an official member of his crew at age seven. In the most dysfunctional way, he helped me overcome my grief. At night, I learned all the skills necessary to successfully execute a high-value heist while tackling my ABCs and 123s in school during the day.

"Is he planning another heist?" Reggie's boots clomped with their back-and-forth march. "Maybe he's scoping out a new job and hasn't told us yet."

Every cell in my body rejected the suggestion. Uncle Liam may have withheld information from Reggie and Gretchen until he was ready to share, but he *always* told me everything. Or so I thought. "He hasn't said anything about accepting a new job. All I've heard lately is his ranting about how we succeeded with the last one."

Reggie snorted. "*We* didn't succeed; *you* went off the rails." He paused with a half smile. "But damn, that was fun. I didn't mean to catch the props van on fire, though. My bad."

I blocked the memory of the inferno. "It worked."

Squeezing the phone, I willed it to ring. When it suddenly rang, I almost dropped it.

Gretchen and Reggie raced to stand in front of me as I held the phone between us, but I didn't recognize the number.

"Thriving Plants," I chirped like a bubbleheaded receptionist. We created the business (on paper only) to weed out misdialed callers or, God forbid, sexy FBI agents who may have tracked us down. "We pledge to keep your office flora healthy and beautiful. How can I help you?"

"*Holly,*" Uncle Liam wheezed, then coughed wetly.

My gaze shot to Reggie's, then Gretchen's. "Uncle Liam—"

"*I just wanted you to hear for yourself he's alive,*" a male voice smoothly intoned, one I heard too often on the news. "*Now you'll take seriously what I have to say.*"

"What have you done to him?" The edges of my fingertips whitened from squeezing the phone.

"*Only what I promised if he refused my request.*"

The bastard delivered the line as if asking his admin assistant to take a memo about the break room coffee.

Reggie's skin flushed while Gretchen gasped behind her covered mouth.

Swiping the face of the phone, I checked to make sure our safety measure hadn't failed. On every phone, we installed an app that automatically recorded incoming calls. That little gem hadn't let me down. This call spooled into our online backup account.

"And what request would that be, *Darien*?" I purposefully used Darien Burton's first name to warn the powerful head of a multibillion-dollar conglomerate that I wasn't one of his sycophants.

"Careful, Holly." His tone lost some of the silk, revealing a taste of the true monster the rest of the world had no clue existed. They thought he was a humanitarian, bordering on a saint. My crew knew better. *"Your uncle can't take much more...incentive. Your disrespectful mouth might cause me to lose my temper. Who do you think I'll use as a target to vent my frustration?"*

The plastic casing squeaked in my tightening grip. "Duly noted," I forced between clenched teeth. "What are you asking us to steal this time?"

"Have you heard of the Infostrata Cryptix?"

Reggie shook his head. *Myth*, he mouthed.

"It's a myth," I repeated, desperately hoping Darien's ego would force him to explain what this thing was.

The CEO chuckled. *"I assure you it's real, and you're going to obtain it for me."*

"I'll need Uncle Liam—"

"No. You have enough experience and contacts to pull the heist without him." Another wet cough filled the background. *"He's your compensation. Your uncle will remain with me until the job's complete."*

I opened my mouth to argue, but Darien kept going.

"If you fail, I'll kill him. If you double-cross me, I'll kill him. If you give me anything but the Cryptix, I'll kill him. Get the picture?"

"We've had a solid business relationship in the past. Why are you coming back now and destroying it?"

"I didn't want it to be this way. I tried to hire your crew with a payout of seven million dollars on top of expenses, but your uncle wouldn't listen. He forced my hand."

"Surely there's someone else," I tried to negotiate. "Another crew—"

"You're just like your uncle." Darien chuckled, causing my skin to goose bump from the evil. *"I need the best. Certain business adversaries need to be taught I don't like to lose or be challenged."* A pause. *"And you and I both know no other crew comes close to matching your skills."*

Bile rose to the back of my throat. "I need time to research, surveil, and plan the job. Two months at least."

"You've got one," Darien countered flatly. *"I need that Cryptix before the next round of negotiations on a merger begins. The countdown starts today."*

Dammit. That didn't give me much maneuvering room. "You're not to hurt Uncle Liam anymore." It was an empty demand. We both knew I had no way to keep Darien or his henchmen's hands to themselves.

"Keep me regularly updated, and I won't have a reason to touch your uncle." The CEO hung up.

"He's going to kill him anyway," Reggie fumed, stating the fear plaguing my thoughts. "And you, too, the second you hand the Cryptix over."

"Are you seriously going to go after this, this *thing*?" Gretchen's hands shook.

"I'm seriously going to do whatever it takes to save Uncle Liam."

For hours, we debated how to proceed. Gretchen and Reggie spouted ideas, but none were practical or even feasible when we drilled below the surface. The moon and stars took over the sky, and still we postulated plans. Sporadic images of Kendrick's face flashed into my head, as if trying to tell me something important.

I pushed him out only to be bombarded by a collage of memories of Uncle Liam taking care of me. Air seized in my lungs. I hadn't been without him since I was five.

Unbidden, a replay of Kendrick jogging down the steps with the sword rammed its way in. *You need an expert.* Expectation burned through my veins, and an idea rose above the noise. In the past six months, Kendrick had shown determination and versatility I shouldn't, *couldn't*, ignore.

Am I crazy for even pondering the possibility? Have I gotten that desperate already?

Uncle Liam's wet coughing gave me the answer.

"The kind of help I need, neither of you can provide." Setting plates beside the steaming box of pizza Reggie had just returned from buying, I eyed my crewmates seated at the dining room table. "None of us are versed in handling sociopaths or whatever you call Darien. We don't tangle with killers or have contacts who can storm a lair and grab Uncle Liam."

"Where are you going with this?" Reggie's tone told me he'd guessed what I had in mind.

"I need an expert." I lifted my chin. "I need Agent Kendrick."

"Are you insane?" Gretchen exploded, dropping her slice of pizza back into the box.

"We have no experience with kidnapping and death threats." I might truly be nuts for talking myself into this plan. Earlier, I'd almost dry-heaved at the thought of coming face-to-face with the FBI agent, now I was rallying to recruit him. "I can't risk Uncle Liam's life, but I won't give Darien what he's asking for either." Reggie couldn't explain what the Cryptix did, but he implied the CEO should *never* get his hands on it.

"Kendrick'll arrest you before you even have a chance to talk to him." Gretchen looked to Reggie who sat scowling with his arms crossed.

"Not if I bait the trap right."

Chapter 4

With Agent Kendrick knowing my first name and my face, I couldn't exactly walk into the Manhattan FBI office and request an audience—and yes, when I learned the biggest threat to my freedom lived in the same city, I seriously thought about moving.

Now I intended to lure the man to me. On purpose. My queasy stomach protested for the millionth time since the horrible phone call yesterday.

Reeling Kendrick in needed finesse. If I made the bait too obvious, he'd smell the trap, but if I was too careful, I risked him not showing up at all.

The clock ticked loudly on Uncle Liam's life, leaving me no time to come up with an elaborate plan. The bulk of the month had to be devoted to freeing my uncle. That left me with two hasty options: One, full-out stalk Kendrick, then break into his home at night—not a choice that would incline him to listen...but just imagining him bare-chested in bed (preferably naked beneath a thin, practically see-through sheet) made that option seriously tempting; or two, pull off a heist...or at least a sham of one.

Guess which option I chose, much to my libido's despair.

Hugging my stomach, I rested my elbow against my forearm. Beyond my windows, the Hudson River churned in the end-of-October wind, and thick, gray clouds obscured the afternoon sun.

"Michael," I stated after a single ring on my burner phone, "thank you for calling."

"Can't say how I feel about a courier showing up to my office," the attorney responded warily, *"with a package containing this phone and a Post-it with 'Call Me' on it."* A clink like the lid of his crystal decanter being lifted chimed in the background. *"Good thing you gave me a hint about your identity, or I'd have smashed the phone and beefed up security."*

I chuckled, unable to hide the strain. "You might just do that anyway. Are you somewhere you can talk freely?" I gnawed on my bottom lip, watching a freighter full of shipping containers chug slowly by.

Silence. I pictured the handsome fifty-eight-year-old taking a healthy swallow of his favorite Scotch. Michael had more money than the GDP of a small country. He didn't have to work but loved uncovering and hoarding secrets. *"Holly, where's Liam? He handled everything when I needed your crew."*

My heart panged, and I swallowed against the sudden lump in my throat. I couldn't tell Michael about the kidnapping. The less he knew, the better, especially with what I was about to ask of him. "I need you to help me set up a fake heist."

"You've got my complete attention." Ice rattled against glass. *"I owe you guys for finding and returning the Matisse swindled from my great-grandfather."*

"You compensated us *generously*," I countered. "Well above the contracted fee." An image of the Matisse painting rose in my mind. The sheen in Michael's eyes when Uncle Liam and I handed over the recovered family heirloom still warmed me.

"I've got more money than I need in this lifetime, and I'm not particularly thrilled with my choice of heirs," he answered dismissively, referring to his nieces and nephews since he had no children of his own. *"How can I help with a fake heist?"*

"The Vermeer delivered yesterday—"

A choked breath echoed through the phone. *"Do I want to know how you knew I purchased the painting? And more disturbingly, when it arrived?"*

"Probably not." My contact at the auction house had no problem handing over a list of all the deliveries in the past two weeks for a hefty fee. "But rest assured, I have no intention of stealing it." I cleared my throat. "I just need the FBI to think I am."

"Okay. Not what I expected." Another audible sip. *"And you want me to do what?"*

"Host a party," I responded simply.

"A party."

"Yep. A large, catered affair to show off your latest acquisition." I turned away from the window and lazily strolled through my loft. "But, uh, it has to be this Friday."

"This Friday?" he repeated. More ice clinked against the glass. *"As in, four days from now?"* He snorted. *"Well, at least you're not asking me to look desperate or anything."*

"I'm sorry, but look on the bright side," I chirped. "Halloween's tomorrow, so you don't have to worry about tacky costumes in the planning."

"You are too good to me," he deadpanned. *"So host an impromptu party to show off the Vermeer. That's it?"*

I bit my lip. How far could I push it?

Michael sighed. *"Out with it."*

"Can you leak the guest list to your favorite gossip reporters? If you'd include the name 'Florence Mantle' within, like, the first five names to be sure it's announced, I'd be grateful."

"I take it that's you?"

"Yep. I need to catch FBI Agent Jackson Kendrick's attention." And what better way than to use the alias from the Georgia heist? That name should act like a Times Square billboard, telling him exactly where to find me.

Michael paused, and I faintly heard liquid pouring. *"You have a job somewhere else and need this agent's attention diverted, don't you?"*

That would definitely be something I'd do, but I hesitated answering. The war between telling him everything and keeping him in the dark raged strong. I didn't know much about attorney-client privilege, but I was pretty sure I had to actually hire him for it to go into effect. "The less you know, the better." My next words tasted like ash. "It's critical Agent Kendrick attends."

"Critical, huh?" More ice clinked. *"I hope you know what you're doing."*

"So do I." I rubbed my forehead.

Michael sighed. *"All right, then. I'll throw a We're Rich So Who Gives A Shit It's Last Minute, black-tie soiree at my home to help you fake a heist of the Vermeer."*

I plopped onto a barstool at the counter between the kitchen and dining room, my rubbery knees unable to hold me anymore. Holy crap. I was really doing this.

"Michael," I ventured once I figured out how to inhale again, "if you have anything you don't want the FBI to find—like, say, a certain Matisse—I'd relocate it if I were you."

"That goes without saying, my dear." Michael chuckled warmly. *"But thank you for your concern. I'll keep you posted."*

⚬⚭⚮⚯⚬

"Ow." I jerked, the sting in my waist catching me by surprise.

"Hold still, and I won't stick you," Gretchen groused around a mouthful of pins.

Reggie sprawled along the length of my couch, alternately glaring at me and at the low-budget sci-fi movie on TV.

The cheesy dialogue and laser-gun effects were grating on my frayed nerves.

"Sure are going all out for this fake heist," he drawled in a terrible Texas accent, not surprising given the man hailed from New Jersey. His eyes scraped down the body-hugging formal gown Gretchen had created to flatter my short-but-toned frame. "I think you want Kendrick's eyes to pop out of his head before he hauls you off to jail."

True about the eye-popping, dammit. To hide the secret desire, I scowled at Reggie, then had to give it up when Gretchen motioned for me to turn around. "You're just sore you can't be a part of the plan."

I couldn't afford to jeopardize Gretchen and Reggie in case Kendrick refused to listen. Someone had to remain free to help Uncle Liam. That meant I'd be on my own at the party.

"It's *not* a plan," Reggie shot back. "It's an extremely stupid suicidal mission—"

Ring-riiiiiing. He clamped his mouth shut at Michael's ringtone on my phone.

"Can you answer that? But *don't* say a word." I motioned for Reggie to pick up the device off the coffee table.

He did as told and held it in front of my chest.

"Michael." I kept my body as still as possible to avoid being stuck again.

"Your FBI agent contacted me today," the attorney stated with glee.

Yes! Yesterday, Michael had leaked the list of his "impromptu" party. "He say anything interesting?"

Michael chuckled. *"Asked if I minded if some agents mingled among the guests. He's smooth, I'll give him that. He sold the party-crashing as free security on the federal government's dime."* Admiration poured through his words. *"How could I refuse an offer like that?"*

"Excellent news." I barely stopped my arm from thrusting into the air. "I owe you. Let me know the final cost of this party, and I'll reimburse—"

"Not a chance," he snapped with no real heat. *"I haven't had this much fun in a while. I can't wait to see how this plays out."*

Neither could I.

Tomorrow night, I prayed I didn't acquire a new silver fashion accessory in the form of handcuffs...they would totally clash with my dress.

Chapter 5

M ichael owned a seven-floor brownstone (including basement) off 5th Avenue with enviable views of Central Park. If the address alone didn't scream money then the elegance and wealth he invested in decorating slapped a person with it.

My black, sixteen-hundred-dollar, five-inch, Giuseppe Zanotti stilettos with butterfly wing appliqués clicked smartly across the black-veined white marble. Jazz music crooned softly from the speaker system arrayed throughout the house. Guests floated between the first and second floors, utilizing the impressive curved staircase to see and be seen. The catering staff had taken over the kitchen and sent an army of tuxedo-clad waitpersons to roam with silver trays full of hors d'oeuvres and champagne.

I sipped on the only glass of alcohol I could allow myself—liquid courage and all that—while blending with the hundred or so attendees. So far, I had identified two FBI agents trying to blend in with the obscenely wealthy but neither were Jackson Kendrick.

The burgundy silk of my dress conformed to my hips then flared mid-thigh, giving me the ability to walk without waddling. A small separate train of the same material attached to a decorative ribbon encircling my waist and flowed over the floor as I slowly tackled the steps to the second floor. The scandalous bodice made up of strips of lace caught a person's attention until he or she realized it was flesh-toned fabric and not my skin that was visible between the strips.

Gretchen had helped me with my hair. My real hair. No wig this time. I prayed showing Kendrick the real me would sway his decision in my favor. Gretchen left the cinnamon-colored tresses down and styled them into big, fat curls, then secured one side with a sapphire and diamond encrusted comb. The gems weren't real and probably looked gauche compared to the genuine baubles in this crowd, but the comb belonged to my mother. It was the only item I had of hers, and I treasured it. I needed to feel the connection to family more than ever now that my only known relative's life hung in the balance.

Please bring me good luck, I told it, still winding up the stairs.

At the top, I caught sight of the Vermeer featured prominently on an ornate easel at the side center of the expansive gallery. Discreet spotlights attached to the ceiling made it impossible to ignore the masterpiece.

Quite a feat given all the diamonds, emeralds, and other nearly flawless gems adorning women's necks, ears, and wrists, on top of the insanely expensive gowns. Men had also spared no expense with their designer tuxedos, over-the-top watches, and cuff links.

A thief's paradise, if she were inclined to let her fingers free, but I had graduated beyond pickpocketing. I had a much bigger prize in mind. And speaking of prizes, I'd bet my next payout Agent Kendrick had found a niche somewhere on this floor. He'd want to stay close to the Vermeer and possibly have a sight line to the stairs.

Boisterous male laughter shattered the status-quo murmuring. My gaze flew past the bodies packing the room and landed on Michael with his head thrown back, framed by the night beyond the bay window beside him. Amber Scotch sloshed inside a crystal highball glass as he clutched his stomach with his other hand.

A small answering smile involuntarily lifted my lips. Michael had the kind of laugh that invited others to join in.

The crowd shifted as attendees resumed their conversations, and my lungs froze. The champagne glass threatened to shatter in my tightening grip, but I couldn't pull my gaze from the man standing rigid next to Michael. Staring at me.

Aqua-blue eyes, the color of Caribbean waters, pierced my very soul. I shivered at the tingles skittering down my spine then exploding inside the most intimate part of me. Golden blond hair was neatly combed, and his jaw was smooth as if he shaved right before donning his tux...and, oh, what a sight he made in that tux.

Holy shit. My nipples *yearned* against the stick-on cups keeping my unbound breasts from jiggling.

No department store sold that tux. It had to be custom. And top of the line. The black fabric molded around his broad shoulders and biceps, narrowing to his waist in such a way as to accentuate his trim, muscular build without making him look like a caricature. I envied the crisp white shirt beneath getting to lay against his warm chest, or maybe I wished I could be the pants wrapping around those powerful legs...

Okay. Rein it in.

A man didn't have to be over six-feet tall to command a powerful presence. FBI Agent Jackson Kendrick topped out at about five-foot-ten and exuded so much testosterone and authority, every man in the room paled in comparison.

And now all that power was directed at me.

Like a rabbit ensnared by a wolf's predatory gaze, I couldn't make my legs move. Oh Jesus. Since this man started stalking our trail six months ago, I had never been this close for this long before. Proximity while running for freedom didn't count.

Come on, Holly. Get it together. This is not the plan.

A guest shifted, blocking the wolf's eyes and freeing me from his hold.

Whirling, I crashed into a forty-something woman. Champagne flew from my glass, splashing down the front of her black velvet gown.

She squawked and screeched, lifting her arms as if I had completely doused her from head to toe.

Drama queen much?

A commotion behind me kicked my flight instincts into overdrive.

"I'm so sorry," I gushed, plopping my empty glass onto a gaping waiter's tray. "Let me find you a towel or something."

Not waiting for a response, I lifted my skirt and attacked the steps up to the third floor. I had to draw Kendrick away from the rest of the guests and avoid the other agents certain to be tightening the net. Convincing Kendrick to help would be hard enough; having to do so in front of an audience would be impossible.

"Florence Mantle, stop where you are," Kendrick growled, his hard-soled shoes pounding after mine, vibrating the marble stairs.

Stupid high heels! I could run so much faster if I didn't have to worry about breaking my neck in a fall.

Bypassing the third floor full of bedrooms, I kept going to the fourth. At the landing, I darted right. The master bedroom dominated the front half of this floor, but I didn't want that space. I raced into the two-story library made up of wood and leather that I had already covertly visited earlier to plant a few items. A door on the other side of the large room lead to a covered balcony packed with plants and plush furniture. A last-resort option to escape if I needed it.

"Holly, freeze," Kendrick ordered, his breath practically puffing against my neck.

Ingrained fear of arrest juiced my legs. I dashed into the empty center of the room.

Thick arms clasped around my chest a scant second before my feet left the Oriental rug. I barely comprehended what that meant before I was turned as I crashed on top of Kendrick in a tangle of limbs.

"Oomph," I wheezed, then the world tilted and rolled once again.

Kendrick pinned my wrists above my head and pressed his entire length against me, using his weight to hold me in place.

I could have fought to get free. Uncle Liam made sure I knew how to defend myself, and we regularly sparred to keep in shape, but I didn't want to. I had chanced too many things to have Kendrick alone just to blow it by racking him in the nuts.

Still winded, I sucked in air, trying to calm my racing heart. With every inhale and exhale, my breasts smashed into his chest, giving me more action in the last minute than I'd gotten in the last six months.

And dear God, he smelled good. Musk, spice, and wicked sexual promises. I wanted to jam my nose against his skin and snort him like a drug.

The sound of our heavy breathing filled the room while the jazz music played softly from a speaker overhead. Neither one of us looked away from the other, creating an intimacy so powerful with our mingling air, I couldn't help zeroing in on his mouth.

His muscles stiffened, and my gaze flew to his eyes to find his lids at half-mast. Those amazing blue irises drifted down to my lips and lingered.

Every cell in my body responded. My breasts grew heavy, and my center swelled, readying itself for him as I grew wet against my thong. My tongue darted out and licked my lower lip. I almost groaned at his tightening grip on my wrists.

Inches. Our mouths were mere inches before they connected. Did he dare breach that space? Did I?

"Give me a minute," he muttered, his tone husky and raw.

While not earthshattering, his words stroked my inner ear, and I had to hold back a purr. I had never heard his voice before...outside of a shout for me to stop. Pure masculinity laced his tone, surprising me with its almost musical quality. I wondered if he ever sang in school. I bet if he had, he'd scored a lot of solos and probably a lot of ladies.

The thought of him in bed with some other woman soured my mood. "Get off." I squirmed, trying to roll out from under him.

"Jesus," he breathed, his legs clamping around mine. "Stop moving."

A hard and heavy thickness pressed at the exact perfect spot, causing fireworks to shoot from the top of my swollen clitoris. I closed my eyes and groaned.

His breathing turned ragged.

A few more strokes, and I'd go off like a rocket.

"Be still and give me a minute," he repeated gruffly.

My eyes flew open. Was he talking to me or someone in his earpiece? A bucket of cold water couldn't have doused me faster than wondering if his FBI buddies were listening to me moan like a cheap date.

I dutifully froze, and my mind decided to review the last few minutes. "You didn't land on top of me."

His eyebrows slammed down, and he lifted his head higher. "What?"

"When you tackled me." I unabashedly studied his face and surreptitiously inhaled another shot of his scent. "You twisted so I'd land on top of you first." My mouth quirked into a small grin. "How chivalrous."

The left side of his lips tilted upward. "I'll probably have a bruise from your elbow nailing me in the sternum."

I sniffed. "That's what you get for manhandling a lady."

His eyes instantly darkened, and they roved down my face to where the top of my breasts were still smashed against him.

If I let my thoughts go naughty again, I'd never get out what I needed to say before he remembered to arrest me. "I need to talk to you."

Those expressive eyebrows pulled down again.

"*You*," I emphasized again, then pointedly stared at his ear before meeting his eyes again.

He kept my gaze prisoner as a war raged in his mind, and I didn't blame him for it. To trust the thief or not?

"I swear," I mouthed, not wanting the rest of whoever was linked in to hear, "no tricks. I just want to talk."

His mouth flattened, and his grip tightened to a painful level. I poured sincerity into my expression.

"Please," I begged in a low voice.

He cursed softly and rolled off.

I instantly missed the hard planes and warmth of his body.

"Everyone, hold position." He fluidly launched to his feet, keeping me in sight through every movement.

I slowly sat up so he wouldn't think I planned to attack. Pointing to his ear, I slashed a finger across my throat in the age-old charade of "kill it."

He scowled. "Keep the fourth floor clear until I say otherwise. Guard all the exits and be on the lookout for the rest of the crew."

Stalking toward me, I got trapped by the wolf's predatory gaze again. He had me so ensnared, I couldn't even allow a flight of fantasy at how my head almost lined up with his crotch before he grasped my biceps and lifted me effortlessly to my feet.

"Whoa," I breathed with my stellar wit just as a cold sensation encircled my wrists, followed by the unmistakable clicking of handcuffs.

Huh. The flat matte metal really did clash with my burgundy gown.

"Florence Mantle is secured." He tapped his ear to shut off his earpiece, then he led me rather forcefully by the arm to an oversize leather chair, but I didn't sit. "Now I'll listen to what you have to say."

Chapter 6

Relief swept through me so hard, I blinked to clear the sheen of moisture coating my eyes. Up until those words, I couldn't figure out if he intended to interrogate me before taking me to a tiny room in some basement holding facility or grant me my plea.

I covered my gratitude by lifting my chin and smiling saucily.

His eyes slid down my entire length as if memorizing the detailing on my dress. Aqua eyes turned almost turquoise as they carefully roved upward again, pausing on my rounded hips, then again on my heaving breasts—the blatant perusal had so much heat, he had my engines revving without a single touch. Damn, I bet he knew exactly what to do with a woman in bed. Way too many parts of me wanted to test that theory firsthand, but I clamped down on them. An FBI agent and a thief sleeping together had disaster written all over it.

His gaze moved to my arms. They had a feminine definition that said I was strong enough to pull myself up the side of a cliff-face but not so hulking that I looked like I ate nails for my iron intake.

Ever so slowly the left corner of his mouth lifted as he focused on the silver bracelets.

"I think you're enjoying me in your handcuffs a little too much for it to be professional," I teased, needing something to break the growing tension in the room.

His mouth awarded me a full, flirtatious smile, lighting up his entire face.

Holy. Jesus. I might not survive him if he decided to help.

"You imagining me handcuffing you to a headboard, Holly?" he murmured, stepping closer. Even with my five-inch heels, he still looked down upon me in a truly delicious way.

What was the damn question? Oh. Handcuffs. Headboard. "No." I cleared my throat and tried for less bordello vixen. "I get the sense *you're* the one imaging handcuffing me to a headboard, Kendrick."

His eyes narrowed, and the smile disappeared. "Kendrick. Why use that name for me?"

"Why use Holly for me?" I countered, unable to resist fishing for the intel he had on me.

He lightly traced his forefinger down my cheek, and I shivered. "I'm still pissed about you getting away in Georgia," he responded, punctuating his words by cupping my chin in a tight grip. "I suggest you use the few minutes you have left wisely."

The comb in my hair slipped another inch, the tines now digging into the top of my ear.

He noticed and plucked off the piece. I sucked in a breath and gritted my teeth. Every cell in my body wanted to shout at him to give it back.

Tapping the comb against his fingers, his expression told me he caught my reaction and knew the comb meant something to me.

"Let's start off with something easy." He waved the comb as he talked. "How did you garner an invite to Michael Henderson's party?"

Interrogation after all. Forcing my eyes off the treasured item, I stuck to the story Michael and I had come up with for just this reason. "I saw him at the auction house and chatted him up right after he finished inspecting the Vermeer to put a bid on it." I had to make sure the FBI believed he had been duped and thereby remained innocent of any suspicion of colluding with me.

"You didn't know Michael before then?"

"No." I shook my head and my newly freed hair swished against my shoulder. "I saw an opportunity and took it. I needed to get your attention."

Kendrick's head jerked back. "What? Spell it out for me."

"The second I heard Michael had bought the Vermeer, I called to congratulate him. I then encouraged him to throw a party to show it off and celebrate."

The comb stilled in his hands. "This whole party was...what? An elaborate scheme to get me here?"

"Yes." My gaze slid to the comb, and I wanted to warn him to hold it gently. "I had to talk to you, and I couldn't exactly walk into the FBI building and ask for an appointment."

A crease between his eyebrows formed. "Is Michael aware of your plan or actions?"

"Hell no. He thinks I'm a useless, rich, socialite looking for my next sugar daddy."

Kendrick's eyes flashed, and his mouth thinned. "Are you?"

"Am I what?"

"Looking for your next sugar daddy?"

I burst out laughing. I couldn't help it. If Kendrick knew how much money I had squirrelled away around the world, he'd be begging me to be his sugar mama. "Um, ew." I scrunched my nose for full effect. "Michael's a good-looking man and all—"

Kendrick's eyes narrowed.

"But he's old enough to be my father." I shuddered to really drive home the point that I had zero attraction to the attorney. "So that's a big no. I don't need or want a sugar daddy."

His shoulders lowered, and he resumed tapping the comb against his hand. "I can't stall the rest of my team for much longer." Aqua eyes pierced me with their directness. "Why would you risk setting up this elaborate plan? What's so important you'd go to jail over it?"

"My uncle," I answered quietly, swallowing the sudden lump in my throat. I shoved all the coy games and flirtations to the side. The time had come for me to plead my case.

"Liam Bell."

Shit. Just how much did Kendrick already know about the crew? "Yes," I uttered hoarsely. "Uncle Liam's the only family I have left."

The crease between Kendrick's brows increased. He slid the comb into his pants pocket and smoothed his tux jacket back in place. "What about him? Did something happen?"

"Yes." I ripped my gaze off the pocket containing the last link to my mother and met his eyes. "He's been kidnapped. He's the incentive to force me to steal an item I have no business going after. If I don't deliver, the man holding him is going to kill him."

Kendrick's entire body went rigid.

"I've come to you—" the handcuffs rattled as I motioned to his chest, "—FBI Agent Jackson Kendrick—for help." My gut quivered at his too-still pose. "Kendrick is a thirty-four-year-old honorable man who graduated from Quantico at the top of his class. A man who dedicates his life to the job. His hard work has been rewarded with a promotion to the special unit chasing art, jewelry, and historical artifact thieves."

"A man whose reputation has been shredded," he continued flatly, "because of his constant failure to catch Holly and Liam Bell, Reginald Scoval, and Gretchen Jost."

Oh fuck. He knew way too much, and he barely divulged a thing. "Looks like we've both done our homework." I didn't know what else to say. I had to steer this conversation to something else fast, or he'd say my time was up and haul me in.

"If you know I'm dedicated to the job, why let me catch you?" He grimaced. "Shit, that sounded pathetic. I would've caught you on my own, you know."

I gave him a half smile. "Believe me. Your dogged pursuit and constant showing up where you're least wanted has kept me awake at night." I leaned forward and whispered conspiratorially, "I thought for sure you had me in Georgia."

He dropped his chin. "That still burns. If my arms were three inches longer, I would have...but you still haven't answered the question."

"You're an honorable man." I shrugged to wipe out the embarrassment of sounding like a groupie. "I'm not trying to butter you up. My instinct said you would at least listen to me, and I was right. My intuition also said that once you knew the details, you'd help me. I can only hope that's right, too."

He rubbed his chin, then swiped a hand through his hair, leaving it much messier and delectable. "I've delayed for this long," he sighed. "Hit me with the high points. Did your uncle try to make a deal with a thug that went wrong?"

Heat spots tinged my cheeks. It took an extra second to swallow my indignation at being lumped together with common convenience store robbers. "Not even close. Darien Burton summoned my uncle and proposed a new job. When Uncle Liam refused, Darien took offense and beat him for days. When my uncle still wouldn't cave, he called me and offered Uncle Liam's life as compensation for completing the job."

"Darien Burton," Kendrick repeated with so much derision, the words practically dripped. "You expect me to believe the CEO of a multibillion-dollar corporation needs to hire a crew of thieves? That he couldn't just buy whatever this item is?"

I lifted my chin. "Yes."

He laughed. "Darien Burton's been awarded the Humanitarian of the Year award three times. He has hospital wings and libraries named after him." Kendrick paced away then back. "And you want me to believe he not only kidnapped your uncle but tried coercion through pain to get Liam to steal something?"

"Yes."

"Bullshit." Kendrick loomed in my face. "I don't know what kind of con you think—"

"I can prove it," I answered calmly, unable to stop every nerve ending from lighting up, responding to the fire and passion radiating from his eyes and body.

He snapped his mouth shut and eased back. "How?"

Lifting my bound hands, the cuffs rattled when I pointed at a bookcase on the left side of the room. "Lift the lid to that vase, and you'll find a cellphone. On it is a recording of the call he made to me saying exactly what I described to you."

"I thought you said Michael had no knowledge of your plans." His eyes speared me with distrust.

"He doesn't. I snuck in here when the caterers arrived and hid it."

"My team and I staked out this house all day; you did not come in with the caterers."

Pride swelled my breast, and I let a piece of it show. "I am *very* good at what I do, Agent Kendrick. I assure you, I did come in with the caterers. Then I left and came back as a guest hours later."

"Shit." Kendrick stomped to the indicated vase on the fifth shelf from the bottom and lifted the lid. His eyes slid to me as if ensuring I hadn't snuck up behind him to knock him out or something.

"It's not in my best interest to do anything stupid right now. Reach inside."

Grumbling, he did as he was told and brought out a brand-new burner phone. Surprise etched his beautiful face.

"See, I didn't lie." I motioned for him to come back. He marched toward me but stopped well beyond my reach. "I'm not going to take it. It's yours. Do whatever you need with it. Just pull up the generic music app and hit play. The recording's the only thing on the phone."

Reggie had made sure nothing on the device could be traced back to us or reveal our online cache of recordings.

Within seconds, Darien Burton's voice blasted through the tinny speaker, causing goose bumps to pebble my skin.

Bile rose to the back of my throat at having to hear Uncle Liam's wet coughing and Darien's sinister voice again.

The color leached from Kendrick's face when Darien mentioned the Infostrata Cryptix, then his cheeks flushed when Darien uttered, *"If you fail, I'll kill him. If you double-cross me, I'll kill him. If you give me anything but the Cryptix, I'll kill him. Get the picture?"*

The message continued for another minute, then the recording stopped, and silence rang in the library.

"I don't even know what this Infostrata Cryptix is," I admitted after giving him a moment to absorb the shocking message, "but I can intuit that it'd be bad if Darien got his hands on it."

Kendrick swallowed hard and studied me, inching closer. "It's a device that contains...I guess the easiest description is a virus. Once activated and set loose on the internet, it gives the owner unlimited access to *everything* connected to the internet as if no firewalls existed. It can even parse information together to give the owner complete control over whomever he wanted. It's the ultimate tool for identity theft with the ability to utterly rob and destroy a person."

The blood drained from my head. I grabbed his exposed wrist to keep from falling over. The cold seeping from his skin helped center me. "My God. Someone invented that?"

"Yes." His other hand wrapped around my forearm, offering me support. "Nothing and no one is safe from it." His gaze intensified and bored into me. "You're not bullshitting me with this, are you?"

"No. I swear, this is not a trick or a con or anything other than what you've heard."

"Fuck."

I nodded. "I have no skills handling kidnapping and death threats. My uncle's life is at stake, and I can't afford to make a mistake." Squeezing his wrist, I dropped all my walls so he could see my desperation. "You asked why I risked this elaborate scheme to draw you out. Why I risked going to jail when I've stayed one step ahead of you." I thrust my chin at the phone. "That's why. I need your help."

"What do you expect me to do?"

"Work with me," I answered honestly. "Not only would you be saving Uncle Liam's life, you'd be taking down a much bigger criminal than me. And trust me when I say Darien Burton is rotten to the core."

Praying Kendrick believed me, I added the rest of Darien's crimes to the list. "Those hospital wings and libraries you mentioned helped launder his ill-gotten money. He's deep in the black market and deals in bad shit daily. In the very beginning, we accepted a few of his job offers, but over the years, his megalomaniacal tendencies have been shining a little too bright, and we've stayed away." I tightened my grip. "You heard how he's planning on using the Cryptix against his adversaries in this merger—and who knows who else after that. Helping me take him down would cause a ripple effect, allowing you to nail a ton more bad guys than you even knew existed."

"In exchange for what?" He tucked the phone inside his tux jacket.

"Immunity for me and my crew."

He let go of my hand. "You have to give me something more. Right now, I only have a phone recording and your word."

"You've already got my most prized possession." My hands shook as I indicated his pants pocket. "That's the only thing left I have of my mother's. I want it back."

"Not good enough." He jammed his hand in his hair. "When I present this to my boss, I need to be able to follow up with a gesture that shows you're willing to cooperate."

"What do you want?" I asked warily, dreading the price he'd exact.

"The sword—"

"I can't. It's already gone, and I won't sell out our client." I bit my lip at the flash of anger in his eyes. "How about the Rodin statue that walked out of the museum in Philadelphia in broad daylight last year?"

His jaw dropped open. "That was you?"

"No, but I know who did it and where it ended up." I hated narcing on another crew, but they'd recently started escalating their heists with violence, and I couldn't stomach anyone hurting innocents.

Rubbing his mouth, he pondered my offer. "You're going to have to give up your clients at some point."

"We'll cross that bridge when we get to it." Hope blossomed, and I couldn't hold back any longer. "You're going to help me?"

He looked at the ceiling, then back at me—and I saw it. The *yes* lingering behind the doubt.

I threw my bound wrists over his head and hugged him tight. Tears of relief once again sprang to my eyes, and I blinked them away.

He stiffened, then wrapped his arms around me. "I don't trust you, and I'm positive you're not telling me everything."

Smart man. Just another reason why he was such a dangerous adversary.

"But, yes." He sighed into my hair, ruffling it. "I'm going to plead your case with my boss and see how we can free your uncle."

The urge to kiss him overwhelmed me. My body vibrated with the need, but I managed to refrain. Instead, I awkwardly untangled myself and stepped back.

Lifting my leg, I rested the front of my heel on the edge of the leather chair's armrest.

Kendrick's eyes darkened and he swallowed at my skirt bunching to reveal my leg from mid-thigh downward. "What are you doing?"

"Have you heard of the five-star steakhouse, Prime Chophouse in Miami's South Beach?"

He ripped his eyes off my exposed leg. "Can't say I've had the pleasure of visiting South Beach."

"The Kobe filet literally melts in your mouth." I withdrew a tiny syringe hidden behind the row of spread wing appliqués on my shoe. "You're going to love it."

"Holly," he drew out with plenty of warning, his hand opening his jacket to reveal a gun tucked inside a shoulder harness.

Lowering my leg, I faced him. "I can't sit in jail while you and your boss dicker over whether to save my uncle." I lifted the small syringe. "This is completely harmless, I swear. No one's going to believe I overpowered you, but if I knocked you out with a sedative, that'd be plausible."

"The fuck you're giving me a drug."

"Kendrick." I stepped closer, but it only made him tense up more, so I stopped. "I've come to you for help. I'm not going to risk Uncle Liam's life by harming you, but I need to remain free. Darien can't realize I've cut a deal with the FBI. He'll kill my uncle. This," I shook the syringe, "gives you a way to let me go without having to admit you let me go."

"Shit." He let released his tux jacket. "How long will I be out?"

"Ten, fifteen minutes *tops*." I closed the distance, taking the cover off the needle. "Meet me at Prime Chophouse in two days. Sunset." I invaded his space and whispered in his ear. "I know you don't trust me yet," a shudder rolled through his large frame, "but I'm trusting you not to double-cross me and show up with a team to arrest me."

He clutched my elbow and leaned forward to my ear. "Same goes for you, Holly. I'm taking a big risk. Don't make me regret it."

"I'll type the details of the Rodin statue into the phone and put it back in your jacket." Unable to resist, I placed a soft kiss behind his ear, then slid the needle into his neck.

His knees buckled, and he was already out by the time he hit the carpet.

I had minutes to get out of the cuffs using Kendrick's key (dropping them both in front of him), type in the Rodin details (which took forever since my eyes kept sliding to the gorgeous man crumpled at my feet), war with myself about whether to take my mother's comb back or not (I didn't, hoping that would show Kendrick I could be trusted to keep my word), and escape (utilizing a backpack I had stashed behind the wet bar in the corner).

All in all, a successful night.

Chapter 7

S ipping my iced latte, I futzed with one of the long, bottle-blond braids itching the top of my chest. Damn wig. The low pigtails were supposed to be cute, but all I wanted to do was snatch the stupid thing off and toss it into the trash can. Disguises usually didn't bother me. I wore them so often, I barely thought about them, but all day, I couldn't seem to settle into my own skin. Everything rubbed me wrong.

Adjusting my large, trendy sunglasses, I ensured the shade still dominated my little hiding spot out in the open. In South Beach, even in the first week of November, humidity soaked the eighty-eight-degree air. I'd lucked out finding the covered spot. Sitting back in the white plastic chair of the outdoor seating section of a hotel's cafe, I lifted my chin to the breeze wafting down the crowded street. South Beach had a vibe all its own. I loved Miami. Sun, sand, and no snow made for some strong selling points to give up the hustle-bustle of New York City. Though, when I finally retired, I'd probably settle into my villa on the island of Nevis.

With my strapless, flower-patterned sundress, espadrille wedge sandals on my freshly pedicured feet, and bright Coach bag sitting on the small round table in front of me, I blended in with the mixture of tourists and locals filling the space.

I had arrived in Miami yesterday after a sleepless night thanks to Michael's phone call waking me at two-thirty in the morning. He told me how Agent Kendrick's supervisor had arrived at his house to grill Michael like a slab of meat. Ever since, I'd obsessed over what the boss showing up meant for this evening's rendezvous. Had Kendrick gotten in trouble for "losing" me? Had he been able to convince the FBI to help? Were they going to show up in force to arrest me instead? The questions wouldn't end.

My nerves were shot, and tension continued to coil.

Even this damn latte tasted wrong. Slapping the cup onto the table, I yanked an e-reader out of my bag and pulled up the romance book I'd randomly down-loaded this morning. The half-naked guy on the cover made my mouth water, and I figured if anything, I'd be entertained while I waited.

For an hour and a half, I tried to enjoy the story about a famous rock singer and a small-town bakery owner, but I couldn't concentrate. My vigil of noting every person around me prevented me from paying attention. I couldn't even tell you the hero or heroine's name or why the singer was staying in...Small Town (I should've known this name, too, but didn't).

Shifting for the dozenth time, I eyed the hotel's main doors. I really needed to pee, and my iced latte had long since turned into a watery mess. Did I risk searching out a bathroom? I had a primo spot to see Prime Chophouse across the street and a general sense of the people around me. No one radiated I'm An Undercover FBI Agent Setting Up To Ambush Holly, but that could change if I moved.

Tall, black, decorative streetlamps along both sides of the two-lane street flickered to life, making the choice for me. No way could I leave now.

Sunset had arrived. Now all I needed was Kendrick to appear.

Crossing my legs, I casually swung my sandal and tried not to think about my full bladder.

Focusing on the entrance of the restaurant, I studied every person approach-ing the door. 5:50 P.M. was still early for dinner, but Prime Chophouse was one of *the* hot spots in Miami, popular with celebrities, the mega rich, and those really wanting to experience exquisite food—

Every single nerve ending zinged, and my mouth instantly dried. Strid-ing confidently along the sidewalk, Jackson Kendrick approached from the north. Even with his chin held high and black sunglasses covering his amazing eyes, he turned heads. Women all but drooled as he passed, while their dates'/boyfriends'/husbands' postures didn't seem too happy.

My heart fluttered at the tiny lift of his lips as he acknowledged a few of the more brazen people staring his way.

Damn the man and his fantastic looks. He paired perfectly tailored black dress slacks with a blue button-down shirt. *Seriously yum.* In this weather, I didn't blame him for ditching the jacket and tie.

As he walked, he casually rolled up his sleeves, revealing a mouthwatering set of forearms.

Shit. If I was this worked up over that little bit of skin, I had no hope of remaining cool when I confronted him. *If* he checked out. *If* he didn't have a team in place to arrest me.

Lowering my face toward my e-reader, I peered over the top of my sunglasses. Kendrick paused just outside the glass doors to the restaurant and openly surveyed both sides of the streets. Cars steadily passed, and the area continued to fill with diners and couples browsing the shops.

His gaze skittered over me, and I had to stop myself from flinching...or waving like a loon because I wanted those women still eyeing him like candy to know he came here for me.

Turning his back, he opened the door, and I finally made an observation I should have noted before. He didn't have his gun. No shoulder harness or side holster clipped to his belt.

Did that mean something? Was he lulling me into trusting him before he sprang the trap?

I'd find out in about thirty seconds.

Slipping the burner phone out of my purse, I held it in my lap and used the e-reader to cover it. By now, I imagined Kendrick approaching the hostess station and giving his name. The perky, adorable woman would smile at him—my blood pressure spiked at picturing her fluttering her eyelashes and flashing her pushed-up cleavage as she leaned forward to "hear" him better—then give him a smallish, square gift box held by a burgundy ribbon with the instruction for him to open it outside.

As if on cue, Kendrick appeared with the box just as my phone vibrated. I casually lifted it, doing my best to ignore Kendrick's deep frown as he scanned the area again.

"Hello?" I answered softly, kicking my foot as if I hadn't a care in the world. Hopefully throwing off the vibe I was just another pampered princess waiting on someone to meet her, not a nervous Nellie with a queasy stomach who seriously needed to pee.

"Mr. Kendrick has the present," the perky female voice of the hostess informed me. *"He didn't say anything other than 'thank you.'"*

"Was he on a cellphone at any point in the lobby? Or did he seem to be talking to himself?" I pressed, holding my breath.

Kendrick peered back down at the present. By his tense shoulders, I got the feeling he was debating the wisdom of opening it.

"No," Ms. Perky answered. *"He only took a second to look around when he entered, then came to my station. He left immediately after I gave him your instructions."*

"Thank you." I exhaled at no overt use of an earpiece or some other communication device. "I'll be by in a moment to give you the other half of your tip." Two hundred dollars: one hundred to bribe her into doing the bizarre action, the other upon completion and report.

Hanging up, I hid the phone in my lap and queued up the text app. I had the first one ready to go.

Kendrick finally pulled the end of the bow and lifted the lid. His eyebrows snapped down.

I hit send on the text.

His mouth thinned as he gazed at the message on the screen. It took him eight more seconds before he lifted the phone out. Heading north again, he veered to a trashcan and threw the box away.

I forced my eyes off his incredible ass and paid attention to everyone around me. No one put reading material of any type down, or abandoned drinks at tables. No one seemed to care at all that Kendrick had left the area.

I stood just as the phone pinged in my hand with a responding text.

Kendrick: I'm alone as promised. You can come out now.

We'll see, I silently answered, shoving my e-reader back into my bag.

Chapter 8

S lipping the strap of my purse onto my shoulder, I fell in step behind
Kendrick, trying to keep plenty of people between us but still see his blue
shirt.

Again, no one seemed to give a shit I left the table and followed an FBI agent.

Lifting the phone, I tapped in the next instruction: Turn left at 2nd Street.

His long strides remained even, but mine were another story. Why the hell
had I chosen four-inch, wedged espadrilles? Sure, they complemented my short
sundress and blended in with the crowd, but I could *not* walk swiftly in them. I
looked like a wobbling idiot taking up too much space on the cramped sidewalk.
And damn if all the jarring hip action hadn't jostled my bladder to critical levels.

Yanking the slipping purse strap back into place, I grumbled. My erratic path
through the joyous traffic resembled that of a drunk butterfly.

What the—

I scowled at the stupid trash can that had the nerve to park itself right in the
middle of my way. Managing to squeeze between it and a laughing group who
didn't care that they were hogging most of the sidewalk, I glanced ahead.

No.

Jerking my head right, then left, I panicked. Where the hell had Kendrick's
blue shirt gone? Had he turned already? Dammit. Attempting to jog, I clattered
against the concrete with all the femininity and grace of a rhino out for a stroll.

I managed to make the left without busting my ass or taking out the streetlamp that had the gall to remain planted at the corner. My eyes slid away from

the fluttering leaves my purse had stripped off a baby tree's branch. Why had the city planted the poor thing at the edge of a sidewalk? Straightening, I ignored my burning cheeks.

Scanning the lesser traveled side street, I couldn't find his blue shirt anywhere.

Son of a bitch! I pulled up short, embarrassed at how silence from thumping greeted my ears the second I stopped.

A wall of heat filled my back just as a pair of meaty arms encased in blue wrapped around me, pulling me against a hard body.

"That had to be the worst attempt at a tail I've ever seen," a male voice whispered against my ear.

All my organs morphed from terror to goo the second my brain registered Kendrick, not a murderer, had gotten the drop on me.

"It was not," I argued for form's sake. Of course he was right, but damn if I'd admit it.

"Where did you get the stupid idea to have me walking for God knows how long?"

Lifting my chin, I stiffened in his arms—those deliciously glorious arms still holding me tight. "It worked for Jason Bourne. I figured if he could flush out a team of agents waiting to capture him, I could, too."

His chest vibrated against my back as he laughed.

Oh, that deep, wonderful sound did wicked, wicked things to me.

"I should have guessed you've studied the highly acclaimed Hollywood method of spycraft," he rumbled against me.

A thirty-something couple passed us, smiling wide and winking.

Shit. How stupid was I to just stand there while an FBI team could be closing in?

"Vanilla cake with white frosting," he murmured, his face pressed against the top of my head.

"What?" I paused my efforts at twisting free.

"How the hell do you smell like my favorite cake?" His arms tightened, fitting me flush against him again. "You have a wig on, yet I still smell it. I thought I had imagined it the other night when I tackled you."

My nipples and vagina went nuts. His statement produced so many images and memories, I longed to drive my fingers into his hair while pulling his head down for a no-holds-barred kiss.

Get a grip!

Wrenching out of his hold, I whirled, cursing at needing an extra step to find my balance so I could face him.

He plucked his sunglasses off and hooked the arm into his open collared shirt. I mimicked his action but jammed my sunglasses into my bag.

His exquisite aqua eyes flitted over the blond braids of my wig and down my dress before stopping at my shoes. "No wonder I heard you so easily." He lifted his gaze back to my face. "Do me a favor, leave the stealthy stuff to me."

"Hey, I'm a damn good...*thief*," I hissed the last word, leaning forward. "I can do stealthy when I need to."

He lifted a golden blond eyebrow as his eyes twinkled. "Really," he drew out, his grin widening. "So your plan was *not* to stalk me silently but stomp like an escaping elephant to get my attention?"

Did he just call me an elephant?

Laughter rumbled out of him again. "How's that a Jason Bourne plan?"

"Hmfph." I folded my arms together.

He tweaked a braid. "This is a cute look, Cupcake."

Cupcake? Dear God, had he just given me a pet name? *Warning! Alert! He could be roping you in.* "Am I to believe your team's not waiting in the wings to drag me off to jail?"

Golden highlights caught the streetlamp's glow as he shook his head. "It's just me. As requested. No one knows I'm here."

Not exactly what I'd requested. "What happened after I left Friday night?" I wanted to see what he'd admit and if it lined up with Michael's accounting.

His eyes dashed to the left and right as his face shuttered. "We need to get off the street." He wove his arm through mine and "encouraged" me to move back toward the main road. "It's not safe to talk about this openly, and I'm starving." His fingers squeezed my forearm. "You promised me a five-star steak, and instead, I received a phone."

Tottering like Bubbleheaded Barbie, I leaned a little harder into his hold so I could maintain my balance while keeping up with his steady stride. (That's my reason and I'm sticking to it.) "Speaking of steak, we have to stop in. I need to give the hostess the rest of her tip." I bit my lip, destroying the last bit of gloss remaining. "You're really here alone?"

Kendrick guided me off the sidewalk, and into a condo building's alcove beside the free periodical bins that hocked real estate and discount coupons to local attractions. He backed me up against a deeply shadowed section of the wall and flattened his left palm beside my ear. Only a scant inch of space was left between us as I looked up into his gorgeous face.

His scent, that same damn musk, spice, and dirty sex, invaded my nose and instantly made me high. My four-inch wedges only raised me to his chin, and I shivered at the way his body crowded mine.

"The shit hit the fan after I woke up," he murmured, placing his other hand on my hip.

Fire crackled beneath his touch. "What happened?" I croaked, cringing at how my horrible dry spell had me panting this hard.

He grimaced. "Let's just say my boss was pissed you slipped away, and he showed up to question everyone."

That lined up with Michael's report. "Yikes. That doesn't sound good."

"No. Then yesterday, we got into it." His eyes betrayed just how heated that conversation had been. "He didn't want to hear about Darien taking your uncle or listen to the recording. He accused me of falling for a scheme you cooked up with fabricated evidence and of incompetence for not keeping you secured once I had you."

"Shit. I'm sorry."

"It's done." The warmth of his hand left my hip as he reached into his pants pocket. "You kept your word, so I'm here to keep mine." Pulling out my mother's comb, he held it between us. "I thought for sure this would turn up in our database as stolen."

My gaze zeroed in on the fake gems. "I told you, it was my mother's." My fingers itched to snatch it out of his hands. "It's essentially worthless, but I value it more than anything I've ever been asked to...appropriate."

Kendrick's eyes darkened and he purposefully placed the comb into my hand. "I don't trust you." His voice was husky, and his palm returned to my hip.

I gently placed the comb in my purse, then kept my hands at my sides to keep from pulling him in tighter. "And *I* don't trust *you*."

He nodded. "Given our history, it's to be expected, but I can't walk away." His muscles tensed, and an edginess crept into his vibe. "We need to come to some kind of understanding that will get us off these streets."

"That's the second time you've mentioned that." The tension rolling off him made my own nerves twist into a knot. "Is there something you're not telling me?"

His body turned to stone, and his grip was bound to leave a mark. "I'm not here to arrest you, but I don't have the FBI's blessing not to."

Air refused to inflate my frozen lungs. "What?" I wheezed. "What does that mean exactly?"

Jamming his hand into his hair, he paced away with a growl, then marched back and crowded me again. "It means I've lost my damned mind." His eyes flashed with something I couldn't interpret before they flattened. "It means I'm in, but I'm all you're going to get."

"Kendrick," I whispered, not sure why or what I even meant.

He stepped closer, pressing his hips into mine, anchoring me to the wall. "For six months, I've dedicated every waking hour to you," he whispered with a hard edge. "Finding you, I mean. I've gotten close so many times, but you've always slipped through my fingers." His eyes searched mine, but I had no clue what he found. "Now I have you. Literally in my hands, and a small part of me wants to drag you to the closest police station for processing."

Terror seized me. The blood drained from my head, making me see spots.

"Then I remember the recording you played for me," he continued, "and the fear and desperation in your eyes as you asked for help."

That same fear and desperation stole my ability to speak or even swallow to relieve my parched throat.

"I can't just blithely stand by while you dive headlong into a situation that could mean death. Yours. Your uncle's. Whoever's." He lowered his face until his lips were centimeters from mine and our eyes were level. "But know this, Holly. If I find out this *is* some giant scheme, I will make it my mission to see you're thrown into the deepest, darkest hole our legal system has."

I inhaled, my lungs suddenly released from their terrified prison, and blinked away the blackness taking over my sight.

Relief so profound, I honestly felt the synapses firing in my brain, loosened my muscles until I had to rely on Kendrick to keep from pooling on the ground.

Call it lust. Call it being high on his scent. Or call it gullibility. But that scary-ass warning convinced me he really was here to help.

Cupping his cheeks, I grinned. "Want to go back to my place?"

Chapter 9

Waltzing out of the hallway leading to the bedrooms, I swished my fingers through my hair, relieved to have the wig off and an empty bladder. I had wanted to spend time styling my hair, maybe wash and curl it instead of hastily running a brush through my thoroughly flattened tresses, but I held back. This wasn't a date. Kendrick and I could never happen on a romantic level. That would be a train wreck waiting to happen. I may lust after him, but I had to remember that when all was said and done, he'd still attempt to haul me to jail.

Trekking to the carefully packed takeout meals I'd managed to talk the chef at Prime Chophouse into providing for a *hefty* fee, I snuck a peek at the dangerous man permeating every inch of the three-point-six-thousand-square-foot condo.

Kendrick stood in front of the screen door that led to the balcony running the length of the living and dining rooms with his jaw dropped.

Okay. To call the four-point-nine-million-dollar condo with an ocean view "my" place might've been an exaggeration...or flat-out lie. The man who really owned the condo was based in Switzerland and only visited a couple times a year. With him currently partying in Amsterdam, he shouldn't mind me borrowing the refuge for a few days—or even know.

"There's an excellent selection of reds in the wine rack," I tossed over my shoulder, heading for the unit built within the bar at the outer edge of the minimally furnished living room.

"You own this?" Kendrick turned his back on the view, giving me something else amazing to stare at.

Framing him, the rising moon glistened off the tranquil ocean while lights, eight stories below, twinkled as the nightlife began to ramp up at the bars rimming the massive pools on the property. Pulsing breezes carried the scent of salty air, exotic flavors from the myriad of restaurants, and Kendrick, making my mouth water.

Grabbing a random bottle, I paced back to the glass dining table in my bare feet. "Come on." I ducked the question. "Food's going to get cold, and that would be the biggest crime of the century." The wine and glasses clinked as I set them down. "I wasn't kidding when I said the Kobe filet will literally melt in your mouth."

Kendrick lazily moved to the other side of the table, his dress shoes still adorning his feet. A small part of me felt vulnerable in my bare feet, but I brushed it aside. My sparkly blue nail polish looked awesome against the white marble floors, and the cool surface helped keep me from combusting—either from the hot weather or from Kendrick's overwhelming presence saturating way too many of my senses.

He reached across and grabbed the wine. After de-corking the bottle, he set it down to breathe.

I couldn't help but be impressed that he had enough knowledge to let the wine breathe. It made me realize I knew next to nothing personal about him other than his relentless dedication to a goal. "I figured you'd be a beer man," I teased, handing him a specialized takeout container.

"Stereotyping me, Cupcake?" He took the container and sat in the white ornate chair.

"Cupcake," I grumbled, popping the lid off my meal. Closing my eyes, I appreciated the aromas of the four-ounce filet, roasted garlic mashed potatoes, and sautéed spinach fusing together.

"Do you need a minute alone with your meal?"

"Would you mind?" I purposefully wafted the scents toward my nose with my hand.

He snorted, then poured the wine into both glasses. Lifting one, he toasted, "To great food and health."

I clinked my glass to his, then took a sip to seal the toast. "A bit of a boring sentiment, but nice."

He popped the lid off his container and picked up his utensils. "At this point, I figured it was the safest thing to say and much better than my usual."

"Do I want to know your usual?"

The tips of his ears pinkened, and the left side of his mouth quirked. "I doubt it, but I'm sure you can figure out the gist."

"It's either some frat-boy type of saying or a vow to arrest us next time." My knife slid through the steak like butter, and juices pooled beneath. Reverently putting the bite into my mouth, I groaned at the explosion of flavors on my tongue.

It wasn't until I swallowed that I realized silence pervaded the room. Opening my eyes, I found Kendrick staring at me with a white-knuckled grip on his fork.

Ducking my head to hide my burning cheeks, I grabbed my wine glass.

He cleared his throat and popped the piece he had on his fork into his mouth...then promptly groaned loudly.

I giggled, then laughed outright when those aqua blues flew open to land on me. "Told you."

"That you did." He sliced another piece and tasted it.

Digging in, I sampled the spinach and potatoes—

A phone rang, shattering the peace. I snapped my head up. Kendrick peered over my shoulder, toward the hallway. We both slid our chairs back, and I wasn't surprised to find him on my heels as I jogged to the master bedroom.

On the dresser, my purse rang, and I ripped it open. The ringtone dedicated to my uncle—which now indicated Darien—blared, turning the orgasmic flavors of the steak to ash.

"Speaker." Kendrick's tone brooked no argument. Not that I had one. I *wanted* him to hear whatever Darien had to say.

Swiping to answer, then pressing the speakerphone icon, I barked, "What do you want, Darien?"

Holding the phone between us, I checked to make sure the call was recording.

Kendrick's eyes narrowed, but I quickly switched back to the caller ID screen so he couldn't memorize anything while making a mental note to contact Reggie. He needed to set up a dummy account for this phone's calls.

"Why were you trying to steal a Vermeer from some society twit's party when you should be focusing on the Cryptix?" Darien clipped as if I was a wayward child.

My blood pressure spiked, but I reined it in. His even knowing about my appearance at the party made me shiver at his contacts. "I *am* focused on the Cryptix. I used the party to contact a source I needed."

"What source could possibly be useful at that soiree?"

Kendrick shifted, his brows drawing down as he placed his hands on his hips.

Like I'd be stupid enough to answer that honestly. "Look, Darien," I snapped. "I don't come to your work and second-guess or demand an explanation for everything you do. Don't do it to me."

"Be careful, Holly," Darien warned in a low tone. *"Your uncle's well-being rides on your actions."*

The skin at my fingertips whitened as I clutched the phone. Kendrick forced my chin up with the side of his finger and mouthed, *steady.*

I inhaled through my nose slowly.

"If at any point I think you're not being honest with me, he'll suffer the consequences before I kill him."

"You son of a bitch," I exploded, all traces of Zen gone.

Kendrick cupped both my cheeks and bored his gaze into mine. *Steady,* he mouthed again.

Gritting my teeth, I bit out, "Darien, you don't need to keep threatening me. I'm working on a plan, but it takes time and resources to pull it together. Sometimes that means I have to use unconventional methods."

Good, Kendrick mouthed, his fingers spreading into my hair.

Silence for a beat. *"A contact tells me you were captured by the head of the FBI task force assigned to hunt you, but you escaped."*

Fear slid down my spine at just how connected Darien was. Spots broke out on Kendrick's cheeks, and his eyes shared his unease at Darien's knowledge.

"That's right," I answered. "I got away."

"You can't take risks like that again," the CEO scolded. *"I'm going to take care of Agent Kendrick once I find him."*

Kendrick jerked, his fingers spasming before he yanked them off my head with a huge scowl.

The Kobe burned a hole in my stomach. "What do you mean 'take care of'?" Only an idiot wouldn't know what he meant, but I wanted it spelled out on the recording.

"I can't have him fucking up your ability to steal the Cryptix. According to another contact, Jackson Kendrick has been suspended. He's also under investigation for losing you."

I whipped my gaze off the phone to Kendrick. *Suspended?*

His lips thinned as his eyes flashed, and his hands practically strangled his waist.

"He's not been home all day, but I'll find him."

Oh Jesus. Darien knew where Kendrick lived? "You can't go killing people—"

"I can and will," Darien promised. *"I'll do whatever it takes to get what I want. Don't ever forget that, or it'll be Liam's and your last mistake."*

Darien hung up, and I stared at the rigid man in front of me. So many emotions flooded my body, I could barely breathe.

"Holly—"

"You're suspended?" I pushed past the lump clogging my throat. His fingertips whitened, and it hit me again he didn't have a weapon. "That explains why you don't have your gun." I paced to drop the phone back into my purse, grappling to assimilate all the new information and push the terror of screwing up out of my head. "And why the FBI still wants to arrest me. Jesus." I marched to stand in front of him. "Why didn't you tell me?"

His eyes flattened, and his skin flushed. "It's not important."

"Not important?" My voice rose. "Kendrick! *Of course* it's important." I jabbed a finger toward him. "I've got to worry about the FBI tracking me down and now Darien finding out you're involved with me."

His pupils constricted. "This isn't—"

"How are you going to help me anyway?" I steamrollered over him, verbally vomiting the thoughts crashing in my head. "You've been suspended. You don't have the resources of the government behind you, and you can't stop the manhunt for me." I poked him. "From where I stand, you're more a liability than an asset."

"I realize you're lashing out because you're scared for your uncle." His expression hardened as he knocked aside my finger from hovering between us. "But I don't see anyone else in this condo willing to risk his life to help you."

My jaw slammed closed. I had no snappy comeback for the blunt reality check.

"You came to me because you have no experience handling kidnappings and death threats." He pointed at my chest. "Your words."

Another point to Kendrick, his cold logic worming its way through the chaos of my brain.

"I do," he clipped, his body hard as granite.

Everything about him screamed confidence and competence. Terror ebbed from my body, and the maelstrom of feeling overwhelmed left with it.

"Nothing about this is a typical circumstance, but I'm not without my own skills, and I'm the only one standing in front of you." Kendrick's tone softened. "We can be allies or adversaries. You have to decide. Friday, you wanted a partnership, but now... Are we going back to being adversaries?"

Biting my lip, I shook my head. "No. You're right; I need your help, but," I narrowed my gaze on him, "you should have told me the truth. I can't believe you got suspended."

"What did you truly expect?" The corners of his eyes tightened. "You want to be hit with the truth? My boss has been itching to kick me off the unit. He practically tap-danced when he took my gun and badge. He gloated about the investigation he's launching into my failure to bring you in after my team heard I had you secured."

My heart plunged. "I'm so sorry."

"Why?"

"Because I am, dammit." I instantly regretted the passionate outburst that revealed a little too clearly how I wasn't indifferent to him.

He blinked. "I thought you'd be overjoyed. My boss wants me gone and now, apparently, your psycho client wants me dead. I'll be out of your hair for good if either succeed."

I curled my lips between my teeth and softly chewed on them, debating whether to be honest or not. "I'm not overjoyed, okay?" My palms itched with a thin sheen of sweat. "I hate that I'm the reason you're in trouble, even though the only way for you to win is unacceptable for me." Why the hell did I insist we go the truth route?

Kendrick cocked his head, studying me.

I let out a sound of frustration and pulled the top of my strapless sundress higher. "Forget it. Can we just move on and figure out our next move? Did you check into a hotel when you arrived?"

Kendrick didn't say a word. Slowly, his shuttered eyes began to lighten, and a smile crept across his lips. "You like me," he breathed in revelation.

"I do not," I snapped, cringing at the defensive tone. I wanted to mount him like a jockey, but I couldn't say I liked him.

"You do!" He chuckled, his whole gorgeous face lighting up.

"You're a pain in my ass." I pivoted, striding back down the hall to the dining table. "Maybe I should call your boss and help speed your dismissal along."

Kendrick's shoes clipped on the marble floors right behind me. I had the urge to run around to the other side of the table, but I squelched it. Knowing my luck, he'd turn it into a game of tag, not stopping until he had me under him again. Son of a bitch, that visual shot jolts of pleasure through me, and I seriously thought about taking off for half a second.

What is wrong with you?

Stopping by my chair, I faced him, lifting my chin and doing everything I could to hide my runaway thoughts.

He stepped into my space and leaned forward until only inches separated our faces.

Drat! Why couldn't I control my pulse, and why the hell did he smell so *good*?

"I think you like me chasing you."

I schooled my expression to not betray my surprise. He had just verbalized a key element I hadn't put a finger on until he said it.

"No one else has ever gotten close to catching to you." His lids closed halfway. "I wonder, is it the thrill of trying to stay one step ahead or is it that it's *me* pursuing you that turns you on?"

Fuck. That throaty tone drenched my already-wet panties to the point where they were useless. I inhaled his addictive scent and couldn't stop the shiver rocketing down my spine. Which he noticed. The bastard.

"Hmm," he murmured in that damn sexy voice, his eyes darkening to show a raging sea. "So it's me. Good to know."

Goddamn it. "A little arrogant assuming I'm turned on or that it's by you, aren't we?" I tossed out, needing to head this conversation off pronto.

"Oh, Cupcake," he whispered, running a finger down my cheek.

"I'm not your cupcake." I pulled my face back to escape the chills his touch ignited.

"But you *really* want me to lick your frosting, don't you?"

"Oh my God." I jerked backward, putting at least a foot of space between us. "I do not like you. I do not want you licking my *frosting* or anything else, and you do not turn me on."

A slow smile full of mischief set my warning bells clanging. "You forget I've had extensive training in detecting lies. Do you *really* want to make that claim when I can see the honest answer for myself?" His irises slid to my breasts, heaving against my dress. I didn't have to look to know my nipples were trying to poke him, the vein at the base of my throat was pulsing erratically, and my flushed skin was giving me away.

"Yeah, well, a wolf respects the deer right before it becomes the meal." *What?* Why did I say that? What did it even mean?

"Interesting response." Kendrick's gaze swept up from my breasts to linger on my lips before meeting my eyes. "Tell me, am I the wolf in this scenario?"

Argh. I cocked an eyebrow. "You'd like to think so, wouldn't you? But alas, no. I'm the alpha bitch of this pack."

Kendrick threw his head back and laughed. The rich, deep tones burrowed into my pores, nestling into places I didn't want him to touch.

Was it too late to change my answer and call off the partnership? I had the distinct impression of staring stupidly at the surface of the water while I allowed Kendrick to steadily pull me deeper beneath.

Chapter 10

Rubbing a dish towel over the last ceramic plate, I slapped it on top of the stack in the cupboard, wincing at the clashing clang.

Dinner of less-than-savory reheated takeout had been a nonstop battle in silent warfare. Neither of us spoke, but I told him plenty with my body language, and he answered in kind. Usually that meant countering my volleys with knowing smirks that made me want to resort to violence, which only tickled him, ramping up my need to wipe the glee off his face until I realized I was playing right into his game and shut down. My mind deftly switched to churning over Darien's phone call and obsessing on all the implications his threats portended.

Kendrick plucked the stopper from the sink, and the soapy water slowly drained. A quaint domestic scene that set my already-thrumming nerves on edge.

Lively salsa music from one of the pool bars trickled through the screen door, blending with the ocean waves crashing against the beach. Very romantic...and exactly the opposite of the mood we needed.

Spreading the towel over the oven door's handle to dry, I pulled my gaze off his muscled forearms showing beneath his rolled sleeves.

"I've been thinking—"

"Who owns this condo?"

Kendrick and I spoke at the same time.

"What?" I padded around the island, into the living room. With the open floorplan similar to my loft, no walls impeded Kendrick from watching me as he dried his hands on a second cloth.

He spread the towel over the edge of the counter. "The master bedroom's closet is full of men's clothes, and the bathroom is bare of the typical women's products." He strolled into the living room and sat in the white leather recliner angled to see both the TV on the wall and the view out the screen door.

I plopped onto the end of a matching three-cushion couch and curled my legs beside me. "Snooping, Agent Kendrick?" I purposefully used his title to build a wall back between us. Things had gotten way out of hand, and I had to reestablish firm lines in our temporary truce. He'd exposed a vulnerability I hadn't realized I had. I *did* covet the chase, and only because of *him*. The lead agent before Kendrick hadn't caused so much as a ripple of attraction. Kendrick washed over me like a tsunami. Now that he'd brought it to my attention, I could strengthen my guard to keep him from getting past my defenses. I couldn't forget we stood on opposites of a huge chasm: law and outlaw.

"Dodging the question, Thief Bell?" He quirked an eyebrow, tossing the title back at me as if he knew my intent to reestablish our roles. "What happened to the demand for honesty? Or does that only apply to me?"

No way in hell he'd let me get away with saying yes. Tracing a random pattern into the armrest with a fingertip, I sighed. "No. It goes both ways, but before we go any further, I'm going to beg a favor. Please don't ask me to name my clients."

He shifted in the chair, a crease forming between his brows.

Blowing out a breath, I hooked my hair behind my ear. "I'm sorry about my outburst earlier. I *am* grateful you're willing to help me, but your suspension changes things." I lifted my gaze to his. "You're in no position to promise immunity, and you demanding those answers will destroy this truce."

The crease deepened, and he tapped a beat against his thigh. "For now, I'll respect your request, but I won't promise questions about them will never come up."

When you go back to hunting me, I silently added. "I can live with that." I scanned the room. "A businessman in Switzerland owns the condo. I'm just borrowing it for a few days."

"Does he know?"

I smirked. "Do you really want the answer?"

His mouth thinned. "I guess that says it all." He sighed and shook his head with a small chuckle. "I should've guessed you'd steal a condo."

"Nah. Stealing would be if I pretended to be a real estate agent and sold it, pocketing the money."

His body stilled.

"No. My crew's never pulled that scam, but I do know a few individuals who are experts at it." Twining my fingers together, I gave him my full attention. "It seems our list of problems is growing."

"You're referring to Darien's call?"

"Yes."

Kendrick rested his ankle on his knee. "Asshole actually did us a favor. With him revealing he has a mole inside the FBI, my suspension has become a blessing." His fingers stiffened on the words "my suspension," then went back to silently tapping his knee and thigh. "Had I convinced my boss to throw the resources of the FBI behind you, it would have gotten back to Darien."

Holy crap. I hadn't even considered that possibility. The blood drained from my head, and I clutched the armrest against the dizziness. Uncle Liam could have died—

"Holly." Kendrick snapped his fingers, cutting through the panic pulling me deeper. "We can use this to our advantage." He waited until I blinked the black spots away and focused on him. "Darien will never suspect I'm helping you. As long as we play this smart, we can take him down."

We. That word took on a huge meaning, comforting me. Kendrick and I may have different visions of my future, but for now, I had a partner committed to seeing this through.

"Hell," Kendrick continued sardonically, "his ego's so big, you should have no problem pulling information out of him. He's a bragger needing an audience to laud how smart he is. You'll be able to find out what he's doing in his search for me, which will give us an idea of the scope of his contacts."

"He wants you dead." I leaned forward, swallowing against remembering Darien's words. "And the scope of contacts he's revealed so far is terrifying. He knew I was at the party, and he knows you're not at home."

Kendrick's jaw ticked. "I'm not that easy to kill."

"I sure as hell hope not, but we can't take any chances." Unwinding my feet, I thwumped them to the floor. "He's now proven the bigger threat over the FBI getting in our way. He's not going to stop until he finds you."

Kendrick dropped his leg and shifted to the edge of the recliner. His eyes moved in a way that showed calculations and possibilities whipping through his mind. "Fuck. I led him right to us." He jerked out of the chair, and I jumped to stand, my heart suddenly pounding. "With what he's demonstrated so far, he should have no problem finding out I flew out of JFK to Miami International. The flight was under my name."

"Did you book a hotel room?" I rubbed my roiling stomach, dinner no longer playing nicely.

"Yes. And I checked in under my name about an hour before our meeting."

"He'll know you're in South Beach but not why." I rested my arm onto the one still clutching my waist and paced. "Let's assume he'll believe you refuse to give up the search for me. I doubt he'd have gotten the information in that hour, but he could have since sent someone to monitor you. Is there anything in your room you can't walk away from?"

"My cellphone."

Pausing a few feet from him, I cocked my head, not expecting those words.

The corner of his mouth tightened. "I am smart enough not to bring something that can be tracked to a meeting with a wanted felon."

Snorting, I rubbed my cheek. "Is it FBI issued?"

"Yes." The light in his eyes shifted. "Damn. It's got to stay behind for good."

"Yep." I nodded. "Anything else in the room?"

"No. Clothes can be replaced. I left my laptop at home, figuring I could pick one up if you didn't have one."

"All right." I dropped my arms. "Good. We need to strategize how we're going to handle the Cryptix—"

Kendrick's warm palm smoothed over my bare shoulder. "First, we need to get somewhere safe."

"We'll be safe enough here tonight." I pulled up the bodice of the strapless dress as an excuse to free myself from the fire erupting beneath his touch. I couldn't allow a repeat of the conversation earlier. "I can't be traced to this condo or even to this state."

A small smile lifted Kendrick's mouth. "No one is untraceable, but for once, I'm damn glad for your frustrating ability to make the process arduous."

I couldn't stop the full grin from taking over. I gave him a bow. "Thank you."

The rich laughter rumbling from him curled my toes.

He rubbed his face with both hands. "A part of me still wants to hit the road, but I'm going to trust your assessment." He dropped his arms. "We do need to strategize, but not tonight. I propose we come up with a plan once we've gotten some sleep. I don't know about you, but I haven't gotten much these last few days."

Walking to the screen door and closing it, I turned to Kendrick after I locked it. "We'll leave the area first thing tomorrow morning. Come on." I padded down the hall. "Claude's an obese man, but he should have something you can sleep in, and you can take your pick of the guest rooms."

Forty-five minutes later, I still laid awake in the king-size master bedroom's bed. Kendrick had found a T-shirt and gym shorts, then took a shower in the guest room that had its own bathroom. I had hopped in the shower as well (my own, not his), and the entire time, my imagination wouldn't stop picturing beads of water trailing over his magnificent body or his masculine hands rubbing soap all over his skin. It took all of me to keep my hand from sliding between my legs and relieving the pressure.

I pushed the thousand-thread-count cotton sheet off of my overly sensitive body. My tank top scraped against my hard nipples, and my fresh panties were already wet.

Only a thin wall separated us now. I moaned softly and pressed my thighs closed but that just added pressure to my swollen center. Pieces of Kendrick's dead-on accusations haunted me, overlapping with my vivid shower imaginations, and the sensations of every single touch we shared—

No. I turned on my side and punched the pillow. Regardless of my previous transgressions, I would not masturbate tonight. I did not trust my face not to give me away in the morning, and knowing his eagle eyes, he'd figure out what I had done and lord it over me.

Burying my face into the pillow, I huffed out a frustrated groan. How the hell did my life get so complicated, my enemy now sleeping under the same roof as an ally?

Chapter 11

Having already attacked the condo building's impressively stocked gym to work off my frustrations and the heavy meal (I hadn't forgotten the elephant comparison), I tossed my toiletry bag into my fully packed suitcase sitting open on the bedroom floor. Fresh from a hot shower that eased the strain in my muscles, I smirked at the contents. Kendrick had been extremely careful, but the traps I set had all been sprung. I would have been disappointed if he hadn't taken the opportunity to search the room, my purse, and the suitcase. I bet he wasn't too happy about not finding anything but documents for my latest alias: Savannah Jolly.

Padding toward the kitchen, I tightened my still-wet ponytail.

I inhaled deeply, the rich aroma of coffee filling my nostrils. "Please tell me you have enough of that divine elixir of life to share with me."

Reaching the end of the hallway, I found Kendrick standing behind the kitchen island, motioning to the second mug sitting in front of him. Steam wafted off the black brew, calling to me like a siren.

"I don't know how you take it." His deep, sexy morning voice sent a shiver down my spine. He pushed an etched crystal bowl of sugar forward with his finger to rest beside my favorite flavored creamer, which I'd picked up when I'd settled in two days ago.

Up until this point, I had managed to keep him in my periphery, focusing on the coffee. Stopping on the other side of the island, I stretched the lines of politeness by scooping a spoonful of sugar and adding the creamer to my mug.

"I would have gone with you to the gym." He set his mug on top of the hastily scratched note I had written so he wouldn't think I'd run out on him.

Shifting my gaze to the blue button-down shirt tucked inside his black dress pants, I rolled my eyes up the length of his body (he had to know the color of his shirt magnified the aqua in his eyes) and took in the neatly combed, damp blond strands curling at the edge of his ear. "Um. I think the gym has a rule about men working out in walk-of-shame clothes. Just saying."

"Smart-ass." Kendrick leaned forward a few inches, and his eyes flickered just as a small shudder rippled through him.

Did he...just...smell me?

Lifting his mug like he did nothing out of the ordinary, he eased back. "I would've only had to rig Claude's 5XL shorts to keep them from falling off. I wouldn't have needed a shirt."

Nope. Nope. Nope. I refused to allow my mind to latch onto that visual of him bare-chested and sweating, lifting a set of weights...

I took a fortifying swallow and banished the growing fantasy. I seriously needed the caffeine hit. I only managed to catch a few hours of sleep last night, and the punishing workout I put my body through didn't purge the tension. Having Kendrick in my personal space, standing across from me like a lover might after a night of sweaty, orgasmic sex, rattled my foundation. For six months, we had defined roles as adversaries. Now the lines were blurring, and I thought I had a handle on that.

Seeing him in my kitchen this early in the morning looking as delicious as sin, offering me coffee like an attentive boyfriend, smashed my illusion of having accepted the change.

"This is weird," I blurted, then took a swig to keep from saying anything else. I shifted to lean my back against the counter, needing some distance.

"Agreed." Kendrick swallowed his mouthful and scraped his eyes down my length.

With this being a travel day, I hadn't put on anything special. My beloved cross-trainers cradled my feet, my favorite pair of cropped black yoga pants hugged my legs, and a loose tank top with the Disney Robin Hood fox on it knotted at my hip over a green sports bra.

"Robin Hood," Kendrick chuffed, taking another sip. "Is he your patron saint?"

Peering down at the character who had an arrow notched with the bow drawn back, I grinned. "More like my liege. After all he is the Prince of Thieves."

Kendrick laughed and lifted his mug in a salute. "So I've heard." He drained the last of his coffee. "You eat breakfast?"

"Sometimes." I shrugged. "I figure we can grab something on the road."

Kendrick moved to the sink and took a moment to wash his mug. Right before I hit the gym, I'd remade my bed (and I'd noticed on my way to the kitchen, Kendrick had done the same), wiped the dining table, and took the trash out in an effort to hasten our departure. Claude should have no clue anyone ever stepped foot in his condo.

Kendrick held his hand out, and I quickly swallowed the last bit of coffee, savoring the flavors as the caffeine raced through my blood, then gave him my cup. Damn, the man just kept getting better and better. Twice now, he'd washed dishes without a complaint, and he'd done a thorough job at that. Either his mother taught him right, or he—

Wait. I rocked back into the counter. He didn't have a girlfriend or wife, did he? Why didn't it occur to me before this second that he could be taken? Now I couldn't stop obsessing about it. Every touch, near miss to close the distance for a blistering kiss, and heated stare swamped me.

"Are you single?" I blurted, then cringed. *Way to be cool, Holly.*

The mug clattered against the stainless steel sink. His chin shot up, and his eyes whipped to mine. "What? Why would you ask that now?"

Flames burning my cheeks, I pointed at his soapy hand. "You know your way around a sponge."

He blinked. "Because I'm a courteous roommate, that must mean I have a girlfriend?"

Not backing down, I waited for the answer. I'd already embarrassed myself enough just by asking; no way would I reveal how much I wanted the answer.

If only my mind and heart could be on the same side. My mind hoped he'd say yes, my heart bleated for him to say no.

He picked the mug up and casually rinsed it. "Are *you* single?"

"Yes." I saw no reason not to answer. What I didn't say was since the minute I clapped eyes on a certain FBI agent with amazing aqua eyes, no other man could hold my attention.

The muscles in his back loosened, and shoulders I hadn't realized bunched, dropped. He shut the water off and plopped the mug into the drainer beside its mate. "Yes, I'm single." He shot me a wink. "All my time lately has been focused on my job."

Me. Little jolts radiated through me, and my heart rejoiced at getting the answer it wanted. *Stupid organ*, my mind groused. FBI agents and thieves did *not* mix well.

"We can't go after the real Infostrata Cryptix," Kendrick announced, turning from placing the sponge back into its holder shaped like a seashell.

Snatching the towel off the oven handle, I grabbed a mug. The shift in conversation threw me, and I hated that it took me an extra second to force my inner romantic to stop visualizing me and Kendrick together.

"Not only is it buried deep within a military instillation," Kendrick continued, "the security, both in manpower and electronic tech, make getting in and out with it impossible."

"Nothing is impossible," I retorted. "And I'm not bragging, but we'll move on before you mistake that statement as a challenge for me to prove it." I vigorously wiped the other mug. "I agree Darien shouldn't have it, but how can we get my uncle back without it?"

Kendrick stared at me as if he really wanted to accept the challenge, then sighed and shook his head. "I've been thinking about possibilities." He rested a hip against the sink and dried his hands on the same towel he'd used last night. "I had a couple of strategies in mind, but after Darien's phone call last night, I can only see one viable solution."

"We can't go after him directly," I croaked, my mouth so dry with fear I couldn't swallow. The second mug clanked into the first as I set it into the cupboard with a shaking hand. "He'll kill Uncle Liam before—"

"We're not going to take him head-on." Kendrick pulled the ends of the towel tight. "I'd need the backing of the FBI and a specialized task force to even entertain that plan, and my boss has made it clear I'm to stay away from the 'pillar of society,' so that'll never happen."

I deflated, slumping against the counter. "Then how?"

"We're going to use his own plan against him. We'll make him think we're giving him the Cryptix, but in actuality, it'll be a device that will scavenge the internet to reveal every dirty secret, bank account, and contact *he's* got."

"And my uncle?" I would not let Kendrick devise a plan that restored his reputation at the expense of my only family member.

"Obviously, this is a work in progress, but we'll get him out. I promise."

Biting my lip, I reminded myself I went to him because he was an honorable man. So far, he had kept his word. I had to believe he wouldn't lie about freeing my uncle...and I had no better plan to offer. "To make Darien think he's gotten the real Cryptix, we'll need a computer programmer." I tapped my fingertips on the counter. Exposing any of my contacts to Kendrick meant gift wrapping him or her to the FBI. "I—"

"Not just a coder," Kendrick cut in, "but a person who has tremendous skills and zero problem hacking into whatever database we need to pull this off."

The coffee turned to diesel fuel in my stomach. "I've got to be honest, I can't help but think you're going to arrest whoever I bring in after we rescue my uncle."

The towel stilled in his hands, and he frowned. "You're putting me in a tight spot."

"So are you," I retorted. "I won't stab someone who'll do what we're asking in the back. You have to promise me every single person we rope in walks away."

"I can't make that blanket promise." Kendrick straightened, his frown deepening.

"Then I guess we do go back to being adversaries." Acid rose up my throat, and my chest hollowed.

"Holly." Kendrick tossed the towel onto the island. "Be reasonable. I can't make a blanket promise your contacts will never be arrested."

I rubbed my aching heart. Until this second, I hadn't realized how much I was counting on his support and expertise—

"I *will* promise not to reveal their names unless I have an ironclad assurance their involvement in our plan will *not* be held against them. That's the best I can do."

That left a lot of wiggle room. The FBI could set up stings later to nail them, but I could get Reggie to help them go to ground and set them up somewhere else.

"Holly?" Kendrick's hands tightened against his hips.

"Fine. Still allies." I met his direct gaze. "I'm trusting you on this, Kendrick. Don't screw them over."

His stance loosened. "As a show of good faith, I'm going to offer our first recruit."

The hollow ache in my chest lessened, and hope began to seep in. "Oh yeah? Who?"

He rubbed his chin. "He's a black hat hacker who had *all* his internet privileges revoked seven years ago. The government got tired of him sliding past firewalls that're supposed to be impenetrable. To keep that fact quiet, he avoided prosecution and jail but had to agree to the internet ban for life."

"Oh wow." I blinked. "You're talking about Stuart Stewart, aren't you?"

Kendrick's head cocked. "You know Stuart?"

"Not personally." I crossed my arms.

Hackers generally came in two classifications: white hats, who businesses or individuals hired to knowingly search (and attempt to hack) their online security to uncover weaknesses; and black hats, who sought out weaknesses to take advantage without the business or individual's permission.

"Logistics aren't usually my part of a heist, but *everyone* who plays in the different shades of gray knows about Stuart." I racked my brain, trying to remember anything Reggie might have told me. "Didn't he get married, like, four years ago and invited the FBI agent who shadowed him to be the best man?"

A snort fell from Kendrick's throat. "That he did, if I remember the office gossip correctly. The agent accepted, too."

"You know where to find Stuart?"

"Not yet." His mouth thinned. "I'll need to sign onto the FBI's servers to review the last reports, then begin a search."

Shit. "And to do that safely, you'll have to sign in through an anonymous server that'll bounce your location all over the globe to prevent the feds from locking onto you."

"I'd bet my next paycheck you have access to just such a server."

Well played, Agent Kendrick. I jabbed a finger toward his chest. "Don't think you'll be able to learn all my secrets."

He chuckled and held up his hands. "You are an exquisitely complex woman. I'm realizing it'd take eternity to unravel all your mysteries."

Ooooob. Smooth. "You can research your guy while we're on the road."

"You have a destination in mind?"

"No matter where Stuart is, we're not going to reach him until you're off the grid. That means a road trip to obtain a whole new identity for you."

Kendrick blinked, and a spark lit those aqua blues. "Do I get to pick the name?"

"We'll see." Reggie had received the text message I left before I fell asleep last night and had called while I ran on the treadmill this morning. He grumbled about having to set up a new dummy profile for my burner phone but understood the need once I explained how Kendrick watched everything with an eagle eye and had seen that I recorded calls. He also provided contact information for a forger located in Alabama and promised to smooth the way to avoid problems once we arrived.

"I've never worked with the man before," I continued. "I don't know his rules, but I have to use someone new."

"Why?" A small crease formed between his brows. "I told you I wouldn't say anything."

"It's not that. We can't use anyone who has ever been connected to the crew for anything. Darien could pry that information from Uncle Liam. If he decided to question them, he could learn we're working together." I shuddered, imagining my uncle bound to a chair, broken and bloody as Darien's thugs beat him into giving up secrets.

Kendrick enfolded me into his arms. "Shhhh." Smooth, soft cotton caressed my face, smelling way too damn good. His heart beat steadily against my ear, and his warmth seeped into my chilled bones. "We're going to save your uncle."

"You're entirely too handsy," I mumbled, working up a defense against wanting to absorb his strength. "I bet your boss gets a lot of complaints from the people you haul in."

A bark of laughter tickled my ear with its vibration through his chest. "Ah, Cupcake, I reserve this kind of handling only for the pain-in-the-ass, hazel-eyed thief who taunts me mercilessly, even in my dreams."

I sucked in a breath. "You dream about me?" I pushed out of his arms, needing to see all of him after that admission.

He nodded, a smile I was starting to covet drawing across his face. "Usually wearing my handcuffs. Sometimes I'm marching you in front of me, other times you're secured to the interrogation table—"

Letting out a disgusted sound, I pivoted and left him chuckling. "We're leaving in five minutes."

Chapter 12

S tanding my suitcase upright on its four wheels in the master bedroom, I castigated myself for the third time.

"...hazel-eyed thief who taunts me mercilessly, even in my dreams." His words echoed in my head again.

I'd chomped on that bait like a naive guppie, ecstatic to have a morsel dangled in front of her.

Yanking the retractable handle up—

A warm hand clamped over my mouth as a wall of heat pressed against my back.

I stiffened, adrenaline flooding my veins.

"Quiet," Kendrick whispered into my ear, stopping my elbow from nailing him in the ribs. "Someone's unlocking the front door."

Shit. I nodded to let him know I understood.

He removed his hand and grabbed my suitcase, hauling it with him as we ducked against the dresser that shared a wall with the door. He forced me behind him and curled his arm around my body, sandwiching me between him and the furniture.

I blinked, my lungs frozen in shock.

"—right. I've just reached my place in Miami," an effusive voice with a heavy accent boomed deep in the condo.

"Claude, I presume?" Kendrick asked under his breath, peering over his shoulder at me.

I gaped at his profile atop a pair of broad shoulders. No one had ever put his body between me and a threat before. After I joined Uncle Liam's crew full-time, I had always been on the front line, usually by myself. Occasionally, I'd have a partner during the actual heist but ninety-eight percent of the time, it was me handling the danger.

"Cupcake?" Kendrick twisted deeper to peer at my face with both eyes. His brows drew down. "Hey," he continued whispering. "What's wrong?"

You protected me, I opened my mouth to say, but the words got stuck.

"Ja, good flight," Claude responded to a query I presumed to be from a phone call.

"Holly." Kendrick's fingers dug into my hip. "Talk to me. I can't assess the danger unless—"

"Shit," I muttered in a low tone. "I'm sorry." My cheeks burned at wigging out over the stupidest thing during the most inappropriate time like a newbie thief. "You're right, it's Claude, but he's supposed to be partying in Amsterdam."

Kendrick studied me a beat longer. Lord knew what he saw, but he shifted so that both our right hips dug into the edge of the dresser while he still maintained almost complete cover of my body as we looked toward the door.

Out of the corner of my eye, I caught something odd sticking up from my purse. Reaching forward—which plastered my breasts against his muscular back in too delicious of a way—I grabbed the bag and lifted it to me.

"Ja. Ja." The sliding glass door to the balcony swished open. "This better be worth it. I cut trip short."

"Do I need to have Claude investigated?" Kendrick whispered, closing the little bit of distance I managed to put between us after spotting the creamer bottle and both dish towels shoved inside my bag. Good man, covering the last trace of our intrusion.

"What?" I placed a hand against his waist, right above his belt. The skin beneath his shirt quivered, and a swift intake of breath broke the silence. *Well, well, well. Not so immune to me after all.* I grinned at the little pleat at the top part of his dress shirt. *No wonder you hammered at me so hard. You tried to hide your recognition of our explosive chemistry.*

"Should I investigate Claude?" he hissed, spoiling my revelation.

"Why?"

"He cut a party trip short, and if he's one of *your* friends, that doesn't exactly give him a glowing character reference."

"Ha, ha." I playfully rocked his hip forward, then back. "We're not friends. Claude's clean, as far as I know. Way too rich and ugly as sin, but harmless otherwise."

"I slept on my plane," Claude continued, his heavy footsteps vibrating the marble flooring.

From my estimation, he was moving closer.

Lifting on my toes to reach Kendrick's ear, I murmured, "We need a distraction."

A shiver skittered down his body as his hand fisted. I seriously wanted to blow on the lobe to really drive him nuts like he had me last night, but this wasn't the time.

Soon, I promised myself. Revenge was a dish best served for maximum enjoyment.

"I have an idea." The strain in Kendrick's tone made me happy. "The second you have an opening, make a break for it. I'll follow the minute I can."

"Meet me at the outside patio of the hotel across from Prime Chophouse."

He squeezed my hand at his waist. "What's Claude's last name?"

"Ten A.M.?" Claude asked, definitely getting closer.

"Geissler," I whispered.

Kendrick lifted his chin and strode out the door. "Mr. Geissler?" His dress shoes tapped over the marble floors, indicating he'd stopped Claude at the edge of the hallway.

"Eh!" Claude yelled, the vibrations halting. "Who are you? How you get in here?"

"Can we talk privately for a minute?" Kendrick asked, pure confidence in his tone.

A thrill stole down my spine. I had a weakness for confident—not cocky—men. Dammit. Kendrick pushed all the right buttons. Why did he have to be an FBI agent?

"I got to go," Claude stated, I assumed to the person on the other end of phone. "Ja. Meet at ten."

Dropping my purse strap diagonally across my body, I gripped the handle of my suitcase and snuck to the side of the doorway.

"Why you in my condo?" Claude's tone rumbled with belligerence.

"I'm sorry to catch you unaware like this," Kendrick responded so apologetically even I believed he meant it. He probably did. "I'm with the building's management company."

Brilliant. With his clothing and authoritative presence, he could totally sell that lie.

"We've had some calls about suspicious people on the premises," Kendrick continued.

I slapped a hand over my mouth to hold in my snort. He lied by telling the truth. I'd bet my next payout he had us in mind as he spoke.

"Suspicious people?" Claude repeated.

"Yes. But since we haven't seen anything ourselves," Kendrick explained, "we decided to check in on our tenants who are out of town before we called the police."

Claude sighed, sounding like a trumpet. "I do not have time to deal with police."

"No one does," Kendrick responded smoothly. "That's why we figured we'd take a peek to see if there were any signs of a break-in. So far, we've found nothing."

"Good. Good."

Damn, Kendrick was a natural grifter. Who knew?

"Would you humor me and take a walk through your condo just to be sure?" Kendrick asked so politely. "Since you're here, I can know for sure everything's okay."

"If I must."

"It won't take long." Pause. "We can start with the guest bedroom here." Silent pause. "After you."

I peeked around the doorjamb and found the hall empty. Hoisting my *heavy*, oversized bag (Why had I packed so much?), I thanked God my workouts included lifting more than my body weight, and jogged down the corridor. Carrying the awkward luggage avoided a wheel potentially squeaking. As long as I didn't bang the wall I should be okay.

"Check the closet as well," Kendrick's voice drifted into the hall.

I slowed, peered into the room, then took off when I saw Claude's massive back.

"I never put anything in there," Claude complained.

"Okay. No problem." Tapping of Kendrick's hard-soled shoes and Claude's heavy vibrations spurned me to pick up the pace.

I ducked behind the kitchen island and peeked around the edge.

"What about the next bedroom?"

"You stay out here," Claude ordered. "I can check faster without you hovering."

I snorted.

Kendrick appeared at the end of the hall and spied my hiding spot. He waved a hand, and I took it as a sign to get gone.

I headed for the building's stairwell the second I slipped out of the condo. I only needed to go down one flight, then I could take the elevator and disappear into South Beach's tourist traffic.

Fifteen minutes later, I rose from my chair on the hotel's patio. On the other side of me, a family of five crowded around two of the tables with plates full of food, and a couple gazed only at each other over frothy drinks in the corner.

Kendrick loped up to me with an easy gait and wide smile. I couldn't see his eyes behind his sunglasses, but I imagined they twinkled.

"Impressive performance." I clapped, earning a curious peek from the little girl at the family table. "I'm seeing you in a whole new light."

Sunlight glinted off natural highlights in his golden hair as he held his stomach and took a bow. "My high school drama teacher would be so proud."

"I'm suddenly feeling a lot better about our partnership." I pulled a set of car keys out of my purse. Why did rental companies insist on securing both keys together? It would make sense to separate them so if I lost one, I could still get into the damn car with the other.

He pointed a finger at me. "Don't think this means I'm switching sides."

"Don't worry, I'm not foolish enough to believe you're becoming a career criminal." I lowered my oversize, trendy shades and grinned at him slowly, deciding to mess with him a little. "But you've just proven once again you're not a rigid, arrogant robot like your brethren. And that, Agent Kendrick, is sexy as hell."

Chapter 13

Four hours into our thirteen-hour journey (that total included stops for gas and meals), Kendrick had pulled off at the exit for a large outlet mall. I needed food and a bathroom. He needed a new wardrobe and toiletries to replace the stuff we'd had to leave behind.

The beginning of our road trip hadn't started off smoothly. The argument about who got to drive had been silly but expected. Authoritative men did not like giving up control, and the passenger seat would be eternal punishment. I argued for form's sake, but it really didn't matter to me. We planned on switching every few hours anyway, so what did I care if he drove first? With him at the controls and the steady hum of the tires, I had dropped my seat back and gone to sleep. The restless nights had finally caught up to me, and I fell into a coma until he woke me at the planned stop.

Two hours later, I tossed my empty soda cup into the trash can—my body now buzzing on carbonated caffeine and a turkey sandwich—and turned to the grumpy man trudging behind me. "Thank your sugar mama for buying you pretty things." I inwardly fist pumped at turning around his dig about me wanting a sugar daddy.

The two armfuls of crinkling paper and plastic bags bulging his impressive biceps stilled, and Kendrick lifted an eyebrow.

"I can afford to buy my own things." Male pride bristled like a puffed peacock.

"Pish." I waved my hand regally. "And deprive me of outfitting a real-life Ken doll...*Ken*-drick?"

His brows cranked down, the sight even more reminiscent of the doll with his sunglasses perched on top of his blond head. It took all of me not to laugh.

Honestly, he may be able to afford it financially, but he'd cost us everything if he whipped out his credit card. We might as well paint a target on our backs for Darien's forewarned pursuit. "Why should you take the monetary hit when it's my trouble you're roped into?" I tried to mollify his ego.

His stern expression lifted, and he resumed walking toward our perfectly ordinary, silver Toyota Camry buried deep in the busy, gigantic parking lot. I learned quickly you didn't mess with seniors on the hunt for good deals with Christmas only seven weeks away. Those octogenarians could get vicious, and they weren't above using canes and walkers to inflict pain and force a person away from a sale bin.

I pushed an empty, brand-new suitcase beside me and peeked at him out of the corner of my eye. Another hot flash made me burn from the inside out. Jesus, how the hell could a man look as delicious in a simple pair of sneakers, cargo shorts, and a fitted V-neck shirt as he did in a custom tux?

"When you put it like that," Kendrick rumbled, pulling my tongue off the pavement. "Thank you, sugar mama, Cupcake."

"Cupcake," I grumbled, secretly loving the damn nickname. We had a special thing now. I couldn't afford to get attached to this man, but having that small, private connection with him warmed a piece of the vast loneliness filling my soul.

He flashed me a grin, his good mood obviously restored.

Standing by the trunk, I waited until he hit the button on the key fob, then I opened it. "You want to put your stuff in the suitcase now or when we get to the hotel?"

With two people, we could've handled the thirteen-hour drive straight through, but we decided to stop for the night in Tallahassee. The extended shopping trip, along with refuels, bathroom breaks, and food pit stops, would push the bar too far to keep going when we had no reason to rush. The forger had a boiled peanut stand he operated during the day in a city park. He would be long closed by the time we arrived.

"Now." Kendrick set his bags on the ground by his feet. "I don't want to draw too much attention to us at the hotel."

Made sense. Being weighed down by shopping bags here was normal. At a hotel, people tended to gawk...and remember.

Muscling mine to the side, I added his suitcase to the trunk, then stepped out of the way. Taking a quick peek at my phone, I exhaled at seeing nothing new. No missed calls from Reggie or Darien.

Kendrick took organization to a whole new level. He played Tetris with his stuff, and I gaped at how he managed to fit every single thing into one medium-size bag. Of course, it helped he didn't have to pack a bazillion pairs of shoes or all the crap it took to style hair or keep up with makeup and skin regiments. Men had it so easy. The dogs.

Balling the empty shopping bags together and stuffing them into one, he slammed the trunk closed. Turning, he grabbed my forearm and tugged me forward into his space. Heat that had nothing to do with the southern sunshine blasted through me, and I took advantage of the opportunity to stare at his gorgeous face instead of constantly sneaking peeks.

His thumb brushed lightly across my forehead. "You get little lines right here when you're disgruntled about something. Care to share what just went through your head?"

"Packing—"

Adding the rest of his fingers, he smoothed them over my temple to rest on my cheek.

I shivered at the fire crackling my blood.

His eyes darkened and flitted to my freshly glossed lips.

My mouth parted in a bid to find air. The tension around us rose, pressing in on every side. My hands hovered inches from clutching his hips. I wanted to touch him so bad, my skin itched with longing, but I knew the second I grabbed him I wasn't letting go.

I don't know how long we stood, staring at each other, registering nothing but this moment. A minute. An hour. Who cared? My world narrowed to Kendrick's gaze and his caress on my face.

Kiss me.

No. Walk away.

Kiss. Me.

No. Walk. Away.

My heart and mind battled while my fingers trembled to latch on.

His lids drew down, and his eyes smoldered, spearing me with aqua sparks. I searched to see if he warred with himself like I did, but only fell deeper into his hold.

Ever so slightly, his head dipped forward.

Soft cotton filled my hands. I dug my fingers into his waist, anchoring myself to survive the kiss I *knew* would blow my mind—

BEEEEEP. BEEEEEEEEEEEEP. A car horn blared obnoxiously. "Get your prescription checked!" the driver yelled. "This is not a crosswalk!"

The spell enveloping us shattered. Dizziness gripped me at the sudden withdrawal of his attention, and I blinked, snatching my hands back.

I couldn't read anything from his blanked expression, but his rigid muscles told me something. What, I wasn't sure. But something.

He dug into his pocket and held out the clump of keys. "Your turn to drive."

Grabbing the keys, I made sure I didn't touch any part of him. Pivoting on my heel, I tromped toward the door, my mind cluttered with preteen statements.

Oh my gawd! He almost kiiiiiissssssed you. You were going to let him taste your frosting.

I started the car, thankful the disaster had been avoided.

Merging onto the highway, I kept my eyes on the road and not on the man cranking his seat back to take a nap.

If I'm happy the near disaster has been avoided, why is there a deep pang throbbing in my chest?

Ten minutes after Kendrick took back over for his turn, I curled into the passenger seat and sucked on the cherry slushy I grabbed—much to Kendrick's amusement—at the impressively stocked and popular fuel stop.

Taking his cue that we were ignoring the almost-kiss (easy enough when he slept the entire three hours of my turn...during which I *may* have had a problem keeping total focus on the road with him looking so peaceful in his slumber), I found a radio station playing a mix of current pop hits and soft rock and turned the volume to soft background noise.

"Can I ask you a question?" I ventured after another few minutes went by. We had to break the weird vibe brewing since the near-kiss, and if I was honest, I missed his teasing taunts and inappropriate goads.

Kendrick's fingers tightened on the steering wheel, then he loosened his grip. "Only if I get to ask you one in return."

"Fair enough." My guts quivered at what he might ask. "How the hell did you know we were going after the claymore?"

His shoulders dropped, and he leaned back into his seat. Propping his right arm on the center console, he...grinned. Grinned!

Changing lanes to pass a full-size RV, he smoothly slid in with the traffic. "Didn't you guys wonder why a sword that hasn't seen the light of day in over a century ended up on a movie set?"

"Of course." I thumped my frozen slushy into a cup holder and wiped the condensation off my hand with one of the napkins stuffed into the door pocket. "We're not dumb, but the story of the screenwriter and producer of the film checked out. He was the owner of the claymore who wanted to add authenticity to the movie and generate buzz so ticket sales would soar once it released." I chafed feeling into my numb palm by rubbing it on my leg. "He even had a publicity tour with it planned."

Kendrick's smile widened and even with the sunglasses on his face, I could tell his eyes sparkled.

A pit formed in my stomach, and I balled the napkin. "No."

Laughter rumbled from his throat, and he slapped his thigh. "Yes. The minute I heard about the movie production, I approached the writer/producer.

He agreed to help me set a trap to catch a crew of highly intelligent and daring thieves."

"Son of a bitch," I breathed, my respect for him deepening. "I hate to say I'm impressed, but I am. We didn't suspect a thing."

The smile faded, and his body tensed. "It *should* have worked. The people on my team are the best."

"It almost did. Uncle Liam had called an abort the second I recognized you as the sword-carrying guard."

His eyes bored into me. "Obviously, that's not what happened."

"No." I shook my head, then exhaled when he refocused that tense gaze on the busy road. "My uncle's railed at me every day for refusing to leave and changing the plan to the chaos you witnessed."

"Your getting away cost the government millions." He opened and closed his fist with his dangling right hand. "The insurance company refused to pay out the policy since the owner knowingly put the claymore at risk to help us. To avoid a huge public lawsuit, we had to give him the money."

I rubbed against a guilty ache growing in my chest. "I'm sorry." I swallowed against the regret lumping in my throat. "Is that, coupled with Friday's loss of me, why your boss wants to kick you off the unit and why he's so giddy about your suspension?"

Kendrick swiftly inhaled. "Have we arrived at the sharing stage of our relationship?"

The sharing stage sounded dangerous. The more I got to know him, the harder it became to see him only as the man trying to put me in jail. All my wins now had consequences and a name: Jackson Kendrick. He paid for each and every loss. And I was dangerously starting to care about that fact.

Peeking at me, then back at the road, he added, "You'll owe me three questions instead of one if you say yes."

"But you only answered one," I countered, suddenly sure I didn't want to say yes, but I wouldn't refuse. As stupid as it was, I really wanted to learn everything I could about the man who kept me so captivated, who stirred feelings I shouldn't even acknowledge let alone have. Yes, I lusted for Kendrick to combustible levels, but every minute in his presence had scary, deeper emotions layering underneath.

"If you say yes, I'll answer the last set." He drew his sunglasses down his nose and peered at me over the lenses. "But then it's my turn."

Yanking the generic white plastic shopping bag off the floor behind me, I snatched out the bag of Skittles. My comfort food and sugary security blanket. "Yes. Let's share."

Chapter 14

I instantly wanted to take back those words, but I didn't. I could always refuse to answer if Kendrick asked something that jeopardized the rest of the crew.

"I think we've progressed beyond the bullshitting." Kendrick's tone brooked no arguments. "We state only the absolute truth. Agreed?"

Oh boy. "Agreed." I popped a handful of Skittles into my mouth, then grimaced at how they clashed with the cherry slushy.

He slid his shades back up and grabbed the opened water bottle taking up the other cup holder. "Growing up, I had this one older cousin who I looked up to."

"Where?" I interrupted, fascinated to learn how his childhood related to his boss's nasty actions, hungering for every detail he'd divulge.

He took a swig, and for a moment I wondered if he'd clam up. "That makes four questions you owe me, Cupcake."

"Worth it," I breezed, pouring more Skittles into my hand to hide my nervous stomach. It didn't take a genius to realize he planned to ask personal questions, too.

He snorted. "Remember you said that during my turn." He tipped the bottle in my direction as if to underline the point. "My parents own a Victorian they're forever restoring in a sleepy little town between Cleveland and Akron, Ohio."

I immediately imagined a gigantic blue house with tons of white-painted gingerbread adornments and a massive porch with rocking chairs and a swing.

In this vision, a yellow Labrador lounged by the top step watching kids play in the yard with their musical laughter and shouts. A sigh curled in my lungs, and a longing to visit settled in my heart.

"Anyway." A small smile curved the corner of his mouth. "At all the family events and holidays, I used to follow my cousin everywhere and with our eight-year age gap—"

I laughed. "I can just see it now." A vision of an adorable little boy with unkempt blond hair streaked by the sun, trekking after an older version of himself like a puppy on a hot summer day. Phantom smells of hot dogs and hamburgers sizzling on a grill invaded my daydream of a boisterous family barbecue the likes of which I'd only seen on TV but had always wanted to experience. "Was your cousin tolerant?"

Kendrick's mouth crooked. "Extremely tolerant, then and now." He eyed all the mirrors, then switched into the fast lane. The Camry sped up as he passed an ancient, white-haired couple dressed in eye-popping neon shirts for some reason. Did the blinding colors help to keep track of each other?

Kendrick merged back into the previous lane. "At the end of my high school freshman year, my cousin graduated from college and was accepted into the FBI."

"Ahhh, so now I get to see behind the curtain." Enthralled, I put the bag of Skittles down. "What happened next, outside of you obviously following in his footsteps?"

"I worked my ass off to make sure I got accepted, too, once I graduated college." Kendrick took another sip of water. "By the time I started my training at Quantico, my cousin was promoted to Deputy Director."

"Whoa." I blinked, not having seen that one coming. "Bet that sucked."

His face whipped to me, and he stared. I couldn't see anything behind the sunglasses, but I could feel the weight of his gaze.

"How did you know... I mean, why would you assume that?" He turned back to the road.

I shrugged. "When I researched you, I found that you graduated at the top of your class in Quantico, but I bet you had to work twice as hard for that spot because people assumed your cousin pulled strings to get you in or something."

The bottle crinkled in his tightening grip. "You're the first person to assume he didn't."

"Then they're utter morons." I plucked my slushy up, waving it as I spoke, flinging condensation drops onto the dashboard. "A person wouldn't even need five minutes around you, especially when you're on the job, to see you're an extremely dedicated, intelligent man who has so much drive and integrity it radiates out of you."

He jolted and lowered his sunglasses to peer over them. "I'm...speechless at the outraged indignation."

I sucked on my slushy, trying to ignore my burning cheeks and his searching gaze.

"I'm also a bit turned on at the lioness ferocity you have for me, Cupcake." A slow smile spread across his gorgeous face.

Sluuurp. Sluuuurp. Sluuuuuuurp—

Aaagggh. Brain freeze!

"You still want to claim you don't like me?" He chuckled, his body relaxing back into his seat.

If I said yes, he'd easily catch the lie; instead, I made the leap to his story. "So let me guess. Your boss is one of those shortsighted men who has more ego than brains."

"He's a good man," Kendrick defended, but his weak tone didn't sell it. "But he couldn't prevent me from filling a spot in the specialized unit. My marks at Quantico, outstanding evaluations from the SAC—er, Special Agent in Charge—I reported to for years, and the myriad of letters of recommendations were too strong and beat out the other candidates. He's hated not getting to make the final decision and has always maintained my cousin bribed others to exaggerate my successes."

"What a pompous prick." I dropped the empty container into the cup holder. "He did make you the team leader of the task force chasing us, though."

"Not as a reward for hard work." Kendrick's hand on the wheel tightened. "For years, he's done everything he could to see that I fail. Given me the worst assignments. Sabotaged investigative efforts by 'forgetting' to tell me crucial details or not passing on vital intel in time to capitalize on it, and giving me unrealistic deadlines on cases no one else has been able to solve. Your crew being a prime example. Assigning me to lead the team to bring you all in is the final knot in the rope he's cinched around my neck to hang me."

The slushy and Skittles leadened in my stomach. I heard everything he said between the lines. If he tried to complain about his boss, he'd have no leg to stand on. His boss could point to Kendrick's less-than-stellar record and claim Kendrick had sour grapes and wanted special treatment because of his relationship to the Deputy Director.

"And now your boss is giddy because he thinks he's finally gotten his way," I summed up flatly. "You'll be kicked off the unit and disgraced." My hands balled into my lap. "What an asshole." I pointed at Kendrick. "We won't let that happen. We're going to take down a villain no one saw coming who will rock the law enforcement world once he's revealed, and you're going to get the credit." I leaned over the console. "No one messes with you on my watch, Jackson Kendrick. We'll show that bastard he doesn't deserve to lick your shoe let alone be your boss."

Kendrick plunked his water bottle between his thighs, then cupped my cheek. "Holly," he uttered, his thick tone filled with emotion.

I swallowed hard as the full import of my impassioned speech sank in. I meant every damn word. How stupid was that? Fighting to restore his reputation and keep him in a position that threatened my freedom should be the *last* thing I wanted, but I'd do everything I could to make it happen. For him. I hated injustice. Built a career—albeit an illegal one—around ensuring those who needed a champion had one, and Jackson Kendrick deserved to keep his honor.

His fingers roved my jaw. "You're making it tough for me to remember we're supposed to be on opposite sides."

"Yeah, well, as alpha bitch," I retorted, retreating behind wit so he didn't see how I clung to his words, interpreting them to mean he struggled with having deepening feelings behind the attraction, too, "it's my duty to protect the pack from threats."

He let out a bark of laughter and dropped his arm. "Duly noted, Alpha Cupcake."

Sitting back, satisfied with the tension evaporating between us, I retied the knot at my hip on my tank top.

Kendrick shifted in his seat and turned the air conditioning up. I covered my delight. A completely innocent reason for the sudden need to cool off could be attributed to the way the sun poured in through his side now that the arc moved firmly toward the west, but I chose to believe I got under his skin as much as he got under mine, and the last half hour had caused a fundamental shift in our relationship.

"Now it's my turn," Kendrick announced. "You owe me four questions."

Butterflies swarmed my stomach. A light sheen of sweat coated my palm at the array of possible topics he could ask about, and I suddenly wished we needed a fuel stop to give me more time.

"Remember," he shot me a look, hampered as it was by his shades, "no bullshit."

"And no asking about my clients," I retorted, reiterating what he'd already agreed to.

"I didn't forget." He rubbed his chin. "Okay. Since we dipped into my childhood, it's only fair we talk about yours. Why did you join your uncle's crew?"

Oh man. "You don't pull punches, do you?"

He shrugged. "I told you why I joined the FBI; this is no different."

Shit. When he put it like that, I really didn't have room to balk, but I didn't talk about my childhood. Ever. The subject was too personal. I had never dated anyone seriously enough to tackle this level of intimate detail, and I dodged Reggie and Gretchen's clumsy attempts when they tried.

"Holly," Kendrick drew out, sliding me another look over the top of his sunglasses.

The man was too sexy for my health. Grabbing the Skittles bag, I poured the remainder and spread them on my palm. We had a deal about no bullshit, but could I trust him with this? *You've trusted him to save your uncle. You've trusted him to come up with a plan to thwart Darien. You've trusted him enough to sleep without fear of finding yourself in the closest lockup. And for the last six months, you've been engaged in a dangerous dance with this man to the point where he's been your sole focus, excluding all other men (outside of the crew) in your life. The skittering pulse throbbing in your veins tells you how much you want to trust him with something special.*

"Hey." He peered at me again as he stroked a finger down my cheek. "You promised."

Heat speared my skin, and I swallowed against the conflicting emotions of lust and vulnerability. "I guess you could say it was inevitable."

"Explain." He jabbed the radio's power button and ominous, er, blissful silence swamped me. The station had gone to mostly static now that we'd moved beyond its reach anyway.

"I don't remember my mom's face," I began, staring at the candy. Red, orange, green, and two purples dotted my palm. Focusing on the colors gave me the strength to divulge a piece of me I've never shared. "When I do think about her, I have the strongest impressions of peace and love tangled with strain and exhaustion."

"She died when you were five, right?" Kendrick propped his arm against the center console.

"Yes." I rubbed my chest to soothe the pang, then fiddled with a purple Skittle, making it flip against the green. "After she died, when the days got rough, I used to surround myself in pillows." My breath hitched. Damn. I'd have to share even more than I'd intended for him to understand the quirk. "My mom and I didn't always have the best accommodations, so mom would make sure I had the softest place to sleep by using pillows."

"Sounds like your mom took you on an adventure each night," Kendrick softly replied. "Kind of like when I used to build forts out of sheets and chairs."

Tears pricked the corners of my eyes. No condemnation, no sarcasm, just understanding and acceptance. I blinked back the moisture. Kendrick had annihilated another piece of loneliness in my soul. "Yes. Exactly." Clearing my throat, I forced my trembling hand to steady. "Anyway, when I missed my mom, I'd surround myself with pillows and curl into a ball, racking my brain to the point of a headache trying to recall her features, but they never came."

"I'm sorry."

"Those five years I had with her, we never stayed in one location for long. Now that I'm older, I understand we would stay with people who didn't mind opening their homes to a woman who'd become a maid in exchange for room and board for the two of us."

Needing to rise out of the maudlin, I skipped ahead. "I met the only family member I know of for the first time on my fifth birthday." I smiled at one of the few clear memories I had of that time. "Uncle Liam showed up at the house my mother worked in with a bright yellow bakery box containing my favorite cake and a Barbie wrapped in Barbie paper under his arm."

"Where?" Kendrick asked, fingering his water bottle.

"Queens," I rattled off without a thought. Curling my hand around the candy, I coughed, trying to swallow the disbelief sitting at the edge of my throat. Why the hell did I give him a straight answer?

The water bottle crinkled in Kendrick's tightened grip, and his left leg began to bounce. "New York City." He peered at me, then back at the traffic. "Is it too much to hope you'll tell me if you still live in one of the boroughs?"

I gave a strained chuckle. "You've already expended question number two by asking where I lived with my mother. Don't push it."

"Worth it," he smirked, repeating my words. "Not that you've answered the first one yet, but I'm thinking I *want* to push it."

I might have decided to trust him with a piece of my history, but I couldn't speak for the rest of the crew. I risked him putting the FBI's resources behind uncovering our sanctuaries like my warehouse after we parted ways. "Nice try. Do you have a different third question before I go back to answering the first?"

He sighed long and loud. "Can't blame me for trying." His leg stilled, and he relaxed his death grip on the bottle. "Fine. What was in the bakery box? I'm curious to know your favorite cake."

My muscles quivered as they loosened, grateful he let the subject go. Opening my hand, I smirked at the dots of colored sugar staining my palm. "Chocolate and vanilla marble cake with white frosting." I plopped the two purple Skittles into my mouth. "When Uncle Liam opened the bakery box, I squealed at all the pretty frosting flowers covering the top. The owners of the house were *not* happy with all the commotion, but my mother ignored their disapproval and made a big deal out of cutting the cake and presenting the first slice to me."

"I can just picture you in cinnamon-colored pigtails and a flowered dress. You're standing on a kitchen chair because you're so short, clapping."

I laughed. "You're not far off, I'm sure. I don't remember what I had on, only that it probably got dirty by the end of the celebration." I chomped on the green Skittle. "That's also when she gave me the comb you held hostage. While she worked, I used to sit and hold it, fingering the sapphire and diamond gems and making believe it was a tiara."

"Aww. You're killing me with that visual, Princess Cupcake."

I attempted a smile, but it fell flat. "Anyway, about six months later, I lost my mother to cancer. With us not having insurance and her working under the table, she didn't know she had it until too late. My father was never in the picture, and she didn't divulge his name, so I was lucky when her younger brother, Liam, took me in even though he had no clue what to do with a grief-stricken little girl."

The water bottle crinkling again pulled me out of the mental replay of leaving the hospital with Liam, not understanding why I'd never see my mom smile or feel her hug me again.

I focused on Kendrick's hand strangling the plastic and stuffed the old heartache deep. I had long since come to grips with the loss, but every now and then, the longing to see her again struck me. "Uncle Liam lived the bachelor life, not surprising since he was only twenty-six at the time. He had girlfriends when he felt like it and a core group of friends that always hung around." I later learned those friends were members of his crew. They changed throughout the years as members retired, moved on to new ventures, or were thrown out for stupidity. "He enrolled me in school, but it was the time I spent with him in the evenings that helped me work through losing my mom."

"I can just bet I know exactly what you're going to say he taught you."

I grinned, tossing the rest of the Skittles into my mouth. "Yep, and by the time I was seven years old, I became a member of the crew."

"Seven?" Kendrick jerked to face me. The car swerved, and he cursed as he righted us back into the lane. "You're fucking kidding me. *Seven* years old?"

"Yep." I popped the "P." "I learned my ABCs during the day and studied heist techniques and executions at night." I leaned across the space and smoothed my finger over the muscle ticking in his jaw. "Don't be mad or feel sorry for me. I may have had an unconventional upbringing, but I was loved. I had a stable roof over my head, food in my stomach, and a good education."

I dropped my hand, laughing as a memory gripped me. "I remember this one time, my uncle decided to test me. I was ten and had a three-day weekend for some holiday, and my uncle drove us to another state." New Jersey to be exact. "He placed a box inside a rundown five-story office building and told me I had three hours to retrieve it without getting caught."

"Jesus," Kendrick murmured, but his mouth lifted. "Tell me you got the box."

"Hell yeah!" I crowed. "In two hours, seventeen minutes. I evaded the crew members he had stationed in and around the building and crept through every room. I won't give you all the details." I winked at him. "A girl has to keep some secrets. But let's just say I made my way to the next floors unconventionally." Via the elevator shaft mostly. With my short height, reaching high places had been a bitch and had inspired more than a few tragically unsafe inventions to get where I needed (not that I ever really grew out of that). "On the fourth floor, I spied my uncle hiding inside a cubicle just outside a glass wall office and knew I'd found the box."

Kendrick grinned. "How'd you get it?"

"Climbed into the HVAC ducks and crawled to the vent inside the office. I waited until he hovered just above the cubicle wall, sweeping the rest of the floor looking for me,before I silently jumped on top of the desk and claimed victory when I grabbed it off the chair's seat."

"What was inside?"

I laughed. "Carefully packed with a ton of Bubble Wrap and an ice pack was a can of Coke and a bag of Skittles."

"Ahhhh. A treasure worthy of your efforts."

"You get me." I pretended to wipe a tear. "I love how you get me."

Chapter 15

"**D**id you save me any hot water?"

I paused beside the left of the two queen beds and eyed the delicious specimen sprawled on top of the other. He had his eyes closed and his hands interlaced on his chest. His shoes and socks had been kicked off and his sunglasses tossed on top of the three-star national chain hotel's dresser containing the TV centered between our two beds.

"I didn't take that long." I dropped the spare plastic bag I used to collect dirty clothes onto the edge of the mattress. In truth, I might have pushed the bar on the "quick" shower I'd promised. Once I'd turned the water on, I'd realized I needed to shave my legs. My recent bikini wax covered *that* area, but my hair on my head happened to get wet in the process so I *had* to wash it, which meant using the blow dryer to fix it nicer than a ponytail—

Son of a bitch. I'd totally justified glamming myself up for dinner out with Kendrick.

I licked my lips and cringed at the fresh coat of gloss. I wouldn't acknowledge the foundation now covering my face or the time I spent applying eye makeup that didn't look like I spent time applying eye makeup. The full-length mirror attached to the wall heading to the bathroom—just deep enough in the hallway so it couldn't be utilized during sex—shit. Not that I wanted to get kinky with Kendrick.

Dammit. Why even bother lying?

The mirror had remnants of steam from when I'd opened the door.

The scent of vanilla cake with white frosting permeated the air, and I scratched my bare arm. Kendrick's favorite cake was also the fragrance of my favorite soap. When I discovered a shampoo and conditioner also containing the scent a few years ago, I had bought cases to ensure I'd never run out if they discontinued them. That I liberally used both the soap and shampoo was like waving a cape in front of a bull.

"Be careful, Cupcake."

My eyes flew open, and I jumped at the low growl, then stilled at Kendrick standing inches from my back but not touching. He had moved without me hearing so much as a rustle of clothing, and that display of stealth sent tingles racing through my center.

Lightly scraping the end of his nose along the top of my shoulder, he audibly inhaled. "You're playing with fire."

A spark burned low in my belly.

A faint touch grazed my dress's bow tied behind me at my waist. "I have the overwhelming feeling you want me to tug on one of these ends."

Oh God, I did. I wanted him to take the decision of us crossing the line out of my hands. Getting involved with him would be stupid on so many levels, but I had become too invested in him to think clearly.

The dress was the most provocative thing I'd packed, and my hands had refused to pick out anything else from my suitcase. Playing with fire? Hell yes. For hell was where I'd been living since the first time Kendrick pinned me to the floor in Michael's house, and I wanted him to burn along with me.

I held my breath. If he tugged on the bow, it'd ultimately unravel my whole dress. With just a few simple movements unwinding the material, the mid-thigh-length, navy fabric would puddle to the patterned carpet, leaving me in just a pair of panties since I couldn't wear a bra with the backless dress.

"Holly," he whispered in a throaty groan. His ragged breath assaulted my skin, sending chills coursing through me. "We can't—"

"Wait to eat?" I cut him off, not wanting to hear the rest of that statement. "Agreed. I need real food. Somewhere that serves entrées with vegetables and has real silverware."

A low chuckle mixed with half a growl speared down my spine. "Yes, broccoli was exactly what I just pictured sliding across my tongue."

My mind blitzed.

His heat disappeared, and a moment later the bathroom door shut.

I opened my eyes and slumped against the bed, catching myself with my hands. "Jesus," I exhaled. My panties were completely soaked, and I couldn't tell if I wanted to rage at missing out on the mind-blowing sex his body promised or drop to my knees in prayer, thanking God for dodging that bullet.

Water pounded against the shower stall, and a new aroma of musk and spice, the same scent I wanted to snort off his skin like an addict, mingled with the vanilla cake in the air.

"Jesus," I muttered again, clenching my hands against the trembling. Kendrick just loved toying with me. How had he figured out I had a weakness for this particular scent, but only once it soaked into *his* skin—like it was doing now? From his hands rubbing over his naked—

I hung my head, panting. Why the hell did I agree to share a room?

Yes, I had to be the one to book the reservation since Kendrick didn't have a new ID yet, and no, the hotel wouldn't let me have two rooms without Kendrick showing some kind of identification...but our chemistry just kept getting stronger and more vivid.

Our sharing truths in the car had strengthened the bond growing between us. The fundamental shift in our relationship had me trusting him to the point where I'd confided details of my personal life with him. Why did I keep doing things like that? No one got those secret pieces of me, yet I couldn't hold back with Kendrick.

The minute he figured that out, too, I'd be in a world of trouble.

A wince-worthy squeak, followed by the water shutting off made my brain instantly cough up a vision of him waltzing out, dripping wet in just a skimpy white towel.

Straightening, I grabbed a fresh pair of panties out of my suitcase, which I had shoved in the closet. I tossed the useless ones into the bag with the rest of the dirty clothes. At this rate, I'd need a washing machine or a store in just a few days.

"I'll meet you in the lobby," I yelled, escaping for fresh air and a public place to keep me from jumping him despite his weak protest.

Chapter 16

C urling my feet beside me, I nestled deeper against the ugly wooden head-board bolted to the wall. Pillows squished behind and around me—I may have stolen a few off Kendrick's bed—allowing me to lounge in whatever position I wanted.

Dinner had been mostly silent, and the second we got back to the room, I scooted into the bathroom to wash off the makeup—not an easy decision, but I had my pores to think about—and put on the most sedate pair of pajamas I'd brought with me.

The pink ribbed tank top with a picture of a white sheep on it hugged my chest and I pondered again if I should also wear a bra (it wouldn't take much of a glance to see my rosy nipples through the thin fabric). The matching shorts weren't too skimpy (just mostly), but I didn't plan on parading around the room any more than I had to.

Flicking through the channels, I searched for something to take my mind off the near-misses today. We had two doozies we currently were pretending hadn't happened: the almost-kiss at the outlets and my golden engraved, not-very-sub-tle invitation for him to show me just how dirty and raw sex with him would be. Which he turned down. Gracefully, but a no all the same.

My eyes slid to the infuriatingly complex man hunched over my thin ultra-book computer at the table shoved against the wall beside the dresser. He pecked on the keyboard like a chicken scrabbling to pluck up seeds. His two forefingers smashed down on the keys like they'd offended him somehow.

The army-green T-shirt with a surfing graphic he'd donned while I was in the bathroom draped deliciously over muscular shoulders and a defined back that left me salivating. I could barely see the black jersey shorts, but my memory supplied a visual of the tight ass they showcased before he sat in the ergonomic office chair.

Look away. I scrolled through the channels and settled on *The Goonies*. Uncle Liam got me hooked on eighties films, and this one was a classic that fit any occasion or mood.

Unfortunately, Mikey, Mouth, Data, and Chunk could not keep my attention. My toes wiggled, and I played with the remote, flipping it constantly on my thigh. Had the room gotten smaller since I stretched out?

I drummed the fingers of my other hand against a pillow and tried to focus on the Goonies pack discovering a pirate's treasure map and goading each other into finding it.

The walls had to be closing in.

I launched off the bed and paced to the bathroom. Moving helped the restless burning festering inside me. Tucking my forearm beneath my breasts to keep them from swaying—my eternally hard nipples already called enough attention—I propped my elbow onto my closed fist and paced back to the bed.

Pivoting, I swished the closet door open and bent over to fish inside my suitcase for a sports bra and decent shorts. "I'm going for a walk," I called, trying not to destroy the careful packing that minimized the wrinkles on my clothes as I searched.

"Huh?" Pause. "What did—"

Silence except for the low volume movie.

I almost cheered out loud when I finally spied the spandex shorts and sports bra set I liked to run in. Straightening, I slid the door shut and turned to Kendrick—and froze.

Swiveled to face me, his eyes were so dark they were turquoise and lasered on my ass...or where my ass had been a second ago. Now they fixated on my crotch, covered in cartoon sheep on my small shorts.

All the moisture fled my mouth as his gaze *slowly* tracked up my quivering abdomen to my aroused breasts. The tip of his pink tongue slid across his bottom lip, and he pulled at the hem of his T-shirt as if to ensure it covered his lap.

My eyes flew to the spot, but his loose clothing hid the prize I really wanted to see.

"What did you say?" he garbled as if he'd chewed on glass for dessert.

I pulled my gaze up and found him swallowing hard as he met my eyes.

White knuckles appeared and he crossed his feet at his ankles.

"I..." I choked and worked to find some saliva to quench the desert in my mouth. "I'm, uh, going for a walk?"

He scrubbed his hands over his face, then combed his fingers through his hair. "I have a lead on Stuart."

That halted the restlessness inside me. "You found him?" I padded forward, my bare feet barely making a sound on the randomly patterned, industrial carpet.

"Ah, yeah." Kendrick cleared his throat and leaned farther back in his seat.

I stopped at the end of the dresser. Neither one of us should really be that close to the other right now.

"I was afraid Darien's mole might be able to get a log of my movements once I signed in," he explained hoarsely, motioning to the screen that showed he'd logged off the FBI's server. "Your program might work to hide where I used the computer, but I didn't want him learning who I'm interested in."

"Excellent point." I pulled my bottom lip with my fingers.

Kendrick's pupils dilated and followed the movement.

I dropped my hand and wrung my workout clothes. "What'd you do to cover it up?"

"Huh? Oh, I cleared my emails out." His mouth flattened, and his body tensed in a different way. "My boss sent a warning that I'll be summoned to formally answer questions in front of a committee soon."

Shit. That could really screw with the tight timetable. We had to deliver the Cryptix before Darien killed Uncle Liam.

"We'll deal with that when it happens," Kendrick answered, obviously reading my expression correctly. "I also checked your file—"

"Can—"

"No, you cannot see it." Kendrick deleted the browsing history and all traces of the FBI's web address. The rat.

Not that I had his sign-in information but Reggie might have been able to hack in.

"Nor can you see the files on the other crew members, which I browsed, too, just to keep up appearances." He slapped the lid closed. "Westbrook, my number one guy, has been promoted to keep up the search for your team." He rubbed his jaw. "We can't underestimate him. He could become a problem."

"We'll add him to the list."

Kendrick snorted. "Then I randomly chose nineteen other names outside of Stuart's with no rhyme or reason and spent an equal amount of time in their files so no one would get a clue I'm targeting the hacker."

Can I just say how much I love a smart man? Brains are such a turn on.

"And?" I rocked up to my toes and back. "Where is he?"

Kendrick followed the move with his focus on my still-erect nipples. "Where... Oh. He's headed for Saint Croix."

I blinked. "Really? Why?"

A grin started at his mouth and filtered up to his eyes, which now sparkled with glee. "You're going to love this."

I couldn't help but smile at his infectious joy. "Don't keep me in suspense!"

"Stuart hasn't had an FBI shadow for years now. He's been pretty much locked down in a no-name town in Missouri with a regimented schedule and a job that gives him zero access to a computer."

"His poor wife."

"Funny you should say that." Kendrick laced his hands behind his head. "According to the notes in his file, assistance has been granted for an FBI agent to accompany Stuart and his wife, Melanie, to a four-day conference in Saint Croix."

"You're dragging this out on purpose, aren't you?" I narrowed my eyes. "I bet you were one of those kids who took all day unwrapping his presents at Christmas, weren't you?"

Kendrick laughed, his whole body shaking from mirth. "Guilty. Drove my parents crazy. Still does, actually." His grin turned devilish. "Prolonging the suspense is a huge part of the fun."

My breath caught. I got the distinct impression we weren't talking about reindeer-paper-wrapped presents anymore.

"Tearing the paper off and digging into the box can be fun, but savoring each step heightens the enjoyment when I finally peek inside." Kendrick's voice deepened. "I find I like to study the present first. It could take hours, even days to admire the wrapping and the shape. My imagination takes over, guessing and visualizing what could be inside."

The Sahara found its way into my mouth again.

"How does the pattern of the paper fit with the gift?" he continued. "Will I discover a surprising number of layers hidden beneath? What do I hope to find inside, and am I ready to accept it?" His eyes locked onto mine. "To help answer those questions, I may touch it," he uttered in a low tone. "Just a graze or maybe a caress. Nothing that will give away the contents but enough to really drive my imagination wild."

Jesus, I would never look at a present under the tree the same again.

"When I can't take it anymore, I'll finally hold it." The muscles in his arms stiffened on top of his head. "Molding my fingers over every inch until I've memorized every curve, line, and edge. I'll get to know this present with all my senses before experiencing it."

Fuck, I wanted to be one of those damn presents. Imagining him using his hands and mouth on me as he learned my body made me ache all over again.

"I'll know when it's time to slide my finger beneath the first piece of tape." He shifted in the chair. "This part shouldn't be rushed. Exposing the layers warrants my respect and full attention." His aqua eyes raged the color of the stormiest sea. "When the wrapping has been fully peeled and the paper lays discarded at my feet, I'll take exquisite care parting the flaps and entering the box. You see, the gift means so much more for having thoroughly understood and learned everything about it. I'll play with it that much harder, cherish it that much deeper, and prolong the enjoyment that much longer."

I gaped, then pivoted on my heel. "Excuse me," I croaked, marching to the little refrigerator tucked inside the dedicated cabinet. Tossing my running clothes on the bed, I grabbed one of the three bottles of water Kendrick had stocked from the supply in the car when we first arrived.

Cranking the lid off, I tipped my head back and chugged half the bottle. When the raging fire finally doused to a simmer, I held it out. "Want the other half?"

"Hell yes." He lowered his arms, and as I got closer, I noticed the fine tremor running throughout his body.

Driving my fingers through my hair after he took the water, I exhaled a shaky breath. "It's a wonder your family doesn't switch to gift cards."

Kendrick choked on the water and coughed. "Special presents receive special treatment." He finished the bottle. "But there are times when I'm inspired to rip the wrapping off and dive right in."

I pointed at him, narrowing my gaze. "*You* need to quit teasing me."

"I don't know what you mean." He grinned, totally unrepentant. "We're talking about gifts under the tree."

"Do you really want to start this battle with me?"

If anything, his eyes sparkled even more.

"No." I jabbed toward him. "The answer is no, you don't." My quota for sexual innuendo and frustration had reached its limit. "You were telling me why Stuart, his wife, and an FBI babysitter are headed to Saint Croix."

Kendrick tossed the bottle into the blue recycling trash can and shifted in the chair again. I caught a glimpse of a *very* impressive bulge pushing at his shorts before his hips settled with the T-shirt covering him again. "I'm not sure how you're going to feel about this next part."

I forced my eyes back into my head. My warning bells clanged, drowning out the rampant tingles swamping my lady bits. "Stabby if I don't hear it in the next two seconds."

"Starting this Thursday, they're attending a four-day marriage boot camp for relationships on the rocks."

My jaw dropped.

"I wish I had a camera."

"Are you serious?"

"About the camera or the couples boot camp?"

I propped my hands on my hips.

"Right. The boot camp." Kendrick rose, his height, now that I didn't have shoes on, had me staring at his pecs. "I've skimmed through the retreat's website and only married couples can attend."

It took an extra second to really understand the meaning of those words. My eyes whipped up to his.

Kendrick cradled my left hand between his hands. "What do you say, Cupcake? Would you do me the honor of becoming my wife for a few days?"

Chapter 17

T apping the plain 5x7 manila envelope end over end on my thigh, I stared absently out the window of our private jet to the water below on our way to Saint Croix. Forced to beg a favor from a former client, he agreed to fly us way below market value (pretty much the equivalent of gas money). With only the pilot (my client) locked up front, Kendrick and I had the plane to ourselves and complete privacy.

"Would you do me the honor of becoming my wife..."

My bare toes curled against the carpeting, and my thumb worried the underside of the simple gold band now circling my ring finger. After two days and two *long* nights, I still hadn't gotten that question out of my head. Add to it our insane chemistry and his taunting Christmas present metaphor, the tension surrounding us remained high. Plus, I had become an official addict of that damn scent mixture of musk, spice, and...Kendrick (the promise of no-holds-barred sex radiating from his skin). I'm pretty sure that first night in Alabama (after a silent car ride to finish the road trip, the forger appointment, and pretending to be tourists), we had an aroma war with our soaps and shampoos, each trying to see if we could make the other break. I barely held on by the tips of my short, unmanicured fingernails, but I did it. The key to my sanity had been trading childhood stories. My adventures with Uncle Liam's tests and his growing up in rural Ohio.

My heart still pattered at the tale he told over slices of veggie pizza about him tromping through the creek one summer with his friends and discovering a family of frogs. I could just picture him covered head to toe in mud from "rescuing" them and bringing them home to his mother, stuffed in pockets and both hands.

A soft *thwump* and a flash of blue returned my focus to the man that adorable boy had grown into as he placed my laptop on the side table and pushed up from the couch across from my two-chair row of rotating and reclining leather luxury.

To help pass the time waiting on the forger to process my document request for the past two days, I'd had our clothes laundered and dry cleaned. Kendrick now wore the same outfit that had kicked off our partnership: impeccable black dress slacks, blue button-down shirt rolled at the sleeves, and dress shoes. Only now I'd caught glimpses of that incredible body underneath. Drool. Worthy.

"Would you do me the honor of becoming my wife…"

Kendrick eased into the oversize beige seat beside me and dropped his forearms onto the armrests. My eyes zeroed in on the simple gold wedding band circling his ring finger—a match to mine.

"It's been almost seventy-two hours since I popped the question," Kendrick rumbled. "How long are we going to wig out about being married?"

The punch to my stomach hit me all over again. "We're not married for real."

"You sure you don't want to change your answer about that?" His aqua eyes danced as he twisted our chairs to face each other. He scooched forward to bracket my knees between his. "Imagine the hell of a wedding night we'd have."

I snorted, not needing him to prompt that particular fantasy. I pretty much imagined him naked, doing all kinds of wicked things to my body and me returning the favor, All. The. Time. I tried to sit back, unable to think with him taking over my space, but I had nowhere to go. The soft cloth of his pants rubbed my bare skin exposed below my mid-thigh-length, full-skirted dress with mint green splashes of color. "Like you'd want to be legally tied to a thief."

"Yeah." He nodded, his gaze sweeping the jet's interior. "That'd be something to explain at the office Christmas party coming up." He slapped his thigh and chuckled. "I know what I'd say." Mimicking holding a drink, he adopted a fake serious face. "What can I tell you, boss, the thief snuck in and stole my heart."

Laughter rippled out of me. "Okay. I have to give you points for coming up with that on the spot."

"You never know," he mused. "It could happen."

"Sure, but I'd bet on probability over possibility."

After we'd dropped the rental car off, but before we'd entered the airport to board the jet, Kendrick had pulled a velvet bag out of his pocket and presented the rings. My heart attack had been subtle but still noticeable. He hadn't helped matters by insisting on sliding my band over my finger and me doing the same to him. It had felt a little too real.

"Hmmmm." His eyes scraped over me. "I do wonder if it's just our cover or my job that has you so freaked out about being my wife."

"Kendrick," I drew out, clamping my armrests.

"Oh, come on. Play along with me."

I didn't want to play along. My feelings for him were still too new. Too jumbled. Too scary to put labels on them. And unfortunately, they were still growing deeper and more encompassing by the second. I couldn't let myself be that vulnerable. Especially since I *wanted* to imagine a future where I could one day have the honor of claiming the title of Mrs. Jackson Kendrick.

"Fine. Be that way." He petulantly pouted with all the drama of sullen teenager, making me laugh.

"That's better." He pointed to the envelope now laying across my right thigh. "I still can't believe you dropped a hundred grand for the IDs and added an additional twenty-five K rush fee on top of that."

The meeting with the new forger in Mobile, Alabama, had gone as well as I hoped. The guy's eyes had all but popped out of his head when I gave him my large order and time constraints, but he had the full packages (including licenses, passports, social security cards, and working credit cards) at the dead drop by nine this morning. The timing made my teeth clench, but I understood. Quality could not be rushed, and our lives depended on not getting caught. The conference began at three o'clock this afternoon, and we were now pushing it with a four-hour flight and travel to and from airports to make it before it started.

"Why so many?" Kendrick pulled me back into the present. "I get that we need a set for our married personas, and you're smart to have a backup individual set for us, too, but the others?"

As much as Kendrick tried not to show it when we were with the forger, I could tell by the way he held himself he had not liked taking another step over the line he had already crossed when he agreed to help me.

"I believe in being prepared." Outside of the ones Kendrick had just listed, I had full sets for Stuart and Melanie as well as Oscar Brudney, the computer hardware guy who was next on the recruitment list to build our fake Infostrata machine.

Scowling at Kendrick's beautiful face, I jabbed a finger against the package of IDs. "How in the hell did you talk me into using Ken and Barb Roberts as our married names?"

"You said I was your real-life Ken doll," he smirked. "Figured you'd enjoy making it a reality."

"I can't believe you vetoed my backup name, too. There was nothing wrong with Charlotte Church."

"I have a good reason, but I'm invoking my fourth question." His expression lost its mirth, putting me on guard. "It's one question, but I have to ask it in two parts."

"No. Uh-uh." I waggled my finger. "If it's two parts, then I get another question."

His head cocked, and after a moment, he gave a nod. "That's fair, I guess, but only after you answer mine."

"If you insist." I sighed with gusto to hide the giddiness at getting to invade his life again.

"I do." He smoothed a hand along his freshly shaven jaw. "I'm curious about the naming convention for your aliases."

I already didn't like where this was going.

"London Grace, Paris Eve, Sydney Frost, Dakota Garland, Florence Mantle, Savannah Jolly, and now Charlotte Church." He ticked them off with his fingers. "Just to name a few."

Holy shit. My stomach gurgled with sudden queasiness. I had no clue he'd uncovered that many.

"Why do you always pick locations for the first name?" He held up one finger, then added a second. "And part two, please put me out of my misery and tell me the code for the last name." He unleashed puppy-dog eyes on me. "It's haunted me too many nights trying to crack it."

"Ha! You *do* have dreams about me that involve more than just your hand-cuffs and an interrogation table." I kept my tone light to cover the disquiet unsettling me. "Although, Agent Kendrick," I tapped his thigh, inches above his knee...and bounced off rock-hard muscle, "that sounds really dirty from over here."

His chuckle was full of raunchy, wicked sex. "Cupcake, if you only knew what I did to you in those dreams to make you sing for me."

Heat blasted through me, sweltering me from the inside out. More than one trail of sweat fell along the edges of my fully styled hair.

He winked, his mouth crooking into one of my favorite grins.

One of us was going to crack and finally cross the line. I feared it'd be me. Soon. And I wouldn't bother with glamming up for a seduction; I'd just attack him.

"I'm assuming those aliases are documented in my file?" I wanted to pat myself on the back for remembering the conversation that could be the difference between jail and freedom in the future.

"Yes." His legs shifted, pressing mine harder together for an instant. "And even though that was a question, I'm going to be magnanimous and not take away the one you get to ask me later." He waved a hand as if bestowing a decree. "That list is the reason I insisted you have something completely separate from what you've used before. Your pattern has become noticeable."

Holy wow. I owed Kendrick a *massive* debt for passing on that vital piece of intel.

"Okay." He clapped, startling me out of my gobsmacked haze. "I've allowed your distraction from answering long enough. Spill." He pointed at me. "The same rule applies—no bullshit."

I blew out a breath and stared out the window across the aisle at blue sky. "It's not that easy."

In the growing silence, I warred with myself on how to answer.

He placed a warm palm on my forearm. "Holly?"

I had already confided in him about my mom, and he hadn't sneered or made me feel small. I guessed I could share one of my best and most treasured memories. He'd hopefully accept it, too. "Mom and I didn't own much." I glanced sharply at him. "Probably not shocking news since you know we didn't have a home and moved around a lot."

He stilled, then without a word, stood. Quiet interest and appreciation etched lines in his forehead as he gently pulled on my forearm until I stood beside him.

Wha...?

Sliding his fingers downward, he laced our fingers together, then slowly walked us toward the couch.

Lowering my head, I stared at our linked hands. I had been pinned to the floor by him, crowded against a building, and gazed deep into his eyes, but the simple act of holding his hand felt more intimate than anything I'd experienced so far.

"I've never held a man's hand like this before," I whispered, digesting the sensation. Warmth—the kind from the heart not the temperature—encased my fingers, and that could only be coming from him since my soul carried so much loneliness. I hadn't realized how much emptiness filled me until Kendrick had awoken the craving to have someone to love and love me in return.

"Never?" He stopped in front of the two-cushioned couch and peered at me. "How is that possible?"

"My growing up years with Uncle Liam don't count, though he never held my hand like *this*." I made a small adjustment, fully immersing my fingers into the hold.

"Okay, but you're a beautiful woman, Cupcake."

My heart leapt to my throat, and I bet he could feel the pulse rippling through our link. *He thinks I'm beautiful?*

"Why haven't men held your hand on a date?"

I shot him a shy smile. This hand-holding thing heightened my aware-ness of him. "My lifestyle doesn't exactly cater to finding and keeping worthy boyfriends. The crop of men I've attempted to date haven't been that keen on anything remotely romantic."

"Sounds like you need to break out of the box and look elsewhere."

I snuck a glance at him. "Apparently I do." Too much of me wanted to believe I'd already found the perfect man, but that kind of thinking lead to heartache.

"I'm sorry." Kendrick squeezed my hand and plopped us onto the cushions. I fell, pressed completely against his side with our interlocked hands resting on my thigh. "I didn't mean to interrupt your explanation, but this is important, and I wanted to be closer for it. Your mom and you didn't have your own home and moved around a lot..."

I blinked. "Right. My single pink suitcase wasn't big enough for many toys, but I didn't know to care about that. Outside of my mom's comb, I had one other cherished item." I absently traced a finger over and around his, enjoying the weight of our link pressing on my leg. "A foldable, ratty map of the world. The laminate coating had frayed so much, pieces of Scotch tape held it together.

"At night, after my mom dragged herself to our room, she'd tuck me into my pillow bed and unearth that map from the front pocket of my suitcase. Spreading it in front of me, she'd have me close my eyes and point. Wherever my finger landed, we'd pretend to have a grand adventure as explorers or invaders or use it as a basis for our kingdom. You get the idea."

"I really wish I could've met your mom." His tone was full of respect. "She sounds amazing."

I cleared my throat. "I like to think she was. Others would probably criticize how she raised me, but she did the best she could. Anyway, I use locations for my aliases' first names because I like to feel connected to my mom as I embark on an adventure. Or contracted heists nowadays."

"Cupcake."

I untangled my hand. "If you want to know the rest of it," I lightened my tone, to hide how safe and accepted I felt in his cocoon of warmth, "you'll have to wait until I get back from the bathroom." I bolted to avoid making a fool of myself at the way he crooned my pet name. The urge to close the distance between our mouths raged strong.

How the hell was I supposed to spend more nights locked in the same room with him and keep my hands off? Or avoid being tempted to share some more?

This had to be a special kind of hell created just for me. Only the devil could deliver the perfect man, have our chemistry raging to the point of distraction, make my heart swell and soul blossom, only to dangle him out of reach by making him an FBI agent. A thief's nemesis.

Chapter 18

The multi-toned taxi sputtered away from the curb in a cloud of black smoke, leaving me and Kendrick standing at the end of the beachside resort's curved driveway with our luggage at our feet. The ham and cheese sandwich I did more picking than eating on the flight sat in my stomach like a rock, adding more weight to the tension coiling tighter in my body.

Salty ocean air mixed with grilled vegetables and seared meat lingering from lunch should've been amazing except they were overpowered by exhaust fumes. Peppy island music pumping through speakers hidden throughout the property beckoned a tourist to forget her troubles and integrate into paradise. I couldn't wait to sink into the crystal-clear, blue water—way too reminiscent of Kendrick's eyes—I'd spied from the plane.

Another taxi (this one in *much* better condition than ours) meandered up the short, curved driveway to stop underneath the salmonish-pink portico. The weird color pink must be a favorite of the owner, or the hotel should fire the marketing company. It was everywhere, even in the staff uniform of pink bowling-style shirts and white shorts.

Long Reef Resorts in Christiansted might have started out as a three-star hotel seventy years ago, but it had since devolved into a two-star...and that was being generous. Yellow Ginger Thomas (Saint Croix's official flower) and colorful hibiscus blooms burst a little too wildly from the flower beds lining the driveway and along sections of the just-shy-of-rundown, seven-story building while the bushes and tropical trees had overgrown to the point where they gave a creepy vibe.

According to their website, the hotel boasted having one-hundred-eighty rooms (a mixture of single rooms and two-bedroom suites) with half those having an oceanfront view, all having air conditioning and satellite TV. They also offered three meeting rooms, an on-property seafood and steak restaurant, a pool with a sundeck, and beach activities like scuba diving and boat tours. I had to wonder about the businesses who chose this seedy place for their corporate events. Not that I should be judgmental. The counselors of marriage boot camp may have had no choice in order to keep costs low enough to attract suckers, er, those hoping to rekindle marital bliss while working on their tan.

Whatever the case, the age and lack of initiative to make improvements could work in our favor. Security features were probably woefully out of date, and I'd bet they had massive gaps I could exploit if I needed to.

"Christmas?"

I peered at the scowling man beside me. Kendrick's grumbled question about the code for my aliases' last names pulled me from my inspection. "For the third time. Yes."

"It's too fucking simple." He crossed his arms and spread his legs shoulder-width apart.

"What did you expect?" I lowered my voice to barely a whisper. "With a name like Holly Bell, I had to use the holiday somehow."

"I should have figured that out." Kendrick swiped a hank of my hair trying to invade my mouth from the constant breeze. My eyes zeroed in on the gold wedding band wrapped around his finger. It still caught me off guard to see the thicker match to my own.

"Cupcake, we've managed to cover a lot of topics, but we've run out of time for the most pressing one."

An older couple shuffled toward us to use the hotel's sidewalk on their way to the entrance, and Kendrick crowded into my space to let them pass. I took advantage and inhaled his exquisite scent.

Once he shifted back to his previous spot on my right, I closed my eyes and soaked in the sun. "How we're going to play this, right?"

"In my experience," Kendrick started in a low tone, "it's best to go with the truth as much as possible."

Flashes of his performance with Claude flitted through my brain. He was right, and his answer fit with the Uncle Liam's lessons from an early age.

"We won't have to keep track of the lies this way." His fingers threaded with mine, and his ring bit into my skin. "Obviously, we'll have to deviate where required."

I snorted, clamping my dress with my free hand, the hem fluttering dangerously close to exposing my panties. "Yeah, we can't exactly go around spouting you're a suspended FBI agent and I'm a wanted thief." I worried the underside of my ring with my thumb; the weight and constriction felt so foreign.

He squeezed my hand. "Good thing Barb married Ken, then. He's a simple man living in Wisconsin, who just wants to get laid by his wife."

My eyes popped wide. "And does Kendr—"

"Welcome to Long Reef Resorts!" a male voice trilled with so much joy, I gaped.

A porter in salmonish-pink and white (shocker) hustled toward us from beneath the portico. Strands of gray curled through his short black hair and glistened under the sun's unforgiving rays.

"I still owe you an answer to a question," he murmured. "Were you about to ask it?"

I shook my head, glad the porter had cut me off. I hadn't been able to ask on the jet and didn't want to waste it on something stupid.

Kendrick winked. "I'm in fear of what your curious mind is going to demand. Will it be about my first kiss?" He held up a finger to the porter who had finally reached us with a huge smile, signaling to the man to wait. Using our linked hands, Kendrick turned me to face him. His shoes tapped the tips of my four-inch black heels, putting us a breath apart as he bent to whisper in my ear. "How about the first time I got a girl to go all the way with me? Or maybe you want to know if I've used my handcuffs in the bedroom?"

Air refused to circulate in my frozen lungs. I wanted to know all of that and yet none of it. I didn't exactly want to picture him with another woman.

His cheek pressed against mine, and I shivered at the puff of air rushing past my lobe. "I'll answer that last one as a bonus." His breathing turned ragged. "You'd be the first. No one else has inspired me to fantasize about using them, let alone try." He stepped forward until our bodies were flush against each other and his addictive scent washed over me. "And, Cupcake, I *really* want to try."

My mind blitzed. Just completely checked out. That son of a rat fink.

He pivoted to greet and shake hands with the porter, leaving me throbbing and thinking about nothing else but him naked, me writhing, and a pair of handcuffs secured to a headboard.

The porter pulled the handles on both our bags with such delight, I wondered if he truly got pleasure out of hoofing suitcases or was angling for a bigger tip. Sweat dripped over his dark brown face but he didn't seem to care. His steps all but skipped as he led us up the sidewalk.

The second the main doors automatically slid open, air conditioning blasted so hard my hair blew back, and goose bumps dotted my skin. A cursory glance showed aging furniture in a small seating section to the right and an outdated check-in desk along the left wall. A seven-foot-tall waterfall that cascaded down a cheesy glass monolith with rotating gel lights in the rock bed took up valuable real estate on the way to the elevators.

A fiftyish woman with a loose bun holding silver hair and a beautiful cream-colored business suit blocked our path, forcing me to pull up short or ram right into her.

She lifted a clipboard, skimmed it, then peered at us. "I hope you're the Robertses."

"Ken and Barb." Kendrick smiled as he extended his hand.

"Dr. Patricia Day." She shifted her clipboard to her other hand, then shook Kendrick's before vigorously shaking mine. "You're the last ones to arrive, but seeing as we start in twenty minutes, you're okay."

Kendrick placed his left hand at the small of my back. "See, honey, I told you we'd be fine."

"But, Kenny, I wanted to check out our room and freshen up from the trip," I whined with an extra annoying tone, assuming that was my role after that comment.

"Oh, I'm afraid you wouldn't have been able to do that no matter when you arrived." Dr. Day's brow crinkled. "We're not letting any of the participants into their rooms until tonight."

"What?" I straightened. I wasn't prepared for that disconcerting announcement. I had banked on easing into this conference and maybe catching Stuart in the hallway or something. Then Kendrick and I could split, moving on to the next name on our list.

"We're serious about this being a boot camp to tackle your issues."

That sounded ominous.

Dr. Day plowed forward with her disclosure bombs. "If we allowed participants into their rooms, they could skip out on the first evening's activities. And that's not why we're here."

Dear God, what the hell had we gotten ourselves into?

"We're kicking off boot camp with an orientation." Dr. Day read from her clipboard. "Followed by our first group therapy session, then a break for dinner."

My eye really wanted to twitch.

Kendrick's fingers dug into my back.

"After dinner," Dr. Day barreled on, "we'll break into smaller groups to tackle some ice breaking exercises that should really help you two remember why you fell in love."

Dr. Day beamed.

Kendrick remained stiff and looked like he kept his smile through sheer determination.

I wanted to cringe and prayed my burning face didn't give us away. *Fell in love?* *Shit.* I wasn't there yet, but damned if I wasn't sort of, maybe falling, and from my bird's-eye view, I saw asphalt, not a fluffy cloud, rushing up to splat me.

Kendrick's fingers curled the material of my dress as he inched closer to me. "Sounds like we're getting our money's worth."

I scowled. It sounded like hell. And this was only day one.

Dr. Day's expression turned sly. "Let's hope you remember that when we're into the heart of the conference, Mr. Roberts. Please be in the Reef Room in ten minutes." She turned, then paused, looking back. "The staff will have your luggage placed in your room by the time we break for the night. Even though you registered so late, we were still able to reserve you an oceanfront room as promised to all our attendees."

"Thank you." Kendrick dipped his chin. "We really appreciate it."

"Honey?" I asked the second Dr. Day zipped out of sight, hating the change. "You called me 'honey,' not Cupcake." Damn. My voice trembled a tiny bit, giving away just how much that stupid pet name meant to me.

Kendrick enfolded me into a hug that comforted rather than seduced. "Only Holly Bell is my Cupcake," he murmured.

Oh. My. God. How did I defend myself against this? I wanted to push him away and cross my arms to stop my heart from lurching out of my chest and into his hands to keep.

"That's my signal." He rested his cheek on the top of my head, and I breathed him in. "When you hear me call you Cupcake, you'll know I'm talking directly to *you*."

I swallowed. Twice. "What should my signal be?" Damn husky hussy took over my voice again. "What do you want to hear me call *you*?"

He shifted just as a fine tremor rippled over him. "You can't say what I want to hear, so how about 'sweetheart'? Think you can tolerate calling me an endearment for a while?"

What did he want to hear? Curiosity flooded my brain. "I think I can stomach that, but 'sweetheart' is way too generic." I pulled back and blinked at our faces lining up so perfectly, we'd only have to close mere inches for the kiss I couldn't stop fantasizing about. "I'm going to come up with something better."

"The thought of what you'll choose terrifies me a little bit."

"As it should." I already had one in mind. If anyone in the crew ever found out I gave it to Jackson Kendrick, they'd assume the world had ended or I'd been struck with brain damage. Tightening my arms around his waist, I bit my lip. "I hope Stuart is worth all this and that he agrees to help."

Kendrick ran a thumb along my jaw. "We'll just have to be very persuasive."

"We don't take no for an answer?"

"Not if we can help it." His thumb retraced its path. "We're a team. Between the two of us, he doesn't stand a chance."

A team. I loved the sound of that and hoped he was right. I couldn't lose sight of what was at stake. My uncle deserved my doing whatever it took to save him from Darien.

Chapter 19

The Reef Room wasn't anything spectacular except for the view. The 16x30 space had the typical stained industrial carpet in a geometric pattern including beige, navy, and pale yellow. White walls had canvases utilizing the ever-popular salmonish-pink and a line of windows starting two feet from the floor and ending a foot from the drop ceiling. Outside, a patch of green grass lined with Ginger Thomas flowers gave way to a chipped, decorative stone footpath which led to the expansive pool deck and the white sandy beach with the ocean beyond.

Aqua waves called to me as they crashed to the beach, leaving their white foamy goodness behind only to crash again. Sunbathers in every assortment of sizes and colors soaked in the late afternoon rays, and I longed to be one of them.

"Take your seats please," Dr. Day announced from behind me.

Soon, I promised the ocean. *I'll come see you soon. Uncle Liam needs me now.*

Turning, I surveyed the eleven couples (not counting me and Kendrick) jockeying to claim seats that faced the ocean view in the massive oval. No tables were in sight. Just the same salmony-pink, stiff-backed, padded chairs found in most hotels (outside of the color).

Sauntering to the closest set of chairs, I sat with my back to the windows and plunking my purse on the seat next to me. Facing the door (okay, it was actually across the room and to the right, but I could see it easily), I searched for Kendrick while pretending I cared about not wrinkling my dress. Once I couldn't stall with that anymore, I made a production out of searching the purse I had bought at the outlets for some mysterious item that didn't exist.

Dr. Day cleared her throat, then leaned to whisper to a cute, thirty-something man sitting next to her. By his suit (complete with a tie), posture, and their familiarity, I figured him to be another therapist, same with the mid-forties, black-haired woman in a sexually repressed outfit (including Birkenstocks and a well-loved beige cardigan buttoned to strangle her neck) sitting on Dr. Day's other side, holding a notepad and pencil.

I stuffed my bag under me as Kendrick slid into the seat next to mine, earning a censorious glare from Dr. Day. Oh, goody. We really knew how to make an impression. Late to register for the conference. Last ones to show up to the hotel. And now making everyone wait to start orientation. Awesome. That should make our turn during therapy a ton of fun.

"We caught a break," Kendrick whispered, totally invading my space. "I don't know the FBI agent."

Hurdle number one conquered. Kendrick had hidden behind everything he could on our way to the Reef Room. He had to check out Stuart's government babysitter to make sure our cover wouldn't be blown.

"I chatted with him for a minute," Kendrick kept going. Somewhere in the moments since he'd left my side, he had found something minty to chew on. Now I wanted a Tic Tac. "I got his name," he murmured, "then I did a quick internet search on him. Chet Seymour has way too many personal pieces of information on social media, but that works out for us. No girlfriend or wife. He's into brewing his own beer and is barely a year out of Quantico, assigned to a satellite office in St. Louis."

Hallelujah, a rookie. That meant he probably wouldn't be entrenched enough to know or care about me or my crew.

"According to the conference website," Kendrick's breath kept tickling my ear, causing pulses of pleasure to thrill me inappropriately, "Chet's not allowed inside the room during therapy since that's protected by confidentiality and he's not an active participant—"

"Now that we're all here," Dr. Day took a swipe at us, then smiled broadly at the rest of the circle, "we can begin."

Kendrick straightened and placed his hands on his thighs, then ruined the "good student" pose by giving me a wink.

Dr. Day welcomed us to the retreat, then launched into a list of rules like a seasoned drill sergeant. I wouldn't be surprised if she had been in the military before retiring to offer counseling to civilians.

Despite the gentle voice, she hurled Dos and Don'ts at us with all the grace of a grenade. My respect for Patricia Day grew. This woman knew she was an alpha bitch and had no problem claiming her position—

"...sex."

I immediately tuned in. What about sex? Damn. What had I missed?

"While we hope you all rekindle that spark in your marriages," Dr. Day continued, "please remember this is a not a private resort nor a private beach. Explicit intimate moments such as intercourse should be enjoyed in your rooms."

I would not look at Kendrick. I would not look—

My eyes slid to Kendrick. He sat rigid beside me, his cheek dimpling from what must be him biting it from the inside. His aqua irises danced and flicked my way. It took all of me not to start laughing at how good he was trying to be.

Challenge accepted. Leaning my chin on his shoulder, I surreptitiously inhaled to get my scent fix and murmured, "Guess I've got to cancel the surfside orgy scheduled at midnight."

His shoulders silently shook as he grabbed my hand and squeezed. "Damn," his strained voice whispered. "I was really looking forward to that bonus workshop."

"Kisa," I pronounced it as Kee-sa, "I had a bonfire planned and door prizes of vibrators and condoms."

"Kisa?"

"K.I.S.A.," I spelled out. "The acronym is my signal for *you*." I jabbed his ribs, giving him the pet name that'd make the crew suck in air in shock.

"What—"

"*Respect,*" Dr. Day said sharply, turning piercing brown eyes toward us, "must be given to every person in this room. When someone is speaking, we *all* will give our attention to him or her."

D'oh! I let go of Kendrick and slunk in my chair like a child, properly scolded. It didn't help to find every eye planted firmly on me...while more than a few of the wives slid their gazes to Kendrick with a little too much appreciation. Not that I blamed them, but it raised my hackles (Whatever the hell hackles were I had no clue, but mine were standing up). I threw a whole lot of *Hell, no, he's mine,* into my eyes and stared them down until they looked away.

Kendrick donned an "avid listener" pose, but proved he'd witnessed my claim-staking showdown by the way his mouth crooked and his posture loosened as if totally pleased, but not before I caught him glaring at a few men, which eased my embarrassment tremendously.

Dr. Day moved on to lecture us about being on time for therapy sessions, blah, blah, blah. I studied my fellow prisoners instead of listening. I easily spotted Stuart and Melanie Stewart on the other side, two couples left of center. The twenty-nine-year-old slouched in his chair sullenly. He had at least a few days' worth of growth on his round face and his meh brown hair really needed a trim. Melanie, on the other hand, had her shoulder-length ginger hair styled and nails polished, and she wore the type of designer threads found in department stores, usually on sale. She'd be pretty if her hands weren't tightly laced together and her mouth pinched unpleasantly. Yikes. Trouble was definitely in paradise. Would our proposal make things better or worse? I'd have to ask Kendrick for suggestions on how to approach them. As an FBI agent, he had to have had training in hostile negotiations. My expertise fell more into puzzling out how to obtain things from supposedly secured places.

Unfortunately, we had inadequate windows to talk to the couple without the FBI newbie hovering. Before and after therapy and maybe during a break, if we got one. My stomach clenched. I doubted that would be enough time to convince him to help. We had to come up with a Plan B—

"Barb and Ken, let's start with you," Dr. Day announced, making me sit up straight.

Start with us doing what? Son of a bitch. I shouldn't have tuned out that far. Kendrick cleared his throat and shifted in the chair, uncrossing his ankles.

"Active listening," Dr. Day peered at the rest of the circle, "is the goal of our first therapy session."

Oh Jesus. We're rolling right into group therapy? No break? No wheeling in a liquor bar to help us loosen our tongues? Shit. I could use a stiff drink—or ten—right about now.

Dr. Day placed her clipboard on her thigh. "When we talk to our partners, we hope they are paying attention and hearing what we're telling them. Unfortunately, most people tend to listen only so they can respond. Utilizing active listening forces us to listen so we understand." She eyed all of us to underline her teaching point. "By *showing* your partner you are hearing him or her, you'll avoid arguments and misunderstandings later."

I already hated this exercise.

Dr. Day smiled at Kendrick and me. "Let's try it."

No. Let's not. Why did we have to be the guinea pigs anyway?

"Barb."

DAMMIT! She couldn't start with Kendrick?

"Please turn in your chair and face Ken."

I dutifully did as instructed, and Kendrick shifted so his knees knocked against mine as he faced me. His aqua eyes danced, and I wanted to slap the smirk off his face. *You'll get your turn. Just you wait,* I silently told him.

His eyebrow lifted. He did not seem properly cowed. The rat.

"Tell Ken what brought you here, to boot camp," Dr. Day instructed. "Is there something you wish he understood or appreciated?" She held up a finger. "This is not the time to hold back. Be honest, but take care not to go on the attack."

Like I could truthfully say: *I'm here because I need to recruit a black hat hacker the government has on a tight leash to help save my uncle...* I cleared my throat.

It's best to go with the truth as much as possible. Kendrick's words played in my head, giving me an idea.

Focusing on my "husband," I answered, "He doesn't see the value in my work." Kendrick's brows cranked down, and he leaned forward a touch. I kept going. "He doesn't understand what I really do or why I do it."

I had to refrain from rubbing my sweaty hands on my thighs. Stupid exercise putting me on the spot. I may have confided in Kendrick why I started stealing, but we'd never talked about why I stayed in my uncle's crew.

"Ken," Dr. Day cut in, "what are Barb's concerns?"

"I heard what she said." Kendrick's expression brimmed with speculation. "I want to talk about these points my wife wishes I valued and understood."

I jolted at the "my wife."

He leaned into our space. "Trust me when I say I can't wait to learn everything I can about her."

Yowza. With that tone, I believed he truly meant it. The trick would be not giving him something to use against me later.

"That's not this exercise," Dr. Day shot back, not giving an inch. "Please say out loud what you understand Barb's concerns to be."

"She thinks I don't understand what she does or why," Kendrick dutifully regurgitated. "She thinks I didn't listen when she told me how she fell into her line of work, but I heard every word."

But you don't know why I continue to pull heists, and that's a huge part of me I haven't shared.

"Ken, why don't you tell Barb what you wished she understood or appreciated," Dr. Day prompted.

Oh boy. This ought to be interesting.

He rubbed his mouth. "Cupcake, I need you to know that no matter how far you run or where you go, I will find you." Kendrick reached forward and laced his fingers in mine to rest over our knees. "That's not a creepy stalker statement, either. She knows she's become my entire world. My dedication to the chase has been well documented, and she loves it. What she needs to understand is no matter what, I won't give up."

I sucked in air. My heart pounded at all the romantic implications in those words, clutching the innuendo that we'd be able to forge a future after we freed

Uncle Liam. My fight-or-flight instincts shivered at him telling me that whether he still had a job with the FBI or not, he'd come after me. What the hell he did with me once he caught me remained a scary question.

"Barb." Dr. Day annoyingly broke into my scrabbling to unravel his meaning. "What are Ken's concerns?"

"Kisa knows I do love him chasing me, *but* he's also just as addicted to the chase." A tremor flitted through his hand to mine, and he raised an eyebrow. "He loves the pursuit. The thrill of the hunt. Pitting his wit against my intelligence." I bit my lip and voiced the fear that had been lurking in the back of my mind since he pointed out my weakness. "I worry he'll get bored once he's caught me."

"You're married," a belligerent voice snarked from across the circle. "I think it's safe to say he caught you."

"Ah," a woman two couples down from Kendrick chirped. "But they're at a marriage boot camp. She's got a legitimate concern about him being bored." The late-thirties wife with bitter eyes leaned deep into the circle to capture my gaze. "What'd he do, honey? Cheat?" Those eyes slid to her husband, a dejected lump of a man slumped beside her. "That's what they do. Bang the intern, then blame *you* for it."

"Okay." Dr. Day clapped her hands. "This is great interaction, and we're going to have more dialogue in future sessions, but we need for everyone to have a turn telling their partners why they're here."

I tuned out the therapist forcing the couple to Kendrick's left to publicly spill their guts.

Kendrick pulled me forward with our still-linked hands and whispered, "For the record, we only have male interns at the office right now. Since I'm not into men, you're safe from me banging one of them."

I clapped a hand over my mouth to silence the snort. I appreciated the levity, but my concern still remained. Kendrick and I had quite a few obstacles in our way, but that didn't seem to slow my soul from allowing him to replace more pieces of loneliness.

Chapter 20

"Now's our chance," I whispered, whapping Kendrick in the gut. "Whoa, mama. You're ripped." Jerking my eyes away from the abs hiding beneath his dress shirt, I pointed at Stuart and Melanie skulking back into the Reef Room.

Kendrick caught my hand from bapping him (fine, attempting to feel those bricks) again and threaded our fingers together, his eyes dancing with amusement.

"You love doing that, don't you?" I held our entwined hands up. "Just 'cause you claimed my hand-holding virginity doesn't mean you can take advantage of me, Kisa."

"Cupcake," Kendrick murmured against my hair, laughing. "How much wine did you consume?"

"I lost count after the third glass." Dinner had been a prearranged tasteless, rubbery chicken with barely steamed broccoli and some kind of rice mixture in the banquet room of the resort's restaurant. It totally sucked. I thought we'd get to enjoy island cuisine. Not the typical conference catering found the world over.

"The waiter should've just brought the bottle like I asked," I complained. "Dumbass had to keep running to the bar for quite a few of us."

He kissed the back of my hand, and I goggled at the feel of his lips on my skin. "It's never a dull moment with you. Now enlighten me as to what Kisa means."

"Nope. Come on, we've got to catch them before the drill sergeant comes in and calls us to order."

Kendrick let out another bark of laughter and let me pull him across the room. "Drill sergeants don't call people to order; that's a court—"

"Whatever. You got the meaning." I dragged him right to Stuart and Melanie. "Hi, there," I chirped to the sullen couple. They should have taken advantage of the alcohol when they'd had a chance.

Warm fingers squeezed my shoulder as Kendrick drew me tighter against his body. "Barb and Ken Roberts." He offered his hand to shake.

"Stuart and Melanie Stewart," Stuart answered, taking Kendrick's hand.

"We know." I smiled. "We need to talk to you."

Leery concern filtered into Stuart's eyes, and Melanie frowned. "Why would you want to talk to us?"

"Are you asking philosophically or because I just said we did?"

"Okay, Cupcake, my turn." Kendrick's fingers bit into my skin.

"Ow." I scowled, wiggling my shoulder to get him to let go. He didn't, but the pressure eased. "Disclosure." I focused on the couple. "In order survive the icebreaker games next, I have consumed a larger-than-usual amount of alcohol."

"Told you we should have ordered another round," Melanie hissed to her husband.

"We need your skills," Kendrick lowered his voice, stopping Stuart from defending his abstention.

Stuart's eyes narrowed. "I drive a trash truck for a living. I'm sure your city has enough sanitation workers already."

"You do now," I chimed in. "But not seven years ago."

The black hat hacker jerked and whipped his head around to see if anyone else heard me. "What do you know about that?"

"Your friend outside is an FBI agent sent to ensure you don't touch a computer." Kendrick pointed toward the door, indicating Chet lurking somewhere beyond.

Stuart's eyes flashed, and I wondered if he planned to deny it. His posture tightened, and he ran his fingers along the buttonhole placket of his chambray shirt. "Fine," he spat. "Then you know I'm not allowed to even so much as have a cellphone made after 1991." He fished inside his khaki pants pocket and withdrew a bulky phone. (Whew. I'd been worried he walked around with a constant hard-on. Talk about awkward and distracting.)

The hacker thrust forward the large, thick phone that had a pull-up antenna and a section that flipped down to reveal the keyboard and rested against the chin as the microphone. "Look at this thing."

I couldn't stop looking at it. "How do you text on that? There's barely a screen."

"You can't," he responded flatly. "That's the point. I'm not allowed to be near *any* computer."

"Well, we very much need you to not only be near a computer," I soldiered on, amazed the ancient phone actually worked, "but create a program that will scour the internet."

Melanie covered her mouth, her eyes nearly popping out of her head.

"Oh, shit." My stomach dropped. "Did your wife not know about your other life?"

Stuart snorted and shoved the phone back into his pocket. "She knows. How could she not with all the restrictions I'm under in order to stay out of jail?"

"I won't let you risk Stu's freedom." Melanie dropped her shaking hand.

"Okay, everyone," Dr. Day yelled, breezing through the door with the other therapists in tow.

Dammit. "I need to explain."

"No." Melanie shook her head and wove her arm through Stuart's.

"We're going to break up into three groups of four couples." Dr. Day waved her arms as if that would magically sort us. "When you hear your name called, please follow the therapist to one of the conference rooms."

Oh, this already sucked. We couldn't maneuver ourselves to stay with Stuart.

"I have to explain," I whispered, leaning into the hacker's space.

Melanie pulled Stuart away, just as mine and Kendrick's names were called.

We followed Cute Therapist Guy into the Ocean Room (the hotel really must not care about originality with these names) at the end of the hall. It looked very similar to the Reef Room, only this one had a frayed maroon color scheme and showed more of the lighted pool beyond its windows. Night had fallen, and I couldn't see the ocean anymore, which bummed me, but I always had tomorrow.

Dr. Daniel Hechler (Thank God he reintroduced himself; I did not remember that *at all* from orientation) had us sit at a large round table big enough to seat ten people, by the windows.

"Okay," Dr. H. stated in a friendly, Midwestern voice. "The last exercise of the night is all about reminding you why you fell in love with your partner."

I peeked at the other three couples (which did not include the Stewarts). None of them appeared any more thrilled than I felt. That stumped me. I knew why I paid to be here, but why did these guys fork over the cash if they didn't want to do any of the sessions?

Dr. H. met every eye. "Question one, tell us your first impression of your husband-slash-wife on the day you met." He let that soak in, then turned to me. "Barb, why don't you kick us off?"

Shitdammit. Why did I always have to go first? I hoped this pattern didn't continue for the rest of the conference.

With my head pleasantly swimming, I shrugged off the unfairness and had no problem coming up with the answer. "Oh, that's easy."

Kendrick placed his elbows on the white tablecloth and laced his fingers together. "I *can't wait* to hear this."

I sighed, staring at him, lost in his rugged beauty. "That's my favorite smile in your wicked arsenal."

He blinked, and two red dots appeared on his cheeks, then, if anything, that playful smile grew. "Good to know."

Dr. H. chuckled. "Okay, well, you skipped ahead to question three, but let's come back to the first."

"Oh." My face flamed. "Sorry. Right. My first impression." I leaned forward to take my tablemates into my confidence. "I'd glimpsed Kisa many times before, but I didn't get my first *true* impression until I got close to him." I dropped into a storyteller tone. "Imagine a very suave, very luxe black-tie soiree. I'm in five-inch heels that cost me sixteen hundred dollars and this gown I had specially designed by my friend because I'm so short."

Kendrick choked and coughed. "Sixteen-*hundred*-dollar shoes?"

"You loved them, don't lie." I eyed him, then went back to my audience. "Anyway, I'd just entered the second-floor gallery of this mega swank townhouse to see the Vermeer painting on display." I paused. "It was the reason for the party, but whatever. Moving on. Just like out of a movie, I'm standing by the stairs when the crowd shifts, and there he is."

I shivered, remembering that intensity. "Piercing aqua-blue eyes held me prisoner, and I couldn't move. This gorgeous, decadent man in a custom-tailored tux took my breath away, but my *very first* impression when the crowd parted was that I felt like prey trapped in a wolf's stare."

Kendrick wove his fingers beneath my hair and across the back of my neck, turning my shiver into trembling. "Cupcake," he uttered with so much meaning, he managed to have a full conversation with one word.

"Then what happened?" One of the wives pressed her ample chest against the table to peer around Kendrick at me.

"I did what any good prey out to catch a wolf would do." Warmth shot through me, hardly any of it from the wine. "I ran so he would chase me."

"Caught her on the fourth floor," Kendrick added, beaming with pride.

"Tackled me, to be exact." I laughed, slapping the table. Seeing shocked faces, I clarified. "Oh, he was completely chivalrous about it. While in midair, he twisted so he took the full brunt. I landed on top of him. Then he flipped me over and pinned me to the floor with my wrists above my head." I sighed and laid my head on his meaty shoulder. "I'll never forget it."

Dr. H. cleared his throat. "I guess not." He appeared to struggle for a second, though I couldn't imagine why. Wonder what he'd think if I told him Kendrick also put me in handcuffs that night. "Well, I'm almost afraid to ask, but Ken, is that the same night you had your first impression of Barb?"

"No, actually, it wasn't." Kendrick's answer rumbled against my ear. I wanted to stay put, but I wanted to see his face even more for this answer.

Dr. H. perked up. "Tell us about it."

"The first time I formed my impression was months before the soiree." Kendrick talked directly to me even though he should be addressing the others. I didn't care. I loved being the focus of those amazing eyes.

"Where?" I asked, curious which job had started Kendrick and me on this wild path.

"Portland, Oregon."

The African Mask job. I remembered that one well, but not Kendrick. Huh. How could I have missed him?

"I had seen pictures of her before," Kendrick continued, "but nothing prepared me for seeing her with my own eyes for the first time."

My heart skipped at the way his voice softened along with his irises.

"This small boutique museum had a grand opening for an African collection the curator had worked years to put together."

More like the crooked woman had swindled, bribed, and strong-armed families to give up their heirlooms.

"I had gone with some coworkers, but after an hour, I needed fresh air." Kendrick traced a finger down my arm. "And there she was, standing at the edge of the sidewalk, off to the side of the main entrance, talking to a friend of hers."

My breath caught. Gretchen. He had seen Gretchen tell me we had to postpone the job because the FBI had gotten wind of the heist. My comm device had failed, forcing her to come after me directly. So many bad things happened that night, I was glad we went back a week later and reclaimed the mask for the family who had been its guardian for generations.

"I froze," Kendrick admitted with a small smile. "Completely caught in her spell. I couldn't tell you my name in that second or care about the reason I'd attended the opening in the first place. The most beautiful sight I had ever seen stood beneath a streetlamp, robbing me of coherent thought."

Tears pricked the corners of my eyes. I'd had no idea. No idea Kendrick had seen me and definitely no idea he'd had such a visceral reaction to me.

His thumb traced over my cheek, then he turned to the therapist. "She's been stealing pieces of me ever since."

Chapter 21

"*S*he's been stealing pieces of me ever since.*"

Holy shit. I couldn't stop replaying that line. A goofy, sloppy grin spread across my lips. "You think I'm a beautiful thief."

"That I do." Kendrick put his hand against the elevator door to keep it open while I tromped out to the second floor. "And you called me a gorgeous, decadent wolf."

I swayed my hips as I followed the signs for our room number grouping. "You're a part of my pack, remember?" I pivoted and walked backwards, carefully picking my feet up so the ugly carpet wouldn't catch my heels and knock me on my ass. "But I'm still the alpha."

Kendrick prowled after me, his eyes turning wolfishly intense. "I love it when you turn all warrior on me."

A hot flash roared through me, and I wanted to tackle him against the wall—

"Cupcake," Kendrick growled.

Lifting my chin, I almost went through with it but managed to stop the impulse. A tacky, salmony-pink-painted hallway was *not* where I wanted my first kiss with Kendrick. "One day, Kisa," I warned. Righting myself, I paced beside him without the seduction. "We need to come up with a Plan B."

He scratched the back of his head and swiped his mouth. "Plan B. Right. To talk to our favorite couple?"

"Yes. I think we'll need more time than a few stolen minutes between sessions to convince them."

"You up for a little recon?"

"Oh, you *do* know exactly how to sweet talk a girl."

Another small growl fell from his throat. "I'm a fast learner, and that seems right up your alley. I'm assuming you'll want to change first?"

"Of course."

He stopped outside our door and hovered the card key above the slot. "What did you mean when you said I don't see the value of your work?" He cranked his head to face me. "Or how I don't understand what you really do or why you do it?"

I slumped against the wall. "Can we talk about that another time? We've had enough therapy today, and besides, it's not your turn to ask a question."

"You want me to know." He straightened, gearing up to dig in. "Or else why mention it tonight?"

"Kisa, please." I did want to tell him for some stupid reason, but not now. "I'm asking you to let this go."

He didn't move for what felt like an eternity but was probably only ten seconds. Finally, he nodded. "I won't badger if you *promise* me the answers."

I scraped my shoulder along the wall and crowded his space. "I promise."

The creases in his forehead cleared, and light drifted back into his eyes. He jabbed the key into the slot.

I opened the door to an ugly rectangular room with a single light on somewhere beyond the hallway containing the bathroom and closet. Partially closed, gaudy curtains revealed a sliding glass door that showed a balcony with a simple railing and the dark ocean beyond.

Marching deeper inside, I slammed to a halt beside the dresser. The setup was reminiscent of our Tallahassee room except for two notable differences. The balcony and...

"There's only one bed." I stared stupidly at the king-size mattress.

Panic rose to squeeze my heart, and I gripped the strap of my purse.

Kendrick stopped behind me, having peeked into the bathroom first. "Nothing gets by you, does it?"

I whirled and jabbed a finger at him. "We cannot share a bed."

"Worried you won't be able to keep your hands off me?"

"More like *you* won't be able to keep your hands off *me*." I stared pointedly at the appendage currently reaching to touch my face.

He didn't hesitate to smooth his palm over my cheek and bury his fingers in my hair. "And we had made so much progress in therapy," he teased.

Exactly. That icebreaker session had really shaken me. I couldn't stop replaying his confessions. *"The most beautiful sight I had ever seen..." "She's been stealing pieces of me ever since..." "Her eyes radiate like she has so much energy inside it's bursting to blanket everyone in her light"* (which was part of his answer to question three).

His eyes sparked with mischief. "I found the perfect wedding present, and you're already getting into the role of not sleeping with me."

"You got me a present?" The last one he'd bought was the wedding rings. Call me leery, but I wasn't sure I wanted whatever he picked up.

"I did." He cocked his hip. "I'm thinking I should make a trade for it."

"Then it's not really a present, is it?"

He halved the space between us, his lips now only inches from mine. "You know how I treat my gifts," he crooned in that damn sexy voice that hit me in all the right places. "Are you saying you don't want to become one?"

I fished my hands up through his arms and caressed both his cheeks in return. "Are you saying I'm not one already?"

The slow smile spreading across his mouth promised so much naughty fun it stole my breath. "Touché."

Not a denial. Oh boy. To be this man's single-minded focus...

"Um. What did Ken get Barb?" Was that my voice? I swallowed against the husky tramp.

"*I* got *Cupcake* something that will make her so thankful, she may incorporate this giant bed to express her gratitude."

My fingers spread into his hair, and I almost moaned at the soft, silky strands. "What if I wanted to use the wall or maybe the edge of the desk?" I teased, unable to help myself.

His eyes darkened to turquoise, and he gripped my waist. "I'm flexible."

The heat radiating from his palm added fuel to my own fire. "This present would have to be something amazing."

"Reach into my front left pants pocket and find out."

Swallowing hard, I shook my head.

"Coward," he chuckled, his voice full of glass shards.

"As you pointed out, unwrapping a gift should not be rushed." I forced myself to step away, hating to lose his touch. "Rooting around inside the wrapping would be cheating if I don't get to actually enjoy the present."

"Damn. Trapped by my own metaphor." He drove his fingers into his hair, then pulled out the phone I'd given him in Miami and handed it to me. "Go to the picture gallery."

I did as instructed and found only one picture. My eyes widened as I comprehended what he'd captured. "How did you get this?"

"*You* are a bad influence." Kendrick pointed at me. "Dr. Day left her clipboard on a table in the restaurant, and I happened to see it when I headed to the bathroom. Figured it'd come in handy, so I snapped a quick pic."

Sending the photo to my phone, I handed his back to him. "You are turning into an amazing partner." I pulled up the picture and skimmed the list of all the boot camp couples with their room numbers written beside their names. "This makes recon so much easier."

Relaxed in my cross-trainers, black spandex shorts with a pink line on the sides, and a matching sports bra (pink with black accents) with a loose white tank covering it, I meandered beside Kendrick as if we were out for exercise and fresh air. A family of four and one other couple (not part of our conference) took advantage of the lighted pool to cool off from the still-eighties temperature. I couldn't believe the light worked given the condition of the rest of the hotel.

We moseyed to a section of concrete deep in the shadows between the two sparse spotlights at the edge of the pool deck. If I hopped a foot down, I'd be on the white, sandy beach. Tempting, but as I'd lost my buzz, I had to stick to work. "What's your count for the cameras inside?"

"One in the elevator," Kendrick answered as a breeze whipped off the ocean. He had chosen a pair of gray jersey shorts, a snug, red, clearance T-shirt with a motivational quote about crushing competition, and, resting backwards, a black Ohio State baseball cap (his alma mater) he snatched up the second he spied it in an all-sports store at the outlet mall. He looked so deliciously male, I had trouble concentrating. "And a camera at each end of the long stretch of hallway."

Stuart and Melanie had scored a two-bedroom suite on the seventh floor. No way would the FBI babysitter stay in a different room when he was in charge of making sure Stuart stuck to his agreement.

We had ridden up in the elevator and pretended to be drunk and lost, finally "stumbling" into the stairwell to jog back down.

"I didn't see any cameras in the stairwell." I tightened my ponytail and casually turned to face the hotel. "Do you think they all actually work?"

Kendrick stood beside me and peered up at the monstrosity. "Debatable, given the condition of this place, but at least one or two on each floor have to be active." He lightly tugged a strand of my hair. "Isn't this your area of expertise?"

I snorted. "Absolutely, but I try never to pull a job without doing extensive research and recon first. One walk-through doesn't cut it." I turned in a slow circle, staring up at all the fixtures, poles, and building.

"What are you thinking?"

"That I'm damn glad I had Reggie send me a care package." The large, beat-up cardboard box had been sitting on the floor beside my suitcase in the room. I had asked him for it the second we settled on coming to Saint Croix to recruit Stuart.

Kendrick exhaled and shuffled his sneaker clad feet. "I'm going to hate this next part, aren't I?"

"I doubt it." I shrugged, pausing my circuit back at the hotel that had no curves—it was just a seven-floor rectangular box with fifteen balcony rooms per level facing the ocean and the other half facing the road, starting with the second floor. The first floor had all the amenities (check-in, business center, conference spaces, restaurant, etc.) and service areas (housekeeping, management offices, etc.). I calculated the heights and widths between the white metal railing balconies and studied options. "It's nothing too far out of your comfort zone, but I say we move on to Plan B if Stuart won't listen to us tomorrow at a session. Personally, I doubt he'll give us a chance."

"And Plan B is what?"

Waves crashed against the shore. Somewhere in the distance, authentic Saint Croix music played. And the kids squealed in delight as they cannonballed into the pool—much to the couple's dismay.

"The hotel went cheap, not surprisingly." I pointed up at certain areas around us. "There're only two cameras out here. One has an odd angle of the pool, and the other's aimed at the restaurant's patio tables. None on the hotel itself."

Kendrick checked out the horrendous security, his brows drawing down. "How do they get away with that?"

"I'm celebrating that lapse in good judgment." My ponytail whipped in the breeze, slapping my cheek. "Plan B is we wait until this time tomorrow night or a little later, and I sneak into Stuart's room to have a quality chat with him."

Kendrick scrubbed the back of his head. "And how are you going to make sure it's quality with Chet in the picture?"

I grinned. "I think you're familiar with the drug."

"Of course. How stupid of me." He swiped his mouth. "How are you sneaking in?"

"By taking advantage of the resort's golden invitation." I grinned. "You'll see. But those two lights on the roof there," I motioned to the ones I meant, "need to go to make all my options easier."

"Let me take care of that."

I jerked and blinked at him.

"What? I can pull my weight in this partnership." He jammed his hands into his pockets. "Have a little faith I can take care of some damn lights."

"Okay. You're right. I'll leave them up to you." I weaved my way to the sparse row of worn chaise lounges scattered along the backside of the pool. Loud scraping made my teeth clench as I straightened one, then Kendrick did the same. "Let's see if we can learn which bedroom is Chet's."

I plopped onto the chair and gazed up at the Stewart suite.

"So, Kisa." Kendrick broke their silent stakeout (not counting the pool commotion) after twenty minutes. "What's it stand for?"

I chuckled, thoroughly enjoying driving him nuts. "You're a smart man. I have faith you'll figure it out."

Silence reigned for another five minutes. "K.I.S.A.," he spelled out. "Kendrick is supremely awesome."

Laughter burst out of me. "Clever, but no."

"Kendrick is super adorable?"

"Try again."

"I have an idea for a place to make the swap for your uncle."

"Way too many letters." My feet hit the smooth paving stones, and I gave him my full attention. "Where?"

He sat up and situated his legs on the outsides of mine, bookending my knees. "I had an email congratulating and naming all the agents invited to attend an annual event, and something about it's been niggling at me. On the plane, I found the event's website and navigated the tabs listing the information such as the sponsors and location, etcetera."

"Okay." I trusted Kendrick to know the best place for the swap. He had the training and the experience, and I'd be dumb to argue against his suggestion. "Where?"

"Every year," Kendrick continued, "law enforcement officers from all over the country, from federal to municipal, are invited to a black-tie ball held the first weekend in December at a hotel in Times Square. It celebrates those who've had an exemplary year or who are receiving an honor." He snorted. "My invitation must have been lost."

I placed a hand on his knee but kept my mouth shut. It didn't stop my toe from tapping at his love of drawing things out.

"Anyway," his mouth quirked, "it has some official name, but we call it the Blue Balls."

I cackled, then it hit me. "Darien sponsors your Blue Balls?"

Kendrick clapped a hand over his stomach and roared with laughter, falling onto his side. "Dear God, I hope he has nothing to do with *my* blue balls."

I continued laughing. "You know what I meant."

Straightening, Kendrick got himself under control and wiped his face. "Yes, Darien is a sponsor. This year, the ball's held on December second. That's three days after the deadline, but he wants the Cryptix so bad, I don't think he'll say no."

"But why would he bring my uncle to a place filled with law enforcement?"

"You're telling me the guy is a money launderer and more, right?"

"Yes." I rubbed my hands on my thighs.

"It takes a sociopath or an egomaniac to stand up in front of a room full of law enforcement officers and give them a giant finger by sponsoring them with dirty money." Kendrick clasped my cold hand. "That is *exactly* why he'll jump at the chance to have you—a known felon—sneak in with a highly coveted, stolen object, and him bring to the hotel your uncle who he's kidnapped. It'll be an ultimate high when he gets away with it...or so he'll assume."

It made sense and lined up with what I knew about Darien. "Okay." I nodded. "When should we call him?"

"That's going to take some strategizing." He scratched his forehead with his thumbnail. "We have to time it so you don't look like you're stalling, but we can't rush it so he can say no to the meeting spot. We'd risk losing out on having twenty-three-hundred extra pairs of hands to keep Darien from getting away if our plan goes to hell."

In the Stewart suite, a light switched on, catching my attention. "I trust you to tell me when, Kisa." And I did. Swinging my legs back up, I relaxed on the chaise, pushing Darien and Blue Balls from my head. My mind needed to be focused on how to make the hacker see he needed to help save my uncle.

Chapter 22

I surfaced from the warm ocean water, smoothing back my hair. Glorious mid-morning sun soaked into my skin, and I lifted my face to accept its heat.

Kendrick and I had fallen asleep by the pool and crawled into our room in the wee hours of the morning. Neither of us did much more than the minimum bedtime prep before dropping onto the king-size mattress and falling back into our comas.

We suffered through an early morning group therapy session, then learned the organizers had given us all the rest of the morning off to commune with our partners. Naturally, everyone gravitated to the beach. As Kendrick and I spread our towels, he murmured he had an idea to distract Chet so I could talk to Stuart, but he wouldn't tell me anything other than, "Be ready."

That had been a half hour ago.

A cheer rose up, and I snapped my attention toward the beach. Two much nicer hotels sat on either side of ours. Their properties were bigger. They both offered beachside, thatch-roofed cabanas with romantic white, gauzy curtains for sides, and they both had poolside bars.

Long Reef Resorts had a wooden-and-thatch-roofed shack against the property line of the left-side hotel that advertised snorkeling lessons and boat tours. A few rows of faded and worn fabric chaise lounges in salmonish-pink and green with equally-rundown umbrellas spiked into the sand between them were spread within their section of the beach. A few guests had taken advantage of the amenity, but I balked at the cost. The resort charged an additional fee to use them, and I banked on my towel being more comfortable than a rickety chair anyway.

Another cheer echoed.

I scanned the beach and found a crowd growing not too far from where the Long Reef Resort's pool deck ended and the beach began. But no Kendrick.

Wait... I hustled out of the water. One, two, three, four...

I ran toward the commotion.

My breasts swayed uncomfortably in my coral-and-white triangle bikini top (I specifically wore the tiny scrap of material to drive Kendrick mad). Sand glued itself to the back of my wet legs and scorched the bottoms of my feet, but I ignored it all. Almost every person from the boot camp was in that crowd, including the cutie therapist, Dr. H.

Reaching the edge, I lifted on my toes but couldn't see a damn thing. Sometimes I really hated being short.

Lurching along the back of the circle, I forced my way through a wedge and kept pushing until I got to the front.

"Hol-ee shit," I breathed, my eyes gobbling up the sight before me. I'd found Kendrick.

"You are one lucky woman," a female said from my left.

I couldn't look away to acknowledge her very valid statement.

In the center of the "ring," Chet and Kendrick circled each other (the friendly sparring match must be Kendrick's "distraction"). Neither man had on a shirt (when Kendrick had spread his towel, he had been wearing a T-shirt). They each wore a pair of swim trunks; Chet's were eye-blinding neon swirls, and Kendrick's were solid red with white stitching.

Sweat glistened off both their toned bodies, and they sized each other up.

My tongue hung out of my suddenly parched mouth. Serious yum. Kendrick had a body straight out of a fantasy. Jesus, I couldn't stop staring at the perfectly proportioned Adonis. Not an ounce of fat dared mar his muscular physique that was a cross between swimmer and gymnast (definitely not one of those overly puffed men who looked like a walking steroid ad).

Kendrick went in for a strike.

Chet threw his arm up and danced back, grinning.

The crowd cheered the movements. Money began to exchange hands, and the betting got heated.

Some lauded "Ken" for having at least ten years on Chet, stating that meant more experience, while others jeered at Ken's age, saying Chet's youth gave him more scrappy stamina.

I'd put all my money on Kendrick. Not just because I was biased, but because the man had a lethal determination to win. Chet came off as an overeager (but adorable) puppy who hadn't had the time to learn enough tricks to beat a man like Kendrick.

Chet snapped his foot up, but Kendrick blocked and countered by pushing Chet's leg, forcing him off balance. He then swept his foot behind Chet's planted leg and slammed his palm into the younger agent's chest. The younger agent went down, and Kendrick followed, quick as a snake as he struck his heart and throat. Pow. Pow. Lightly, since they were only sparring, but enough to show Chet would be dead in a real situation.

The crowd went nuts, and the betting soared once again for the next round.

Kendrick helped a grumbling Chet up, and they went at it for real (still at a sparring level but just as lightning quick). Punches. Kicks. Blocks. Strikes. Jabs. Everything.

A primal rhythm rose from their moves, and it called to my body. Holy Jesus, I wanted this man with a fierceness I hadn't experienced *ever*.

Kendrick's cutthroat style made me want to jump in and spar with him myself. I hadn't had a good session since Uncle Liam disappeared, and I'd love to pit my skills against his. No doubt, he'd wipe the floor with me, but I'd learn a thing or two as I went down.

Catcalling and jeers flew from the spectators' mouths.

Out of the corner of my eye, I spied Stuart and Melanie, two people down.

Be ready. Damn, Kendrick's plan had scored one for our team. I'd never get a better shot at talking to Stuart. With everyone focused on the match, no one would care about my conversation.

Wending my way to the hacker by going behind people, I pushed my way to a spot right in between the couple, then leaned forward. "Stuart."

He jumped and whipped his head around. The second he registered my presence, he scowled. "No."

"Please." I placed a hand on his back to keep from falling over. The crowd kept shifting and knocking into me. "I just need you to listen. If you still want to say no after you've heard what I have to say, I'll respect that."

Melanie glared. "You can't talk about anything here—"

"Of course not," I shot back, cutting off what was sure to be a tirade. "I'll come to your room late tonight. Leave your balcony door unlocked." I could pick the flimsy lock with no problem, but it would save me the trouble if he just opened the damn thing for me.

Stuart chewed on his lip.

"Please. I wouldn't ask if my uncle's life wasn't in jeopardy." I showed him the same desperation in my eyes that I'd revealed to Kendrick. "Please. Just hear me out. That's all I'm asking for now."

The crowd surged and went nuts. I desperately wanted to see what had just happened, but getting Stuart to cooperate was way more important.

"And how are you expecting to talk freely when we've got Chet constantly hovering?" Melanie hissed.

"I'll take care of that. Painlessly and with *no* harm. I promise," I tacked on when Stuart's eyes widened.

"Fine." Stuart slicked back his sweaty hair. "I'll listen to you, but this is it. When I say no again, don't come back to me tomorrow to change my mind."

"Deal." I rubbed my cramping stomach. My pitch had to be so persuasive, Stuart wouldn't be able to say no.

The couple nudged past the spectators to the left, leaving me a wide-open view of the men in the circle.

Kendrick ducked beneath a right hook and lurched up with an uppercut that caught Chet square in the chin. The younger agent's head snapped back, and Kendrick took advantage of Chet's exposed chest by striking once in the heart and shouting, "You're dead."

Chet shook his head vigorously, then hung it in defeat.

Betters cheered or grumbled, handing or collecting money. Even Dr. H. had gotten in on the betting and happily collected from more than one disgruntled husband.

I ran into the ring and launched myself at Kendrick. He caught me easily and lifted me off my feet, laughing as he tightened his hold on me.

"You're good, Chet," Kendrick praised, not bothering to put me down. "But I'd suggest adding Krav Maga and boxing to your workout. With your street skills and timing, you'll be unstoppable once you have those under your belt."

I wondered if Chet would ever learn he'd just sparred with a fellow FBI agent. Shrugging the thought off, I wound my legs around Kendrick's extremely sweaty and sandy waist to give my aching ribs a breather.

The second I did that, I instantly regretted it. Too much of my skin rubbed against his and my teeny-tiny suit didn't do squat to give me a layer for sanity.

His left arm slid down to settle at the small of my back and his fingers spread, causing fire to rip through my nerve endings.

"That was so hot," I whispered into his ear when the other FBI agent wandered away, playing with the ends of Kendrick's wet hair at the base of his neck. "My man's a badass, and all the girls on the playground are jealous of me."

Kendrick growled and hustled us toward the ocean. He didn't stop when we hit the water; his powerful legs just kept wading deeper. "Aren't you all handsy this morning?"

A wave crashed into us, but he held me firm, then continued beyond the breaking line.

"And yet, just last night, you complained about your wife not sleeping with you." I pulled back grinning, the clear water now coming to the middle of my back. "Make up your mind, Kisa."

Without warning, he dropped, dunking us both under the surface.

I pushed off him and came up sputtering. Water had shot right up my nose. I coughed and squeezed my nostrils against the unwanted sinus cleansing.

"I'm liking this forward side of you, Cupcake." He floated beside me. "Feel free to launch yourself at me whenever you want, preferably with no clothes on."

I splashed him in the face. Rat. I wanted him overcome with desire, not with the ability to tease me about my blatant attempt to make him ravenous with my itty-bitty bikini.

He laughed, then disappeared under the water. Popping up on my other side, he went back to floating with his toes peeking out of the water. "Does Kisa stand for 'Kendrick is sexily awe-inspiring'?"

I snorted. "Definitely not it."

"Kendrick is such a babe?"

"Kisab?" I squatted so the water covered my shoulders.

"Maybe the 'B' is silent." His hand lightly grasped my arm to remain floating in front of me.

"What's with all the self-adoration in these guesses?"

That smile I absolutely loved, the one that made my knees weak, peeked out. "Just trying to channel your thought processes, Cupcake."

I rolled my eyes. "Well, you're way off base."

"Fine." He gazed through the crystal-clear water toward the sandy bottom. "Don't tell me, though. I want to figure it out. In the meantime, what did Stuart say?"

I dipped under the water to readjust the mess of my hair. "We're on for Plan B tonight. He's convinced he'll still say no." I bit my lip and rubbed my aching heart, standing back up.

"Hey." Kendrick cupped my cheek and planted his feet on the sand, his height cocooning me along with his mass. "We're a team, remember? We'll do whatever we have to do to get him to say yes." A crease formed in his brow. "Short of pulling a Darien."

"He *has* to say yes." I searched Kendrick's eyes, clinging to the certainty and conviction shining within.

"He will." Kendrick squeezed my bicep. "Look at how you convinced *me* to help you."

I wrapped my arms around his waist and laid my cheek on his chest. Thank God I had him with me. And he was right. If I could make my adversary my ally, then I could convince a revoked hacker to touch a computer again.

Chapter 23

S triding into the Ocean Room for the last session of the day, I wished I had thought to sneak wine inside a to-go cup.

Three ugly, salmony-colored chairs sat in the center of the meeting room. Two waited side by side, facing the third. This did not portend good things. I had no clue what to expect from our first (and, I prayed, only) couples' therapy session, and the mahi-mahi fish I'd had at dinner suddenly didn't feel so good in my stomach.

"I thought there'd be couches or something," I murmured to Kendrick who had his hand at the small of my back, gazing out the window at the night sky.

Amused eyes peered down at me. "Exactly what do think the therapist is going to make us do? This isn't a setup to some cheesy porno."

I snorted. "Watch enough to know their setups, huh?"

His fingers dug into the material of my simple, sleeveless pink dress I paired with black flats. "Is that what you really want your fourth question to be? You've only got the one left unless you negotiate for more."

I slammed my mouth shut and shook my head. I hadn't decided on what I wanted to ask, but learning his porn habits did not even rank on the list.

He didn't have much in the way of dress clothes or summer attire (we'd had to buy enough to cover any climate since we hadn't known Stuart's location at the time of outlet shopping while still keeping it limited to a suitcase amount), so after a day of scheduled (required) couples beach activities, he chose khaki cargo shorts and a hunter green polo. It seemed no matter what color he wore, it flattered his eyes.

The door closed behind us, and I whirled to catch Sexually Repressed Doc turning on a small black machine next to the doorframe. A strange whirring, annoying noise filled the room as she marched toward us. Her Birkenstocks clopped across the carpet, and if her cardigan had another button on it, I'm sure she'd have that one secured up her neck too. I sucked in a breath.

Waves of tremendous restraint and bottled-up emotions rolled off this woman so harshly, I feared for her. She seemed so uptight, I wanted to take her to the closest male revue, then buy her a hooker to release some of that tension. I worried if she didn't do something soon, she'd snap, and whatever poor man ended up in her bed might be left with a broken noodle.

Catching my glance at the machine, the doctor explained, "White noise. No one can hear us once it's turned on."

"Oh." Made sense with the confidentially thing and all.

"Dr. Helen Lynds." She held a hand out, and we dutifully shook it, then took our seats with her in the single chair.

Placing a pair of glasses at the end of her nose, she picked up her notepad. "Ken, can you achieve and maintain an erection?"

Kendrick jerked and blinked. "Excuse me?"

I snorted and swiped my nose to hide my wanting to laugh from the therapist.

"What kind of question is that?" Kendrick challenged, his skin flushing.

"Oh. I'm sorry." Dr. Lynds glanced up from her pad. "I thought you knew. I'm going to ask you both some basic questions for our sex therapy session."

Sex therapy? By a woman in serious need of getting laid? What the hell?

Kendrick goggled.

"So." Dr. Lynds readjusted her glasses. "Ken, your erections. Can you achieve one and maintain it during sex?"

I. Am. Dying. Holy shit. I wanted to roar at Kendrick's horrified face.

"Yes," he bit out, his hands clenching together on his lap. "I can maintain an erection. I've had no problems whatsoever in that department."

Dr. Lynds scribbled a note, then she put me in her sights. "Barb, can you experience an orgasm?"

Holy cow. "Um, do you mean by myself?" I squirmed in my chair, sliding then retracting my gaze from Kendrick.

Kendrick twisted toward me, his eyes losing their offended flatness to alight with interest.

"Or, um," I continued, scratching my nose, "with a man?"

"With your husband." Dr. Lynds pointed helpfully...you know, in case I had married more than one guy.

Wait...

Oh, this is too good to pass up. I settled, crossing my legs at my ankles and smoothing my skirt.

"Barb," Kendrick drew out, obviously sensing the shift. "Cupcake. Don't—"

"But, sweetheart," I implored, widening my eyes so innocently. "She may be able to help you." I flung my hand toward the doctor, then turned to the woman. "Kisa has yet to give me an orgasm."

A low growl rumbled in his chest, and red spots brightened his cheeks. Two aqua eyes pierced me, but no way in hell was I stopping there.

"It's nothing to be embarrassed about." I wrapped my fingers around his stiff forearm as if to soothe him. "I'm sure lots of guys can't satisfy women."

"I swear to God," he whispered under his breath, the skin around his fingers whitening.

Dr. Lynds scribbled like mad, then paused and focused on Kendrick. "What types of stimulation have you tried? Oral? Fingers? Toys?"

Hol-ee shit! I deserved an Emmy for not falling out of my chair, roaring with laughter.

Kendrick's shoulders lifted higher, and the muscles in his forearm turned to granite beneath my hand. A red flush crept up from his polo to encompass his neck.

I cleared my throat. Twice, trying not to lose it. "He's never done any of those with me."

"Revenge," he uttered so low I wasn't sure I actually heard the word, but I got the message—and it made this so much sweeter.

"Ken." Dr. Lynds paused writing. "How do you touch Barb sexually?"

His mouth flattened, and I'm pretty sure I heard teeth grinding.

"He doesn't," I answered woefully, trying not to ruin it by cracking up at the death rays shooting from those aqua blues. I turned to the therapist. "He'll hold my hand, graze my cheek, even hug me, but not touch me...you know, *there*."

Bones creaked in Kendrick's fingers, and a soft growl curled from his throat.

Dr. Lynds' brows drew down, and she bowed her head to scribble on her pad.

"Payback," Kendrick barely murmured through his ticking jaw, "is going to be sweet."

Yes, it is. And I was taking full advantage of my opportunity.

"Ken." Dr. Lynds glanced up. "Were you a virgin prior to your marriage?"

I whipped my face down to my lap to hide my expression and doing everything I could to rein in my laughter. My shoulders still shook, but I tried to get myself under control.

"No."

That one growled word conveyed so much.

"Okay." More scribbling on the notepad. "Did you have many partners?"

"Yes."

"Really?" Dr. Lynds blinked, then her cheeks flooded red as if she hadn't meant to ask that out loud. "Right. Okay." She loosened a button on her cardigan—*alert all single men: be wary!* "Barb, men don't come out of the womb knowing how to please women. They learn by communicating with their partners. For some," her gaze shot to Kendrick, then back to me, "the learning curve is, uh, *steeper*."

I. Am. Going. To. Lose. It. Moisture coated my eyes, and I curled my free hand into a fist to keep from jamming it into mouth.

"I do not suck in bed," Kendrick snarled, puffing out his chest.

"Of course not," Dr. Lynds soothed weakly, and I lost my grip on my composure. "But maybe you need guidance."

OH. MY. GOD! I smashed my fist against my mouth and coughed, trying to hide the laughter roaring to break free. "Please," I croaked, really wanting to turn the screws, "help him, Dr. Lynds. Maybe you have some tips or tricks you could share with him?"

"I. Do. Not. Need. Tips. Or. Tricks." Kendrick untangled his fingers and dropped a hand over mine that was still on his forearm. His grip turned bruising.

"Okay." Dr. Lynds leaned forward. "I can see you're getting upset, Ken. Understandable. It's not easy to hear you're not satisfying your wife. But that's why we're here."

"I am more than capable of satisfying my wife."

"That's the spirit," Dr. Lynds crowed, beaming. "We're going to help you learn how to give her an amazing orgasm."

"I—"

"With some coaching and effort," Dr. Lynds barreled over what was sure to be Kendrick's ego-infused protestation, "in your case, maybe *multiple* sessions, you'll master what it takes to give your wife the sex life she dreams about."

"Doesn't that sound rewarding?" I asked, wide-eyed. I blinked to hold back the tears trying to fall. "Imagine how studly you'll feel once you've gained some skills in the sack."

"*Cup. Cake—*"

"Barb." Dr. Lynds loosened two more buttons, and I *really* wanted to send a memo to the men on the island: *Run. The beast is breaking free.* "Ken needs your help. It's, uh, *obvious* he's not grasping what turns you on and, er, what to do about it."

Kendrick lasered his beautiful blues to beam through me.

Dr. Lynds got up and grasped the side of a beat-up banker's box and dragged it behind her as she retook her seat. "Inside here are some toys and videos that may, uh, enlighten and broaden Ken's understanding of foreplay."

Chapter 24

1:34 P.M. I slipped the communication device Reggie had sent in his box of goodies into my ear. "Testing."

On the bed in our room, I flipped my favorite black backpack over and flicked open both snaps residing about four inches below the curve of the shoulder harnesses.

"Kisa?" I tried again. "Can you hear me?"

"Yes," he clipped through my earpiece, *"but I'm still not talking to you."*

I snorted. Laughter welled up inside me again, and I clutched my stomach as I let it out for the millionth time.

"It's not funny," he grumbled.

I moved to the balcony and peered across the deserted pool deck. Kendrick had pulled a chaise lounge into the shadows, well out of sight of the pool camera and sprawled, facing the hotel. He had been out there for a while sulking by himself under the guise of watching for the last guest to leave the area and the last employee to call it a night.

"You made me sound like an incompetent asshole who couldn't find a woman's clit if his life depended on it."

Slapping a hand over my mouth, I tried to quell the cackle dying to break free.

"Charts," he snarled. *"I'm going to have nightmares starring those damn illustrated diagrams of women's erogenous zones."*

Yeah, that had been bad. "Awwww, Kisa, you know you're my stud muffin even though you have trouble with orgasms."

"Cupcake, don't push me," he growled, sitting forward. I caught a piece of his fierce expression off the pool light.

A sizzling jolt ripped through me, and my breath caught. Gorgeous.

"My pride's demanding I set the record straight." He flopped back into the shadows again.

Pivoting, I marched back to the bed so he wouldn't catch just how much I wanted him to restore his ego...preferably all night. Snatching the backpack off the mattress, the newly freed bottom half of the straps fell downward, revealing two cleverly disguised J-hooks hidden inside the shoulder harnesses. I zipped the dangling straps into the specially designed compartment at the bottom of the pack and ensured I had all the basics a good thief carried for unexpected eventualities inside the main section.

"We good to go to execute Plan B?" I shut off the single lamp on the night-stand to plunge our room into darkness, then stepped onto the balcony with the backpack in hand.

Movement from his shadows had me guessing he'd picked up the binoculars we'd bought this afternoon as we explored the quaint shops (before the most awesome therapy appointment ever). *"Ninety percent of the rooms are dark with no movement."*

Not surprising given the crappy hotel was barely booked to half capacity. "You ready?" I whispered.

Kendrick had made sure I knew he didn't like not being in the same room when I talked to Stuart. It wasn't lack of trust but more feeling left out that fueled his disgruntled grumbling. I understood, but we both had our strengths, and scaling the side of a hotel definitely fell into my territory. And me opening the suite's main door for him was out because we didn't want to him caught on camera if something went wrong.

"Seeing you in action and not having the stress of thwarting your plan to steal something is freeing," he answered, his voice losing some of the petulance. *"I can't wait to sit back and watch the show."*

Great. I didn't want to give him any insights he could use against me later. A pang skewered through me. I loathed the thought of us going back to being adversaries after this. I couldn't imagine it, and a growing sentiment in the back of my mind had me contemplating leaving the crew. Kendrick had opened my eyes to see that he paid for every victory we celebrated. He didn't deserve that, and I didn't want to go up against him anymore.

But the idea of just walking away made me break into sweat. My feelings for the FBI agent may be strengthening to imbecilic levels, but I couldn't...wouldn't give up a fundamental side of me. Our relationship had no happy ending. Staying meant jail. Remaining free meant ditching him to disappear. Either way, I'd lose him.

Shivering, I stowed the thoughts that had no solution nor business tangling my head up right now.

Swinging my body on top of the metal railing, I balanced my weight over my feet on the two-inch square bar, and peace swept over me. Tackling a job that pitted my wits and body against the frightening and/or impossible was my domain. A tiny slice of giddiness invaded me at showing off the skills I'd honed over the last twenty-one years to a man who fully appreciated the expertise.

"Balcony above is clear."

Dressed in all-black spandex (plus a knit hat for my hair), I rose to my full height with my backpack in my thin-gloved hand. A constant breeze off the peaceful ocean helped keep me cool in my body-covering clothing. Extending my reach, I lifted the backpack overhead and hooked the two shoulder-harness J-hooks onto the lower railing, threading it through the vertical bars. All across the front of the backpack, black, one-inch nylon strips crisscrossed, giving the bag a rugged style...or so the uninitiated thought. Grabbing the lowest nylon strips at the center where they crossed, I hoisted myself up.

Kendrick inhaled, the sound really carrying in my earpiece.

I fed my fingers into the next grouping up, showing Kendrick I had a portable ladder no one would ever suspect.

"Cupcake," he breathed, *"that's genius."*

Hand over hand, I pulled myself up the almost two-foot-tall backpack.

"What is that? Where did you get it?"

Pride tore through me as I transferred my grasp to the closest vertical railing. The rubbery pads lining my gloves helped keep my grip on the smooth metal, and I'd long since strengthened the muscles in my palms and fingers to give me a further edge. (Fingerprints were a hazard in my line of work, so going without gloves was not an option.)

Using pure upper body strength, I climbed up the front of the railing (thanks to the thousands of pull-ups during workouts). Once my soft-soled shoes silently landed on the cement, I answered. "It's my design," I whispered, waddling in a crouch to the sliding glass door and peering inside.

Empty single room.

"Inside the cushioned shoulder harnesses are strong but lightweight polymer resin poles that won't set off an airport scanner." I hopped onto the top balcony railing. "They're strong enough to hold up to two hundred pounds, and inside, I can remove the supports running down the back if I need the pack to be soft. The cushioned sleeves are adjustable and completely removable so I can adapt to different widths. The fabric is a blend of Tyvek and Kevlar, and the quadruple-reinforced seams have nylon thread, so nothing will rip or tear." In essence, I could completely rely on it to hold my weight.

"You continue to awe me." After a beat, he gave me a report. *"Balcony above is clear, but the room to the right still has its light on."*

"Got it."

"You still need to work your way three rooms to your left as you climb."

"What's the path look like?" I jumped back down and leaned over the railing with my back pressing into the metal. "By the way, should I ask how you got the roof lights turned off without shattering them like a street rat?"

Two silent beats passed before he answered, *"Given our last session, I don't know if I want tell you."*

"Oh, this must be good." I strained to see around the foot-thick cement walls separating the balconies that gave guests a modicum of visual privacy from their neighbors.

He sighed heavily. *"I explained to the maintenance guy who's been married for twenty-seven years that one of my wife's fantasies has always been to have sex on a hotel balcony. Since I'm already in the doghouse, as evidenced by my having to come to this boot camp, could the guy please help a desperate husband out and turn off the lights tonight."*

Damn. I totally wanted that fantasy, and I was totally avoiding all maintenance men for the rest of this trip. "What the hell are you going to tell this guy tomorrow?"

"I don't know." An evil chuckle filtered into my ear. *"The night's not over with yet. Especially after witnessing how totally fucking hot you are scaling the side of the hotel with seeming ease."*

Cruel. Cruel man. As much as he touched me *every chance he got*, he still had too much discipline to cross the line...though I suspected his control was about as frayed as mine. I wasn't sure who was going to crack first, but one of us was going to...soon. *All the more reason to crank up the heat so he'll live in my world for a while.* "You know," I uttered in a low tone, mindful that the guests in the room adjacent above could stroll out at any minute. "Dr. Lynds said we should embrace telling each other our fantasies." I hopped back on top of the railing. I couldn't really see anything from my position anyway. "Maybe I should describe, *in full detail*, this one fantasy I have where I'm a thief and you're the FBI agent trying to catch me."

His breath caught, and that little tell spurned me to continue.

"It's late at night, and I've just scaled a multistory building." I pictured tonight's venture to help give my bullshit fantasy some framework. "I could have sworn you had just arrived to stop me, but you surprise me. When I pick the lock to open the sliding glass door, you're already inside, standing beside a king-size bed. Your legs are shoulder-width apart, and your arms are crossed with a pair of silver handcuffs dangling by your waist."

Silence descended through the comms, and I shuddered at the image of him in his blue dress shirt and black dress pants, waiting for me.

"The way you stand there, oozing authority with your gun holstered at your side and your badge clipped to your belt, makes me instantly wet." My toes curled, scraping over the railing as I maintained my balanced crouch, though just barely. "I could run, but I don't want to. Instead, I allow you to grasp my bicep and force me to lie down on the bed."

A low growl rumbled between the heavy breaths.

"I roll onto my stomach and stretch my arms straight above my head." My panties were soaked, and I closed my eyes, clinging to the scene. "You secure one wrist, then feed the chain into this special bolt made specifically for it on the headboard and ratchet the second cuff closed on my other wrist."

"Cupcake," he gritted, and I turned my head to stare into the shadows hiding him, knowing he could see me with the binoculars.

"You're not gentle when you shove an arm beneath my hips and raise them into the air." I spoke directly to him, unable to stop the bullshit fantasy from turning into one I desperately wanted to come true. "I kneel with my forehead on the mattress and my knees spreading—"

"Stop," he commanded, his ragged breaths filling my earpiece. *"Guest just wandered out of the room one floor below, one room over to smoke a cigarette."*

I hopped back off the railing and crouched, resting my forehead against the metal. The cool sensation did nothing to extinguish the inferno raging inside me.

The stench of tobacco permeated the air, and I wrinkled my nose. Ten long minutes went by, and I still hadn't wrangled any form of control over my need. The fantasy insisted on playing beyond what I'd described.

"He's gone, and the room lights have gone out. Can you maneuver to the next balcony on your left? Same floor."

"Easy peasy," I croaked, clearing my throat as I jumped back on top of the railing. Grabbing the little handle on top of the backpack, I stood, holding onto the cement wall, then swung my leg around the one-foot thickness and transferred my weight so I now stood on that balcony railing.

"It's my turn to take over this fantasy you were taunting me with." His voice sounded like he just ate gravel. *"As I gaze down at your amazing ass raised so fucking beautifully, waiting for my touch, I'm flooded with the need to cut those*

spandex pants off. I've waited too long to see you naked, and another second of your body hidden from me is unacceptable."

I hurriedly hooked my backpack onto the balcony above and clung to the strips so I wouldn't fall off the damn building. Holy shit. Why the hell had I started this game with him? I resumed climbing with shaking arms.

"Your darkened hazel eyes peer up at me through your bound arms, begging me to..."

For the next ten minutes it took to wend my way over to Stuart's balcony, Kendrick wound the fantasy around us.

Never in my life had I scaled a building drenched with so much need. Kendrick had better run the minute I entered our room tonight, or he'd face being attacked. Gripping the railing to Stuart's balcony, I pulled myself up, trembling with wanting Jackson Kendrick. Now.

"Kisa," I whispered, the strain strangling my voice. "Please."

He stopped mid-description of flipping me over and sliding back inside me again.

I wasn't sure what I was pleading for. For him to stop tormenting me? For him to make his words a reality? For a release of all the tension coiled so tightly I could barely breathe? Something. Anything.

But I had run out of time.

Throwing my leg over the top of the railing, I landed silently on the concrete in a crouch, then peered through the bars at Kendrick's shadow.

Air still moved heavily in his lungs, the comms broadcasting his own raging desire.

"You've got this, Cupcake," he encouraged.

I appreciated the effort even as he growled the sentiment at me, neither one of us really in the right frame of mind to negotiate. I chuckled under my breath. "We weren't exactly too smart about our scaling topic."

His gruff laugh made me smile. *"I don't know. I've never had this much fun on a comm device before."*

"Ditto." Inhaling twice to clear my head of all the visions Kendrick had just filled it with, I rescued my backpack and put my game face on. I had one shot at this. My uncle deserved my complete focus.

Chapter 25

Slipping silently to the screen door, I paused to peer inside the darkened room. I couldn't really make out much; all the dark blobs melded together.

"It's unlocked," Melanie whispered, suddenly appearing on the other side of the door.

I stood as she slid the screen open.

"I can hear her just fine," Kendrick informed me. I gave a silent thank you to Reggie for sending me the good stuff even though he still hated this plan.

A shaft of light pierced the darkness and Stuart strolled out of the bathroom, not bothering to turn the light off. He marched across the room wearing a ratty concert T-shirt from an early-two-thousands band and old gym shorts. Melanie was in much the same, though her T-shirt boasted of a bar in North Carolina.

"Where's Chet?" I asked softly, needing to settle that detail ASAP.

Stuart's mouth thinned, and he crossed his arms. "What are you going to do to him?"

I didn't blame him for being suspicious. He didn't know me at all, and I respected him a little bit more for standing up for the agent's health.

Opening the smaller front compartment on my backpack, I pulled out a small syringe identical to the one I'd used on Kendrick. "This is completely harmless. It's a fast-acting sedative that'll give us at the minimum ten minutes, maximum fifteen minutes to talk before he wakes up."

Melanie's frown deepened. "Does it have side effects?"

I paused, and Kendrick understood I needed his expertise.

"No. My roiling stomach had nothing to do with the drug and everything to do with second-guessing my wisdom in letting you go."

Thank God he had, and thank God he went through with helping me. "No side effects," I answered Melanie. "I swear." Feeling a bit of déjà vu, I kept going with the conversation. "I've come to you for help. I'm not going to risk you saying no by harming Chet."

Stuart scratched his chin (the hair coating the bottom half of his face desperately needed to visit a razor), then stepped out of my path. "He's in the living room, snoring in front of the TV."

Not ideal, but doable.

"The curtains are closed tight. I can't help," Kendrick informed me.

Damn. Setting my pack on the floor by the bed, I carefully opened the wooden door.

The suite had a simple layout. Two bedrooms bookended a large communal room that consisted of a fully furnished living room and small kitchenette (a whole whopping counter with a cabinet, a medium-size refrigerator, a sink, and a microwave). Behind the TV stand, curtains hid another set of doors that led out to the balcony running the length from Stuart's room to Chet's.

I padded across the ugly carpeting to the back of the couch that acted like a hallway/room divider to the kitchenette. Ducking behind the fabric-patterned nightmare, I looked left and found Melanie and Stuart crowding their doorway like anxious parents.

Motioning for them to get back inside their room, I uncapped the syringe's lid and rose, staying as hunched as possible to minimize exposure. Chet had fallen asleep sprawled across the cushions. Tucked against the armrest, his head had slumped against a salmonish-pink throw pillow leaning on the back of the couch.

I shuffled to the corner and kneeled, carefully positioning the needle at a meaty part of his neck. With his seriously short hair, I had a lot of real estate to choose from. The needle gauge was super thin so it shouldn't feel like anything more than a mosquito bite. I inhaled to steady my hand, then zapped him.

He flinched, but before he actually woke up, his body slumped into a heavier slumber.

"Chet's out," I whispered, capping the syringe again. "Kisa, can you start the clock for ten minutes?"

"Done."

I jogged back to the room, not surprised I had to force Melanie and Stuart to move out of my way.

Yanking my backpack up, I dropped in the used syringe and pulled out the other item in the small compartment, then thrust it at Stuart. "Hide this."

His eyes popped, and he jammed his hands behind his back. "No way am I touching that."

Feeling the countdown already ticking, I marched to the dresser, pulled a small drawer all the way out, and taped the thin burner phone to the back by using two crisscrossing pieces of electric tape from my bag.

"I'm not out to frame you with fingerprints on it," I defended, refitting the drawer. "I'm hoping we're going to need it to negotiate and work out details because you said yes."

Now that the moment was here, my mind blanked, then swarmed with a thousand chaotic points that would only confuse the Stewarts if I vomited them all out at once.

"Breathe, Cupcake," Kendrick soothed. That he knew I needed him in that moment just showed how much deeper our connection had gotten. *"You can always put me on speakerphone to help."*

Right. We're a team. "As I mentioned before, I need your help to save my uncle's life." I tossed the electric tape back into the bag and fished my phone out, then queued up Darien's initial call. "Before I get into the details, I want you hear something first, so you'll understand why I pressed so hard to talk to you."

Hitting play, I swallowed around a lump of bile at having to hear Uncle Liam's obvious pain and Darien's sinister voice pouring out of the speaker.

Stuart snapped his chin back and blinked while Melanie covered her mouth, her eyes horrified as she stared at the phone in my hand.

Once it ended, silence rang for too many thunderous heartbeats.

"He wants the Cryptix?" Stuart jammed a hand through his hair. "Fucking Christ."

It didn't surprise me he knew what the Infostrata was. Computers were his thing. He'd make it his business to keep up with the changing world even if he wasn't allowed to play in it.

"Who are you really?" Stuart dropped his arm. That man called you Holly and talked about your crew pulling heists for millions among other disturbing things."

It had been a gamble to play the recording first before explaining, but when I'd asked Kendrick's advice this afternoon, he'd thought the message would get their attention and make them more apt to listen. His instinct had been right about getting their attention; now I needed to rely on his advice again.

"Kisa?"

"Kisa?" Melanie repeated, her brows drawing down over eyes still clouded with disquiet. "Isn't that what you call your husband?"

Kendrick sighed. *"I don't like having to put my faith in them keeping our identity a secret, but I think we'll lose them if we're not completely honest."*

Pressing send on the number for Kendrick's phone, I put it on speaker.

"I'm here," Kendrick answered, his voice both in my head and on the phone. *"Hello, Stewarts."*

Stuart moved to stand by his wife and pulled her against his side as he stared at me. "Where is he?"

I pointed at the balcony. "By the pool, keeping an eye on the hotel so I can talk to you safely."

"You owe me an answer." Stuart demanded after pulling his attention off the screen door and placing it back on me.

Inhaling to center myself, I met his gaze. "My real name is Holly Bell. I'm part of a very successful, four-member crew who perform contracted heists under specific circumstances. Every single one of us are wanted felons."

Melanie's breath caught, and her eyes widened. Stuart didn't blink.

"My name is not Ken," Kendrick chimed in. *"It's really Jackson Kendrick, and I'm an FBI agent out of the New York City office. We've come here posing as a married couple specifically to get your help."*

"FBI agent?" Melanie looked from me, to the phone, to Stuart, then back to me. "What? How is that possible if you're a wanted felon?"

"It's a long story," I answered. "I wish I had time to tell you, but I don't. Suffice it to say, Agent Kendrick is risking his career to be my partner in freeing my uncle and taking down Darien Burton."

"Holly," Kendrick drew out, discomfort lacing his tone.

"It's the truth, Kisa." I refused to let him downplay his role and laid it out for the Stewarts. "For his troubles, Darien's painted a target on his back and has men searching to kill him as we speak."

"What?" Melanie fell into Stuart's hold. "But Darien Burton's, like, a humanitarian."

"No, he's really not," I retorted, trying to keep the heat out of my voice. I couldn't blame her for buying into the façade he suckered the world into trusting. "That's the side he wants everyone to see, but he's a monster who's currently holding my uncle hostage, as you heard."

"But *kill* an FBI agent?" Melanie persisted.

"I could play the recording of that phone call, if you'd like." I split my gaze between the couple and simplified with a mostly true explanation. "He's targeting Agent Kendrick because Kendrick is the head of the task force seeking to capture me and my crew." They didn't need to know about the suspended part; it'd muddy already treacherous waters.

Stuart's eyes popped, and his face whipped to the balcony, then back to me.

"It's true. I heard the death threat myself," Kendrick stated coldly.

I nodded. "In Darien's deluded mind, he believes killing Kendrick will remove the biggest obstacle so my concentration can remain one-hundred percent on stealing the Cryptix. He's already let it slip he has contacts in way too many places and has shown he can learn about my movements. His reach is not to be underestimated."

Stuart let go of Melanie and paced. "Let me see if I've got this straight." He glanced at me as he moved. "You're a wanted thief, the man sitting by the pool is the FBI agent in charge of hunting you down and arresting you, and a humanitarian who's really an evil dude wants you to steal the Cryptix to basically hold the world hostage." He paused by the screen door, but I knew he wouldn't be able to spot Kendrick in the shadows. "But instead of arresting you, Ken, er, Agent Kendrick has teamed up with you to save your uncle and sets his sights on taking down Darien Burton."

"Right so far." I bit my lip and prayed I had enough time to convince him to join our crusade.

Stuart tracked to the bed, then pivoted and paced back. "Since you're still wanted, and you say Agent Kendrick is risking his career, I assume this is not a sanctioned mission or whatever it's called by the FBI."

My stomach flipped. Was that a selling point or not? "That's also correct."

"And that's why you needed to knock out Chet?" Melanie joined in on Stuart's pacing, but not in sync. The discord made me dizzy.

"Yes," Kendrick answered. *"It's imperative you keep your silence about us and this conversation. If you talk, it'll put everyone in danger. Darien's not a man to mess with lightly."*

"We need your skills, Stuart." My fingers tightened on the phone. "In therapy, you both talked about feeling stifled and boxed in." I gambled on bringing up their personal issues. "Helping to take down an extremely bad man and saving my uncle would be a way to break free from the chains you're under, and it should go a long way to helping you two reconnect."

I had no clue about that last part, but I prayed it sounded logical enough.

Stuart stopped. "What are you expecting from me?"

"I need you to write a program that'll scour the internet." The hairs beneath my hat tingled; my instincts said I didn't have much time left. "I can't show up to the swap empty-handed, but I can't give Darien the real Cryptix."

Stuart snorted. "I should say not."

"What's this Cryptix?" Melanie's eyebrows furrowed.

"I'll explain later." Stuart swished a hand.

"That's where you come in," I implored. "We're going to make Darien believe he's getting the real Cryptix, but instead, it'll be a trap that'll expose him."

"The program you write," Kendrick tag-teamed, *"should mimic the Cryptix but instead of holding his adversaries hostage, it needs to target Darien specifically and reveal all his hidden bank accounts, secrets, underworld connections, etcetera."*

Stuart rubbed his hairy jaw. "You're talking about building artificial intelligence."

Unease skittered down my spine. "Isn't there a lot of controversy around AI?"

"Yeah." Stuart nodded. "But what I'm talking about is different. I'd be creating a program that can make correlations and connections on its own as it rips through the internet. Something that can continuously learn and skew off into as many branches as are needed to put everything you're asking for together."

My breath caught. "Is that possible?"

"Absolutely." Stuart's eyes glassed as if thinking, then cleared. "It takes time to code, but it's possible."

"How much time?"

The hacker glanced at Melanie who stood with her hands clenched together. "Two weeks, but it could probably be scaled down to nine or ten days if I dedicated myself full-time."

Hope wiped out the fear. "You'll do it?"

Stuart's gait ate up the carpeting to his wife. "Excuse us." He grabbed her hand and pulled her into the bathroom, firmly shutting the door behind them.

"How much time do we have left?" I opened the screen door and moved to lean against the railing. Peering at Kendrick's shadows made me feel better.

"Two minutes." The phone and my earpiece relayed his response.

"Damn. What do you think?"

"We need more time." He sighed. *"There's still so much to cover. We don't know his needs for programing, how this would all go down—"*

The bathroom door swung open, and I whirled, gripping the phone and my backpack in each hand.

Stuart marched closer, still holding onto his wife who now had a green tinge to her skin.

"I'll do it on one condition," the hacker responded flatly.

Shit. I didn't like this already.

"You have to kill me and Melanie."

Chapter 26

"*What the hell?*" Kendrick barked and I leaped to get inside the bedroom before our conversation could drift to any night owls. "*Kill you?*" he hissed.

Stuart lifted his chin while Melanie chewed on her lip and stared at the geometric patterns on the carpet like they held the key to life.

"Not literally." The hacker didn't back down. "But in every way it counts, make us disappear." His eyes hardened. "I can't live like this anymore. I've paid my penance, and I've grown up. I understand the more I touch a computer, the greater chance I have of getting caught, so believe me when I say my random hacking days are done, but if you want my help, you need to kill off Stuart and Melanie Stewart."

Son of a bitch. I didn't blame Stuart for demanding a high price, but...shit. Had he really thought through his request? A person couldn't come back from death...duh. Did he think of how he'd be cutting them both off from their family and friends forever?

"*Stuart, what you're asking for goes way beyond creating a program for us,*" Kendrick argued.

"What do you think is going to happen to me once Darien's caught?" Stuart shot back.

Melanie's hand flew up to cover her mouth.

"*I'll shield you in every way I can,*" Kendrick offered. "*I'll fight to make sure nothing blows back on you.*"

"That's a nice thought." Stuart voice was cold. "But let's be real, Agent Kendrick. The FBI will never let me go. No matter what you say, once the dust settles, you're never going to convince the federal government to keep me out of jail for violating my agreement."

A soft sob choked out of Melanie, and her shoulders shook.

Stuart pulled her into his arms. "Melanie deserves to have a full life with a husband who can order a gift off the fucking internet or send a goddamn email." His brown eyes lasered into mine. "You want me to break the agreement to build your artificial intelligence...which I *can* deliver, then you're going to have to make this happen."

"We'll get back to you." I hung up on Kendrick and tuned out his squawking in my earpiece. "Silence, Kisa," I snapped, straining to hear—

SHIT! "Chet's awake," I bark-hissed, shoving the phone inside my pack and pulling out a thick coil of rope with a single insulated hook on one end and a set of gloves that could withstand a ton of friction. "Can one of you unhook this in five seconds and let it drop?"

"I'll go out and distract him." Stuart let go of Melanie and hustled to the bedroom door.

"Aim for the middle, between the two bedrooms," Kendrick instructed in my earpiece. *"The way down is clear."*

Running for the indicated section of the railing with Melanie dogging my heels, I anchored the hook onto the upper bar, praying Chet didn't snap the living room curtains back. I'd be a sitting duck.

Jamming my hand through a set of the crisscrossing strips, I pushed the backpack up my forearm since I didn't have time to reestablish the loops of shoulder harnesses.

The second I crammed my hands inside the thick gloves, I swung my leg over and grabbed onto the rope, fast-roping down like the military did out of helicopters. Thankfully, with only seven floors, it took seconds for my feet to hit the ground. The rope suddenly loosened, and the hook came rushing down to land in a flower bed.

My heart slammed against my ribs with a ton of after-action adrenaline, and I leaned my butt against a separator between two darkened conference rooms.

Kendrick materialized out of the shadows, and I motioned for him to head toward the ocean. Without a word, he jumped off the pool deck and disappeared from view.

I rescued the hook from the middle of a patch of pink (shocking) hibiscus and methodically re-coiled the rope. Placing it into my backpack, I also tossed in both sets of gloves, my knit hat, and the comm device. I needed an extra second to allow the adrenaline queasiness to pass, so I refastened the nylon straps back onto the harnesses and looped the pack over my shoulder like a student.

I did not look forward to the coming conversation with Kendrick.

"We'll get back to you?" Kendrick repeated by way of greeting when I caught up with him at the edge of the water a half mile down the completely deserted beach. No lights from the nearby hotels shined on the sand. Only the half moon in the partly cloudy sky gave us any illumination.

"What did you want me to say?" Wind ruffled my sweaty head, helping to cool me off.

"How about, hell to the fucking *no*." Kendrick slapped his hands on his bathing-suit clad hips, worn in keeping with the cover of being by the pool. He had his Ohio State hat on backwards to minimize the light catching on his blond hair, and the breeze rippled his plain black T-shirt, molding it to his body.

"Can we at least talk about this before you make your ruling?" We were one step closer to freeing Uncle Liam, and I refused to walk away without a good goddamn reason.

"I'm an FBI agent." Kendrick's eyebrows cranked down. "Are you asking me to participate in a highly illegal stunt that would give a felon a clean slate and have him walk free without any supervision?" His aqua eyes were dark with emotion. "He's a hacker. Who knows what he'll get himself into? I don't want to shoulder the blame if or when he does something stupid or evil."

"*I'm* a felon," I answered, my stomach turning to lead. "You're participating in an illegal venture with me."

"Yes." He hit his hat trying to jam his hand into his hair. "But you're different. *This* is different."

"Only if you count that he's been caught, and I haven't."

Kendrick's jaw began to tick. "You two are nothing alike. His actions have caused international incidents and hurt a lot of people."

"I've hurt people—"

"Insurance companies paying out claims don't count," he snapped.

"I'm not talking about insurance companies." My heart rate kicked back up, and I wished my mouth would shut up.

"The victims—"

"I'm not talking about them, either." Why oh why couldn't I let this go? "And trust me when I say, there have been no victims. At least not how you're referring to them."

Kendrick's mouth slammed closed.

I drew on the rhythmic pounding of the waves hitting the beach and forced myself to keep holding his gaze. "I hurt *you.*"

He shook his head, then waved a hand as if to wipe away my confession. "I can't do it, Holly. I can't give Stuart what he wants."

My heart flipped in my chest, and my mouth lost all its moisture. "What's that mean for Uncle Liam?"

"I don't know." He sighed, the corners of his eyes tight with tension. "We'll have to find someone else—"

"*Is* there someone else? Do we have time to recruit them?" The weight of my uncle's life pressed on my shoulders, forcing the blood to drain from my head.

Kendrick softly cursed. "I don't know that, either."

There wasn't anyone else, and we both knew it. The contacts I had at my disposal weren't up to building artificial intelligence, and now that Stuart had mentioned it, I knew he was right. That was the only thing that could bring Darien down.

I lifted a shaking hand to my mouth. I couldn't look at Kendrick right now. Stepping around him, I bowed my head and marched along the waterline. Jabbing my arm through the other harness, I settled the pack on my back and kept walking.

"Cupcake, wait," Kendrick called, but I ignored him.

Heavy footsteps thumped behind me, and I had the urge to take off. Tears crowded the corners of my eyes, and I didn't want him to see them.

Uncle Liam's life rests on my shoulders—

"Holly."

"No." I ran. My soft-soled shoes were not designed like my cross-trainers, but the sand helped cushion the impact.

"Goddamn it." His footsteps pounded into the beach after me.

I spurred my legs to move faster. The tears fell from my eyes, and for the first time since Darien's initial call, I wept. All the pain, the fear, the outrage, and the grief of the unknown could not be contained or shunted to the side anymore. *What am I doing? How did I get here?*

A fresh round of tears blinded me. I could *not* lose the only family member I had left. Just the thought of being completely alone in the world terrified me.

Uncle Liam was only forty-nine years old. He had way too much life still to live. If I failed, he'd never fall in love or get married or finally retire from the crew and live out his dream of traveling the world.

My mistakes are costing Uncle Liam everything. A keening wail broke free, and I stumbled.

Strong arms caught me, sweeping me up in one smooth motion. My head thumped against the top of his chest as Kendrick cradled me by my knees and back. I turned my face into his shirt and sobbed, unable to stop.

"Cupcake, you're breaking my heart," he whispered, tightening his hold.

Then we'll have a matching set. My fingers dug into his shirt, and I bawled.

He left the wet sand and carried me over the soft white beach into one of a row of thatched-roof cabanas the fancy hotels provided for their guests. With a gentleness that was a testament to his strength, he eased us both down onto a fabric-based, armless chaise lounge. Unsnapping the fasteners on my shoulder harnesses, he plucked the backpack off me and tossed it on the sand, against the chair. He cranked the back of the lounge up to a reclined position, then resituated me on his lap as he stretched his legs and dropped his hat on top of my pack.

I settled onto his chest and rested my hand above his pec. Without a word, he hugged me tighter and rocked me slowly.

"Kendrick," I pushed through my raw throat.

"I've got you," he murmured, his slow swaying and warm body cocooning me. "Let it out."

To my mortification, I did. I wanted to stop crying. *Needed* to stop crying, but I couldn't shore up the dam. Soft kisses pressed into the top of my head every so often, and I selfishly absorbed his strength.

"I can't lose Uncle Liam, too," I whispered after a time, wincing at my torn throat and cringing at my runny nose. "He's all I have left."

A small shudder rippled beneath my face and traveled down Kendrick's body.

"I've tried to be open about enacting our plan," he answered softly, "but Stuart's request goes too far." His hand smoothed over my spine. "You called me an honorable man. Would I still be one if I crossed that line?"

Pain lanced through me once again, and a fresh onslaught of tears fell over my rims. "I can't fail. He's counting on me to save him."

"I know." The remorse lacing his tone ripped through me. "We'll figure out a new plan." He laid his cheek on top of my head. "I'm not giving up, Holly."

The lead running through my veins deadened my heart. "But you are," I croaked.

His muscles stiffened.

Taking my long-sleeved shirt off (I had a black sports bra underneath), I used it to wipe my face so I wouldn't keep leaking my grossness on him. "All this time, I worried about getting Stuart to say yes." I searched his aqua eyes in the moonlight and found so many emotions brimming within. "But we did it. We convinced a forcefully retired hacker to pick up a computer again, only now you want to say no."

"Holly." His fingers resettled on the back of my ribs and fisted. "Would you honestly respect a man who compromises his morals?"

"To save a life? Yes."

He peered toward the water over my shoulder.

"We're running out of time." I stroked the stubble on his jaw. "I will do whatever it takes to save Uncle Liam."

Kendrick dropped his forehead against mine, his eyes awash with pain and conflict.

I cupped his cheek. "If I lose my uncle, I have no one."

His breath caught, and his body trembled. "That's not true," he murmured, hugging me tight. "You have me."

"For how long?" My heart hammered. Our personal feelings had no business clouding this discussion, but hell if I could stop the question. "How could we ever make this...us...work?"

He twisted his forehead against mine. "I don't know, but I'm learning I want to give you everything you ask for."

"Kisa." I caressed his cheek and blinked at the sting of air passing over my sore, puffy eyes. "I'm learning the same lesson too, wanting to give you the world."

A ragged breath passed over his parted lips. "Please," his grip became bruising, "don't ask me to compromise my integrity. I'm committed to saving your uncle, but I need to be able to live with my choices afterward." His hand curled into my hair and gripped it tight. "It's true the clock is ticking down, but it hasn't run out yet. Don't give up on me." His trembling became more noticeable. "I'm not read—"

He cut himself off with a soft curse. "Don't give up on us. Please. We're a team."

I closed my eyes and dropped my head to curl into his shoulder. *Give up on us?* I wanted to find a way to keep him forever, but I could not be responsible for my uncle's death. I had no problem destroying my morals to save Uncle Liam's life.

Exhaustion swamped me and I slumped against him, maybe for the last time. I had a choice to make. One that gutted me more than I ever imagined. Did I sever my partnership with Kendrick and give Stuart his freedom in exchange for his help, or did I risk chancing we could come up with another solution before the deadline?

Chapter 27

"You can't be in here."

I batted a hand at the source of the heavily accented male voice invading my sleep. I smacked into something hard and unforgiving, making my pinky finger throb. *Wha...?*

A groan uttered from above my head just as my mattress rippled beneath my body.

Huh? My eyes popped open, my mind springing awake.

Through a tangle of hair, a broad, black T-shirt-covered chest filled my vision and I swallowed hard.

Kendrick and I had slept through the night in the cabana.

"Seriously," the male voice pleaded. "If the manager finds you here, he'll call the police."

My "mattress" rippled beneath me again, and I clambered to sit up.

"Christ, Cupcake," Kendrick uttered sleepily, clamping a hand on my flailing arm. "Stop moving. You already nailed my jaw."

A certain member...Happy Jackson dug into my bare stomach—*yowza, he's well-equipped*—from my sprawled position on top. My elbow accidently drove into Kendrick's chest, trying to lift off—

"Ow." He jerked upright, the sudden movement toppling me over.

I couldn't catch my balance and ended up falling off the side of the chaise, landing on my ass in the sand. "Well, that was a graceful way to wake up," I muttered.

A golden-skinned man wearing a maintenance uniform scurried into my sight and thrust out his hand. I grabbed it, and he helped me to my feet.

"The manager is making his rounds," the maintenance man warned, his brown eyes shooting toward a beautiful resort rising above a row of waist-high bushes planted behind the cabanas with the pool area on the other side. "You two have to go."

"Thank you," Kendrick answered, his voice husky with sleep. He rubbed his eyes with the heels of his hands and planted his feet onto the sand. "We're leaving."

I snatched my balled shirt off the edge of the chair, but before I could grab my backpack, Kendrick clamped onto it. He shoved his hat on his head (brim in the front this time), then looped a harness over his shoulder as he stood, having no trouble reconnecting the straps and adjusting it to fit comfortably.

Swiping the sand off my butt, I followed Kendrick out of the shade and into the bright morning sun. I crammed my shirt inside the pack and plucked out the single water bottle. Saint Croix had gifted the tourists with another beautiful day, but I couldn't appreciate it. Grit from last night's embarrassing crying lapse coated my eyes, and they still felt puffy. Not attractive whatsoever.

Walkers and joggers hogged the wet, hard-packed sand by the water, and a few industrious family members staked their spots for the day by setting up towels and beach chairs for later.

Kendrick motioned toward a ramp between two resorts, and I nodded. I had no gumption to put my calves through a punishing workout walking in the loose sand.

"What time is it?" I swished more water around to clear my fuzzy mouth, wishing I had my toothbrush, a comb, and a tissue. No way did I want to see myself in a mirror yet. I could feel the tangled clumps in my loose hair, and knowing the way my tears had washed away my makeup, I wasn't up for another knock to my confidence.

Kendrick fished his phone out of his bathing suit's pocket. "Eight thirty-nine."

"What? Wow." I gave him the other half of the water, and he took advantage of it like I did.

We reached the sidewalk, and I appreciated how only a few folks were out and about for a walk. Most were probably on the beach for their exercise.

Tossing the now-empty bottle into the trash, Kendrick determinedly laced his fingers with mine. "We needed the rest."

I bit my lip. I wanted to yank my hand back at the same time I wanted to savor the contact like a hoarder storing up for Armageddon (in other words, when we parted for good).

Tense silence surrounded us for at least a mile. Geez, I hadn't realized how far I had run last night. Steady traffic cruised by us, and we had to stop and start as cars entered and exited parking lots, but the buildings kept us in the shade and a breeze helped clear the cobwebs tangling my brain.

"Are we still a team?"

Shit. Kendrick wasn't pulling any punches this morning. I looked toward a decorative water fountain display outside the main entrance of a colorful hotel.

"Your hesitation slays me." His raw tone hit me hard.

Guilt slithered into my gut, and I hung my head. Last night, I'd banked on the answer to my heart-wrenching choice being clear this morning. But I was no further knowing which direction I should take.

"You mentioned you have a hardware guy," Kendrick persevered, his voice ladened with strain. "Someone who could build the replica of the Cryptix itself."

"Oscar Brudney." I stopped staring at the sidewalk cracks to peer ahead. Long Reef Resorts in ugly salmony-pink was on the road sign was only feet ahead. "I'll need to get in touch with Reggie, but if I remember correctly, he lives in Pennsylvania."

"Oscar. Right."

Fuck. We sounded so stilted. Like a couple trying to find their footing after breaking up but forced to still interact.

"I think our next course of action should be to head there." Kendrick rubbed his chest, over his heart. "He may be able to recommend a coder capable of building an AI program like Stuart described."

I remained silent. The thought had crossed my mind. I also wondered if I leaned on Reggie harder, he might be able to quietly find someone, too. But I hadn't ruled out accepting Stuart's demand, either.

"Cupcake."

The whispered way he spoke my pet name sliced into me. So much longing and worry dripped in that tone.

Stopping, Kendrick pulled against our interlocked hands. I didn't want to face him, but I didn't want to drag this out either, so I turned to stand in front of him.

He trailed a finger over my check, then swiped his thumb gently beneath one of my puffy eyes. "You've already made the decision to leave me."

I exhaled as if he'd punched me in the gut. Hearing it said out loud made my heart scream, *NO!* "I haven't, actually," I answered, my tone low and hoarse.

He whipped his face toward the road, blinking repeatedly as his shoulders slumped and he swayed.

"But I'm not going to lie," I soldiered on. "I truly respect you, Jackson Kendrick."

His eyes snapped back to mine, and he tensed all over again.

"I shouldn't have asked an honorable man to go against his integrity." My free fist clenched at my side to keep from reaching for him. "You're right to demand that line stay firm. I just don't know if I can win against Darien by playing fair." A lump formed in my throat, and it physically hurt to swallow. "I care too much about you to drag you down to my level. It may be for the best if we part now before you're drawn deeper into this mess."

"No." The word ripped from his throat. "There have to be other options." His fingers squeezed mine. "Don't make up your mind yet. Give us the day to brainstorm."

I didn't have a plan in place if I decided to say yes to Stuart, so I could afford it, and I owed him that much. "Okay."

Every muscle in his beautiful body loosened, and I faced forward again to keep him from seeing how much his wanting to stay with me nestled deep in my soul.

Leading us up the dirty sidewalk to Long Reef's main entrance, I grabbed my nasty hair. "I need quality time with my toothbrush and a long, hot shower. Can we agree to skip the couples' scavenger hunt today and order room service while we hide from Dr. Day and talk?"

"God, yes." He shuddered. "I have reached my therapy quota for life."

Ignoring the scandalized looks from two old women in the lobby, I pulled Kendrick to the elevators and jabbed the "Up" arrow. Letting go of his hand, I scrubbed my face and peered toward the gel lights turning colors slowly up the gaudy glass-based waterfall.

Two men in rumpled suits rounded the corner, coming from the lobby, and I stiffened.

My warning bells clanged to DEFCON levels, making my head hurt. "Pretend to kiss me."

"What?" Kendrick's dazed gaze snapped from the elevator doors.

"Now." I grabbed a handful of his shirt and slammed my back against the wall beside the elevator. He tripped and caught himself by bracketing my head with his hands.

Out of the corner of my eye, I watched the two men get closer. Everything about them screamed wrong. Their aggressive body language, the hard lines on their faces, and how they seemed too intently focused on a set path instead of meandering and taking in the scenery like typical tourists. They didn't add up.

Darting my hands up, I further hid Kendrick's face by covering his cheeks and forcing his forehead to touch mine, pushing the hat's brim up. Damn, I wished I had a Tic Tac or some gum.

"What's going on?" His tone was on full alert, and he pressed the entire front of his body to mine. "What do you see?"

"Two Hispanic men in business suits approaching from the lobby. My intuition is screaming they're up to no good."

Kendrick slid his eyes to the left, and I felt the second he saw them. "Shit," he murmured, sliding his hands down the wall so his muscular forearms blocked my face. "Who the hell are these clowns?"

The floor vibrated with the thugs' heavy footsteps as they neared us. One elbowed the other and jutted his chin in our direction. He said something in Spanish, and they both laughed.

I lost sight of them behind Kendrick, then caught them again when they strode past.

"Did you catch the bruising?" Kendrick whispered, following their path as they headed toward the conference rooms.

"One had a black eye."

"The other had swollen and marred knuckles," Kendrick completed.

My stomach rolled, and my heart jumped into my throat.

"Darien," we said at the same time.

"Shit." I dropped my arms, and Kendrick grabbed my hand, yanking me into the open elevator. "He found you."

Chapter 28

Pacing from one end of the beautiful room to the other, I chewed on my thumbnail while Kendrick took his turn in the bathroom. I'd never packed so fast in my life. We'd raced to the room, thrown our stuff into our luggage, and escaped out a side entrance. Not wanting to be caught on the street with our suitcases, we checked into the four-star resort diagonally across the street, under our backup IDs.

Neither Kendrick nor I could chance that Darien had found out we'd been posing as Ken and Barb Roberts.

Bile lurched up to my throat. Uncle Liam. The implications of everything Darien could and would do crashed into my head. Wave upon wave threatened to drown me.

I covered my mouth and bent over, air suddenly nonexistent, yet my stomach gagging anyway.

"Breathe, Cupcake." A wall of heat curled around me. One of Kendrick's arms encircled my waist, keeping me from taking a header on the floor, while the other rubbed circles on my back.

I sucked in as hard as I could without success. The black spots continued to crowd my vision.

"Breathe. Slowly." Kendrick inhaled and exhaled as if to show me.

My body followed his lead, and I choked on my lungs suddenly expanding. His exquisite, addictive scent poured through my nose, and I inhaled just to keep ingesting a part of him.

"I should call Darien," I wheezed, clinging to his arm.

"Yes. We have to know who those men were after." Kendrick gently forced me to stand, but he didn't move away.

I slumped into his hold and rested the back of my head against his shoulder. His *bare* shoulder which meant shirtless chest. I wished I could be goggling over pressing against his skin, but I couldn't think beyond the implications of the thugs' presence.

"If Darien knows about us posing as Ken and Barb," I rambled, my thoughts still ramming into each other, "then he knows I've teamed up with the FBI. Your suspension won't matter. Those thugs might have been sent to take care of both of us. What if he's killed Uncle Liam already?"

Panic tore through me again, and I gripped his forearm across my stomach.

"We'll deal with it *together*." His deep voice rumbled past my ear. "You can't make yourself crazy playing 'what if'." He waddle-walked us to the bed and made me sit on the edge.

Only a pair of black gym shorts covered his lower half as he marched to our bags clumped against the windows overlooking the pool and flower gardens. "Which one has your phone?"

"Backpack."

He fished out the phone, then grabbed the office chair from the desk and wheeled it in front of me.

With shaking hands, I took the device and pulled up the last number for my uncle since Darien had the burner phone.

"Make sure it records," Kendrick reminded me, leaning forward to peer at the screen.

I nodded and tapped the button to activate the app as well as the one that scrambled my location so I couldn't be tracked easily by the usual methods, then pressed call.

Kendrick cupped my trembling hand holding the phone and supported the weight. Thankfully. The simple device had suddenly turned into a brick in my palm.

The call finally connected, and it rang once. Twice. *"So, you do realize it's not a good idea to make me chase you for updates."*

My eyes flew to Kendrick's. Darien didn't sound like a man on a warpath for betrayal. "How's Uncle Liam?" I couldn't stop the small quiver. Hopefully, Darien's ego attributed it to my cowering in the face of his greatness instead of terror of him learning I was doing everything I could to destroy him.

"Yesterday, things got tough for Liam."

My hand gripped the phone tighter. "Tough? What do you mean? Why? You said you wouldn't touch him."

"I wouldn't have if you'd kept me in the loop," he delivered with a cold edge. *"It's been too long. But don't worry your pretty little head over it. He's just being stubborn about having a simple conversation with me."*

I wanted to reach through the phone and choke him.

"Nothing for you to be concerned about," he continued airily, like he hadn't just told me he'd had my uncle beaten again. *"You need to stay focused on bringing me the Cryptix."*

"I am one-hundred percent focused." *On taking your ass down.*

Kendrick shifted, his face mottled with anger and disgust.

"Excellent," the CEO crowed, and a squeak of a chair rocking back echoed over the line. *"Are you or have you been in Miami?"*

"Miami?" I added confusion to cover the *Oh shit* suddenly making my stomach queasy. "What's in Miami?"

"Not a what but a who," Darien replied silkily. *"Don't ever say I don't look out for you, Holly."*

Kendrick's fingers spasmed around my hand.

"According to one of my contacts," Darien barreled on to brag, obviously not noticing I'd never actually answered his question. *"Agent Kendrick booked a flight to Miami, checked into a hotel in South Beach, then stopped answering his cellphone. When they tracked his phone, they found it in the room along with his luggage. The maids say he never slept in the bed and only used one towel that first evening."*

"Have they found him?" I held my breath, needing Darien to continue spilling his guts.

"No." His tone dripped with disdain. *"Opinion is split, depending on who you ask. Some think he's gone off the grid to look* for *you. Others believe he's gone off the grid to be* with *you."*

I suddenly couldn't swallow. "What?" I choked, forcing a laugh, then cringed at the hollowness. "Team up *with* me? How on Earth did they leap to that bit of fantasy?"

"It's a mystery."

That response did not soothe my nerves. I risked peeking at Kendrick and found him still as granite.

"Either way," Darien's voice dropped its airiness, *"the FBI is not giving up searching for you both. You cannot take unneeded risks that expose what you're after."*

"I'm not taking any extra risks," I defended. "The Cryptix is buried deep inside a military installation with a ton of electronic security on top of all the GI Joes. It's taking time to figure out the right people to approach, and I'm doing that as quietly as I can."

"You better be. Your uncle's life depends on it."

Asshole. "I understand." I gritted my teeth, and Kendrick bookended my knees. The hairs on his legs tickled mine until he pressed harder.

"I debated whether to tell you this, but since you've finally learned to respect my authority, you deserve a reward."

Everything inside me rebelled at that condescending, father-knows-best tone. "Oh? Tell me what?"

"My search for Agent Kendrick has gotten very exciting."

Kendrick stiffened, and this time, I got to be the one to comfort him by smoothing my hand over his freshly shaven cheek.

"One of my contacts was able to obtain a list of names he searched when he last signed into the FBI servers."

"Oh wow," I breathed, hoping to sound appropriately shocked and amazed, not sick and horrified. "Your connections seem endless."

"Years of hard work," he preened. *"Anyway. I've sent men to find every person on that list. He chose these people for a reason. That means he's bound to show up at one of their locations."* The satisfaction in his tone made me want to hurl. *"Don't worry, Holly. I'll make sure you never have to worry about Agent Kendrick again. My guys know how to extract information out of people."*

Kendrick's hand clenched into a fist, and he slammed it into his thigh. *That bastard,* he mouthed, fire raging in his irises.

My phone buzzed, and Stuart's name flashed on the screen. I jolted, and Kendrick's mouth thinned.

"Darien, I've got to go. A man I've been trying to get in touch with is finally calling me back."

"Keep me informed, Holly. Not only will your uncle fare better, but I'll be more willing to share my updates about Agent Kendrick."

"Will do." I hung up and instantly flashed over to Stuart, but he wasn't there.

"Dammit!" I thrust the phone into the air, breaking Kendrick's hold.

Kendrick surged to his feet. The chair flew backwards, hitting the dresser and spinning forlornly. "I've painted targets on their backs." He paced the space between the windows and the bed, jamming his hand in his damp hair.

I pressed redial and willed Stuart to answer.

"That bastard," Kendrick railed again. "Nineteen randomly chosen people who have nothing to do with this are going to pay the price of my search."

"Kisa—"

"Holly, is Agent Kendrick with you?" Stuart's furious voice suddenly blared through the speakerphone.

"I'm here." Kendrick marched to drop beside me on the bed. My body flopped against him, and I had to work to get out of the steep decline his extra weight caused.

"Two armed men waltzed into the resort." Stuart's voice shook.

"Where are you?" Kendrick demanded. "Where's Chet?"

"He's still dealing with turning them over to the police." A clang reverberated, and I winced at the horrid sound. *"He knows I took Melanie to our room, so I don't have long before he comes in."*

"What happened?" I internalized Stuart's agitated rage, which didn't take much on top of Darien's call and the man vibrating with guilty fury beside me.

"Those guys came for me," the hacker pushed out through gritted teeth. "Me. *Not a word was said about either of you. What the hell?"*

Shame flashed over Kendrick's face, and his irises lit with an even deeper fire. Darien was going down. That's what his expression promised.

"The assholes had guns. They could have killed Melanie."

My breath caught. Never in my dreams had I imagined our plan would spiral out of control like this. "Is she okay?"

"She's lying down." He audibly swallowed. *"She's a gentle woman. All this has taken a toll on her."*

"I'm so sorry, Stuart."

"It's not your fault, Holly." His tone said otherwise. *"You're not the one who was waving a gun. At. My. Wife."*

No, but we brought those men to your door. Fuck. "I hate to ask, but how do you know they're connected to us?"

"I'm positive I'm the only one who saw this, and I only paid attention because of our conversation last night," Stuart rambled, *"but the black-eyed asshole had a photo of Agent Kendrick on his phone, then swiped to mine. He put the phone away the second he saw me, and then he accosted me and Melanie outside the Reef Room."*

Kendrick's fist slammed his thigh again, and his jaw hardened.

"Agent Kendrick, I know you don't trust me, and I realize my price probably has you booking the next flight out," Stuart continued, and Kendrick's granite body stilled even more, if that was possible, *"but I'll be at your disposal for life if you help us disappear. Whatever you need, if I can do it, I will."*

So much passion and sincerity rang through the speaker. I had no doubt he meant every word.

"Those assholes had guns. They could have killed Melanie." His voice caught, and he paused as if to get an image out of his head. *"I may not be a ninja warrior like you, but I do have the power to help you take this bastard down."*

"How can I trust you're not going to disappear on me once I've freed you?" Kendrick argued, his voice lethally calm.

"I've already proven my word is valid by sticking to the agreement for the last seven years," Stuart defended. *"That legal document left me with very few choices for a job, but I willingly accepted whatever I could find to prove I had learned from my mistakes."*

I peered up through my eyelashes at Kendrick to find him listening and ruminating on Stuart's point. I didn't know about *his* decision, but mine finally became clearer.

"I could have easily gotten my hands on a computer and taken my revenge on the FBI for smashing my ego, but I didn't."

"You make some compelling arguments," Kendrick answered, a little warmer.

"Glad to hear it." Stuart took an audible breath. *"I want to help you. I need to help you, but understand this, I'm not going to allow this Darian bastard to get away with sending thugs after me and threatening my wife. I will do whatever it takes to break these chains, then I will make it my mission to dismantle this asshole's empire piece by piece. I'd rather do that under your plan and be held accountable to you, be your hacker du jour."*

"Why?" Kendrick rubbed his forehead. "Why me? Why be accountable to anyone if you think you can break free on your own?"

Silence rang for two long heartbeats. *"You're different, Agent Kendrick. You're willing to risk your career and team up with a wanted thief in order to do what's right. That speaks of a strong moral character. You're the type of agent I trust. I realize Holly's way hotter than me, and your chemistry with her is insane, but I can be an asset to you, too."*

I bit my lip, my cheeks flaming at Stuart's way-too-blunt observation about us.

Kendrick bumped my shoulder with his. "Holly *is* way hotter than you."

The hacker cleared his throat. *"Bottom line, I want to be held accountable to you as a way to keep myself in check, so I'm never tempted to do something stupid.*

I know if you asked me for my skills, it'd be for a genuine need. This reformed hacker couldn't ask for a better person to pledge their life to."

Kendrick hung his head, his skin flushing red.

Tears pricked the corners of my eyes. Didn't this man know how special he was? I suspected his boss was actually threatened by Kendrick and that was why he went on the attack to push him out of the unit. Even Stuart didn't take long to see the light shining inside this amazing man. It was no wonder he wanted to stay near it.

"Don't do anything rash yet," Kendrick answered gruffly. "Stick close to Chet in case more goons show up. We'll contact you either through this phone or another late-night visit with the answer."

Chapter 29

U nder the night's moon, I wandered to the middle of the beach and stared at the waves crashing against the shore. The rhythmic symphony of that steady action entranced me. I hugged my arms to my chest, shivering at the ocean breeze seeping through my black spandex "heist" uniform I'd had laundered earlier. All day, the warmth had steadily leeched out the deepest part of me, leaving behind a cold emptiness I couldn't fight. Rubbing my chest, I hated how I now recognized my soul reverting back to the lonely darkness it had known before Kendrick filled it up.

For the last twelve hours, Kendrick and I hadn't had a moment to talk about anything. The conference schedule and all the drama surrounding Darien's goons had swamped us, stealing the time I had agreed to give him.

He hadn't shown any indication in changing his mind about Stuart, but it didn't matter. I knew what I had to do.

"The farewell party is almost over. Your escaping early was commented on."

I closed my eyes and inhaled at that wonderful, deep male voice that had become the center of my world. With the conference ending at eleven A.M. tomorrow, the therapists had organized a final-night event including a buffet and open bar in the Reef Room. "Not really dressed to return to a party."

"No." Heat blanketed my side and warm, rough skin laced with my hand, pulling me gently to walk. "You've got your work clothes on."

I adjusted our hold, savoring the connection, knowing it'd be our last, and peered at Kendrick. He hadn't changed out of his navy shorts and light blue polo shirt he had put on shortly after Stuart's phone call this morning.

"I take it you've made some decisions on your own?"

The guarded question made me wince. "What did you learn about the two goons?" I countered like a coward, not ready to focus on the issue rending my heart in two.

He didn't say a word, and tension inside me coiled tighter.

"I talked Chet into following up with the local police," he finally answered. A wave broke loudly next to him as we curved to walk on the wet sand, heedless of his trendy sneakers. "It didn't take much prompting, and Stuart helped egg the agent on, so I owe him for that." His fingers tightened. "The two thugs are wanted by the Miami police for beating a hotel clerk into a coma."

I sucked in a breath and whipped my gaze up to him.

"Do I have to tell you which hotel?" he snarled.

"Yours." Son of a bitch. "I hope that clerk gave them those bruises before he went down."

All the turmoil and uproar forced us to remain boot camp participants. Chet was more than capable of handling Darien's goons (if he sent anyone else), but Kendrick worried disappearing would make us look suspicious. Any investigator worth his badge would start looking for reasons why the thugs showed up just as we vanished, and that would potentially reveal everything we couldn't afford to have uncovered yet. We kept our new hotel room as a precaution, but we'd scurried over to join in the couple's scavenger hunt that had us scattering to find things all over town. We stomped the crap out of all the other couples and were scolded by Dr. Day for our "competitive natures" even though we were the epitome of the intended lesson of working together. But the activity tore me apart. Every joke, touch, laugh, and heated gaze sliced like a knife. I'd never have this with him again, and my soul crumbled, revealing just how far I had fallen for FBI Agent Jackson Kendrick like an idiot.

"The thugs' appearance doesn't change anything." I forced the words past numb lips. I couldn't imagine continuing without him, but I had to be strong.

"We knew Darien would send men after you." My mouth froze. *Say it.* "You have to walk away—"

"No," he growled, jerking to a halt.

My pulse leaped, and I untangled my hand from his hold, hugging myself in a lame attempt to catch the pieces of my breaking heart. "Kendrick..." My brain jumbled the responses that *had* to follow.

"No." Kendrick's jaw hardened, and he held my gaze hostage with the fire leaping into his eyes.

"You need to stay true to yourself," I pleaded hoarsely, heart-wrenching pain stealing my ability to utter the speech I had come up with earlier that sounded a lot better than the staccato statements falling from my mouth now. "Walk away before you're in any deeper and cross a line you can't come back from."

"Don't you get it?" He grabbed my arms and yanked me against him. I didn't think twice about sliding my hands around him, but I should have. Tears gathered in my eyes, already aching for his touch that I knew I'd never get again. "*I'm all in,*" he whispered fiercely. "I don't care about crossing lines or following someone else's rigid rules. I care about doing what's right. I care about *you.*"

Air clogged my lungs. I couldn't take hearing the words, even though I coveted them at the same time. "You can't do this for me—"

"I'm not doing this just for you." He ran stiff fingers against my cheek. "Although you're a major damn part, Darien *must* be stopped. I have to make sure he doesn't hurt those other nineteen people *I* made targets or anyone else. My boss refused to listen when I tried to follow the proper channels to get help, so I already have to find another way."

"Kisa," I choked, too flooded with conflicting emotions to whisper more. *He's all in? He can't stay. I shouldn't have dragged him into this in the first place. And what does that mean? Does he only mean professionally or personally, too—*

Kendrick brushed a strand of hair that escaped my ponytail, and I hoarded the heat from that trail to combat the ice crystalizing inside me. "Help me, Holly," he whispered gruffly. "Tell me something you've never told anyone else. I need you to feel as vulnerable as I do right now."

My heart slammed so hard against my chest, I wondered if it hit him, too. "You feel vulnerable?"

"Haven't you been listening?" His eyes searched mine.

"Yes, but I don't understand."

"What's so confusing?"

"When this is all said and done, we go back to being adversaries—"

"Fuck that." His grip on my face tightened. "I can't go back—no, I *won't* go back to chasing you like before. You've challenged everything in my world." Aqua irises pierced me. "Now you consume it. Consume me."

The last shred of my willpower exploded into dust. "I haven't had sex since the day I first saw you seven months ago," I blurted with all the grace of a battering ram to answer his request. Mortification devoured me. My brain chose *that* as a confession? What the fuck?

His mouth slammed closed, and a jolt rocked his body.

"How's that for vulnerable?" I attempted to quip, my legs turning to Jell-O. "No other man has interested me or could compare to you, so I stopped trying," I gamely finished my humiliating admission, but why stop there? My stupid mouth plowed on. "I've also never shared my childhood memories or talked about my mom with anyone before." While not a new vulnerability, it was the biggest weakness I had outside of admitting just how deep I'd fallen for this man.

His pupils dilated. "No one? I'm the first?"

I ducked my head and nodded.

"Holly," he breathed. "Cupcake."

I lifted my gaze to find his aqua eyes softening.

"I'm *honored* you shared something so sacred with me."

"I can't seem to stop," I whispered. "You make me reckless, and it scares me."

"You petrify the shit out of me."

"You have the power to destroy me—"

"I don't want to destroy you." He wound his arm around the small of my back and pulled me in tighter. "I fantasize about doing a lot of things with you, but destroying is not one of them. And you have just as much power to crush me, too."

My hand grazed the area just above his pec, and he shivered, his eyes narrowing and boring into mine. Firming my touch, I spread my fingers to feel as much of that hard muscle as possible.

He gently swiped more hair and tucked it behind my ear.

I searched his eyes and got lost in their alluring depths.

"Kendrick," I breathed really meaning, *kiss me.*

"Jackson," he murmured, his grip on my back spasming.

"What?" I croaked. Following a conversation was not in my skill set at the moment.

"My name is Jackson," he uttered as if his throat had become sandpaper. "Jack to those close to me."

"Am I," my voice hitched, "close to you?"

"Cupcake, you're about as close as you can get."

Pressing my swollen and heavy breasts against him, I murmured, "No, I think I can get much closer. Jack."

His irises flared just as he slanted his mouth over mine.

Heaven. My eyelids fluttered closed, and I memorized the weight of his soft, full lips expertly teasing mine. His kiss hit me clear to my toes.

I sighed against him, never wanting this moment to end.

He sipped and sampled, taking his time to explore every inch of my lips. It drove me wild.

More. My fingers curled, grabbing the material of his shirt and pulling him harder against me.

He refused to be rushed. With small little bites, he nibbled my bottom lip until I growled. Only then did the very tip of his tongue touch the plumpest part of mouth.

Desire zinged through me, and my lips fell open in a swift inhale.

His fingers dug into the side of my spine, and I answered by clawing into that same area on his back.

Still not taking the hint to ravish my mouth, his tongue dipped inside mine in teasing little forays. I'd never experienced anything like it. *This man is lethal with his mouth.* Groaning, I raised my tongue to meet his, and his entire body shivered.

"I'm trying to take my time." His breathing was completely ragged. "But I'm about to lose it in another second. I want you so goddamn bad."

"Hell yes. I've been fantasizing about this for too long. Rip the wrapping off the present, Jack," I growled, tearing the bottom of his polo out of his shorts.

"Fuck." A shudder rippled over him. "Hearing my name on your lips in that tone." He scraped his fingernails up the side of my ribs. "You have no idea what it does to me."

"Jack." I tilted my head and placed soft kisses on his chin. "Jack." Kiss on his jaw. "Jack." Little licks up to his ear. "Jack."

His hips rocked into mine. The long, thick length pressing into my stomach had my panties completely soaked.

"Jack—"

He ripped himself away, startling me with the suddenness.

It took me an embarrassing extra second to comprehend him pulling out his phone, the screen lit with a part of a message.

His shoulders slumped, and he growled. "Sorry. I thought it was something urgent, like another attack." He turned the screen toward me to show me the text. "Stuart and Melanie are safe and in for the night. They'll wait up for our answer."

"Oh." I stepped back, trying my hardest to rebuild the wall he'd just smashed to hell. "I need to go see them."

"Hey." He closed the distance between us again. "Not without me watching over you."

Boom. Down went the wall again. Flimsy piece of crap. It had looked like a kindergartener constructed it anyway. "You truly mean it? You're not going to regret staying and come to hate me for making you compromise your integrity?"

"I'll say it again. I'm. All. In, Cupcake." He softly brushed my lips with his, and the shiver that stole through me from the contact was *not* subtle. "I had a chance to look Stuart in the eye. We managed to grab a few minutes alone at the party, and I believe him. I believe he's not escaping to go back to his old ways. I believe he truly wants to protect his wife and will keep his word to deliver the artificial intelligence to take down Darien, and after that, he'll help me whenever I need it in the future." He snorted. "I figure it'd be better to join forces with him and know what he's up to rather than hear about his 'death' and always wonder what or who he's about to strike next."

Cupping his cheek, I smiled. So much joy and relief radiated out of me, it was a wonder I didn't blind him. "You're starting to gather a very interesting collection of personalities and skill sets in your new crime fighting unit."

Kendrick groaned. "Don't even joke about that. You might tempt the universe to make it come true. Then I'll be up to my neck in God knows what crazy schemes."

I bit my lip. "Speaking of crazy schemes, I have an idea to kill the Stewarts." I slid my arms around his neck because I could. Because after too many hours of being convinced I had to give him up, I needed to touch him and assure myself he was still here. Still mine for as long as I could have him. "I have no clue how you're going to take it, but I need your help fleshing out the plan. We don't have much time to put it into play since it requires Stuart and Melanie to go on a second honeymoon straight from here, but I have someone I trust to participate if you approve."

Kendrick made a dramatic show of steeling himself. "Okay, partner, hit me with it."

Chapter 30

A peaceful, calm ocean skimmed smoothly beneath the speedboat. At a little after one A.M the following morning, the moon added a silver mystique to the water and illuminated, *Rolling Deep*, the one-hundred-forty-one-foot, white superyacht anchored ahead.

Running lights made the four deck (three visible: sun deck at the top, bridge deck, main deck, and one lower deck mostly beneath the water line) mega yacht that much more impressive.

I stole up behind Kendrick (I facilitated between calling him Kendrick, Jack, and Kisa, even in my head) standing beside *Rolling Deep*'s twenty-three-year-old first mate currently driving the small speedboat and wrapped my arms around him. Peering around his bicep (I debated hard about licking), I tried to read his expression. He had one of those faces that didn't give much away, but I'd been with him long enough to see through the façade. His heart beating against my forearm and the goose bumps on his skin told me he wanted to grin like a little boy at our ride for the next phase of our plan: Operation: Kill the Stewarts. (Okay. So only I called it that, but it fit.)

Kadmos, the first mate hailing from Greece who I'd met once before, slowed the engines, and I moved away from Kendrick as the boat eased against the superyacht's swim platform at the stern (back).

"I'll take care of your bags," Kadmos offered in smooth, accented English.

My attention was on the five-foot-seven, weathered-skinned, burly man standing on the platform. Gray hair had found its way into the Scot's red-brown beard, and his hairline had receded alarmingly since I'd last laid eyes on the captain.

He thrust a meaty hand toward me and whipped me out of the small boat so hard, I fell against him in a tangle of feet and flailing arm. "You never could stay out of trouble fer long, lass."

"It's not me this time," I retorted, my throat wanting to clog again, but I wouldn't let it.

Captain Jonah Clancy (though only a rare few knew his real name...Lord knew what he'd call himself on this venture) and my uncle went back more than twenty years. Captain (as I usually referred to him nowadays so I didn't have to remember anything else) used to be a part of the crew when I first came to live with Liam. He left when I turned fourteen to strike out on his own. It took him quite a few years, but he built a name for himself as one of the best damn smugglers in the Caribbean, only to be rivaled by his other reputation as being one of the best damn charters to hire if you're rich and want a customized tour of the islands. Retrofitting and using the multimillion-dollar yacht to cater to both types of clients just made sense.

My skin tingled, and I didn't have to look to know Kendrick had placed himself just behind me. Untangling myself, I turned to stand sideways between the two men (with the way Kendrick barely left any space, my shoulders practically touched them both). I rolled my eyes at Captain bristling and Kendrick puffing out his chest. They studied each other in the way predators often did when they sensed an equally dangerous presence in their midst.

At least four sarcastic retorts flew to my lips, but I managed to bite my tongue. Being a wiseass would just make the two alphas dig in deeper. "Okay," I chirped in the growing silence. "If you two are done memorizing each other, I'll introduce you."

Without taking his eyes off Captain, Jack smoothed his hand across my back to my left hip and gently (but firmly) made me turn so we presented a united front.

Seriously? God save me from men's egos and caveman instincts. Although, I'd be lying if I said Kendrick's "claiming" didn't make my blood quicken and my inner romantic sigh. (*I know, feminists are railing, but I liked it, so sue me.*)

A low-sounding motor rumbled, then a ten-foot section of the swim platform and corresponding back wall in the center slid apart. Jack's grip on me tightened as the floor beneath us vibrated, but through awesome engineering, we didn't need to move. Kadmos expertly drove the speedboat through the channel and docked it inside its housing within the yacht. The motor whirred again, and the floor and wall began to close back together. I caught water pumping out as the speedboat lifted higher in its rack.

Supercool, but not important.

"Ken Roberts," I thumbed at Kendrick's chest, "meet one of the finest smugglers ever known and a former member of the crew." I swished my hand toward the Scot, "Captain—"

"Fred," Captain barked, filling in the blank like I knew he would. "Fred Jones."

It took all of me not to laugh. *Fred Jones?* I raised an eyebrow, but the gesture was wasted. "Fred" hadn't looked away from Kendrick once.

Kendrick snorted. "What kind of thieving, seafaring smuggler name is Fred?"

"The kind that does'nae get caught." Captain's brogue hardened, and his eyes turned calculating. "And I suspect yer name is'nae really Ken, so why don't we stick with Captain and Mr. Roberts while ya're aboard my ship."

Yikes. Apparently, these two would not be forming a bromance anytime soon. Captain had always been outspoken and crusty with no filter on his mouth. I should have realized that would trigger Kendrick's wolf tendencies. Neither one would ever back down. *Oh joy!* Didn't that make the next few days sound like a ton of fun?

The superyacht's engines cranked to life—barely audible; I felt them more than heard them—and within moments we began to smoothly turn away from the island to head deeper into the sea.

"All right," Captain Fred crossed his arms, "now that we can'nae be overheard, give me the details. What happened ta Liam?"

Captain had always hated talking on the phone, fearing (rightly) that some-one could be listening in. After playing the recording for him, and giving him a highly edited explanation of how I ended up on the yacht, Captain's stare intensified, and he jutted his chin at Kendrick. "Why's he here? What's he have ta do with this? And why're ya two wearin' weddin' rings?"

The urge to jerk my left hand behind my back gripped me, but I stayed strong. "They're part of the cover we used to get to the hacker." Only days ago, the band had felt so foreign and scary, now I didn't even think about it. Nor did I want to take it off. The only solace I had about the oversight was that Kendrick still wore his too. "Ken's here because Darien's targeting him for reasons you're better off not knowing," I replied firmly, refusing to cow under the stare that used to make me squirm when I was younger. "Just know he's *very* committed to getting Uncle Liam back and taking Darien down."

I made the decision not to tell Captain about Kendrick working for the FBI before I even called to get his help. He would not be amused or generous with his support if he knew Kendrick had ties to law enforcement, suspended or not. Nor would he ever trust my verbal agreement with Kendrick to not go after those who helped us.

Captain grunted, and his lips disappeared in his beard as he crooked them. "Ya've grown up, Holly Bell. Got a backbone on ya. Good. Glad ta see Liam pounded some of that softness out of ya. A bleedin' heart only gets ya broke or dead."

Kendrick stiffened, and his fingers spasmed on my hip. "I completely dis-agree," he answered with a lethalness I hadn't heard before. "When you pair Holly's soft heart with her wicked intelligence and amazing skills, you've got a woman who can thwart the most determined to catch her, execute the most daring of heists, and still have the capacity to love those lucky few she claims with a lioness ferocity."

My breath caught, and I whipped my eyes up to find Jack staring down at me. His aqua blues darkened with an emotion my heart recognized but my brain argued could not be possible. *"I'm all in."* His words played in my head as I fell deeper into his gaze—

"Look at that," Captain boomed with a bark of laughter, shattering the moment. "The lass has finally met a man worth gettin' ta know." His whole posture loosened, and he no longer radiated the desire to kill Ken. Captain slapped Kendrick in the back, and Kendrick blinked as if coming out of a daze.

Maybe there'll be a bromance after all.

"Come on." Captain headed toward the steps leading up to the open-air seating section on main deck. "Let me give ya a tour while I fill ya in on the latest."

I honestly wanted to go to bed. The all-night planning session (part with the Stewarts, part with just Kendrick), the closing sessions of the conference, and all the racing around afterward to get ready for the next phase had drained me, but I gamely followed. Kendrick wouldn't settle until he got the layout of the superyacht, and I didn't blame him. If I hadn't been on *Rolling Deep* many times already, I'd want to memorize my surroundings, too.

Going from room to room, deck to deck, the opulence astounded me all over again. No matter how many times I saw the over-the-top amenities, they still caught me by surprise. I mean, seriously...who needed Italian marble in every bathroom, two dining rooms (one inside, one outside that could have an awning for cover), or five different types of living rooms/seating groups (both inside and out)? Though I planned on hitting the fully stocked gym pretty hard.

"Every stateroom is soundproofed." Captain turned with his foot on the step to head to the top floor and winked at Kendrick. "Ya do'nae have ta worry about...noises escapin'."

Oh my God. My cheeks flamed like a high school girl's. *Meddling bastard needs to learn to put a muzzle on it.* Kendrick and I hadn't been alone since we'd kissed (not counting the nap we stole in our secondary hotel room after the conference ended). As much as we teased and taunted each other outrageously, I wasn't ready for the world to be let in on the new personal aspect to our relationship.

Kendrick chuckled. "Good to know."

His standard response, I'd noticed, when he wasn't sure what to say or wanted to keep his reaction hidden.

Warm air hit my ear on our way up the stairs, and he uttered in a low tone, "I can't wait to see if that blush reddens your skin all over."

I missed a step, and he scooped me up, turning sideways to finish the climb.

"Put me down," I hissed, batting his shoulder. I had a reputation to maintain with Captain. I did not want to be seen as a damsel in distress, especially in my Knight In Shining Armor's arms. (I did love how easily Kisa picked me up without strain though.)

Kendrick stole a quick kiss and winked at Captain when we reached him on the highest floor, the sun deck (moon deck after the sun went down?), then set me on my feet.

"That's a good lad," Captain guffawed in that macho way I hated. "Take care of her properly."

"I can take care of myself," I sniffed, but it sailed right past Captain.

Kendrick caught it and tweaked the back of my neck with a wink and a nod.

Captain breathed in audibly. "We'll stay cruisin' at about eight knots since we've got days ta reach the rendezvous coordinates."

"I'm sorry you had to cancel your charter." I scraped a bit of hair out of my mouth. The cool breeze off the water made my skin goose bump even though the temperature was still in the eighties.

Captain swished his big hand. "Do'nae worry about it. I passed the couple who had more money than brains ta a guy who's just startin' in the business. Now he'll owe me." His green eyes scanned the open horizon. "If I had a cargo run with this charter then it could have gotten messy, but we're good."

"What do you smuggle?" Kendrick's posture was completely loose even though the FBI agent inside him had to be screaming. He'd find out soon enough how this yacht had secret panels and niches large enough to hide quite a bit, even people if needed.

A sly grin filled Captain's face. "I think I'll keep that ta myself for now. When ya're ready ta tell me yer secrets, I'll tell ya mine."

Kendrick laughed. "Fair enough."

Captain scratched his beard. "I hired some additional men who'll meet us later, and I found another charter willin' ta go along with yer plan, lass."

Excitement and worry quickened my blood. I hoped I hadn't gone overboard with my crazy idea. Playing pirates could be tricky, especially when I had to rely on someone else to arrange all the other players to pull it off.

"Alonso De Luca, the captain of the *Livin' Large,* owes me a favor and assures me he'll make port by noon tomorrow, er, today as promised." Captain sighed and wiped his face. "I'm exhausted. I do'nae usually stay up this late anymore. Kadmos takes the night shift."

Where Captain hadn't charged me anything, citing his desire to help save his friend, I had to foot the bill for the *Livin Large*'s lost charter. And apparently my urgent need for the other superyacht to pick up the Stewarts ASAP caused wear and tear on the engines.. Three-hundred-ten-thousand euros. My stomach cramped. I could afford it, but I *hated* paying crooks who took advantage of a situation. De Luca owed Captain the favor but had no compunction about fleecing me. Not everyone who played in the gray looked out for each other. Next time I had business in the area, I would *not* involve Captain De Luca.

"I've not heard of Captain De Luca," I responded, almost purring at Kendrick combing his fingers through my hair. "Is he new?"

"Nay." Captain shook his head. "The Italian's been independently charterin' and smugglin' out of Saint Martin's fer three years." Something flittered across Captain's face, but my overtired brain couldn't interpret it. "He's a hot-headed arsehole, but he'll be fine ta participate in yer scheme."

Kendrick shot me a look and frowned at Captain. "Do you trust De Luca?"

Captain snorted. "About as much as I trust anyone else."

"So not much, I gather," Kendrick retorted flatly, his hand pausing.

Captain shot him a grisly grin. "I can see why the lass's chosen ya."

I dropped my head back, unable to fight the second round of blushing swamping me. I hated being obvious, and my feelings for Jack were still so new and all-encompassing, I wasn't ready for them to be part of a jab or punchline, especially in front of Jack.

Captain finished his statement, "Ya're not as dumb as yer pretty face makes ya seem."

"On that note," I jumped in before he could say anything else or before Kendrick could respond. "I'm headed to bed. We can catch up and plan whatever we need to in the morning."

Chapter 31

With a disgusted grunt, I kicked the thousand-count Egyptian cotton sheet off and slapped my heel onto the heavenly mattress. After forty-five minutes, I needed to give up pretending to fall asleep no matter how much I really needed it.

Peering at the clock, I groaned. 2:32 A.M.

"That's it." My feet sunk into the divine carpeting in one of the four staterooms on the lower deck with the fifth—the massive "owner's" suite—located on the main deck. "I'm officially screwed."

I'd become addicted to Kendrick. Shit. I should be overjoyed at having my space back, giving me time to decompress and clear my head after the whirlwind kicked off by Darien's call, but it was too quiet and wrong. I missed Kendrick's heavy breathing as he slept and the way he held me so tight when we fell asleep (a new aspect)... I wanted that again.

Scrubbing my face, I debated putting on something more appropriate than my blue pajama shorts with little purses, lipsticks, and heels on them and a solid, thin tank top. *Nah.* I didn't want even that much of a delay.

Padding barefoot out the door, I stopped short at finding Kendrick's door across the hall wide open and him nowhere in sight. Damn. Hustling up the steps, I searched the man out like the true addict I'd become, needing my fix.

On the sun/moon deck (of course he'd be on the very top floor), I found Kendrick lying flat on a long steel platform supported by round poles about a foot and a half off the specially coated wooden planks. The entire seating group had plush mint-green cushions and decorative throw pillows. He'd stuffed one beneath his head as he stared up at the stars. Pausing on the top step, I asked softly, "You doing okay?"

His blond head popped up, and he peered down the length of his gorgeous body clad in a T-shirt and loose jersey shorts. "Your friend is not telling us something about Captain De Luca."

I snorted and ambled toward him over the still-warm deck. "I bet he's not telling us a lot. Do you blame him?" But I hadn't forgotten the look that had passed over Captain's face, and I made a note to press the man tomorrow.

"I just hope whatever he's hiding doesn't bite us in the ass." Kendrick's hand curled around the back of my thigh and pulled gently. "Come here. I was just debating whether I should give you your space like you asked or bully my way into your bed so I can wrap my arms around you."

The floodgates of my heart flew wide open, and I had no hope of stopping all manner of feelings for this man from flowing free, but I wasn't ready to show him that yet. "It hasn't even been an hour," I teased, fitting myself between him and the low back cushion running the length of the armless "couch."

"Are you implying I'm pathetic?"

Tucking my head onto his shoulder and curling my leg over his, I smoothed a hand across the white cotton hiding his magnificent chest. "Very."

A low hum vibrated against my cheek, and a soft kiss pressed into the top of my head. "And yet you sought me out, Cupcake."

I chuckled. "I never said I wasn't pathetic or that I didn't need the same thing."

He squeezed. "As alpha bitch, that makes you leader of the pitiful club."

"I guess it does." Humming, the tension inside me drained, and I inhaled his scent again.

We fell into a peaceful silence, and I gazed up at the sky full of bright stars I'd never get to see anywhere else.

"Your life is seducing me," he murmured, pulling me out of almost falling asleep. "Is this how you spend your days? Different cities. Million-dollar condos. Superyachts in tropical settings. Jetting off wherever you want..."

I couldn't stop my chuckle. "Uh, no. Usually I'm rattling around in my loft by myself." I traced a random pattern on his chest, enjoying the valleys and plains my finger discovered. "Uncle Liam visits a lot, and we spar to keep up our skills or argue about which contracts to accept next or both. And Reggie and Gretchen stop by to take advantage of my sixty-inch TV—"

"With a full Bose surround sound?" The boyish hope in his voice made me giggle.

"As if I'd study Jason Bourne's spycraft techniques without it."

He laughed, and my heart squeezed at the rich, carefree sound. I felt like I held the fabled lost jewels of Atlantis in my hands. *New life goal: make him laugh like this over and over.*

"Damn, that was funny." The rumbling from his mirth vibrated my entire body, making me grin at the delicious way every nerve ending got a thrill. "You charmed the shit out of me with those ridiculous, but sexy, wedge shoes, looking so disgruntled when you thought you'd lost me."

I lightly bapped him. "It's not nice to make fun of those not expertly trained to be macho warriors." My chin dug into his pec so I could peer at his eyes. "I'd like to see you navigate a HVAC shaft or climb up the side of a building with just a backpack and a prayer."

"Fuck, that was sexy."

With only a few emergency lights scattered in the walls of the deck, the shadows made his darkened eyes appear dangerous. *Purrrrrrr.*

"I don't think I'll ever forget the sight of you in all that spandex, pulling your body up the railings or the fantasy you mercilessly tortured me with as you climbed." His thumbnail scratched down my spine absently, and I settled against him to give him as much access as possible to keep going.

"I tortured *you*?" I snorted, my skin goose bumping at remembering his filthy words. "You raised the bar and had me soaked by the time I hit the Stewarts' patio."

"Nice," he breathed, male pride bursting through the drawn-out word.

We fell into a peaceful silence again.

"You promised to tell me why you do it," he spoke softly after a time. "You said I didn't see the value of your work or understand what you really do. Will you tell me now?"

Peering at the stars, I gathered my thoughts. I did want him to know, and if we had any hope of figuring out how to make this not end in the epic disaster I feared was coming, I had to share this huge part of me. "The law doesn't always protect and help those who truly need it."

"Explain."

"The world is not black and white but shades of gray." I rubbed my forehead. "Take that African collection in Oregon you mentioned."

"What about it?"

"The curator is a swindler and thug." I realized my finger had dug into his chest, and I eased up. "She put together almost that entire collection by ripping off, bribing, or strong-arming families with all kinds of nasty threats to force them into giving up their family heirlooms."

Kendrick's body stiffened, and I could almost hear his brain working to put pieces together. "You won't give up your clients' names. You said there are no victims in the way I referred to them. The way you describe this curator doesn't sound like a unique experience..." He twisted to peer down at my upturned face. "Are you saying you're...Robin Hood thieves?"

"No." I shook my head. "I'm saying that when people can't turn to the law or the law refuses to help them get justice, they pay us to find and retrieve what is rightfully theirs."

A growl rumbled from Kendrick's chest.

"I can't stand injustice." I punctuated the point by jabbing him lightly. "Everyone needs a champion, Kisa. You have me to help with your bastard boss, and I have you with Darien." His eyes fluctuated with conflict. "My moral compass may not always point north like yours, but since I became old enough to have a true stake in the crew, I have *only* accepted jobs that took from the guilty. And that's why I've stayed. Why I keep risking my freedom. Someone has to stand up for those who have no one else."

He closed his eyes and swiped his mouth. "You just keep pummeling the shit out of my defenses."

I had a feeling I wasn't supposed to hear that last line by the way he barely whispered it behind his hand.

"Kisa...Jack, I'm sorry." I rolled on top of him, allowing my legs to fall on either side of his. "I never stopped to think about what every win for us meant for you." I framed his face with both my hands and rose and fell as his breathing grew heavier. "I'm sorry we hurt you—"

His mouth swooped up to mine and silenced my apology. I fit my lips over his and kissed him with a fierceness he wouldn't allow last night.

Threading his fingers through my hair, he gripped the back of my head. I parted my lips, and his tongue dove inside. Moaning, I adjusted my angle, and he deepened the kiss. *Yes.* My addiction to him was reaching unparalleled levels. I couldn't get enough. Every lick and flick of his expert tongue hit me deep in my belly.

"Fuck, what you do to me," he whispered, adjusting his chin to plunge back in for more. He exceeded every fantasy and dream I'd ever had.

Lust consumed me, and I drowned in him. *No more waiting—I need him to fill me completely.* Tasting his toothpaste and inhaling his scent, I moved my hips to slide over his erection.

Groaning, he circled his hips, rubbing his long length against my sweet spot. My grip on him tightened. *More.*

In contradiction to my demand, he stilled his body and lightened the kiss to soft pecks along my jaw and throat.

Nooooo.

"I have my own confession to make." His tongue traced up the column of my throat, and I blacked out a little. "I haven't had sex since the first time I saw you either."

That cleared my lust-addled head instantly.

"That next day," his lips nibbled behind my ear, "I broke it off with the woman I was casually dating. She couldn't hold my interest, and I've not been tempted by anyone...but you."

Holy shit. My mind blew at that admission. I attacked him, meeting his tongue with my own and dueling with his until I got lost in the kiss.

Surfacing for air, I drove my fingers into his silky hair and pressed my forehead to his. "Jack, you better not say the words 'we can't' or give me some speech about not crossing this final line." My grip tightened. "I swear to God, I will rain hell down on you if you don't rip the goddamn wrapping paper off and enter this present."

He shot straight up, twisting to slap his feet on the deck. Standing with my legs wrapped around his waist, he peered into my eyes. "You have one question to answer, then you won't have to think for the rest of the night."

A shiver ran down my spine at the way he growled those words.

"Do you want to be fucked senseless up here or in your room?"

"You have protection on you?" I rolled my hips over his seriously hard erection.

He shuddered. "Yes. I've had it with me since Tallahassee."

That admission made me even hotter, and I ground his shaft against my sweet spot. "Fuck me senseless under the stars."

Chapter 32

"I can't move, much less walk." I sprawled naked with my arms and legs wide, taking up way more than my allotted space on the king-size bed in my stateroom.

A thoroughly satisfied male chuckle made me pop one eye open.

"Three days, Kisa." I stared into those gorgeous blues hovering above me. "You cannot be human to keep me screaming in this room or on the moon deck that many times for that long. Are there any condoms left on this boat?"

His cheeks pinkened, and he cleared his throat. "Um. We're down to the last few from Captain's emergency supply."

"No." I slapped a hand over my eyes. "You went to Captain?"

"I couldn't exactly pop out to the corner store, now could I?"

"Oh man." Mortification tried to grab hold, but I was too damn sated and happy to give it much energy. "How am I going to face him?"

"Well..." Kendrick fiddled with a curl of my hair, making my eyes narrow. "He, uh, wrangled a stash from Kadmos, too, so...technically you should thank them both."

I most certainly would *not* be thanking them out loud, but silently? Hell yeah. If those two realized just how *extraordinarily* Kendrick had used up their supply, they'd kick him off the ship in a fit of jealousy.

The bed dipped, and I hummed as I ogled his incredible bare ass crossing the room to the bathroom. "It's not like they couldn't figure out what we were doing anyway." He raised his voice over the flow of water thundering into the Jacuzzi tub. "We barely saw them this entire time."

Managing to waddle my way into the beautiful bathroom, I leaned against the doorframe. "I'm going to write Dr. Lynds and let her know you really took her training to heart."

He whipped around. "You wouldn't dare."

I laughed. "I'd think you'd want to be vindicated." Moving slowly, I sank into the tub when he beckoned me. "Ahhhhh, I needed this." I closed my eyes and soaked in the heat loosening my muscles.

"Sore?" Water splashed, and a hard body picked me up, then cradled me in his arms as he settled on the seat.

"Very." I snuggled against him, inhaling his scent to get my fix. "Some of those positions were inventive, but I am *not* complaining."

He flipped the jets on, and I purrrrred, making him laugh.

"Like I was saying." I traced my fingers over the drops of water on his shoulder and down his ridiculously perfect chest. "I'd think you'd want the sex doc to know you were right. You definitely do *not* suck in bed." He squeezed some of my cake-scented gel onto a wet washcloth, and my heart gave a girly flip at the gentle way he soaped my shoulder. "Although, *I* was right about you having trouble with orgasms."

The washcloth paused on my bicep, and he raised an eyebrow. "Want to tell me the number of times you came again?"

A jolt of pleasure hit my core, and it tightened in anticipation of coming for the bazillionth time, but I clung to my straight face. "Your tendency to give mind-blowing lobotomies instead of orgasms could be detrimental to my health."

My favorite smile spread across his mouth right before he butterfly-kissed down my throat. "As do you, Cupcake. Forgot my name and how to speak quite a few times."

Yeah, I definitely made sure I gave back as good as I got and then some. Saliva pooled in my mouth, and I slid off his lap to my knees and worked myself between his legs. Scraping my hands over the hair on his thighs, I continued up until my fingers wrapped around his hard length and stroked upward. "I could make you forget your name again right now."

"Tempting." His hips moved in time with my slow strokes, and he took advantage of my position to wash my breasts, which were peeking just above the waterline. Thoroughly. "I'd rather have your lethal mouth wrapped around me, but we need to be on the main deck in twenty minutes."

I sobered. The time had finally come to enact Operation: Kill the Stewarts.

***

Night had fallen hours ago, and storm clouds filled the sky.

"We've doused our runnin' lights and dropped anchor two miles out from *Livin' Large*," Captain announced the second I opened the door to the wheel-house on the bridge deck. He turned from a row of computers and blinked. "Look at yer skin glowin', lass," he boomed, his weathered face stretching in a wide smile. "Lad, glad ta see ya're takin' proper care of yer woman."

Son of a bitch. That damn lack of filter on his mouth! It took all of me not to slam the door on Kendrick's smug face or choke on all the testosterone filling the room. Even Kadmos wore a smirk as his gaze flitted between me and Kendrick.

Lifting my chin, I waved the pompous, male-self-congratulating off and fought fire with fire. "You two should be more concerned about him." I thumbed at Kendrick. "Older men can have health issues after that much activity. He did his best to keep up with me until I took mercy on him."

"Older men?" The smug smile slipped off Kendrick's face, and he crossed his arms, planting his feet shoulder-width (the authoritative pose gave me shivers and the rat knew it). "I'm thirty-four. And what do you mean, *you* took mercy on *me*?"

It took all of me not snicker at his indignation. Men were so easy to wind up. "Of course I did." My thumb went to the underside of my ring finger and found nothing but skin.

No—

Wandering to the edge of the counter to cover my split-second panic that I'd lost the wedding band instead of taking it off now that we didn't need the cover anymore, I peered out the line of windows wrapping around the room, seeing nothing but a roiling black sea beyond. "I recall a ton of pleading to a certain deity, *lots* of shouted expletives, and a loss of words for periods of times."

Captain clapped a hand against Kendrick's back. "Lad, we should all be so lucky ta have that problem."

"Keep it up, Cupcake." Kendrick prowled toward me. The gleam in his eyes spoke of wicked things to come once he reached me. I shivered in anticipation. His voice lowered when he finally stopped in front of me, so only I'd hear him. "The more you push, the slower I'll get. You already know how I treat gifts; imagine how long I can prolong your finding release." He cupped the back of my neck and bent to whisper, "Hours, Holly. *Hours* of you screaming, cursing, and begging to come, yet I'll keep you on the edge."

My mouth dried, and my fresh panties were already damp. Going up on my toes, I responded in his ear, "Right back at you, Kisa. Every lick, suck, and stroke of my mouth will have you swearing and demanding to explode, but I'll show no mercy, matching every minute you tortured me."

A devilish light radiated from his eyes, and he growled. "Fuck, you're perfect. Tonight, I'm going to make you sorry you just challenged my age—"

"Mayday, mayday," poured out of the speakers mounted in the corners of the room from the emergency channel.

Kendrick whirled, his entire body flipping to full alert.

Captain banged on a keyboard while Kadmos fiddled with something on a complicated navigation display.

"This is Captain De Luca of Livin' Large," the speakers blared. *"Be advised, hostiles are approaching us, threatening to board and harm my crew and passengers. Please send help to these coordinates."* He rattled off latitude and longitude numbers.

"No." All the blood drained from my head. "Stuart, Melanie, and Chet," I breathed, clutching Kendrick. "How can they be under attack? We haven't left yet."

Captain cursed. "Kadmos, undock the speedboat now."

Kadmos tore out of the room.

"What's happening?" Kendrick barked. "He's not supposed to send the distress call this soon."

Captain charged to a radar screen and cursed again. "Three ships are showin' on the north side. One's at least a two-hundred-foot vessel—it's three miles out. And there are two little ones, about twelve feet long, closin' in on *Livin' Large* as we speak." He snatched a set of walkie-talkies and hit some buttons on a panel. "Come on."

"*Real* pirates?" I ran after Captain who had surprising speed and dexterity for a man with his heft. Kendrick dogged my heels, and we raced down the steps to the lower deck. Captain's heavy gait ate up the hallway, then stopped suddenly in front of a blank section of the wall near the gym. He tapped a complicated pattern in various places (I couldn't see how he knew where to tap since it all looked the same to me). A click reverberated, and the panel dropped back an inch, then slid to the side, revealing a small room with an arsenal.

"Holy shit," Kendrick exclaimed, all but drooling at the weapons displayed on hooks and filling clear tubs and drawers.

"Ya know anythin' about guns and shootin', lad?" Captain stared at Kendrick.

"Hell yeah," Kendrick retorted, gazing at the impressive array. "I can handle everything in here with ease."

Call me sick, but that complete confidence in his training made me want to slam him against the wall and kiss the hell out of him in gratitude for his skills despite the urgency to get to the Stewarts and Chet.

"We'll find out—"

The radio in Captain's hand blared to life, cutting off Captain's response. "*Fred, you there?*" A frantic, pissed-off, Italian-accented male voice asked in English.

"De Luca, go ahead," Captain answered, then released the button. To Kendrick and me, he pointed. "Load up."

"*I'm in a shitload of trouble. How fast can you get here?*"

"I caught yer distress call. Who's approachin'?" Captain snatched a rifle off a hook and stuffed it in a black duffle Kendrick found by the door.

"An upstart cartel leader's army. He doesn't understand he can't have my yacht as compensation for a stolen cargo shipment. It's not my fault his cocaine's gone missing from the docks. I delivered as promised."

Kendrick let loose an impressive string of expletives and I seconded every one of them. *Captain got us tangled up with someone who runs drugs for the cartels?*

Captain growled. "I told that arsehole ta stay away from drugs and guns." He grabbed a double-barrel shotgun off its pegs.

Darting to touch Kendrick's waist as he bent to peer in a tub, I whispered, "De Luca's not covered under our agreement. Feel free to go after his ass once all this is done."

"Thank God." Kendrick slapped boxes of ammo into the duffle. "I foresaw a huge fight in our future because I targeted him anyway." He lurched up to pluck two handguns and their holsters off the wall.

I hated guns. I was a thief, not La Femme Nikita. If it came down to a gunfight, then things had already gone beyond sideways, and my pulling out a 9mm would just escalate things to deadly levels.

Not touching a thing, I pivoted and ran into my stateroom. *Where? Where?* I spied my backpack peeking out from beneath the comforter now piled on the floor. Kendrick and I had kicked it off sometime in the last three days. Rescuing the pack and the white shopping bag from the closet, I tore down the hall to catch up to the men hoofing it up the steps.

Kadmos already had the speedboat out and waiting by the swim platform.

I tossed the shopping bag in and leaped over the side, moving out of the way for Kendrick to deftly jump in with the ominous Black Duffle of Death clutched in his grip.

"We're on our way," Captain barked into the radio, then jammed the hook to hang off his black pants and landed in the boat. "Kadmos, stay here."

The twenty-three-year-old Greek didn't hesitate to hand the wheel over to Captain and plant his feet on the deck.

"With authorities on their way," Captain slapped the second walkie-talkie into his first mate's hands, "turn the lights back on and make sure the yacht holds up ta an inspection."

My stomach dropped further. "They can't know about us." I thumbed between me and Kendrick.

"I know, lass." Captain turned back to Kadmos. "Stow their luggage, tidy the rooms as best ya can, and send the additional crew I hired fer the lass's scheme ta meet us at *Livin' Large*. I have a feelin' we'll need their help."

Kadmos shot him a salute, but Captain already had the speedboat roaring away.

Falling on my ass against the back of the boat, I slid to the floor and grabbed the shopping bag. How had this night gone so horribly wrong?

My crazy scheme to "kill" the Stewarts had been relatively simple:

1. Stuart and Melanie would tell everyone at the conference that marriage boot camp had worked. They had found the spark again and were going on a second honeymoon (chartering a yacht to see the islands in style with Chet forced to tag along because he couldn't leave until the Stewarts were back home in Missouri).

2. Kendrick and I would steal out of Saint Croix without telling anyone our plans (boarding Captain's yacht at 1 A.M.).

3. After three days of the Stewarts island hopping, showing Chet how happy and in love they were, Kendrick and I (along with some hired men) would pretend to be bloodthirsty pirates, hijacking De Luca's yacht.

4. We'd "kill" the Stewarts and throw them overboard (where they'd swim to a waiting boat) and knock out Chet so he could tell the tale of pirates murdering the hacker and his wife to the authorities and his bosses in the FBI.

Thus, freeing Stuart and Melanie to build the artificial intelligence I need in peace before starting their lives over with the identities I had forged for them.

Why did the universe hate me so much to send real pirates to attack *Livin' Large* tonight of all nights? And why in the hell didn't I listen to Kendrick when he warned me that Captain had been cagey about De Luca?

Pulling out the first item my hand latched onto in the bag, I vowed to never brush aside anything Kendrick said ever again.

Chapter 33

Holding up an extremely bright, full-head-covering mask, I thrust the plaid (pink, green, and blue) at Kendrick. "Aren't you glad I insisted we buy these?"

His lip curled, and he made no move to take it. "No. We'll look ridiculous."

I dropped into his lap the mask with a cotton cloth that covered the face and a straw hat sewn on and pulled out a second one (this one yellow, red, and blue). "We can't be recognized."

He snatched the yellow one out of my hand. (Okay. It was more masculine.) "No one's going to believe we're innocent Good Samaritans trying to thwart a real hijacking wearing these."

The *Livin' Large* loomed into view. The white superyacht was similar to the *Rolling Deep* in that it had four opulent decks visible above water, but the design said this one offered different amenities to guests.

I plucked the other mask off his thighs and fit it over my head. The small boat crested over another wave and smacked down against the water. My teeth rattled, and my brain bounced against my skull.

"I get it," I gritted. Not usually one to get seasick, my stomach threatened to revolt at taking these waves this jarringly fast.

On our last day in Saint Croix, we had searched high and low, but an island in the tropics did not have a market for ski masks. The only things I could find were the Mocko Jumbie disguises sold everywhere as part of the culture. "Look at it this way." Damn eyeholes refused to stay where I needed them, and the straw hat on top kept tilting wrong to make it worse. "These are supposed to scare bad spirits away. That's like getting double bang for our buck. Chet won't know it's us, and we'll have the supernatural world covered in the event that part's true."

"Do you hear yourself when you're talking? Are you making this shit up as you go?"

"Hey," I protested for form's sake, but he was right. Nerves made me ramble and talk out of my ass.

The corners of his eyes remained tight, and his mouth stayed flat. As much as he professed to be "all in," there was no way his participating in freeing a felon didn't bother him. Add to that, knowing that the very same felon, his wife, and a fellow FBI agent's lives were now in jeopardy had to be making him crazy. And to top it off, that we had inadvertently put those three in the middle of a cartel/smuggler feud had to be ticking him off royally.

Captain owed me beyond belief for this epic disaster, and De Luca should run from me after we freed the Stewarts. I rubbed my trembling hands together. My Knight In Shining Armor had better have donned his hero suit beneath his V-neck shirt and cargo shorts. I needed Kendrick to put all those warrior skills to use and save our asses with his training.

The boat smacked into the water after another infernal wave, and Captain boomed, "Take that shit off and get rid of it. Yer plan's gone ta hell."

Kendrick lifted his chin, his eyes alight with vindication. He tossed his mask overboard, then did the same with the shopping bag containing the rest of the Jumbie suits.

"Fine." I pulled mine off and threw it to die with its brethren. I couldn't see out of it anyway. "How are we going to keep Chet from seeing us?"

Gunfire erupted just as shouts echoed over the water.

"Fuck." Kendrick leaped to his feet and fought the incline of us climbing another wave to stand beside Captain, then clutched the top of the windshield to keep from pitching overboard when we slammed against the water on the other side. "That may not be a problem anymore."

"Don't say that," I yelled, swiping my backpack off the floor. Rummaging inside, I pulled out the comm devices and my climbing gloves (my habit of leaving no fingerprints was too ingrained). Fitting a comm into my ear, I crawled to Kendrick and gave him his earpiece and the larger set of thin gloves I'd bought when we were out shopping for everything else.

"Captain," I held my weaving palm up, "put this in your ear. It'll keep you connected to me, Ken, and Stuart." I only had four. Before we left the planning session, I gave one to the hacker, knowing I might need the other spare in case of an emergency.

Boom. Boom.

I flinched at the rifle reports.

Captain took the earpiece and dutifully inserted it.

Crack. Crack. Crack. Crack.

"Fuck." Kendrick rocked to his toes, then back at the automatic handgun fire. "You have to get me closer."

I finished pulling my second glove on and scraped the black death-duffle across the floor, then unzipped it.

More shouts and yelling, and I began to pick out figures running in the muted lighting of the *Livin' Large.*

Brrrrrrrrrrrrrr. Brrrr. Brrrrrrrrrrrrrr.

"Son of a bitch!" Kendrick yelled (my ear ringing from it exploding in my earpiece). "They've got machine guns. Holly, I need a rifle." He held his gloved hand out.

I plunked the double-barrel shotgun into his palm and fished out a box of large shells. I may hate guns, but Uncle Liam made sure I knew how to handle and shoot the basic assortment.

"Cupcake, can you brace me?"

I rolled to my feet, placed my shoulder against the small of his back, and thrust my arms awkwardly around the two handgun holsters clipped to the belt on his hips. Grabbing the silver hand bar mounted on the dash, I pressed into him as tight as I dared. "Got you," I grunted.

He took me at my word and let go. *Oomph.* The side of my face smashed into his kidney, and I fully supported one-hundred-eighty pounds of solid muscle. I couldn't see a damn thing, only felt his body shifting—

BOOM! BOOM!

Holy crap, I'm deaf.

Kendrick tapped my side.

"Ease up," filtered through the comm from him. Oh. I loosened my grip and realized one of the assault barrages had silenced.

"Ya got 'em, lad. Nice shootin'," Captain praised in my earpiece.

Kendrick snapped the rifle open and slapped in two new shells.

I re-braced him.

BOOM! BOOM!

I eased my grip just as the engine wound down and the boat instantly slowed, knocking my balance off and thrusting me into Kendrick.

Angry shouts peppered the air, and more gunfire drifted down from above.

"FIND THE SHOOTERS," a furious male voice shouted.

"THROW THE DEAD OVERBOARD," another male yelled.

"Oh, Jesus." My heart slammed into my ribs. *The dead?* As in more than one? "No."

Captain eased the speedboat against the side of the yacht, ten feet from the stern. "Lass, can you scurry up?"

Into gunfire? Gulp. The Stewarts' safety came first. "On it." I snatched my backpack, and Kendrick promptly stole it from me.

"The fuck I'm risking your life by having you go up first," he whisper-snapped. "This is my arena."

I grabbed a harness and tugged. "Scaling walls is *my* arena."

"My arena of guns, shoot-outs, and bad guys trumps scaling walls." He ripped the harness out of my hands. He thrust the spent rifle, the barrel still cracked open waiting for the next load, at Captain and unsnapped the straps on the pack to expose the J-hooks.

Before I could take over, he climbed on the driver's seat and extended to his full height with the backpack as far above his head as possible to catch the silver railing on the main deck.

A heavy splash hit the water, farther up from our position. *Dead body.* I slapped a hand over my mouth to keep from crying out. *NO!*

Another round of gunfire erupted, and a woman screamed. *Melanie!*

"Melanie," Chet shouted. "Get—"

Brrrrrrrrrrrrrr. Fully automatic gunfire tore through the air.

Chet screamed in agony, and a thud reverberated.

Fuck this. I plucked a Sig Sauer out of the duffle. A bit heavier and larger than what I'd shot before, but I could wrap my hand around the grip, and the mechanics worked the same. *It'll do.* I checked the magazine to find it fully loaded, racked the slide to put a bullet in the chamber, then slipped silently into the water (Feet first. I wasn't sure if the comms were waterproof and didn't want to fry my brain by testing it out). I frog-stroked to the swim platform, keeping my hands beneath the water so I didn't make a sound. Lifting my body onto the low platform as quietly as possible, I stayed in a crouch.

"Cupcake," Kendrick hissed in my earpiece. *"I swear to God."* He growled. *"Do NOT get hurt. Just keep your head down."*

Duh. Did he honestly think I'd waltz up the steps and introduce myself? Again, *not* La Femme Nikita, but not a coward either.

Crack. Crack. Screams followed the gunshots that had to have come from Kendrick's gun based on how my head rang with the loud sound. *Crack. Crack.*

"I can't hang here much longer," Kendrick grunted. *"One of these assholes is going to notice the hooks and pick me off."*

A heavy presence loomed behind me, and I whirled, lifting my Sig to aim—Captain ducked his big wet body to avoid me shooting his face off.

"Can someone knock Chet out so I can climb aboard?" Kendrick whisper-barked. *Crack-crack. Crack. Crack.*

Captain lurched to his feet and tackled the stairs, pausing at the top. He didn't have to worry about anyone recognizing him. With both hands filled with Glocks, he kept up a steady rhythm, hopefully dealing death with the squeeze of the triggers.

I crept to the other side of the swim platform and snuck up those stairs. Peering over the last step, I spied Chet slumped on the open-air deck, twenty feet in front and to the side of me. A trail of blood followed behind where he'd pulled himself between one of the bolted-down platform chairs that had to be a norm for superyachts and a low table.

"Stuart!" Melanie wailed, and my blood curdled. *No. No. No.*

"AHHHHHHHHH!" Chet war-cried as he lifted his gun and opened fire on anyone that moved. Captain dove back down the steps to avoid becoming a casualty.

Taking my chances, I leaped onto the deck and crept to a spot behind the chair beside Chet. Repositioning the Sig Sauer to hold it by the barrel, I reached around the back and slammed the grip into just the right spot on Chet like Uncle Liam taught me.

SORRY. SORRY. SORRY, I silently cried as he jerked, then slumped into a heap.

"Chet's out," I announced, my voice shaking with remorse, adrenaline, and terror. Forcing my mind to not think about the likelihood of hurting him more, I choked down the bile lumped in my throat at all the blood coating his body and grabbed his shirt collar, dragging him behind the chair to give him better cover in an effort to keep him alive.

My gag reflexes tried to kick in at the fresh spurt of life oozing out of the bullet holes when I let go. "Stuart," I whispered to distract myself. "Can you hear me?" He should've been answering us in the comms by now.

Kendrick popped over the side of the boat. The gun in his right hand constantly fired at the dwindling men scrambling around the deck while holding my backpack and the other gun in his left.

Unable to stay still or remain where small rivulets of blood formed, I snuck to hide behind the long, low-back couch facing the interior salon. With the wall that led to the swim platform just to my left, I couldn't miss the roar of an engine racing closer. "Another boat's coming," I hissed, ducking down to avoid detection by a *fugly* man with missing teeth who was creeping inside the salon that had its glass doors slid back to make one big inside/outside room.

"Reinforcements are here," Captain answered at the top of the stairs from the swim platform. *"They're the men I hired."*

Hallelujah. I rose slowly to peek over the top of the couch in an effort to spy Stuart, Melanie, or Kendrick, then blanched. Missing Teeth leered, finding my hiding spot while slapping a fresh, oversize magazine into his machine gun. He swung the barrel at me, and I flattened to the deck.

Brrrrrrr. Brrrrrrr. Bullets ripped through the white cushions with its spray.

Holy shit! I covered my head, flinching and wincing at the lethal projectiles doing their best to *kill* me. Bits of stuffing and fabric rained over me and the wooden floor as another round *brrrrrrrr*ed around me.

"NO!" Kendrick hoarsely cried.

I flicked the safety off the Sig Sauer and aimed toward Missing Teeth from beneath the steel platform's poles that gave me a foot-and-a-half clearance from the deck. *Crack.* The gun recoiled in my grip, snapping my wrist up. I hated the noise and the uncontrolled motion, and I'd never mastered hitting a bull's-eye.

Brrrrrrrrrrrrrrrr. More bullets slammed into the wall behind me, the deck, and the seat of the couch, keeping me down.

Crack. I forced myself to fire again.

Crack. Crack. My shot melded with two others.

Brrrr—

The barrage of bullets fell eerily silent, and Missing Teeth dropped to the floor amid a scary amount of brass from spent bullet casings.

"Cupcake," Kendrick shouted frantically. *"Cupcake, answer me. Are you hurt?"*

"I'm fine." If you didn't count my heart in my throat or my bladder threatening to loosen. Adrenaline coursed through my system so hard, I shook and blinked at the drunken fuzziness gripping my mind and the nausea flooding my stomach. Pushing my trembling body up, I peered over what was left of the couch.

"When we get back to the ship," Kendrick snarled in my earpiece from his crouched position behind a wide, single chair opposite Chet's, his aqua eyes blazing at me, *"I'm handcuffing you to the bed so you can't give me a heart attack like this again."*

"Love you, too, Kisa." *OH. MY. GOD.* I fell into a mound of stuffing erupting from a destroyed cushion. I did not just say that. *No. No. No.* No, I did *not* just declare my feelings for FBI Agent Jackson Kendrick. Emotions I could barely admit to myself did *not* just blurt out of my mouth, in the middle of a gunfight, on an open communication line, and with the universe stacked against us to make this work. *I am not that stupid. I can't be.*

Kendrick's irises bugged and his expression slackened. *"What—"*

"Figure of speech." I barreled over his breathy response. "Where are Stuart and Melanie? Stuart should be talking to us. He's got a comm too."

Captain tromped to Chet. He crouched and brandished a knife. *"Lass, lad, find yer couple."* He sliced Chet's shirt into strips and did what he could to staunch the blood still seeping. *"I'll watch over the fallin' agent and send my boys once they board ta rout out the last of the cartel."*

Kendrick focused on the targeting bad guys leaning over the back of the bridge deck above. *Yikes.* Slipping out from behind the couch so I wouldn't be a sitting duck for the upper decks, I hustled into the salon. "Stuart—"

"Holly?" Stuart interrupted me in a thin voice, making my knees weak. *"Ow! Stop, Melanie. Damn, my head hurts."*

"Stuart," I cried, pausing beside a beautiful grand piano that now resembled Swiss cheese. I pointedly did not look at the dead man sprawled near the bench. *My bullet could've taken his life. No. Don't freak out about that now. Your aim is worth shit so probably not, but... Focus.* "Where are you? Is Melanie okay? Are either of you hurt?"

"They murdered Captain De Luca," Stuart answered in a daze. *"They also killed the first mate and threw him overboard—"*

"Stuart," Kendrick interrupted in his full FBI authoritative tone I knew all too well without pausing his shooting. *"Can you make your way to the main deck, or are you pinned down?"*

I scanned behind me and found unfamiliar faces surrounding Captain but since he wasn't firing, I took them as being our four hired "pirates."

"Find the stragglers," Captain ordered, the bark reverberating in my earpiece. Three of the new guys peeled off and ran past me with grins on their faces and guns I recognized from the death-duffle in their hands.

"That last order's not for you, Stuart," I clarified, worried he'd get confused. "I'm in the main deck's salon. Tell me where you are, and I'll come get you."

"We're okay," Stuart answered. A door at the top of the room widened slowly, and the hacker's shaggy brown head peeked around the threshold. Blood dripped down his face, and he lifted a shaky hand to a sticky wound at his hairline. He stumbled into the doorframe, then righted himself, leaving behind a bloody hand smear. Melanie peeked over his shoulder, and I slumped in relief. Neither one looked ominously injured like Chet, just traumatized and dirty.

I raced across the expanse and put an arm around Stuart. Melanie clung to his other side, and together, we hustled him toward Captain.

Kendrick appeared at the threshold of the two melded spaces just as we reached the piano. With a gun still clenched in his right gloved hand, the back-pack hanging precariously over his shoulders by the hooks, and his left hand jamming the other gun back into its holster, he resembled every inch of the warrior I had fallen for. His gaze lasered in on me, and he marched forward with a hard expression that made my lower belly quiver and spark with desire.

"Don't take it back." He ripped me away from Stuart and slammed his mouth on mine. I lost the ability to decipher his words. My body fell into his, and I kissed him with everything I had. *No one else but him can make me so crazed or so addicted.* My free hand grabbed a section of his shirt, and I clung to him for all I was worth.

He finally pulled back, his eyes blazing with passion and steely resolve. "I heard it. We're going to have a very thorough and *honest* discussion about all this tonight, Cupcake."

My fuzzy head instantly cleared, and I immediately understood what I shouldn't take back. I'd accept him dressing me down for the risks I took (and would do again)—after all, he was the expert—but I had no desire to be stupid enough to say those three little (GINORMOUS) words again. "Kisa, if you want to *honestly* discuss how badass you are, I'm all in." I added a wink to cover how my legs were about to resemble pudding and mush to the floor as the horror and terror of the events caught up to me. "But talking may be difficult," I plowed on before his eagle eyes caught on that I was one step away from losing it. "I'm going to be busy running my hands over every inch of you to make sure you're not hiding an injury."

I turned (a pivot beyond my current capabilities) and scowled at all the stares directed at us.

"Couldn't have scripted that little scene better myself," Captain declared saucily from his position beside Chet, then sobered. "I can't leave." He held up the walkie-talkie. "Kadmos just confirmed the authorities will be here in minutes."

Damn. I jogged to stop Stuart from falling over when Melanie dropped to her knees, tears falling down her face as she reached toward Chet. "Is he going to make it?"

"Medics will arrive with the police," Captain nonanswered and jabbed a finger at the fourth "pirate." "Jose will drive the four of ya back ta the *Rolling Deep* in his boat. The rest of us'll stay here ta guard yer friend, play the Good Samaritan card, and spin the story as planned. My yacht's too close for me ta play this any other way without a lengthy interrogation. Authorities will board the *Rolling Deep* and every other ship in the immediate area, so follow Kadmos's instructions on where ta hide. I'll get ya out when it's safe."

Chapter 34

Kendrick had to waste precious seconds getting verbally rough with the Stewarts and stripping them of everything from their old life (outside of the torn clothes on their bodies). We couldn't afford to have the investigation hang open because one of them decided they couldn't part with a keepsake. A family member might seize on that and cast doubt on their "deaths."

Jose started up both outboard engines while Kendrick and I helped maneuver Stuart into the twenty-one-foot piece-of-crap trawler I couldn't believe it actually floated. Unable to wait any longer, Jose cranked the engines wide-open, making me hit the floor, once again, on my ass.

I couldn't be mad at him, though my pride wanted to be. We were racing to beat the authorities to the *Rolling Deep* and with minutes on the clock, he couldn't afford to be polite.

Kendrick finished settling Stuart over Melanie's lap, then dropped to the floor, resting his back against the hull. I scooted on my butt (Jose had no fear of launching his boat over the waves despite how hard we crashed to the water afterward) and nestled between Kendrick's bent legs, then he curled his arms around me.

Using Kendrick's meaty shoulder for a headrest, I quipped weakly to the Stewarts, "Congratulations. You're now dead."

Melanie's sickly green tinge could be from the news or the events or both, and I wasn't sure Stuart even paid attention to the announcement.

"It's horrific, and I'd never wish it anyone," Kendrick scraped his cheek against mine until another slam over a wave made him separate or risk knocking me out with a hard hit, "but those drug thugs did us a favor."

"How?" My body bounced with his.

"The investigators should have no reason to look beyond the cartel or doubt the Stewarts were killed and thrown overboard."

A silver lining in the tragedy.

One minute, thirty seconds later, Jose banked a hard left and cut the engines. We drifted at high speeds right into the *Rolling Deep*'s swim platform. *Wham*. I winced and prayed Captain had extra paint stored up to fix the scrape marks bound to be left behind.

Jose flew out of the chair and threw a rope to Kadmos, who waited on the platform. While the Greek tied the bow tight to the yacht, Jose tied a line at the stern to a metal cleat.

I grabbed my backpack, having already refastened the straps, and stood to move out of Kendrick's way. He crouched in front of Stuart and lifted the man, throwing him over his shoulder.

"Hey," Stuart protested weakly, his eyes flying open.

Kendrick ignored him and climbed over the side, then set him on his feet on the yacht's deck. Kadmos ran to grab Stuart's shoulders to keep the hacker from falling over while Kendrick helped Melanie next, then me.

My shoes were barely on the all-weather turf coating when Kadmos motioned. "This way. Hurry."

Didn't have to tell me twice. Kadmos took us (minus Jose) to the lower deck and surprisingly back into my stateroom (now clean with no trace of my three sex-filled days). He shot me a sheepish look. "Sorry. You just happened to pick one of two rooms Captain recently retrofitted to house a larger compartment. Figured you'd find this more comfortable than the other spots."

"Um, I'm not sure how I feel about that." I eyeballed the room for anything he might have missed.

"At the moment, thankful." Kendrick stepped out of Kadmos's way. "Stuart needs medical attention."

"I'll do my best once you two are settled." The first mate stopped beside the left nightstand and proceeded to open the drawer and turn the knob in a random pattern of twists. A click reverberated, and the low hum of hydraulics accompanied the king-size mattress rising at the same time the solid oak wooden bedframe lowering into the floor.

"I'm loving this ship," Kendrick breathed, his face lit up in boyish fascination.

"You'll have to crawl in." Kadmos motioned when everything stopped, leaving a two-foot gap. "Quickly, so I can see to the Stewarts."

I dropped to my knees and lifted the edge of the comforter covering part of the space. Three dim lights attached to the bottom of the steel platform holding up the mattress showed the bed-size hole dropped three feet. I ungracefully rolled (fell) inside with my backpack, and Kendrick followed behind me.

Lying flat on my back, I tried not to wince at the platform coming steadily closer to my face while the sides rose back to their original positions. Kendrick laced his glove-free hands with mine, and his presence made me feel better. Not like I'd willingly crawled into a romantically lit, oversize coffin.

The minute everything stopped, I found I had room to curl against his side, using his shoulder as a pillow.

We listened through Stuart's earpiece as Kadmos cleaned up Stuart's wound, got the couple settled in their hidey-hole, and assured them that both hiding spots had fully integrated oxygen tanks with enough to keep everyone alive for days. Then silence until three minutes had passed.

The shock of the violence, Chet's blood and wounds, and most likely everything else must have finally gotten to Melanie. I did my best to tune out her crying and Stuart's attempts to soothe his wife, but it still got to me. I was barely holding it together myself. The contracts my crew accepted rarely had one-tenth of the assault and bloodshed I'd just experienced.

I wanted to take my comm out but couldn't. With the authorities about to board, I couldn't afford to take the risk. Captain would be back in range soon (maybe), and I felt better having plenty of warning if everything went sideways.

"Thank you, Kisa," I whispered around a lump in my throat, aware Stuart could hear. "Thank you for...everything." Emotions clogged my voice box, preventing me from saying more, which was probably a good thing with my feelings so close to the surface. *I almost died.* Phantom bullets whizzed around me again, but I forced the replay to stop. Chet may still die, and Kendrick...this amazing man, my Knight In Shining Armor, came through, risking his life to save everyone he could.

I blinked rapidly. I didn't want to think anymore. I needed him to make me forget.

As if hearing me, Jack carefully eased me on top of him, mindful of the tight space. My legs automatically split to embrace his sides and my nipples grazed over his chest, hardening to sensitive peaks as he pulled me higher. With our faces perfectly aligned, we stared at one another. Sharing my air with him, no words passed between us, but we spoke volumes:

I heard it. His gaze intensified. *You said you love me.*

It was just a sarcastic comment that popped out in the heat of the moment. Don't put any stock into it.

I'm a trained lie detector (eyebrow raised). *I saw your reaction.*

And I saw yours. (Stunned shock didn't exactly instill me with the urge to repeat the experience.) *No more talking, Kisa.*

After another beat of those aqua blues holding me hostage, his lids fluttered shut, and he slid his mouth gently across mine. Chapped lips from the saltwater and air scraped over mine, sending little jolts through me. Tilting my head, I nibbled on the ocean still clinging to him, then licked at the seam. He didn't fight my request and parted his lips, adjusting his hands to smooth down my back and squeeze my butt.

The last vestiges of the horror dropped away, and I immersed myself in his kiss until I couldn't think about anything else but Jackson Kendrick.

Relaxing against him, I teased him with my tongue dipping in and out lazily. A smile crooked his lips, and he played with me back, licking my tongue and answering with his own foray into my mouth.

I sighed and deepened the kiss again. Showing him everything I couldn't, wouldn't say, I kissed him long and hard, then lightened to soft and gentle. Alternating between the two.

His hands worked my clothing off me and I helped him out of his. Staying true to my warning, I inspected every inch of him (mostly with my mouth) and found no major injuries. He obliged with the same treatment, then we passed the time getting creative with our pleasure since we couldn't make a noise without being overheard and didn't have condoms inside our secret love nest.

After God knew how long and two silent orgasms (for both of us...during which it had been excruciatingly difficult not to scream, whimper, or pound the floor while I lost my mind), I fell asleep with him curled around me.

Chapter 35

S triding through a set of open, leaf-green, louvered doors in the living room, I followed the flow of the white cotton curtains as they billowed to flap lazily outside my personal villa on the island of Nevis. The sun brimmed on the edge of the horizon, showing off a view that took my breath away.

My three-bedroom (all en suites), two-story villa clinging to the side of a cliff had an oval infinity pool built into the center edge of the twenty-foot-wide (at the widest section of the curving design), house-long wooden-deck veranda that overlooked the sea and St. Kitts island. Strategically placed tropical trees and vegetation kept my villa completely private from the neighbors dotting the cliffs.

My bare feet soaked in the warmth as they padded to Kendrick, standing at the left edge in a hunter green polo with his back to me. His hands were shoved in his khaki cargo shorts pockets, and a breeze ruffled his hair.

The last eighteen hours had been a whirlwind of activity and travel. True to Captain's prediction, the authorities had boarded the *Rolling Deep* shortly after we fell asleep and climbed all over the yacht. It took hours, then hours more to reach one of my secret hideaways (the closest one I owned, which worked out since Nevis was under British authority, meaning the FBI couldn't easily search for us or the Stewarts if they felt inclined), wrangle with the customs officials to get everyone's forged passports properly stamped so we could leave the country without being smuggled (again), and deal with Captain.

The entire incident with De Luca had soured my relationship with my former crewmate. He knew he'd royally messed up and had apologized (which in and of itself was a miracle), then made monetary reparations by depositing five-hundred-thousand euros into my account to reimburse my expenses and then some, and another five-hundred-K into an account for the Stewarts (who were now known as Jim and Cathy Martin) to start their new life. It helped, but I'd hesitate to call him again, not that I could anytime soon. He'd decided to head back to Scotland, dry-dock the yacht to alter the ship's appearance and amenities, and go to ground to avoid the cartel's retaliation for his part in preventing the hijacking, which had been documented in the official record.

"Jack." I wrapped my arms around his waist, rested my chin on his back, and peeked around his bicep. "Welcome to Hidden Jewel." I gave him the name of the villa.

"Cupcake." He smoothed his hands over my bare arms. "Are we borrowing again?"

I chuckled and bit his bicep lightly. "After our last experience, I thought I'd utilize one of my own properties."

His jaw dropped, and he twisted his upper body, moving us both to scan our surroundings. "This is yours?"

I nodded as he resettled forward again. "Yep." Not wanting another Claude incident, I'd sacrificed Kendrick learning one of my bolt-holes to set the hacker and his wife up for the next few weeks so he could work in absolute peace.

"Holly," he breathed, lifting my left hand to kiss the back.

"Stuart and Melanie, er, Jim and Cathy aren't interested in dinner," I blurted to stop him from veering into the heart-to-heart I couldn't handle yet. I wanted to live in this fantasy world filled with love (even if it was one-sided), the promise of forever, and intoxicating sex as long as I could. Sharing this villa's existence on top of all the pieces of myself I'd already given him that came deep from my soul, along with the glaring chasm between our roles (no matter how blurred they seemed now, his bosses wouldn't forgive a thief corrupting their agent), were subjects I wasn't ready to tackle. "They're turning in for the night."

Kendrick pulled my hands apart and guided me to stand in front of him. With my back resting against his chest, he fed his arms underneath mine and hugged me beneath my breasts, then nuzzled my ear.

Shivers stole through me, and my toes curled. I had to work hard to remember the rest of my report. "The internet company assures me I'll have the needed upgraded speed by tomorrow morning, and the requested computer equipment should arrive shortly thereafter."

"I'm glad Stuart can't do anything tonight," he whispered against my lobe, and I held back a moan at the tingles racing through my blood. "He's got a mild concussion, and she's exhibiting classic signs of shock. They need time to heal."

"I know." I bit my lipstick-free lip. "I'm not trying to be heartless, it's just the clock is ticking for Uncle Liam."

"Sorry." He sighed, and my shoulders lifted at how the air rushed past my ear deliciously. "I didn't mean to make you feel bad. You're right. He has to start as soon as possible."

"Luckily, Stuart agrees." I rested my head against Kendrick's shoulder and watched the sun dip below the ocean in a spectacular vista of colors. "He's promised that the moment the computer stuff arrives, he'll dedicate every waking minute to getting updated on all the new security protocols. Once done, he'll be able to hack into a scary number of databases, then begin writing the codes that will make up the artificial intelligence program." I closed my eyes. "I barely followed a quarter of what he described. Something about algorithms, data extraction, relevance sorting...and other...stuff. My takeaway is that he needs nine to ten days to have the program finished."

Kendrick rested his chin on my shoulder. "We're going to make the deadline, Holly."

A chill ran down my spine. Tension surrounding him shifted and rose, warning me my attempt to thwart the heart-to-heart had only succeeded in stalling it. He obviously refused to believe my idiotic blurted declaration in the middle of a gunfight was either a figure of speech or a sarcastic response. Personally, I felt I should be absolved of all manner of stupidity after a man tried to mow me down with a machine gun. *Just sayin'.*

Small kisses pressed into the side of my throat. "Now." Kiss. Kiss. "About that honest conversation you owe me."

Called it. I lifted my hands and scraped my nails over his scalp, then gripped his hair. Making his head lift, I craned my face to line my mouth up to his and gave no mercy. He dueled with my tongue and angled his head to intensify the assault, bombarding me with so much electrifying bliss, I ached and demanded more. His amazing fingers worked beneath my tank top and bunched the material as he traced up my exposed ribs to cup my braless breasts. My hard nipples beaded to points, and he played them like a maestro.

Panting at the spikes of pleasure weakening my knees and consuming my thoughts, I moaned against his mouth, "Maybe another day."

I had no intention of talking about anything that didn't involve orgasms. All night.

"The heater doesn't go any higher, Cupcake."

The look I shot Kendrick sitting in the driver's seat (because of course he won the battle to control the rental car) invited him to shut it. I then snatched my purple, fuzzy-knit-gloved hand away from the dial. "It's forty-one degrees outside," I complained irritably, curling my hands around the SUV's vents on my side. "That's the *high* for today."

My body didn't take too kindly to switching from weeks of heat and humidity to biting winds and cold temperatures. It didn't matter that I'd normally be in New York City with these same conditions—the tropical paradises had spoiled me.

Kendrick and I left the villa early this morning on a journey of boat rides, commercial planes, and rental cars to reach Lancaster County, Pennsylvania, home of Oscar Brudney. Donning my white-blond pigtail-braided wig and a purple knit and fuzzy "fur" hat, I used my last backup ID of Elizabeth Duvall (it still felt weird not to have an alias with a location in it) for the trip. Kendrick covered his blond hair with a red-and-white knit hat, (making him adorably delicious with his rosy cheeks) and ditched the Ken Roberts ID to become Mitchell White.

Computers had two main parts: hardware, which was the actual machine itself that included things like intel chips, memory, fans, circuit boards, etc; and software, which included platforms like Windows, Microsoft Office, Internet gateways (Firefox, Chrome, Apple Safari, etc.), music or gaming programs, etc. With the deadline fast approaching, we couldn't wait for Stuart to finish the coding. So, on to Oscar. After hearing Reggie's voicemail yesterday, I did as much research as possible and found Oscar was legendary for building custom computers. With Oscar being Reggie's contact, I'd relied on my crewmate to set us up like he did with the new forger. Reggie had been vague on the details in the message. He only gave me Oscar's address and warned me he couldn't get a hold of the guy, but Oscar rarely traveled so he should be home. Oh, and that the man did *not* like interacting with people. In the gray world, that quirk probably benefited him since Reggie swore he had a stellar reputation for keeping his mouth shut.

"Oh wow." I stretched my seat belt to jam my face next to the windshield. "A real horse and buggy! Look!"

Kendrick slowed the SUV on the two-lane road and eased to pull around the Amish man bundled up on the front, open bench seat of a single-horse buggy. The narrow, dark-gray carriage had four huge, spoke wheels and an enclosed section that probably held his supplies or wares to sell at the local markets scattered everywhere in the area.

"The Amish are so cool." I grinned at the man now beside me as we passed him. Amish Man smiled back, then snapped the reins to make the horse clip-clop in a right turn onto another road.

"It's cold because it's November." Kendrick went back to my weather complaint, highly amused as he resumed normal speeds. "What did you expect?"

"It better not snow." I eyed the thick gray clouds making the adjustment all the more depressing. "I don't want to be trapped here."

Kendrick chuckled. "It's too warm to snow." He ran a finger (bare! How could he stand it?) down my cheek, then playfully tugged on a braid. "Did—"

"In a quarter mile, make a left turn onto Chester Holland Road," the female GPS announced through the SUV's speakers.

Kendrick eased over another steep hill, then complied with the turn instruction. "Did you forget science class and the freezing point?" he teased, pointing
out my "error" in thinking it might snow.

More rolling hills greeted us as we continued. "It'll drop below thirty-two
degrees tonight," I retorted, glancing at the GPS screen. Another three-point-six
miles to go. "I'll accept your apology for implying I have a lack of intelligence
anytime now."

Kendrick laughed but didn't grovel. The bum.

"In five hundred feet, your destination will be on the left."

Finally. Wide-open spaces, massive farms, crop fields, and patches of forest
made up our route from the moment we left the regional airport. If you liked
country living, this was the area for you. As a city dweller, it gave me the creeps.

For example, the white fencing lining the edge of our two-lane road on our
left had these ominous No Trespassing and Private Property signs alternating
on every single post for the last two miles. Did that mean the owner would greet
a wayward interloper with a shotgun and a snarling dog? Or allow the cows and
horses dominating this county to trample the person to death? Was that legal
out here in the sticks?

"You have arrived at your destination," the GPS helpfully informed us.

The hill we'd been climbing prevented me from seeing anything but a break
in the white fencing for a mostly dirt/barely graveled driveway...oh damn. The
No Trespassing/Private Property fencing belonged to Oscar.

Kendrick slowed, then turned in. "Are you sure about this guy?"

From the top of the driveway, I blinked at the sight before me. A dairy cattle
farm sprawled across acres upon acres of land. A two-story red brick house with
a wide front porch perched about a mile in front us near a massive red wooden
barn that had two big doors spread open but no one in sight. On the right, black
and white cows lazily grazed in one meadow, and some horses stood with their
tails swishing in another. I didn't see any animals on the left but spied more
buildings and barns dotting the land.

Stealing a peek at Kendrick, I followed his frowning gaze to another sign
tacked to a 2x2 wooden post:

Last warning!

You are trespassing

on private property

"Um." Unease slid down my spine, and I suddenly felt hot in my peacoat and sweater. Bracketing both sides of the narrow driveway only wide enough to fit one vehicle, the white fencing butted right up against the dirt.

"Um?" Kendrick whipped his eyes to mine, making me even more nervous.

"Uh—"

"Cupcake," Kendrick growled, navigating the bumpy, potholed driveway. "You're not instilling me with confidence, here."

"I—"

"Look out!" I shouted, cutting my stammering reply to point through the windshield.

Kendrick slammed on the brakes. The truck rocked to a stop only feet from a dirty, steel blockade that had shot up from the ground.

Dirt carried in the wind toward the four-foot-tall roadblock spanning the width of the driveway, but not enough to cover the black-and-red sign: You were warned!

"Who is this guy?" Kendrick barked.

Something slammed into the passenger side window, right near my head. I yelped and ducked.

Boom! An explosion erupted, spraying dirt and gravel against my door. Before I could recover, a second blast exploded behind us, nailing the bumper and hatch with debris.

Kendrick grabbed my hand and yanked. "Come on." He shoved his door open and ripped me over the console.

"Wait!"

"We don't have time to wait." He pulled again just as another explosion slammed into my side of the SUV.

"My seat belt." I scrabbled to jab the button that suddenly decided to play hide and seek.

"Quit fooling around!" Kendrick lurched back inside and dove his hand beneath my sprawled body to punch at the seat belt clip.

Boom! Boom! Boom!

The SUV rocked with every charge.

The stupid belt finally sprang free, and he pulled me out of the truck. I had no time to turn or get my feet under me. I had to slap the ground with my free hand to keep from eating the dirt.

Erg. Kendrick muscled me into a standing position, and my eyeballs swam with all the sudden movements.

Boom! Boom! Boom! Boom!

Holy shit. A line of explosives erupted from the ground, starting at the back of the SUV and headed right for us.

"Run!"

He didn't need to waste his breath—my feet were already on the move. I darted around the driver's side door, aiming for the small sliver of an opening between the four-foot-tall blockade and the fence.

"No room," Kendrick shouted from right behind me.

Boom! Boom! Boom!

"Jump it," he yelled, overtaking me. He leaped, planted a hand on the top, and swung his legs over like an obstacle course ninja.

Boom! Clumps of dirt and stones slammed into my back and legs, propelling me forward awkwardly. "Aaaggh." My hands flattened on the top of the barricade and promptly slid forward due to loose clumps of dirt. *Wham.* I landed on my breasts, sending shooting pain everywhere as I lost my breath, then my legs slammed into the steel. "Ow. Shit."

Kendrick wrapped his hands beneath my armpits and pulled me off. "You okay?"

"I don't know—"

Plink. Plink. Plinkplinkplink.

Sparks flew off the barrier.

"Fuck." Kendrick whirled with me still in his grip and darted forward.

Not sparks. Bullets. *Not again!* I pushed him to get free, and he dropped me. I stumbled to find my balance, then almost lost it completely when Kendrick clamped onto my waving hand and yanked me to keep up with him.

"Cupcake," Kendrick shouted over his shoulder, "we need to have a serious talk about these contacts of yours trying to kill us."

No kidding. I ran after him. My new winter boots were made for warmth and style, not running, but I persevered. Bullets and explosives made damn good motivators.

"Go left," I yelled, pointing at the fence's gate just ahead. It hadn't shut all the way. "We can cut through the empty meadow."

Chapter 36

We barreled through the gate with Kendrick leading the way. All along the fence, right up to the gate, small black holes dotted the top rail from the bullets following us.

A niggling thought lurked at the back of my mind, but my adrenaline and fear prevented me from reasoning anything out. The fight-or-flight instinct had taken over and chosen "flight" as the dominant response.

"I wish I had my Glock or something from Captain's arsenal," Kendrick bitched.

The bullets had stopped, and nothing had exploded since we entered the meadow.

"I wish I could wring Reggie's neck," I muttered, hustling to walk beside him.

MERRRRRRRRRRAUAWA!

"What the fuck was that?" Kendrick whirled, then he stumbled. "Run. Run now!"

I turned to peer over my shoulder, but Kendrick grabbed my hand and jerked me forward.

"You said empty," he accused, forcing me to really hustle. "But that's a goddamn bull!"

I almost lost control of my bladder. "BULL?" I shouted, pouring as much speed as I had left into my feet. "Bull?!" I couldn't comprehend it.

Pounding hooves vibrated the ground that had gone hard from the cold.

My mind grasped the picture real fast. I tore my hand from Kendrick's, needing to pump my arms along with my legs. "Holy fuck!"

Kendrick's new Timberland boots dug into the ground, but he didn't leave me in the dust even though he was much faster.

MERRRRRRRRRAUAWA!

"Run for that barn." Kendrick pointed at a smallish red structure straddling the fencing at the end of the meadow.

"We're not going to make that."

"*RUN.*"

I zigzagged to avoid large mounds of shit (literally) and clumps of dried grass that threatened to trip me.

"What is this hardware guy's problem?" Kendrick shouted, doing the same idiotic dodging pattern as me.

"He doesn't like people," I wheezed, jumping over a small dry ditch.

The bull's pounding hooves charged closer.

"Yeah, I got that from this welcome."

MERRRRRRRRRAUAWA!

Terror slid down my spine, and my heart threatened to pop through my ribs. I couldn't keep this pace up for much longer. Already, I could barely breathe and had a huge stitch in my side.

"If we live, I'm knocking that cocksucker right in the face," Kendrick railed, his red-and-white ski jacket blazing a streak like a cape for the bull to follow.

I hope he means Oscar because hitting a bull is nuts. I risked a glance over my shoulder and blanched. *No!* The black beast was within a step or two of Kendrick.

I wailed a battle cry as best as I could with nothing left in my energy tank and veered right. Toward the bull.

"Cupcake—"

"Run, Kisa," I gasped. "Save yourself." I couldn't believe I was actually giving the martyr speech.

My sudden movement made the bull stutter as he changed his focus to me. OH. SHIT.

Kendrick pulled away, and I straightened my path to head for the partially open door on the side of the barn. Vibrating, thumping hoofbeats paced right behind me.

My mind numbed and cut out. The only thought left in my head was, *Go faster. Must go faster.*

MERRRRRRRRRAUAWA!

The bull sounded even angrier than before.

I lost ten years off my life with that animal's breath puffing against my coat.

Kendrick reached back and jerked me toward him. My short legs couldn't keep up with his, and my body pitched forward.

No. I didn't want to die yet. *Uncle Liam needs me. Jack...*I couldn't process the rush of emotions his name invoked.

Kendrick yanked my arm up, keeping me from falling over. Somehow tossing me upward, he grasped my sides and threw me toward the open, windowless door.

I screamed as I landed against the wood, then through it, crashing to the floor in a heap. Kendrick leapt and grabbed the door on its rebound path, slamming it shut and holding it closed with his body barely a second before the bull rammed into it, making the whole wall shudder.

He slammed a bar down to lock the door, then peeled himself off and tromped on unsteady legs to me. "If you ever...attempt...to sacrifice your-self...for me again," Kendrick puffed, his tone full of breathy anger as he leaned over me with fire raging in his irises. "I will do...something you'll truly...hate." Deep breath. "I can't think with...my heart lodged in my boots...but it'll be something really terrible."

"Right." *Inhale.* "Back." *Cough. Hack. Hack. Coooough.* "At you." I rolled onto my back and clutched my chest, praying my heart didn't give out.

"Come here." Kendrick dropped to his denim-clad knees on the rough plank-wood floor and gathered me up. His chest heaved and sweat on his ex-posed skin mingled with mine.

I wanted to rip off my wig, hat, and gloves to escape the inferno blasting inside me, but I needed to hold Kendrick more.

He cradled me in his arms and buried his face into my neck. "I almost lost you," he wheezed, his entire body trembling. "Shit. Another second, and you would have been trampled."

"I would have lost you." I wrapped my arm around his neck and hugged him. "You're faster than me. You shouldn't have held back." I sucked in more air, but it didn't appease my racing heart. "That bull was one step away from taking you down."

Kendrick stiffened. "Save myself?" He pulled back enough to laser furious blues on me. "Don't you know me at all by now?"

I kissed his flattened lips. "Kisa—"

"This is all very touching," a weaselly male voice said from somewhere above us. *"But it won't help save you."*

Clink...clunk...clank.

Kendrick used brute strength to stand straight up with me (uh, wow), then set me down. I ran for the door we just barreled through and found I couldn't lift the bar. Kendrick's boots echoed as he raced to the second door at the back of the small room. He wrenched the knob left and right, but it didn't budge.

Peering up, I found a single-pane window above the rafters on the back wall. Dirt and grime on the glass obscured the weak light from behind gray clouds, and I couldn't tell what kind of locking mechanism it had from my vantage point.

Taking in the room at a glance, I cataloged the space at roughly 12x13. Old and scarred wood planks made up the walls. They might have been painted at one time, but the color had long since worn away. Large 6x6 beams spanned six feet from the ceiling, and dust had accumulated everywhere. A simple wooden table with two spoke-backed chairs pushed in at the ends rested on one side, and an aluminum bucket sat forlornly against the opposite wall. I did not want to speculate about what would create the need for a bucket.

Nothing about our surroundings seemed to have anything to do with farming or animals. Ice slid down my spine.

Craning my neck, I spied a cheap black speaker screwed into a beam overhead and counted four cameras mounted high to capture the entire room.

"You both ignored all the warnings."

"Cut the shit, Oscar," I snarled, peering into the front-right camera.

Kendrick marched to my side, his face a thundercloud of fury. Following my lead, he looked into the same camera. "You put my…" He swallowed and pointed at me. "You put her in danger." His finger shifted to point at Oscar behind the lens. "Whatever the fuck kind of game you're playing, it ends now. Unlock the goddamn doors."

"No."

Kendrick stiffened, then his chest puffed out as he straightened to his full height. "No?" he repeated in a low, lethal tone that caused my skin to goose bump.

"No."

Red splotches broke out on Kendrick's skin, and my own blood pressure spiked. "I will tell you one last time. Unlock. The. Fucking. Doors." He took a step forward. "You're in deep shit, Oscar Brudney."

My gut roiled at how fast the latest phase of our plan had turned to crap.

Kendrick took another measured step forward. "You trapped our SUV, surround it with bombs, shot at us—"

"You have no proof of any of that," Oscar retorted, not sounding the least bit concerned.

That niggling feeling returned, and I concentrated on teasing it out.

"I only have to show the police the bullet holes on the fence or the craters near our SUV—"

A soft whirring filled the room just as four planks in the wall above the bucket slid seamlessly down to reveal a TV behind clear plexiglass. The black screen disappeared, and our SUV sat in the center of a live feed. Outside of a layer of dirt, nothing seemed out of place with the truck or the ground. No blockade and no craters from the blasts. The image swung dizzyingly as the cameraperson turned to walk along the white fence…the *immaculate*, bullet-hole-free fence with a now-locked gate.

"You were saying?" Oscar asked, gloating.

"Special effects," I growled.

Kendrick's hands balled at his sides.

The TV went dark. *"According to Pennsylvania law, Title Eighteen, Section Thirty-Five-Zero-Three, Criminal Trespass."* Oscar's nasal tone was really starting to get to me. *"You two entered an area 'fenced or enclosed in a manner manifestly designed to exclude trespassers or to confine domestic animals.' That means jail time and fines for agricultural trespassing."*

"Son of a bitch," I breathed. "He corralled us."

"Give the lady a prize," Oscar snarked.

I'm going to deck him when we get out.

"I thought you made computers for the rich?" Kendrick asked, his tone still in the lethal range. "No way would they go through this."

"No one is allowed to come here." The speaker crackled. *"And I only take on new clients by referral. Neither of you are on the recommended list."*

"How do you know that?" I challenged, eyeing the wooden beams overhead.

"I've never heard of Elizabeth Duvall or Mitchell White before."

Chapter 37

Kendrick's teeth ground, and he pivoted to face me. Anger lanced through my chest so hot, a fresh round of sweat dotted my hairline again.

"Woooweeeee," Oscar chirped. *"Both your bio levels just spiked."*

I ignored the hardware guy and focused on Kendrick. Praying our silent communication skills held strong, I rolled my eyes toward the table, then at his shoulders, then peered up at one of the wooden rafters.

"Don't you want to know how I know that?" Oscar snapped, testiness creeping into his tone at us obviously not acting the way he wanted.

Kendrick's brows furrowed until he recreated my sight directions. Another second passed, then he nodded slightly. He clomped to the table and didn't hesitate to hop on top. The legs creaked but held firm.

"What are you doing?" Oscar demanded.

Continuing to shut out the asshole, I climbed onto the table and sent up a prayer it would hold out a little bit longer. Taking my gloves off, I jammed them into my pockets. Kendrick clasped my waist and hoisted me up. I tucked my legs and quickly rested my boots on top of his shoulders. He transferred his grip to my hands.

"Stop that," Oscar commanded, fury infused with the whine.

Kendrick widened his stance to fully support my weight as I found my balance. Feeling steady, I let go and raised to my full height. He clasped my ankles, and I raised on my toes and grabbed a beam. The rough wood bit into my hands, threatening to give me splinters, but I couldn't worry about that now.

"Let go," I stated. The moment the pressure released, I lifted my legs to wrap around the wood. It didn't take but a few seconds to work my body to sitting on top. Peering at the window, I mapped a route over the rafters to reach it.

"If you don't get down, I'm releasing the gas," Oscar snarled. *"It will knock you both out, and I'll turn you over to the police."*

Dread iced my veins. We could not afford to tangle with any type of law enforcement. "You had your chance, Oscar." I eased to my feet, keeping my center low. Thank God I'd never developed vertigo or fear of heights. "We came here in good faith. A man's life is on the line, and I need the best-of-the-best computer hardware guy to help save him."

Only thinking about putting one foot in front of the other, I steadily walked the beam with my arms out for balance. Kendrick's heavy boots kept in time with me, and I knew if I looked down, I'd find him right below me.

"You're telling the truth," Oscar answered, his fury subdued.

"And you can tell that how?" Kendrick asked. I wanted to beat him for challenging the weasel now that he sounded like he'd listen.

"Like Elizabeth,"—Oscar snorted—*"or whatever her real name is, said, I'm the best of the best. Hardware, electronics, and computers are my specialties. That entire room is rigged with biometric sensors and so much more. It's a giant lie detector machine on top of a holding cell."*

Reaching the intersection I needed, I gripped the post that bolted into the ceiling. Easing around it, I began walking crosswise across the room. My goal was the window dead ahead.

"Does the name Reggie Scoval mean anything to you?" I asked, keeping my steps even and not rushed. Kendrick below me or not, if I fell, I'd break something.

"Why do you ask?"

"He's the one who sent me to you." I wished I had my soft-soled shoes to help keep a better grip against all the slippery dust. "Said you would be up for the challenge of recreating an exact replica of the Infostrata Cryptix and keeping your mouth shut about it."

Silence.

Okay. He's listening. "I'm under a deadline." I grasped another post bolted to the ceiling and carefully inched around it to keep going straight. "If I don't produce the Cryptix in the given timeframe, the person holding my uncle is going to kill him."

Silence.

I reached the window and roved my hand over the steel frame. A loud click startled me, and I slapped my hands against the wooden planks on the sides of the window to stop myself from overbalancing and falling.

"Cupcake," Kendrick called from directly below me.

"I'm good."

The window slid soundlessly up, and I blinked. I hadn't touched it.

Sticking my head out, I found a middle-aged, pudgy man standing in the middle of a dirt pathway wide enough for tractors or whatever, peering up at me.

"The blond braids threw me off," the man said, and I instantly realized I now beheld Oscar-The-Shithead. "But Reggie showed me a picture of his...friends once. You're Holly Bell, aren't you?"

"Unlock the door and let Mitchell out," I responded instead.

Oscar lifted a tablet dangling in his hand and tapped on the face.

Clank. Clunk.

Kendrick's boots pounded against the wooden floor, and not a second later, he burst through the doorway below to my left. His long strides didn't slow or hesitate in their trajectory to reach Oscar-The-Shithead.

Oscar blanched and held his arms out as if that would stop an enraged FBI agent intent on taking his head off.

"Kisa, only maim, don't kill," I yelled, searching for the fastest way to get down.

Kendrick grabbed Oscar's stained sweatshirt, exposed beneath a long, black coat, and yanked, forcing the Shithead to stand on his toes. Getting in Oscar's face, he threatened, "If her feet aren't touching the ground in the next thirty seconds, I'm tearing your ass apart."

"BUTCH," Oscar screamed, the girly effect making me cringe. "LADDER."

A commotion from the larger barn on the other side of the house reached me just as two bona fide cowboys in jeans, boots, and Stetsons wrangled a long aluminum ladder. They hustled and worked together to fit the ladder under the window frame.

I hadn't even hit the ground when Kendrick plucked me off and squeezed me so hard, I gulped. "I know it's your arena," he whispered against my wig and hat, "but I could barely breathe the entire time you waltzed like it was nothing to be thirteen feet in the air without a goddamn safety net."

My heart melted. It had been so long since anyone was concerned about my safety. Sure, my uncle loved me, and Reggie and Gretchen did, too, in their own way, but no one had ever been terrified for my sake just because they cared that much.

More scuffling and clanging rang out as the cowboys disappeared with the ladder.

Jack planted a solid kiss on my mouth, then set me down. He laced his hand in mine and whirled on Oscar-The-Shithead. "Be thankful I'm not armed like usual. That said, I'm about two seconds away from beating the shit out of you, asshole." He pulled me forward so he could crowd the weasel's space. "Blockades, bombs, bullets, and bulls." He jabbed his finger into the Shithead's chest. "You endangered her life to feed your power trip."

"Just as you endangered his." I pointed to Kisa as I moved beside him to present a united front. "And trust me, Mitchell means a hell of a lot more to me than you."

Oscar opened his mouth, but Kendrick barreled over him, "Did you steal our luggage or just get your rocks off pawing through her lingerie?"

Oh, ewwww! I didn't even think about that. "I'm burning it all."

Red flushed Oscar's skin. "I didn't paw through—" He gulped at Kendrick's menacing growl. "Okay. I did look through *both* your bags and I did see her...stuff, but I'm not a perv. I didn't fondle it or anything."

"Are the suitcases still in the SUV?" Kendrick loomed in Oscar's space.

"Yes. I didn't remove anything other than your IDs." He fished inside his coat pocket and held up our driver's licenses and passports. "Those are incredibly good, by the way. Professional."

Kendrick snatched the documents and handed them to me. "We're leaving." He pivoted, then stopped, peering over his shoulder. "You better pray I never come back."

Yikes. I'd pee my pants if Kendrick ever looked at me like that and said those words.

"Wait!" Oscar scrabbled to get in front of Kisa.

Really stupid or really brave, dude.

"I can build the Cryptix." Oscar peered around Kendrick's shoulder to me. "Reggie's...well, I owe him." His brown eyes turned anxious. "You don't have to confirm you're Holly, but I'm positive you're looking to save your uncle Liam, Reggie's...friend."

I didn't say a word.

Oscar took a step to the left to better look at me, then swallowed. "I just have to say your crew stealing that claymore right off a movie set is legendary. People can't stop talking about it."

Oh shit.

Kendrick stiffened, his grip spasming around my hand. I cringed. What once made me proud, now made me hang my head.

"Not only do I not like you," Kendrick stated in a strained voice, "I don't trust you."

"I get that, but you *did* show up at my house uninvited." Oscar fiddled with the tablet. "I've got a million signs posted to keep strangers out. In my defense, how was I supposed to know you weren't government agents trying to entrap or spy on me?"

"I'm not even going to dignify that paranoia with an answer," I jumped in so Kendrick couldn't say something that might tip the Shithead off to his employer, thereby feeding into the government-out-to-get-him paranoia. "But Mitchell is right. I don't know if I can work with you after this."

"Look, you said you're on a deadline, right?"

My stomach roiled. I really didn't have the time to find someone else or hope that Stuart could cobble together the parts in time.

"I already have all of the basic, high-speed, and large capacity hardware components for my regular orders," Oscar rallied. "What I need are the specs for the machine itself. Do you have those?"

"I can get them." I had no problem asking Stuart to hack wherever he needed to, to find the specs. Flicking a peek at Kendrick, I unlaced our hands to rub mine together for warmth. The scowl on his beautiful face spoke volumes about his unhappiness.

"The faster you get them to me," Oscar pressed, "the more time I'll have to obtain the parts that aren't found through normal channels—like the casing rumored to house it."

Kendrick pulled his cellphone out and looked at the calendar. "We'd need it in our hands by the twenty-eighth."

"Of this month?" Oscar's eyes widened.

"Yes." Tension coiled tighter inside me. If anyone could do it, it would be this man, but I really hated working with him after what he'd just put us through. *Suck it up for Uncle Liam.*

Oscar bit his lip. "I'm already losing days to Thanksgiving and the weekend—"

"We didn't choose the deadline, asshole," Kendrick snapped. "Her uncle's life hangs in the balance. Can you do it?"

Oscar took a moment to work through the logistics of turning it around in ten days in his head. He finally looked up. "If I have the specs today, I can get it done by then."

Hope speared through the disgust at partnering with Oscar-The-Shithead. Pointing to Kendrick's phone, I said, "Type in your contact information, job cost, and your bank's wiring instructions."

Kendrick held onto the phone, spearing Oscar with a deadly gaze. "And your job estimate had better include a *steep* discount in labor charges for today's attempt to kill us."

Chapter 38

S unday afternoon, a full week after the Saint Croix conference ended and
twenty-four hours after surviving Oscar's farm, Jack and I strolled on the
sidewalk toward the hotel we had stayed in the last time we visited the forger
in downtown Mobile, Alabama. Exhaustion seeped into my bones, but we had
one final set of items to procure before we went to ground, waiting for Stuart
and Oscar to complete their parts.

The partly cloudy, seventy-four-degree day helped thaw my body and gave
me another excuse to wear the backless, flowy navy dress that had the single bow
on the back. With a simple tug, the material would unravel and reveal my naked
breasts and the brand-new lacy panties I'd picked up last night to replace the
underwear Oscar might have touched.

"You're killing me with that dress, Cupcake," Jack growled in my ear, giving
the lobe a small lick.

My shoulder lifted at the chills racing through my blood. That reaction right
there was the main reason I wore it along with the wedge sandals that charmed
Kendrick in the beginning with my non-stealth. "I figured this time around, you
won't have a problem pulling on the ends of the bow." I scraped my forefinger
down the three buttons of his light blue polo. "And, Kisa," I whispered in
a throaty voice, "you're going to want to see what I have on...or don't have
on...underneath."

A steely arm banded around my back and swept me off my feet. I landed
against his hard chest and laughed at the growl rumbling in his throat as his

eyes hooded darkened. "What time is Gretchen arriving— Fuck," he hissed, the color draining from his face as he let go. "Go back the way we came. Don't turn around. Now."

I clambered to find my balance. Everything inside me itched to look over my shoulder, but I complied. Lifting my chin, I casually strolled to not draw attention and pulled my oversize sunglasses out of my purse. The skin between my shoulder blades twitched and stung as if someone was staring right at me, *hard*. Like I was a target.

Shit. My instincts screamed at me to run, and I never ignored them. Picking my pace up, I darted right at the next street. Pivoting, I pressed against the side of the florist shop and peeked around the brick corner.

Kendrick stood with his hands on his hips, talking to a man in a black suit.

Dammit. Westbrook. I had seen his face too many times at too many instances when Kendrick almost caught me to not recognize him. The latest being at Michael's townhouse.

The late-thirties black man probably had no problem finding a date. His smooth, bald head enhanced his rugged good looks perfectly, and he stood a little over six-feet tall with an athletic physique.

Westbrook jabbed a finger toward Kendrick, but I couldn't see Kendrick's response. He had his back to me. By the stiff posture and rigid shoulders, I'd lay money the conversation was not a friendly catching up.

I had to do something quick. If this went south, Kendrick could not be carrying a cellphone linked to me or forged IDs. *Think. Think. Think.*

Go back to basics. Pickpocketing. Running as best as I could in the stupid wedge heels—*I'm burning these the first chance I get*—I used the back streets to reach the parking garage that stored our car. It took a lifetime to finally make it to the white Honda Accord on the fourth level. Rummaging in my purse, my heart plunged when I couldn't find the keys. *No, no, no. I know I have them, I drove.* A small miracle that I won that argument—and a lifesaver now.

Giving up, I paced to the trunk and dumped the contents onto the dirty concrete. The keys clattered out along with the rest of the crap, and I scooped them up. Popping the trunk, I hoisted my hulking suitcase out (Again, why had

I packed so much?). Taking a few extra precious minutes, I wiped the car of my existence and gathered the stray items back into my purse.

Yanking the suitcase's handle up, I hustled to a panel van belonging to an HVAC repair company parked in the corner and stashed my luggage behind it. I had to take the risk of it being stolen. If Kendrick had to reveal the location of the rental car, my luggage couldn't be found inside it. Opening the bag, I yanked out a pair of black flats, my blond-braids wig, and a pink, sleeveless flirty dress in case Westbrook had noticed the woman in the navy dress. No cameras could see me in the tight spot, so I changed as quickly as I could and stuffed my clothes back into my luggage. Using the van's oversize side mirror, I swiped my hair up into a wig cap then secured the wig onto my head. I wished I'd packed other disguises, but wishing did nothing to help me now. Sliding the sunglasses back onto my face, I jogged back to the street, my gait so much easier without the wedges.

That gave me an idea. I needed some "drunk" friends to pull off a distraction. Veering toward the park that housed the forger's daytime business, I searched—

There. I pulled two one-hundred-dollar bills out of my purse and held them toward the two youngish women sitting on a bench. Judging by their scanty clothes and shark eyes, these ladies were for rent. "I need a distraction," I announced to their suspicious faces. "See those men over there?" I pointed to Kendrick (I almost wept when I saw he'd remained right where I'd left him and was not in handcuffs or gone) and Westbrook. "Two hundred dollars if you keep the tall, dark morsel's attention for five minutes."

They jerked to their cheap-heeled feet and began smoothing their short skirts. "No soliciting," I warned. "He's FBI."

The color drained from their faces, and they looked at each other.

"Just follow my lead and you'll be fine." I held up the cash. "We're going to pretend we've started partying early."

Auburn Hair snatched the money out of my fingers and gave a bill to Short Black Hair, then the two of them fell in line on either side of me. Ensuring my sunglasses covered as much of my face as possible, I led our trio to the FBI agents squaring off on the sidewalk.

My heart pounded with every step, and I second-guessed the wisdom of my hastily hatched plan, but I kept going. *Please, let me walk away from this.*

Jack's eyes rounded when he spied me behind Westbrook, and his lips thinned.

"...Savannah Jolly's trail lead here." Westbrook jabbed a thumb at the entrance to the four-star hotel Kendrick and I had used the last time. "Rest of the team's inside..."

My mind blanked, and my mouth dried as the blood leached from my head, making me dizzy. Had they gotten ahold of the security feeds?

Kendrick crossed his arms across his chest and widened his stance in my favorite pose as he stared at me. Westbrook whirled, ripping me from my spiraling thoughts. *Showtime.*

"Wooweeeeeeee! The party continues!" I trilled in my most Bubbleheaded Barbie voice. I exaggerated the sway of my hips, which would have looked better with heels, but I made it work by skipping to insert myself between Westbrook and Kendrick. My braless breasts bounced, and my skirt fluttered dangerously high. "It's my birthday, and I just found what *I* want!"

Auburn Hair and Short Black Hair giggled and fell right into the drunk act perfectly, targeting Westbrook. "So did we!" Auburn Hair warbled in a gratingly high pitch.

"Can I have *you* as my present?" I lurched forward and fell into Jack's arms.

He caught me like I knew he would. Not giving him a second to say a word, I forced his head down and kissed him. He stiffened, but played along, parting his lips and taking the kiss up to inferno levels. It took me an extra second to remember I had a reason for accosting him on the street. My skills might be rusty, but I picked his shorts pockets clean and stuffed it all in my purse.

"Jack," Westbrook called from behind me. "Ladies, please." Pause. "Thank you, that's enough." Pause. "Jack, your girlfriend's going to be pissed if you don't knock it off."

Everything inside me died. *Girlfriend?* I tore my mouth away and wiped it with the back of my hand.

Kendrick's grip on my shoulders tightened, but I refused to look at him—not that he knew it with my sunglasses hiding my eyes. *He said he broke it off when he first saw me.*

"Holly Bell is not my girlfriend," Kendrick retorted, squeezing harder. "I'm free to kiss this smoking hot blond."

What? My gaze shot up, and I found his cheeks completely red and ears pinkening.

His eyebrows cranked down. "How many times are you going to bust my balls about her anyway?"

"She's your Achilles' heel." Westbrook's tone lost all traces of humor. "Your obsession with her has already cost you."

Obsession? Life began to pound through my heart again, and giddiness washed through me, especially after seeing embarrassment flushing his skin.

"Calling it obsession's going a bit overboard, isn't it?" Jack's pink ears darkened another shade.

"No. Send Ms. Birthday on her way." Westbrook spoiled my world being rocked. "You still haven't explained why you left your cellphone and luggage behind, or why you've dropped off the face of the Earth only to conveniently surface now that I'm closing in on her trail, or why her crew's gone mysteriously silent all of a sudden."

The corners of Kendrick's eyes tightened, and it took everything I had not to break character. Holy shit. I toyed with his collar, but terror roared through me, and I swallowed against the bile rising in my throat. How the hell could I leave Kendrick to face those questions? Westbrook sounded like he was on the "Kendrick disappeared to work *with* Holly" side of the argument Darien described. He could wind up in handcuffs—

Panic later. Kisa can handle it. And if not, you can come up with something brilliant to save him then. Jabbing my thumb over my shoulder, I pouted. "He's such a downer."

"Sorry, Cupcake." Kendrick eased me off of him, and I made sure to keep my back to Westbrook to cut down on showing him my face. "You're one *hell* of a kisser." He cupped my cheek, and I sucked in a breath at how cold his hand was.

Oh Jesus. The last time he had cold hands, we were on the beach, and he was pleading for me to be as vulnerable as him. Shit. How could I walk away when fear, nerves, and uncertainty had their grips on him? Longing to save him rooted my feet to the ground and stole my breath.

"He's right," Kendrick continued. "You need to go. I hope you have a happy birthday."

I slumped as if dejected, but in reality, it was more in defeat. I couldn't do a damn thing to help. I'd only make things worse. "But I want *you*, Kisa."

He clutched his heart and smiled, his eyes lightening with adoration.

"Let's go, Romeo." Westbrook bumped me in the back to grab Kendrick's bicep.

Though I wanted to follow so bad my chest ached, I stayed in character and started singing at the top of my lungs, "Happy Birthday to me." I wound my arms through my companions' and drifted up the sidewalk, wanting Kendrick to hear my poem. "Happy Birthday to me. You have to a-gree. That kiss was amazing. He'd give me an orgasm or three!"

Chapter 39

I wore a path in the thick grass, pacing from one side of a shady section in the city-block-wide park to the other in my beloved cross-trainers. My luggage sat behind the park bench where my "drunk" cohorts resumed their vigil for business. I had changed yet again into my black cropped yoga pants, sports bra, and Robin Hood tank top. Keeping the wig cap on, I packed away the very noticeable pigtail-braids wig and snatched the black baseball hat out of Kendrick's suitcase to help hide my natural hair coloring.

Waking my phone for the hundredth time, I groaned long and loud. Two hours. Two long, excruciating, nail-biting, appetite-stealing hours spying on the hotel's entrance.

"Come on, Kisa," I murmured under my breath, fiddling with the knot I'd tied at the bottom of the tank.

Birds continued to sing and call to each other in total disregard for the ulcer growing in my gut with every passing second.

Movement jerked my attention across the street, and the air froze in my lungs. An eye-piercing ray of sun glinted off the glass as the automatic door slid to the left and a man strolled beneath the green awning.

"Kisa," I breathed, catching sight of blond hair, light blue polo, and navy shorts.

Auburn Hair shot off the bench as instructed and waved to get Kendrick's attention.

He gave a small wave of acknowledgement but didn't enter the park. He moved his hand in front of his waist and pointed to the left, then dropped his arm.

I slapped a twenty into the woman's hand, as the promised reward for her hailing his attention, and grabbed my suitcase handle. I followed as best as I could without looking like I was stalking the decadent man. The second I surmised he was heading toward the garage, I cut to the left and chose a different path.

By the time I reached the fourth level, he was already there, leaning against the car with legs crossed at the ankles and arms crossed over his chest. I let go of the suitcase and ran to him, my steps echoing against the concrete.

He met me halfway and picked me up, twirling me once, then kissed me senseless, knocking the hat off. "I don't know whether to thank you for robbing me blind," he whispered against my mouth, his tone fierce. "Or toss you over my knee for jeopardizing everything with your stunt. I damn near pissed myself when you showed up. You scared me to death."

"You scared *me* to death."

He swooped in for another long, hard kiss, and I gave as good as I got. "It kills me to say this, but I'm damn glad you came. Westbrook had me searched in the lobby."

I hugged him tighter. "What happened? How did you evade those questions? What do we do now? I called Gretchen and told her to find a hotel on the other side of Mobile."

He rested his forehead against mine. "Bottom line, I'm under suspicion, but Westbrook has nothing but theories."

Relief poured out of me, and I slumped against him. "Are you going to be okay?"

"For now, yes." He straightened. "He can't hold me since I'm on suspension and not required to carry my cellphone. Without an active case, I don't have to account for my movements." He rubbed his face. "I managed to learn two new kernels of information. My cousin, the Deputy Director, is questioning my boss about his full investigation into me, and Westbrook let it slip he can't get a copy of any of the security tapes. He doesn't have evidence to prove Savannah Jolly is really you, which prevents him from obtaining a warrant. The businesses and hotels won't turn over anything without one."

"Oh, thank God." Black spots hit my vision, and I blinked at the lightheadedness.

"Come on." He left me to grab my suitcase. "We can't risk staying in here any longer."

I plucked the hat off the concrete and covered the ugly wig cap again.

He marched my bag to the trunk. "Let's go find Gretchen and a place to lay low for the night." The second he closed the lid, he held his hand out. "Keys?"

I snorted but slapped the set onto his palm.

"You're going to lay down in the back." He pointed helpfully—you know, in case I lost my IQ in the last ten seconds. "I'm not taking any chances Westbrook might see you and put together you're Ms. Birthday." He redeemed himself with the next line. "Holly," his eyes shone with pride, "excellent thinking with the clothing changes."

I beamed. Unable to argue with the logic of my hiding, no matter how unhappy I was about the cramped space and bumps in the flooring, I shut my mouth and climbed in. I'd hidden in worse conditions. At least the rental company had recently vacuumed.

"A-Agent Ken-Kendrick," Gretchen warbled, opening the door to her hotel room. Her skin blanched totally white, and her hands trembled. "I'm, uh... Co-Come in."

"Thank you, Gretchen," Kendrick answered kindly, obviously noticing my crewmate was scared shitless of the man who had been relentlessly hunting us until a few weeks ago.

I followed behind his suitcase, dragging my own in my wake. I pulled up short when I spied Reggie standing at the end of the little hallway with his arms crossed and a mulish expression.

Letting go of my bag, I burst around Kisa and got in Reggie's face. "If you ever send me and Jack into another situation like the one with Oscar, you better never let me see your face again."

A wall of heat enveloped my back, and I clasped Kendrick's closed fist. Tension radiated off him, and I could taste the anger peppering the air.

"Jack?" Reggie's obstinate eyes peered between me and Kendrick. "He's *Jack* now?"

Gretchen squeezed past us, having wrangled our suitcases out of the way to shut the door. She stood behind Reggie, her hands wringing as she stared at all of us.

Kendrick leaned forward, his back pressing into me in his bid to close the distance to Reggie. "Only Holly has permission to call me by my name." His free hand reached around me and jabbed a finger toward Reggie, who didn't have the sense to be nervous about a pissed-off FBI agent in a room full of thieves. "*You*, asshole, are lucky she has you under her protection."

Reggie's chin lifted. "Threats, Jack-off?"

"Oscar almost *killed* her." Kendrick's voice shook with every word.

"He did what?" Reggie's arms dropped, and he straightened, losing the fighting stance.

Gretchen gasped, her eyes widening to the point where I feared they'd pop out.

I recounted the tale with Kendrick chiming in to fill in what I'd forgotten due to the terror.

"A *bull*?" Reggie paced, then cursed. "I'm sorry, Bells. I didn't know his paranoia had gotten that far out of hand."

"You're playing courier," I snapped, relieved to give someone I trusted this "punishment." Kendrick and I had to stop moving around so much. "You need to transport the finished hardware casing to my villa in Nevis. Stuart will load the software and programs on it. Have him teach you everything you need to know to run it, then meet us in New York City. I'll give you details later."

"Fine." Reggie scratched the scruff on his chin. His eyes slid to Kendrick, and his expression soured. "Thanks for doing what you could to save Bells. I take back calling you Jack-off."

"Big of you," Kendrick responded dryly.

"Holly," Gretchen whispered, awed, "in your explanation you called Agent Kendrick Kisa." She covered her mouth as she stared at the FBI agent.

I froze. Shit. It had become so ingrained, I hadn't even thought about it. And now I was about to pay for it.

"How did I miss that?" Reggie whirled from marching to the closed curtains. "*He's* Kisa? Have you lost your mind?"

Kendrick growled. "Watch your tone."

I bit my lip and castigated myself for saying the name in front of the people who knew what my giving it to him meant.

Gretchen cocked her head. "He doesn't know, does he?"

"No." I barreled forward to the space on the other side of the king-size bed, needing the subject changed pronto. "Reggie, can you get a hold of the forger? See if he can meet us somewhere other than the park for the latest IDs. With the FBI swarming the area, we can't risk being seen over there again."

"Already did." Reggie leaned against a bare section of the lined wallpaper, keeping Kendrick, who still stood at the edge of the hallway, in sight. "For an extra grand, he'll come here tomorrow afternoon and will have your IDs at the dead drop Tuesday morning."

"Excellent." I swiped the hat and wig cap off my head and sighed at the freedom. Tossing them on the bed, I peered at the woman who no longer looked like she wanted to vomit. "Then let's get started. Gretchen? You're the queen of special effects and disguises. Where do you want us?"

"Wait a minute," Kendrick announced, causing everyone to still. "Holly, what did Gretchen mean by her question? What don't I know?"

Shit. Shit. Shit. My heart slammed against my chest, and I lost feeling in my hands and feet. I could *not* have this conversation with an audience...or ever.

Gretchen whimpered, her skin losing color again as she peered between Jack and me.

I shifted my gaze to find aqua eyes focused on me. Inhaling through my nose—

"You know it's an acronym, right?" Reggie asked bluntly, his tone suggesting Kendrick had the intelligence of a slug.

"Yes." Those blue eyes remained on me as he answered.

"Do you know what it stands for?" Reggie pressed. I wanted to yell at him to shut up, but my tongue had turned to stone.

Don't tell him. I opened my mouth, but nothing came out.

"Not yet," Kendrick admitted, still looking only at me.

"Knight In Shining Armor," Gretchen answered from somewhere on my right.

Kendrick's head jerked back, and he blinked.

Blood roared past my ears, and black spots dotted my sight. *No. Don't say any more.*

"Holly doesn't talk about her past." Gretchen kept going despite my silent plea. "To anyone. But after she used that name a few times in conversation, Reggie and I talked Liam into telling us the reference."

Oh Jesus. Speak! Make her stop. But I couldn't thaw my frozen lungs or move.

"During her fifth birthday," Gretchen continued, "the last one she had with her mom, she, her mom, and Liam wove together a fantastical adventure of them in Camelot. At the end of the story, her mother told her one day she'd meet a special man who'd capture her heart and treat her as wonderfully as the noble knights. He'd be so exceptional, she'd love him with every fiber of her being, and he'd be her knight in shining armor. Her Kisa."

I crumpled to the floor and rocked. The memory of those words infused with the horror that Gretchen had just laid my soul bare.

Footsteps thudded across the carpet, and I pulled my legs up to my chest. I needed to hide. Burying my face in my knees, I shut my eyes and swayed. I couldn't bear to see the lack of reciprocal feelings, or worse, the pity at my stupidity for falling for him.

Like a tuning rod, I knew exactly when he reached my side.

"Please don't say anything, Jack," I whispered, finding my voice enough to push those words out.

Through sound, I followed his actions. He dropped to the floor to lean his back against the bed and spread his legs on either side of me. Strong arms wrapped around my body ball and scooped me backwards. He settled me on his lap and wormed an arm between my stomach and thighs, forcing me to unfurl. With gentle hands, he caressed both my cheeks and used pressure to lift my face.

"Open your eyes, Cupcake," he ordered softly.

I inhaled and raised my eyelids.

Irises swimming with so much emotion bathed me in their light. "Is that true?" He kept me prisoner with his gaze. "After chocolate and vanilla marble cake with white frosting and opening the Barbie present from Liam, did you visit Camelot?"

He remembered. My heart stuttered, then pounded anew. "Yes."

A small smile lifted the left corner of his mouth. "I bet you weren't some wimpy maiden or damsel in distress, were you?"

I shook my head, fear of his reaction prevented me from returning the smile. "No. I was Sir Galahad."

"Of course you were." Kendrick's smile widened. "The most loyal and chivalrous of all the knights; the one who succeeded in the quest for the Holy Grail." His fingers moved against my face. "Even at five, you had a lioness's ferocity for justice and those you love."

I stilled, waiting for the gentle rejection of my feelings.

"Including me." His grip tightened, and a sheen filmed his eyes. "God," he pressed his forehead to mine. "You said it once, but I had no idea you've been telling me this entire time."

I blinked back tears, unable to respond. Every cell I owned braced for the blow.

He pulled back and searched my face. "Although I still think the word 'obsessed' is too strong, Westbrook wasn't kidding. I've been enthralled by you," he whispered, and I girded myself for the "but" surely to follow. "Holly. Cupcake.

I meant every damn word when I said you've been stealing pieces of me since the first moment I saw you."

A small kernel of light beamed through the darkness seizing my soul. "What are you saying?"

"That I'm not pushing you to declare anything. But when you *are* ready to admit out loud how you feel about me"—his expression softened—"you'll find you may not be as alone in this as you fear."

Chapter 40

E ight days had passed since my soul had been sliced open and left bleeding in that Alabama hotel room. Eight glorious and yet nerve-racking days spent with Kendrick at an extended stay hotel in West Virginia. Neither of us brought up the subject of love again, but it hung heavy in the air between us, shrouding every touch and kiss.

Reggie and Gretchen invaded our one-bedroom, apartment-style suite on Thanksgiving Day and Stuart video-streamed to tell us Chet had survived the surgeries and should make a full recovery after physical therapy. I didn't ask how he found out, just offered a toast of thanks and lifted my glass of wine. Once Reggie and Gretchen left, Jack had utilized the GPS scrambler on my phone to call his family. My heart broke/filled with love when he put it on speaker and let me hear his mom and dad gush about missing him before launching into a hilarious tale involving his nieces, nephews, the dog, the turkey, and some kind of toy that burst into pieces, almost ruining dinner.

He belonged in that Hallmark world, not pulled down into mine.

"You ready?"

Kendrick's question ripped me from my thoughts, and I blinked at the view through the window in front of me. Cars filled the side parking lot, and a thin layer of snow clung to the top the vinyl cover strapped over the rectangular pool.

He pressed against my back and swiped my hair to the side. Kissing my exposed neck, he murmured, "It's time. We can't put it off anymore."

I nodded, my mouth suddenly dry. The nerve-racking part of the eight days had been the helplessness to reach Uncle Liam faster. Stuart and Oscar were working as hard as they could, but I wanted the Cryptix to be finished already. I had to free Uncle Liam from that monster. My imagination kept terrorizing me with visions of my uncle being beaten daily to the point of near death.

Plucking my phone off the windowsill, I willed my hands to stop shaking as I pressed call on Darien's number. I checked to make sure the scrambler app had activated, then opened my recording app to start spooling the call into the online cache.

"Holly," Darien answered. *"I hope for your uncle's sake you're calling to tell me you have the Cryptix."*

My heart seized. "Why for my uncle's sake?"

Kendrick forced me to turn and kept a grip on my hips.

Darien sighed. *"His refusal to share his contacts and clients has really become a problem."*

"You son of a bitch." I wrenched from Kendrick's hold. Pacing, I snarled, "You told me you wouldn't touch him if I gave you updates."

"Yes, but after careful consideration, I realized that wasn't a smart business decision," the CEO stated with all the callousness of a snake. As if my uncle's health rated no higher in importance than what he'd have for lunch. *"The items your crew have stolen over the years are quite valuable, and I want them for my own collection. Why deny myself?"*

Red tinged my vision, and the synapses in my brain erupted to the point where I felt the wave shooting across my skull. "If you kill my uncle, I have no incentive to give you the Cryptix."

Kendrick stomped in front of the couch, his footsteps marking the carpeting as he clenched his fists and growled softly.

"I have no intention of killing Liam," Darien replied as if offended. *"I only promised your uncle as compensation. You weren't savvy enough to negotiate the condition he'd be in when we met."*

My arm cranked back, and Kendrick leaped, seizing my hand before I could hurl the phone against the wall. Furious tears fell from my eyes, and I envisioned wrapping my hands around the CEO's neck. "I'm going to kill him," I snarled into Kendrick's bicep.

He pressed his lips to my ear. "I'll help. Now set the meetup so you can be done with this son of a bitch." His strength muscled my hand holding the phone back in front of me.

"Arranging the meeting place is the reason for my call." I had to unlock my jaw to continue. "You're going to be at the Marriott Marquis in New York City on Saturday night. I will meet you there for the exchange."

Silence for a beat. *"That's three days after the deadline."*

"I'm sure you'd rather have the Cryptix than quibble about a three-day difference. You'll still be able to crush the competition in the merger."

Two more beats of silence. *"You've got balls suggesting a swap at a law en-forcement ball."* Excitement tinged his tone, exposing he was hooked. Kendrick had called it right. *"I love it. It's perfect. No one would ever suspect this deal to happen there that night."* He hummed suggestively. *"I never knew you had such an adventurous streak inside you."*

I gagged at the leer coloring those words.

"You intrigue me," he purred. *"If you survive the night without getting caught, I believe I see a future for us...personally* and *professionally."*

Oh ewwwww. I dry-retched into Kendrick's trembling shoulder. The rage pouring off him fed my own.

"Keep your phone on you," I managed to answer against my gag reflex. "I'll call you again with details." I hung up.

"You're mine," Kendrick pronounced harshly. "We'll take this bastard down and save your uncle." Gripping both sides of my head, his eyes flamed. "I will get you and your crew immunity, I swear it."

"Jack—"

"I swear it, Holly." He emphasized by forcing my head to tip further back. "You will walk away free for helping to reveal and capture this depraved son of a bitch."

Before I could respond, he kissed me with such ferocity that I could only hold on for the ride.

❧

"Thank you, young man," I crooned in a scratchy voice to the police officer in full dress uniform who "helped" me maneuver my walker onto the Marriott Marquis's escalator. Peering up at the eighty-two-ish-year-old man hunched over a cane a step above me, I cackled. "Kisa, you remember when you used to look like him?"

Cloudy aqua eyes—thanks to the contacts Gretchen had supplied along with the rest of her amazing special effects to dramatically age us both—flitted to the officer now a step below me. "Yeah," Kendrick croaked, bobbing his head which made the thin ring of gray hair bisecting his bald head dance. "Got your attention with all my muscles. I remember when you couldn't get enough of 'em." He winked and the officer cough-choked behind his hand as his cheeks flared red.

"Hush, Larry," I admonished. "You're embarrassing him."

"You're making me *gag,"* Reggie bitched in my earpiece, then pretended to do just that. Drama king.

"Watch your step, Margie." Kendrick pointed a liver-spotted, shaking finger at the top of the escalator.

"I know how to walk," I bitched in my best waspish old lady tone. Gripping my walker in my "gnarled" hands, I purposefully rammed the front wheels into the side of the escalator as I wobbled behind. The bright white-and-yellow daisy-flower satchel hooked inside the front of my walker banged into my shins and the aluminum poles, making me glad my eggplant-purple, elastic-waistband pants would cover the bruises I was sure had just sprouted.

Kendrick rolled his eyes to the officer who grabbed my elbow to keep me from teetering backwards. "Been married fifty-two years." Kendrick hobbled with his cane out of the way so more people could exit. The yellow long-sleeve button-down shirt covering his lumpy middle had a coffee stain near the pocket and was tucked into a pair of wretched brown pants held up to his nipples by a worn black belt. The tweed blazer about forty years out of date covered the gun he had holstered to his side (Reggie had howled when Kendrick stripped him of it). "Want to know what I learned?"

The late-twenty-something police officer patiently paused. "What's that?" His deep accent gave away he came from the heart of the mid-west. Oklahoma maybe?

"Shut my mouth and say 'you're always right, dear,'" Kendrick slapped the butt of his cane into the carpeting as he chuckled.

I grumbled, swiping the side of his leg with my walker. Tottering as I pushed forward, I only took a few steps, then halted. "Lorda mercy," I cried, staring at the sea of men and women mingling in and out of the ballroom's opened doors on the sixth floor. According to Kendrick, approximately twenty-three-hundred people were in attendance (that included the plus ones and speakers). "Look at all the fancy dresses, tuxes, and uniforms. Glad I wore my nice cardigan and jewels." I touched my mother's comb tangled in my fluffy, white hair, shaped just like a Q-tip. Having a piece of her with me helped combat my nerves at how everything could go wrong. Turning to the police officer trying to make his escape, I asked, "What's going on? What kind of shindig is this?"

The officer halted, and his shoulders stiffened. I could just see the curse forming on his lips at having been trapped by the chatty old couple. "It's the annual George James Hill Ball."

"Oh yeah?" Kendrick drew out, his bushy eyebrows soaring. "Sounds prestigious. What's it for? How you score an invitation?"

The officer's jaw tightened. "Law enforcement officers are invited from all over the country as a way to reward exemplary service or honor those receiving an award. All the levels are represented from federal to municipal."

Kendrick slapped his cane down again and cackled. "A Blue Ball...s, eh?"

I snickered and the officer barked with laughter.

"Have a good evening, folks." He waved, then bolted (impressively keeping it respectful) to join another man wearing a similar uniform already holding a drink in his hand.

Making the arduous journey to the next Up escalator heading to the seventh floor, I scanned the crowd, looking for Darien and other scary faces like Kendrick's unit.

Kendrick and I had checked into the Times Square hotel yesterday afternoon in full disguise. We needed as much time as possible to recon the massive building and sight the cameras, security, and such. The Marriott Marquis had forty-nine floors above ground with the fourth through ninth floors providing ballrooms, meeting rooms, and function spaces. The eighth housed the main lobby with the check-in/registration desk (a huge multi-station affair), restaurant, bar/lounge, and a few more meeting rooms. Our room was on the twenty-third floor, overlooking a view of Times Square with the blinding billboards, stores, street performers, and endless tourists.

A state-of-art elevator system with way too many glass-front cars shot guests up or down a massive round column in the center of the hotel like an amusement park ride, touching all the floors while escalators carried guests up and down the first nine floors if they wanted or needed a break from the elevator launch or if they were only in the hotel to attend a conference event.

Being so close to home made me long to escape. I wanted to center myself with my things, but I wasn't ready for Kendrick to know about my warehouse, and anyway, I couldn't afford to take any time out for the trip. Uncle Liam's safety came down to tonight's swap.

"I'm in place," Reggie announced through the comms. He'd found a hiding spot that allowed him access to the hotel's technology wiring. *"I'll be spliced into the security feed within the next five minutes."*

"What about the sound system and projection display on the stage of Blue Balls?" Kendrick asked, snickering like a twelve-year-old on the last two words as he caned his way to the Up escalator.

"Yeah." Reggie chuckled. *"I'll be connected to those, too."*

A gigantic stage sprawled across the front section of the ballroom with a podium on the leftside. Taking up fifty percent of the space was a white screen held aloft from above. On the screen, a projector showed pictures of the invited officers taken throughout the year, like a yearbook, with the slideshow set to soft music.

We planned to hijack that and expose Darien's crimes.

I rammed my walker onto the metal stairs as they lifted into place and stepped onto the escalator. "Then I guess it's showtime."

Chapter 41

Not as many people wandered the seventh floor as the sixth, but that didn't mean it was empty. Taking care to keep my posture skewed and off-center like the older woman I studied yesterday, I pushed my walker across the vivid carpeting made up of reds, blues, and gold. Guests in formal gowns and tuxes waltzed in and out of a smaller ballroom's open doors. (By "smaller," I meant it held four-hundred-and-fifty people instead of twenty-four-hundred.) A DJ turned down the music and called for the bride and groom to take the dance floor for their first dance.

Awwwww. I silently wished them well. Moving on, I peeked over the chest-high glass wall that rimmed the elevator column to see more full-dress police uniforms, tuxes, and gowns on people who were moving around on the sixth floor.

"How are we doing on timing?" I adjusted my uber-thick glasses with lilac-colored plastic frames (they even had a metal chain with links in the shape of tiny flowers attached to the sides).

Kendrick cranked his wrist over to expose a cheap black rubber watch. "We've got about ten minutes before he's due to show up."

"Reggie? You good?" I kept my eyes on the men leaning their shoulders against the wall and talking on cellphones. They could be wedding guests, or they could be Darien's thugs.

"All set," Reggie replied. *"I'm spliced into everything we need and can cut the feed off the projection screen and replace it with our own stream when it's time."*

One hurdle down. Kendrick and I soldiered on, staying in character by razzing each other about the stupidest shit, like my burning the tuna casserole last week because I refused to put down my romance book or him not getting around to fixing the dishwasher despite my asking twenty times.

"Are the bathrooms this way?" Kendrick cut me off loudly, pointing his shaking hand at the corridor containing four small conference rooms. "My prostate's acting up."

"How should I know?" I retorted shrewishly. "You think I developed X-ray vision on the escalator?"

"You have eyes in the back of your head," he snapped in a reedy tone. "Wouldn't surprise me none."

"If I did," I shuffled through the propped open doors that would take us to our ultimate destination (not the bathroom), "you think I'd use it on your wrinkled body? No. I'd be drooling over those young bucks down there."

"You two sound just like my gran and pops," Reggie chimed in. *"It's scary."*

Kendrick winked at me and drove his cane into the floor with his steps. A small plaque at the end of the hall announced we had arrived at the "Gotham" Room, and he grinned, mouthing *Batman.*

Leaning into me, he murmured, "Does that make me Bruce Wayne and you Selina Kyle?" He then laughed in a low tone, making my insides quake beyond the nerves roiling my stomach. "That's actually perfect. Selina's secretly Catwoman, the infamous cat burglar."

"Dude," Reggie drawled, *"she's considered a villain, so points off for that."*

I rolled my eyes and pulled the wooden door open, inadvertently banging it on my walker. Stupid thing. I kept forgetting to account for the extra space needed. Hustling inside, I frowned at the completely empty space. If this went south (gut clench), I would have nothing to hide behind. Two doors fed into the room: the one we'd just entered through and one along the back wall that led to the service corridor running the length of the entire floor. No windows looked out on New York City. There were only plain walls with a few simple pictures on three sides and one temporary wall that could be folded up to combine this room with the one on the right.

"I've got to go." Kendrick wrapped his arms around me. I hated all the padding keeping me from feeling him. "Whatever you do, don't get hurt." He pecked my lips. "Play it cool and safe."

I nodded, having trouble swallowing. I didn't want him to leave me by myself with a monster on his way. I hated feeling like the damsel in distress, but having Kendrick beside me made me feel like I could pull this off and save Uncle Liam.

"I'm listening." He pointed to his ear. "I'll coach you as best as I can."

"Enough mushy bullshit," Reggie groused.

"Bite me," I barked, rising to my toes in my orthopedic shoes. I slid my mouth over Kendrick's. He pulled me in tighter and slanted his head, taking the kiss deeper. *Yes.* I needed his strength. A small part of me feared this might be the last time I tasted him, and that really set me on edge.

Pulling away much too soon, he stepped back. "Cupcake." He clutched his heart and swallowed.

I nodded, getting what he wasn't saying. "Kisa."

He jogged (so weird with him looking eighty-something) to the service door and poked his head out, then disappeared.

"Kendrick, the Empire Room was clear when I stashed your stuff." Reggie named the first conference room in this row where he had placed Kendrick's garment bag. Kendrick would change into a tux and dress shoes to blend in with the ball attendees, then swoop in after I left to arrest Darien. All the prosthetics Gretchen had supplied were easily removed in case we had to lose the aliases.

Silence swamped me, ratcheting up my nerves to the point where my swallows echoed in the bright fluorescent-lighted space.

Darien had three ways he could reach the Gotham Room. One, the escalator/elevator: a direct approach I couldn't see him utilizing seeing as he had to cart my badly beaten uncle with him. Two, the stairs inside the Blue Balls ballroom that lead to a balcony rimming the room that allowed a person to exit onto this floor: the door was only feet from the Gotham Room. A possibility but again, he'd be dragging my uncle through a crowd of very astute people, and I didn't see that happening. That left the third way, the service elevator. I was banking on this approach. The entrance and exit were in the service corridor and barely anyone would see him escorting an injured man.

I debated whether I should move to the center of the room or stay near the main exit. Moving closer could give me a better chance to snatch my uncle if I needed, but it also gave Darien easier access to snatch *me* if he chose.

"The doors to the service elevator just opened," Reggie announced, tuned into the security feed. *"That fucker."*

"What?" My stomach lurched as I grabbed the walker.

"Darien's just marched out wearing at least five thousand dollars' worth of threads with his head high. Following is one of his goons, pushing a wheelchair. A hood's over the man's head, but it can only be Liam."

No. I blacked out for a half a second, thankful the walker kept me upright.

"Before you hand over the machine," Kendrick's tone was cold, *"make him lift that hood. Be sure it's your uncle and not some dupe. He may try to force you into doing something else for him."*

Oh wow. This is it. Weeks of hard work came down to this. The only variable was how quickly the artificial intelligence worked. Stuart couldn't test the final program once he finished blending all the pieces together. Without knowing if Darien had security monitoring on his accounts, we couldn't chance tipping him off.

The grinding of the metal door handle engaging rang through the room. My adrenaline spiked.

Gripping my walker until my bones creaked, I faced the back door and balanced my weight evenly over my feet. Sweat pooled beneath my wig and under my clothes, and I was afraid I'd combust, but I didn't move.

The door slowly swung open, and Darien Burton strode into the room.

Chapter 42

Darien stuttered to a stop, blinked, then threw his head back and laughed. I worked hard to hide the cringe at the evil coating my ears.

He slapped his stomach and strolled forward, shaking his gray and brown-haired head. "Amazing." Confidence and authority oozed out of his pores, and I shuddered, not wanting him anywhere near me.

"The goon has wheeled Liam into the room next to you." Reggie's voice helped purge the taint crusting my insides.

Darien meandered around me. My skin twitched at having him at my back. He popped into my view again, smiling wide. The rest of the world saw a handsome, relatively fit, pleasant man in his early fifties, willing to give millions to charities. I saw calculation, greed, and a vile criminal.

"Your disguise is incredible." His hand lifted to caress my arm, but I jerked back.

"Don't touch me."

Light dimmed in his eyes, and his mouth tightened. "I'd never have guessed a beautiful woman hid beneath those layers."

Ick. I vomited a little in my mouth. "Where's Uncle Liam?"

He waved my question away. "We'll get to him in a minute."

"Don't let him control the swap," Kendrick warned.

"I think we should get to him now," I countered.

The light completely extinguished as his lips flattened. "Don't presume you're in charge, Holly. He lives because of my generosity. Don't push me to change his status."

Mother-effing asshole. The skin on my fingers whitened from my tightening grip.

"That's better." He dipped his chin as if a king bestowed the serf a favor. "Now. Where is it?"

"Same place as Uncle Liam," I shot back. "Once I see him, you see your Cryptix."

He cocked his head and studied me. "You and your uncle share a life-ending stubborn streak."

"Darien." I worked to control myself from barking at him. "This will go so much faster if we both make concessions. You bring in my uncle, I bring in the machine, and we're both happy."

I never saw the punch coming. My face exploded with pain, and I fell over the walker, crying out.

"Holly. Bells," Kendrick and Reggie called at the same time. *"What the hell just happened?"* Kendrick demanded.

Clutching my throbbing face, I lifted my head and blinked through the tears streaming down my cheeks.

Darien bent over and sneered. "Next time you mouth off, I'll follow that punch with a kick to your ribs."

Curses exploded in my earpiece and I closed my eyes to find my control. My self-defense training had me wanting to break his nose.

"Play the game, Holly," Kendrick ordered tightly.

Standing my walker back up, I placed one hand on a pole and lifted the other in the air. "Will you help me up, please?" A fresh round of tears streamed down my face at having to use my jaw.

"Aww," Darien drew out, his voice completely soft. "Of course I will, sweetheart. Don't make me hurt you again."

The son of a bitch was a total psycho, switching moods faster than a preteen.

He pulled me up, and I firmly retracted my hand under the pretense of gently wiping the tears with the tissue crumpled in my pocket. I couldn't afford to mess up the disguise more than I already had. Trying to ignore my face throbbing in time with my pulse, I moved to the walker and unhooked one handle of the daisy satchel, then pulled out the replica Cryptix. The four-inch thick, rugged, all-weather, extremely tough black case (the military loved surrounding their toys in armor) was a little over a foot long and a half-a-foot deep. It weighed about twelve pounds.

Darien slithered closer, his eyes burning with greed and delight. "Open it," he ordered, hovering his hands near the latches but not touching.

Balancing the heavy computer onto an arm and front of my walker, I unsnapped the clips on either side of the handle. Lifting the lid, I turned the case to show him the device built within. The lid held the monitor while the bottom housed the computer hardware. Since we didn't really need to store any data on the hard drive itself, we didn't worry about fitting much storage space within. Everything the artificial intelligence found would automatically save to the FBI's servers under a designated folder Kendrick could access. To setup the file properly, Stuart had hacked into the FBI and changed the settings for the folder to have unlimited disk space. He assured me that adjusting the setting was critical since the amount of data the AI program uncovered would be huge. I trusted him to know better than me, so I'd just nodded when he'd talked.

"The signal just went live," Reggie assured me. Stuart wrote into the code to automatically connect to Kendrick's FBI folder through a satellite link the second the lid opened. Using the satellite instead of the hotel's wireless internet cut down on potential connection delays and detection of its existence if someone were looking to stop the program. Only a person with the correct password could shut it off now. Hurdle two complete.

I lifted my eyes, careful to keep the hate from spewing out. "Okay." I flinched at the pain flaring through my jaw. "I've held up my end. Please, bring in Uncle Liam."

Darien ripped his gaze off the machine with a frown. "How do I know it's the real thing?"

"Please," I begged for real because I was starting to freak out. Why was he stalling so much? "Please let me see him. I have to know he's okay." I swallowed the fear and my pride and let the desperation show. "Please, Darien."

His entire body relaxed. He ran a finger over my tender wrinkled cheek that was swelling more and more with every passing second. "You beg so beautifully. I'm going to enjoy having you in my bed."

It took all of my skills not to clobber him with the Cryptix or jerk away.

"I'm going to kill this asshole," Kendrick growled.

Darien pulled a small cellphone out of his pocket and pressed a button. Lifting it to his ear, he barked, "Bring him in."

Twenty eternal seconds later, the back door swung open again, and a thug in a tux wheeled in a man slumped in a wheelchair.

I cried out and raced across the room.

"Don't—"

Reaching the wheelchair just as Darien shouted, I ripped the hood off and dropped to my knees. "What did you do to him?" I cried, new tears rolling down at the sight before me. Uncle Liam's face resembled a swollen, bruised, lumpy mess.

"Is it Liam?" Kendrick demanded.

"Uncle Liam." I gently swiped a clump of stringy hair off his forehead. "Can you hear me?"

He didn't react.

"Say his name again if that's a yes," Kendrick ordered.

"Uncle Liam—"

Darien grabbed beneath my arms and yanked me off the ground. "We're not finished," he snarled. "You can mother him after he's woken from the sedative."

I allowed Darien to march me back to the computer still balanced on my walker. I had one more huge hurdle to jump before I could make my escape. On the screen was an official seal in the middle of a blue background.

"How does it work?" Darien centered his body in front of the Cryptix.

Good. "Just hit any key to activate the password screen." I gently held my inflamed jaw.

He pressed the space bar. I wanted to throw my fists in the air. With that one keystroke, he just initiated his own downfall.

"Excellent," I encouraged, more to let Kendrick and Reggie know Darien had sealed his fate.

The beauty of Stuart's program was that it didn't matter what button Darien (or anyone, it was just more poetic with Darien initiating it) pressed, the artificial intelligence immediately unleashed onto the internet to begin uncovering Darien's dirty secrets. With me already having Darien's work and home address, cellphone number, and at least one bank account from our dealings years ago, the program had a place to start. It would branch out from there to learn and make connections. Stuart had explained how it all worked, but I'd gotten lost about thirty-seconds in. I'd just needed to know it was smart enough to give me the money laundering stuff, for example, versus the accolades of a library dedication.

The best part was that Darien had no clue. The screen didn't show a thing—*wouldn't* show a thing unless a person had the knowledge of where to find the innocuously named program buried in the root system and the coded keys to turn it off.

"What's the password?" Darien pointed at the navy box with a white bar in the middle that would unlock the first screen.

I reached inside the daisy satchel and pulled out a folded piece of white scrap paper. "Type this in." I handed it to him, and he pecked one finger over the keyboard to insert the fifteen-character letter and number sequence Stuart made up to look authentic.

"*Holly,*" Kendrick interrupted. "*You've got to get out of there. We don't know when the program's going to start displaying its findings—*"

"*Shit,*" Reggie cut in. "*It already is.*"

"What?" I asked under my breath, coughing to cover the question.

"*Items are popping up on the projection screen in the ballroom as we speak,*" Reggie continued, his voice tight. "*And the initial phone call you recorded from Darien has overridden the music like we intended. It's pumping loudly for everyone to hear.*"

"Fuck," Kendrick spat.

"Jesus," Reggie drew out. *"You should see what's on the screen. An entire trail from news articles to emails to photos to bank statements with accounts and sums highlighted showing an entire money laundering scheme involving a hospital wing, a major crime family in Ireland, and a shell company traced back to Darien."*

My heart seized. *No.* Stuart's program worked too fast. I'd banked on having at least ten minutes to hustle Uncle Liam out, and Darien being in the ballroom before anything was displayed.

"As you can see," I motioned to the machine, "I've held up my end of the bargain. It's time for me to go."

Darien raised his head from investigating the offering. "But I don't know how this works."

I shook my head. "My part of the deal was to steal the Cryptix and bring it to you." My words slurred at my jaw tightening with swelling. "I was lucky I found that password so you could open it. I couldn't exactly stick around for a tutorial." I pulled my walker toward me, forcing Darien to catch the hardcase. "I'm taking my compensation and leaving before my luck runs out."

"Fuckshit," Reggie snarled. *"Your luck's already run out, Bells. The whole ballroom's in an uproar. Officers and agents are tearing out of there as if they're on the hunt."*

Chapter 43

A second thug burst through the back door of the Gotham Room at the same time Kendrick threw the main door open.

"Freeze!" Kendrick swept a gun over us. "You're all under arrest."

Thug One lunged around Uncle Liam's wheelchair with a black gun pointed at Kendrick.

Jack shot him in the chest.

I clapped a hand over my mouth at the sudden violence and blood. Uncle Liam's chair rocked as the thug fell. I lurched toward him. I had to shield my vulnerable uncle in the chaos.

Thug Two had a huge handgun already lifting as he ran toward Darien.

Crack. Crack. Kendrick fired two deafening rounds. Thug Two jolted twice and dropped to the floor, dead.

No, no. Uncle Liam.

"Darien Burton, Holly Bell, and Liam Bell," Kendrick boomed. "Freeze. You're under arrest."

What? The carpet had somehow turned to molasses, preventing me from moving with any kind of speed.

Shouting and screams wailed beyond the room, but I couldn't think of anything past Jack's absurd demand and my own need to rush Uncle Liam to safety.

Darien grabbed me from behind and whipped me around to become a human shield. The closed Cryptix case banged against my chest as he pulled me in tight. "I'll kill her, Agent Kendrick."

Oh, fuck no. I'd had enough. He had no weapon, making the choice easy. Drawing on my self-defense classes, I elbowed, kicked, and punched. Darien cried out, dropping the hardcase. His hold loosened, and I wiggled free.

"Darien, don't even think about moving," Kendrick snarled, his gun pointed at the CEO. "You're under arrest for a shitload of crimes. On the ground. Hands behind your head."

"You've got nothing on me," Darien wheezed, inching toward me with a hand cupping his balls. I had tried to shove them up into his body.

Kendrick stepped forward. "Touch her again, and I *will* end your miserable existence." The deadly black hole in the gun's barrel centered on Darien's heart.

Hate and menace exuded out of the CEO as he slowly bent his knees to kneel on the floor.

I took a step, needing to reach Uncle Liam—

"Stop, Holly Bell." Kendrick lasered ice-cold aqua eyes on me but kept his aim on Darien. "You, too, need to get down on the ground, hands behind your head."

"You slimy piece of shit," Reggie wailed. *"I knew you couldn't be trusted."*

I slowly lifted my hands, not understanding a damn thing. Had I entered an alternate universe? "Jack—"

"Don't say another word," Kendrick ordered. His eyes slid to my throbbing cheek, and they flashed before deadening again. "You both have the right to remain silent. Anything you say can and will be used against you in a court of law…"

Holy shit. I sank to my knees and put my hands on the top of my Q-tip wigged head. Jackson Kendrick, the man I had fallen in love with. The man who had pressed his hand to his heart and begged me not to get hurt. The man who claimed to care about me…just read me my Miranda rights.

"This is not over, Jackson Kendrick," Reggie warned in a dirty, evil tone.

"Get out of here, Reggie," I whispered, staring at the floor. "Take Gretchen and go to ground."

Kendrick fished the comm device out of his ear and turned it off before putting it in his tux jacket pocket.

Footsteps pounded and vibrated the floor. Police officers clad in uniforms in a variety of colors, interspersed with tuxedos and gowns, streamed into the room from both entrances. Many had guns raised and pointed in all our directions (where they kept them in their fineries, I didn't have the bandwidth to ponder), I feared we'd end up like Swiss cheese if someone accidently got an itchy trigger finger.

"What's going on here?" a deep male voice boomed. So much authority rang from his tone, I bet he never had a problem receiving answers. The crowd parted in a rippling wave, and two men in tuxes marched into view.

The first was a short, black-and-gray-haired man in his forties showing signs of losing the battle to fat. His tanned face had a pinched expression that was probably its natural resting state. The second man was a few inches taller than Kendrick and had the same blond hair coloring and facial features. I'd bet my life this was the older cousin, the Deputy Director.

Pinch-face Man's mouth fell open as he surveyed the room. When his eyes landed on Darien, then me (though I doubted he knew it was *me* beneath the disguise), they lightened with calculation. "Explain, Agent Kendrick."

I knew by the tone this was the jealous, asshole boss I'd thought I was helping Kendrick fight.

"Sir," Kendrick responded. "I've placed Darien Burton, Holly and Liam Bell under arrest after I was forced to shoot those two men when they drew their weapons on me."

"This man's not moving," a female stated, and I twisted enough to see a woman in an emerald gown accessorized with a black 9mm pointing a finger at my uncle in the wheelchair.

"Liam Bell was drugged after he was beaten," Kendrick answered.

"He needs a hospital—"

"I demand to see my attorney." Darien cut the female off as he lowered his arms.

"Lace those fingers." Kendrick narrowed his eyes onto the CEO. "You'll talk to your attorney soon enough. And trust me, what little money you might have left after the government seizes your funds, your lawyer's going to take as compensation. He or she'll have a hell of a time coming up with a defense against all the evidence we're uncovering by the second."

"Your days in the FBI are over," Darien hissed but dutifully put his hands on his head.

"Hollow threats from a sociopath are wasted on me."

"Well done, Jack," Asshole Boss crowed, beaming at Kendrick. "You're a real testament to the badge." He slid a peek at the Deputy Director, then rested a hand on Jack's shoulder. "I knew you could pull this assignment off."

What? Everything inside me froze.

Kendrick glanced at me without a flicker of emotion, lowering his gun. "Thanks."

No. Everything inside me died with that one word. He didn't argue or counter the claim. He didn't fight for the immunity he'd sworn he'd secure for me and the crew. He didn't do anything but accept his boss's words as fact. My entire body went numb, and I barely felt it when someone jerked my arms behind my back and put a pair of handcuffs around my wrists.

He'd betrayed me. Jackson Kendrick wasn't under suspension. He was undercover, and he'd used me to take Darien Burton down—he'd almost succeeded in capturing my entire crew, too.

Who knew how many hours later, I sat in a small, sterile interrogation room somewhere inside the FBI building in Manhattan. White walls, white floor, steel table, and a wide mirror on the side was as depressing as it sounded.

I had been forced to take my wig and all the special effects off my body for a super-fun photo session. It wasn't held in the formal booking studio with the snazzy lined background showing heights, and it wasn't voluntary, either. Someone had raided the fitness center supply closet and given me a pair of black sweatpants and a gray T-shirt with black "FBI" stenciled across my breasts. So, I'm sure those pictures came out awesome, especially with the spectacular bruise covering the lower left side of my face and the attractive swelling I had as a result.

My cuffs rattled against the table as I pulled at the chains secured to the bar running down the center. A draft wafted over my bare toes, and I cursed the FBI assholes again for taking my shoes and socks. What did they think I'd do? Well...never mind. I could've easily hidden a key or lockpick in those humongous orthopedic nightmares.

Youch. I winced at the burn slashing through my clenched jaw. My mind coughed up an image of Uncle Liam's beaten body in the wheelchair.

My leaden heart flipped as I blinked back the hundredth round of tears threatening to form. No one would tell me if he was okay. I was sure I remembered someone mentioning a hospital, but did he make it there? He needed medical attention.

Unbidden, my mind switched to the cold eyes Kendrick had laid on me after he burst into the room. *Kisa*, my soul bleated. My Knight In Shining Armor turned out to be an asshole in aluminum foil.

Dropping my head into my hands, I inhaled. Why had I stupidly read into his innuendos? I believed he had fallen for me, too. Thousands of pieces of conversation flitted through my brain. In reality, he hadn't outright lied, just excluded a shit ton of facts. *Weaselly bastard. He played on my emotions to keep me invested in him.* Pain from his defection tore through me.

The door swung open. I didn't have to look to know the man I'd once dreamed of having a future with had just walked in. My withered heart and soul recognized him instantly. The scent I'd loved so much drifted to me, tingling my traitorous body.

Something slapped against the table, and I parted my fingers enough to see a *very* thick, worn, legal-size file on the other side.

A chair scraped against the floor, the noise skittering down my spine. Agent Jackson Kendrick—the traitor—sat on the edge, directly across from me in the black, tailored tux we'd picked out together in West Virginia. Only it no longer made him look devastatingly roguish. Now, he looked devastatingly at home, as if it was just another day at the office.

Lowering my hands, I laced my fingers together to keep from slapping him. I hated violence, but he'd destroyed me with his betrayal. I had believed him. Believed *in* him. Confided things I'd never voiced before. Fallen in love for the first time, and he'd callously used me.

"How is my uncle?" I slurred, my jaw too tight to move easily. Forcing myself to meet his eyes, my gut clenched as if he'd reached over and punched me. A stranger stared back at me. None of the light, the humor, the kindness I had basked in the past month showed in his irises. *This* man was every bit the dedicated agent I'd encountered when he'd attempted to thwart our heists.

"A qualified team of doctors and nurses have treated him. He's now resting under guard." Agent Kendrick paused. "He's going to be fine."

I slumped and covered my face. A shudder ripped through me, and I inhaled against the relief clawing at the fury, the heartbreak, the deception. *Uncle Liam's going to be fine. I did it. I saved him.*

Clothing rustled, and rage speared through me.

I saved him only to trap him into living out his life behind bars. My chains rattled as my hands clattered to the table. I had trusted this man, and Uncle Liam was going to pay for it.

Agent Kendrick's eyes lifted off my cuffs to zero in on my injured jaw.

"You still owe me an answer to a question," I bit out, working to enunciate. *You're wasting your breath.* "Same rule—no bullshit. Did you have any second thoughts about stringing me along?"

His jaw muscle ticked. "You can't expect me to answer something like that now." He flicked his wrist, and the file opened with a slap onto the table. "Ms. Bell, Michael Henderson is on his way in."

Michael? What? How the hell did he know about my arrest? A chilling thought squeezed my lungs. Did Agent Kendrick figure out Michael had been in on my fake heist ploy? Was this another play to capture everyone who'd ever helped me?

"Before your attorney arrives," he continued in an official tone that made me want to smack him even more. "I thought we could talk."

"I'm not saying a word to you, asshole." I clamped my mouth shut and breathed against the treachery squeezing the life out of my soul.

His eyes flickered, and I swore I caught pain, but that'd be ridiculous. He had me right where he'd said he wanted me from the start. In handcuffs, sitting at an interrogation table. Only I wasn't singing like he'd once teased me I would.

"Right." He shut the file and stood. The chair scraped across the floor again, the noise grating down my back. At the door, he turned with one hand on the handle. "While you're waiting for Mr. Henderson, think about what you told me once as you gazed up at the stars. You spoke about champions and injustice. Compasses don't always point north."

Chapter 44

Thirtyish hours later, I lay on my back in a room agents used to catch some shut-eye when they had intense cases that didn't allow much down time. I bent my legs and laced my hands behind my head.

No matter how many times they asked, I refused to say anything. Not even Michael could prompt me to respond. Eventually, the string of agents (Kendrick and Asshole Boss included) gave up and stuffed me in here.

Compasses don't always point north.

Staring at the ceiling, that line replayed for the one trillionth time. What the hell did it mean? If he thought to convey some type of message, it missed its mark. I had no clue what to take away from that other than him telling me he wasn't honorable after all.

Yeah. Got that memo. In triplicate.

Curling on my side to face the wall to keep off my bruised jaw, I rubbed a hand over my hollow chest. If I had stupidly held out a small modicum of hope that Kendrick—the one who had been my Kisa—had some elaborate scheme to free me, it died when Michael informed me last night I'd be transferred to a federal prison today.

Prison. Terror iced down my spine, mingling with the soul-deep agony. This time I couldn't stop the tears from falling and allowed myself to weep. How had I so royally misjudged him? How could he ruthlessly use me and then send me to jail after everything we'd been through?

God. I sobbed. It had all felt so real. His reactions on Saint Croix, or when we'd barely survived the bull, or when I'd almost been mowed down by the cartel, or when he realized my calling him Kisa was in essence saying, "I love you." His warmth when he held me so tight and made love to me for hours, days, weeks. His confessions in the car, the therapy sessions, the beach, the yacht... No human with any type of soul could fake those, yet somehow, he had. Somehow, he'd made me believe he had fallen for me, too, and wanted us to have a future together.

Prison.

I jammed my fist against my lips to keep from screaming.

The door to the temporary holding "cell" opened behind me. I froze with snot trailing from my nose. *Gross.* And no, it *couldn't* be time to leave already. *I'm supposed to have a few more hours.*

"Ms. Bell," a male voice intoned. "Stand up, please, and hold your hands together in front of you."

I almost lost control of my bladder. *Please let me wake up from this nightmare.*

"Ms. Bell."

I flinched and rolled off the hard mattress. "Can I blow my nose first?" I didn't wait for a response. I grabbed a napkin off the small kitchenette counter and went to town.

The FBI agent's all black attire made me blink: bulletproof vest, guns strapped to his thighs and hips, knives in special holders, combat boots, and a helmet.

That's right, boys, I'm a dangerous criminal. Yep. That's me. I try to corrupt agents—

I cut that thought right off. I did not want to end up bawling again at my gullibility and shattered heart.

Nasal passages clear, I washed my hands in the surprisingly clean sink, then held them out as instructed. The agent gave me back my ugly shoes and socks. Once I had them laced, he used gentle hands when he ratcheted the silver bracelets around my wrists in front of me.

Leading me by the elbow, we took a route that led us down instead of up. Guess that made sense. The parking garage wouldn't be on the roof.

Okay. Focus.

The elevator doors opened, and I sucked in a breath. The transport van sat *right there*. Bitter December cold in the stale lower-level air attacked my bare skin and seeped through my thin T-shirt. Trembling started in my legs, moved up to my arms, then overtook my body. I doubted it was my journey to frostbite that shook me so hard. I couldn't breathe. I couldn't swallow against the dryness making my tongue stick to the roof of my mouth.

Gentle Agent's pressure on my elbow forced me toward the van. Everything inside me wanted to dig my heels in and fight. As if sensing my rising panic, his grip tightened.

Two more agents in full gear swooshed the back doors open. I stumbled at the sight of the two men seated across from each other on the sideways benches in the windowless section, beneath a row of lights in the ceiling. "Uncle Liam? Michael?"

I no longer had to be coerced—I practically ran to the van. "Uncle Liam," I yelled to my jaw's detriment, memorizing his lumpy and bruised face. "You're okay." Gentle Agent let go, and I climbed inside with all the grace of a child first learning to walk. Not caring if I broke the rules or not, I threw my handcuffed wrists around my uncle's neck, and he yelped. Backing off my squeeze, I whispered, "Thank God you're okay."

"Holly," he rumbled, patting me awkwardly on the side of my ribs due to his bound hands. "I thought I'd never see you again."

Another round of tears fell from my eyes as I kissed his cheek. "I'm so sorry—"

"Holly." Michael moved behind me and pried my arms from around Uncle Liam's neck. "Now is the time to be silent."

Forced to stay bent due to the restricted height, I lifted the bottom of my shirt and dried my face as best as I could with tethered wrists.

Darkness descended inside the van. My foot caught against something on the floor when I tried to move. Falling backwards, I landed on my ass. "Son of a bitch. I really need to break this new habit," I grumbled, muscling myself to sit like a normal person beside Michael.

The darkness moved, and my eyes flew to the tall man creating the shadow at the back opening.

"Deputy Director—"

"Kendrick," he finished my stupid blurted statement.

Like he doesn't know his own name. You're on fire today.

Cousin Kendrick raked a cool gaze over me, assessing me with a pair of eyes so similar to Kisa Kendrick—*No. Jackson Kendrick. He's not your Kisa anymore*—it felt familiar and wrong at the same time.

"Deputy Director," Michael began but stopped when the DD held up a hand.

"I will not explain myself," he stated, and I bumped the back of my head against the van at that kind of start to a conversation. "If I'm right, I won't have to—but regardless, I'm delaying your transport."

"Now wait just a minute." Michael sat forward to further see around me.

"Save it." The DD frowned. "All will be made clear soon e—"

He straightened. "Shit." DD stepped back to allow Gentle Agent to hop in, then slammed the doors shut. The agent didn't even have a chance to sit before the van took off.

"What?" I grabbed the seat between my legs since I couldn't move my hands apart. "Didn't he just say we were delayed? Why are we moving?"

The van careened around a turn, and judging from the angle, we climbed to the next level. On and on it went.

Poor Gentle Agent could only brace himself with one hand on a side wall while holding his gun in the other.

Finally, we slowed, and a final sharp turn brought us to a halt.

"Seriously." I winced against the dizziness. "What the hell?"

"Silence," Gentle Agent ordered, then dropped to a knee.

What the...

He jammed his gun back into the holster on his thigh and fished a thin, ten-inch tablet from behind his vest.

They hid computers there? Really? Did the vest honestly stop bullets that spectacularly without shattering the screens?

He tapped a button on the top. Beeping emanated from the speaker on the back with each tap. Gentle Agent swiped and tapped some more on the screen, then motioned for Michael to sit on the floor. "Hold this so we can all see."

All right. I'm dreaming. None of this seemed real, yet it was too weird not to be.

The van engine continued to idle, but I couldn't see the driver since a solid wall existed between the back and the front. Warm air wafted over my bare arms, and I flicked my gaze up to see a line of thin black vents beneath the row of lights. Hallelujah.

Michael slid to the floor as instructed, not seeming to care he might ruin an expensive suit.

"Trust me, please." Gentle Agent pointed to a spot next to Uncle Liam. "If events unfold the way we suspect, this'll be made clear, and you'll owe the Deputy Director your gratitude."

Okaaaaay. Weird, but I'm not arguing with the delay in heading to prison. I moved to the indicated spot and clasped my uncle's cold hand, then blinked when the agent sat next to me. Michael twisted to put his back to us and rested the tablet on raised knees. We all craned to look around his head.

At first, I had no clue what was happening. By the camera's height, the filmmaker had decided to embrace using the security camera angle in his creepily lit movie. I could see another transport van exactly like the one I sat in waiting just beyond a set of elevators that looked just like the ones I'd exited a little while ago...

What was this?

Too many long minutes of nothing but staring at the van and five compact cars parked in spaces to the right gave me no clue and had me squirming. The damn bench had no padding, and my ass started to ache—

Something in the shadows between two cars moved, catching my attention. I squinted. The blob moved again, and I realized it was a person. Okay. It just got interesting. Were we watching a live feed of the garage's lower level? Why? What did the DD and Gentle Agent expect to happen?

The person crept to the edge of the cars, then paused. The black ski mask and dark clothing didn't give away much, but I surmised by the large body type that Creeper was a man.

I leaned forward, wishing I had some Skittles. Suspense and intrigue always paired nicely with sugar.

"He's talking to someone," I whisper-slurred. "See? His mouth just moved."

As if scripted, the others bent closer simultaneously. My uncle squeezed my hand after a few beats. "I think you're right."

Creeper leaped from between the cars and ran stealthily to the back of the van. He flattened a gloved hand on the left door, and I held my breath. Would he open it? Why did he want in?

Interminable seconds passed.

Do it already! I wanted answers.

He finally put his hand on the handle and pulled it open. The door blocked the camera's view, and I silently howled.

Endless seconds later, Creeper backed away as five more blobby shadows moved in his periphery in a surrounding pattern to become more distinct as people fully geared and dressed like Gentle Agent.

The camera flickered, then switched to normal height, catching Creeper from behind. By the subtle shaking it had to be handheld or stashed in someone's body armor. Sound erupted from the tablet's speaker, and I jolted.

"...do it."

Creeper hung his head, then pulled his mask off. Blond hair in the midst of all the black clothing really stood out. *Good call on covering it.*

Wait. My heart thumped against my chest.

Deputy Director Kendrick hopped out of the back of the transport in a dignified way I'd never pull off just as Creeper lifted his face. The cameraperson sidestepped until he caught a very familiar profile.

Jackson Kendrick.

Holy fuck. My eyes tried to pop out of my head. "What?"

"Shhh," Michael admonished, turning the volume up to the max.

"Jack, what are you doing?" Cousin Kendrick asked, concern and anger lacing his tone. "You could go to prison for this."

Jackson Kendrick swiped a gloved hand through his hair. "I know." He sighed deeply. "I didn't know what else to do. I promised she'd be free and then it all went to hell."

The world dropped out from beneath me once again.

Chapter 45

U ncle Liam changed the grip on our hands so *he* held on to *me*. I couldn't process all the hits pummeling my poor heart.

On the screen, Jackson lifted his head. "How did you know I'd—"

"Try to break out two captured felons?" the Deputy Director asked with barely any emotion.

Jackson winced and nodded. "Yeah."

Shock tore through me again. Jack...tried to...free me? I couldn't comprehend it, yet deep within, a sense of balance began restoring itself. This. This made more sense than the last two days.

Compasses don't always point north. His message suddenly became a lot clearer. He had been talking about honor but not in the sense of my arrest. *Champions and injustice.* I swallowed. He'd...sacrificed his integrity, his job, his...everything to keep his promise?

DD swiped his jaw. "I know you, Jack. I stood behind the interrogation room's mirror at one point." He paused as if measuring his words. "You weren't an agent just doing his job. I saw how being in the same room with her affected you and how you looked at her."

Oh yeah? He must be alluding to some other Jack. The man *I* saw in that room looked *exactly* like a heartless agent just doing his job.

"I analyzed the opportunities," DD continued, "and figured if you were going to strike, this would be the most vulnerable point."

"Shit," Jack muttered, strangling his knit mask.

DD crossed his dress-coat-clad arms and leaned his back against the now-closed doors of the van. "I think you better start from the beginning." His eyes narrowed. "This is not the time to bullshit or leave anything out. I need you to come clean about *everything*, Jack."

Jack slid a look at the five agents forming a wide circle around the van. No one had their guns out, but a tension in their postures stated they'd have them in their palms before he could blink.

"Don't worry about them." DD lifted his chin. "Every single agent from the drivers to the people watching the monitors in the security room is loyal to me. In anticipation I'd be right, I made every person scheduled to be on shift attend a human resources seminar and replaced them with my core group. They can keep their mouths shut unless I want them to start flapping." His eyes narrowed. "And, Jack, you'd better be very forthright with your explanation. No one will ever have to know about your attempt to break the law unless you piss me off."

"Fuck. Thank you, Aiden." Jack shoved the knit hat into his coat pocket and looked his cousin dead in the eye. Starting with seeing the announcement about my Florence Mantle alias attending a party at Michael's house to standing in his boss's office the next day, Jack spilled it all, even admitting to allowing me to drug him so I could escape.

"Wait." Aiden held up a hand. "You say you tried to tell William"—I assumed that was Jack's boss's name—"about Darien capturing Liam Bell, but he refused to discuss it? Wouldn't even listen to the recording?"

Jack nodded. "He accused me of incompetence, falling for a scheme with fabricated evidence. He gleefully suspended me and stripped me of my gun and badge."

"That's a very different story than what he's been telling me." Aiden's mouth thinned. "He's claiming he knew about your investigation into Darien from the start and approved you going undercover. Your suspension was to help you move freely without having to report in while he worked to rout out the mole."

Jack's fists clenched, and a muscle ticked in his jaw. "That's so false, I don't even know where to begin."

"I believe you." Aiden put a hand on his cousin's shoulder. "Up until this insanity, your integrity has never been in question. But I'm starting to understand your motivations. Keep going."

To my utter mortification, Jack did. Starting with my hiding in disguise across from the restaurant in Miami (I hadn't realized he had picked me out of the crowd right away), he recounted our journey. Almost every detail poured out of his mouth, and I winced and closed my eyes at spots, not wanting to see any of the others shooting startled, pitying, and embarrassed peeks at me. Thankfully, Jack held back my personal childhood confessions, but he laid the rest of the story out there.

Our having to "get married"? Out there. Group and couples therapy? Blabbed to the delight of everyone (I even got a high five from Gentle Agent for thoroughly taking advantage of the sex therapy session.). Partnership dissolution threat part one on the beach, goon invasion, partnership dissolution threat part two? They all knew it now, including Jack's heartfelt speech about being "all in" and our "pirate" plan.

Three-day sex fest? Nope. Jack remained a gentleman, but Aiden hinted he'd guessed how we'd filled those days. Missing Teeth trying to mow me down with a machine gun, and our fight with the cartel to "kill" the Stewarts? Confessed, and Stuart and Melanie's alive status now known, but not every detail. I exhaled at Jack keeping mum about their new name and about not divulging Captain's whereabouts and plans from the moment he left us. He also left out the existence of my villa in Nevis and how the Stewarts were still there until they decided where they wanted to settle.

Blockades, bulls, bullets, and bombs? That pissed everyone off, and yet again, Jack refused to give up Oscar's name since Aiden wouldn't blanketly agree not to go after the hardware guy (keeping his promise because of our agreement?). On and on it went.

"Christ, Holly," Uncle Liam muttered. "You did all this to save me?"

I jerked my eyes to his. "Of course. You're my only family."

"I don't think that's true anymore." His chin jutted toward Jack's profile on the tablet.

Aiden covered his eyes and sighed. "I can't even... Jack, I know you're holding back, but...fuck. I don't know whether to hug you for still being alive, deck you for putting yourself in this mess, or commend you for everything you've done to get that son of a bitch." He chose to hug his cousin in that manly lean in/slap on the back/separate fast thing they did.

"Aiden..." Jack closed his eyes as if in pain. "I practically destroyed her. Did you see her expression when I arrested her? Ripped my goddamn heart out, but I didn't have a choice. I tried to talk to her in the interrogation room, but she looked at me with such disgust and betrayal." He shuddered. "It took everything I had to maintain my distance so I wouldn't tip anyone off about...this." He motioned to the van. "I had to do it."

I sat forward, my broken heart pounding, the pieces desperate for him to say something that'd glue them back together.

"It all went to hell so fast. I barely had a second to plan, let alone act." Jack balled his hands. "I didn't know how many of Darien's thugs were still lurking, and too many officers were about to swarm the room from both sides. I knew I couldn't get her out."

I hung on every word. Hope speared my chest, and my frozen soul warmed.

"She's like a lioness with those she loves." Jack's face was a blend of torment, anger, and...love? "Thugs were pulling guns, and she was turning to charge in their path to get to her uncle. No way would she have left without Liam, and he was too injured to move with any kind of stealth if he could move at all. That left me with one play to keep her and Liam safe."

"Arrest them," Aiden answered. "To keep them under our jurisdiction and protection."

"Yes." Jack nodded. "Liam needed a hospital, not to have to flee a contingent of law enforcement agents."

"Shit," Uncle Liam uttered. "I hate that I'm starting to like and respect the son of a bitch."

This different perspective floored me, and I struggled to breathe. He'd arrested me to save me...he didn't set out to use me. The warmth in my soul flared into piercing heat. He hadn't betrayed me. I pulled my trembling hands from

Uncle Liam's and covered most of my face—but not my eyes, which remained glued on Jack's beautiful profile.

"Okay, but she knew the risks." Aiden scrubbed his face. "How did we get here?"

"I promised I'd do whatever it took to gain her freedom in exchange for her help taking down Darien." Lines in Jack's forehead deepened. "I tried to talk to the New York State Attorney General, but it was the weekend, and I got nowhere." Jack lifted accusing eyes to Aiden. "Then I tried to reach you, but you shut me out."

"You caused a shitstorm with the fake Cryptix uncovering Darien's secrets and his subsequent arrest no one saw coming." Aiden's chin rose. "I've been running nonstop since...and I have my reasons why I didn't respond to you, but we'll get to that in a moment. Once you're done confessing...which I should be hearing more of right now."

Jack's eyes flashed, then he paused and nodded. "Fine." He cleared his throat and shuffled his feet. "I'm almost positive Michael Henderson's a former client of her crew."

Michael jerked.

I straightened and blinked. Damn, Jack really did have eagle eyes and a wicked intelligence.

"How the hell did he jump to that conclusion?" Michael scowled, showing he was smart enough not to admit it outright with Gentle Agent sitting beside me.

"She doesn't realize her effect on people," Jack continued as if he'd heard Michael. "Anyone who's been around her or been on the receiving end of her fierce loyalty ends up wanting to do whatever they can to help her when she needs it. I'm positive Michael's party was at her request to draw me out." Jack took his gloves off. "I called Michael and told him about her arrest, and he offered to represent her. I then asked him to how to get in touch with Reggie and Gretchen."

"And speaking of them, I think it's time Mr. Scoval and Ms. Jost joined us," Aiden stated, his tone brooking no arguments.

Nothing happened for thirty seconds, then a group appeared, tromping down the steps from some unknown level of the parking garage above. Four agents (two smaller in stature who I took to be women) armed with automatic rifles surrounded handcuffed Reggie and Gretchen as they escorted them to stand just to the side of Jack.

Shit.

Uncle Liam stiffened, and his hand tightened around mine. "They've got us all."

"Long story short." Jack turned to face two of the crew. "I persuaded these two to help me keep my promise."

"Bring the rest," Aiden ordered into the air. The van suddenly rocked backwards, then twirled round and round again, heading down.

Gentle Agent snatched the tablet from Michael's grip and stuffed it behind his vest again. The van's brakes squeaked as it stopped, and I untangled my clammy hands from my uncle's.

I hadn't had enough time to adjust to all the revelations, but it didn't matter. My soul cried for reconciliation, and the adrenaline pumping through me had my legs bouncing.

The back doors swooshed open, allowing the freezing air to steal the warmth from the van. Amid goose bumps, my gaze shot right to Jack. Dark circles blackened his eyes—I didn't catch that on the screen—and a sallowness tinged his skin. In other words, he looked as miserable as me.

Gentle Agent shooed Michael out first, then helped Uncle Liam who winced and cursed with every movement to the pavement. When it came to my turn, he didn't come back, instead, jumped out to stand with his brethren just behind Reggie and Gretchen.

"Holly." Jack strode forward, but he stopped at the edge of the van.

My gaze gobbled him up. His aqua eyes had no trace of the coldhearted agent I'd encountered for the last two days. They were now filled with regret and fear.

"Please," he whispered hoarsely, "let me explain."

"No need." I twisted on the bench to face him. "Your cousin made sure we witnessed your whole confession and explanation."

"What the hell?" He whirled, but Aiden only raised an eyebrow.

"Join your crew, Ms. Bell." The Deputy Director rolled his wrist.

My legs bounced even harder. It took all of me to stay seated instead of launching myself at Jack. "Is it true?" The bones in my clenched hands protested my tightening grip.

"Every word." Light eased into his irises, and he flattened both palms to the floor, leaning into the van. "It killed me to sit across from you in the interrogation room and see that devastation in your eyes."

I scooted to the very edge of the bench. "Your natural gift for grifting is scarily good. I believed you." I swallowed against the tears forming a knot in my throat. "I thought you betrayed me."

"I didn't—"

I shot up unable to wait another second. Racing forward like a hunchbacked track star, I had to reach him. Jack plucked me out of the back and crushed me tightly against him. My bound hands created a frustrating wall between us, but I managed to bury my face into his neck and inhaled.

Home.

Unyielding hands gripped me beneath my armpits and ripped me away.

Jack growled and lunged forward—

"That's enough," Aiden yelled, freezing everyone. "Jack, stand beside me. Anderson, escort Ms. Bell to the rest of her crew."

My orthopedic monstrosities hit the concrete and I twisted to find Gentle Agent—Anderson, who wasn't so gentle after all—behind me.

A heavy weight suddenly burdened my shoulders, and the scent of Jackson Kendrick enveloped me, burrowing all the way to my soul. I turned, and Jack pulled the lapels of his coat over me tighter so it wouldn't fall off.

"Jack," Aiden warned. "Step away from Ms. Bell."

Anderson gave me no choice but to move to Uncle Liam's side.

Chapter 46

I couldn't stop staring at Jack, now standing beside his cousin. Relief soared through my veins while foreboding followed directly behind, leaving a wake of disquiet and fear. Jack might not have betrayed me, but he'd attempted to break the law, and I was still a felon in FBI custody. What the hell kind of future could we possibly have?

Aiden unbuttoned his dress coat to reveal a beautiful, well-cut suit. "So, I've got an extremely fucked-up mess dumped in my lap." He glared at all of us. "I can let my cousin follow through with his idiotic plan, which will have me lose one of my best agents and force me to declare him a criminal. That will break way too many of our family's hearts, including my own."

He paced slowly. "Or I can lock my cousin down in a way he'll hate and send you all"—he jabbed a finger toward the crew—"on to prison for your long list of crimes. I foresee my cousin never forgiving me, and I'd lose one of my best agents anyway."

Ice spread through my whole body.

"*Or* I can offer a solution that won't have everyone on the run or making license plates for the rest of your lives."

Jack crossed his arms. "That one. Number three."

I steeled myself for the blow, not confident number three would be any better than the other two.

"Number three." Aiden planted his feet in the same pose Kendrick favored. "Jack, that means I transfer you out of William's unit. You move to another floor to cut down on run-ins—or move to another location, we can discuss." He waved the detail away. "You become the new Special Agent in Charge of a specialized unit overseeing consultants Holly and Liam Bell, Reginald Scoval, and Gretchen Jost."

What? I whipped my head to see if the others had heard what I just did.

Uncle Liam's eyebrows were in his hairline, Reggie scowled, and Gretchen looked ready to cry. So, on par with our usual.

Jack's arms dropped along with his jaw.

"Great," Aiden said wryly. "I can see my working out a fucking miracle with the Attorney General is really getting the accolades it deserves."

"When you say the unit is made up of consultants—namely, us." Uncle Liam recovered his faculties first. "What exactly does that mean, and how would it work?"

"Excellent questions." Aiden pointed to Michael. "I'll draw up an agreement, and your attorney will look it over"—he stopped and swept us with a hard glance—"and no, you can't use anyone other than Mr. Henderson. He's not officially charged with anything, but the suspicion surrounding him alone makes me want to keep an eye on him."

"Be happy to offer my services," Michael sarcastically quipped, giving a small salute.

"Glad you see it my way." Aiden turned back to Uncle Liam. "That agreement will bind you to work with the FBI"—his gaze moved to his cousin—"specifically with Jack as your supervisor of record. You'll help us rout out more criminals like Darien. Work to put away the ones we don't know about or don't have access to."

"And why would we risk our lives doing that?" Reggie challenged.

"In return, your past criminal history will be expunged. Wiped clean. Cease to exist. Whatever you want to call it."

"How long would we be indentured with this agreement?" I tried to work through the implications as fast as I could, the roller-coaster emotional ride of the last few days having taken its toll on me.

"Three years."

Okay. I'd expected a lot longer than that.

"We sign this document, and we can go on living our lives until you call on us?" Reggie scoffed. Gretchen put a hand on his arm.

"In essence, yes." Aiden rebuttoned his jacket. "You can't take on any more jobs unless Jack approves them, but you won't have babysitters to watch your every step. You renege on the agreement, your ass is going to jail. No second chances. That should be enough incentive to stay out of trouble and show up when you're called."

"Agent Kendrick?" Uncle Liam turned to Jack. "What're your thoughts on this?"

Jack crossed his arms, the black, long-sleeved T-shirt molding to every muscle in a delicious way.

"I have to be honest." Jack planted his feet shoulder-width and focused on his cousin. "Being with Holly has changed me."

Reggie snorted, and my cheeks burned at the same time the little girl in me who just wanted to be special perked up.

"Get your mind out of the gutter," Jack snapped, sliding his gaze off Reggie back to Aiden. "Fundamentally, I'm no longer the same man who slapped a pair of handcuffs on her in Michael's house."

Air caught in my lungs, and I stilled.

"I can't, no, I *won't* go back to William's or any other unit and play the game anymore."

"If you take on this new role," Aiden responded, "you won't have to—but explain."

"My transformation goes deeper." Jack's large hand smoothed up to cover his chest. "I didn't realize how disillusioned and frustrated I'd become until Holly opened my eyes. She made me see that I had lost a very basic part of myself." His attention turned, and he took a step toward me. "Pursuing justice and being the underdog's champion is who I am, who I want to be. Over the years, dealing with William's mistreatment and being surrounded by agents who work the system for political gain, I've become soured. Justice shouldn't have agendas other than taking bad guys off the street and protecting the innocent."

I devoured every word. I had shown him this?

His large gait ate more steps toward me until he stood only two feet away. "This amazing woman has more honor and guts and determination to stand up for what's right than I do. She doesn't stop fighting until the true victims she's championing have been saved or vindicated." He halved the distance. "If I could channel even a quarter of this humble, caring, funny, determined alpha bitch"—he halved the remaining distance again—"I'd be a better agent than I've ever been."

Tears crowded the corners of my eyes. I was not this good of a person, but that he saw me this way filled my soul.

"To answer your question, Liam..." Jack lifted his voice but didn't move his gaze off me. "I'd be honored to work with the crew as long as you understand something first."

"What's that?" Uncle Liam answered.

I couldn't look away from the light shining in Jack's eyes. It radiated with so many emotions, I wanted to bask in their rays.

"For a glorious few weeks, Holly called me Kisa."

My breath caught, and Uncle Liam inhaled swiftly.

"Only at the end did I learn the true meaning of that name." His eyes darkened as they roved over my face. "If you all accept the agreement, there won't be any lines or rules keeping us apart. I want to be her Kisa again. I'll do my best to live up to all it entails, but I'm getting my title back."

He halved the distance again. My bound wrists scraped against his hip, and I looped a finger into his belt. Cupping my uninjured cheek, he continued only loud enough for me and possibly Uncle Liam to hear, "I don't have a fancy nickname that says 'I love you' every time I utter it, so I'm just going to say it. I love you, Cupcake."

The air whooshed out of me, and my legs turned to mush.

"I'm hoping you'll choose option number three so we can continue righting those wrongs you're so passionate about—"

I lunged up and kissed him. His hands gripped my shoulders to keep us from tipping over, then he tilted his head and claimed my mouth. Pain shot through my jaw, but I ignored it. All the love and light Jackson Kendrick had steadily filled me with burst free, burning out the last of the darkness from the past two days.

Giddiness swamped my mind to the point where I felt drunk. I giggled as I pulled my mouth back and squiggled my tethered wrists up his chest so my fingers could touch his chin. "I love you, too," I slurred as coherently as I could. "And the title of Kisa is yours."

He growled, tightening his hold as a sheen fell over his eyes.

"But," I continued with a mock sternness, "I have a condition of my own."

His irises narrowed, and my favorite grin spread across his lips. "Oh yeah? I can't wait to hear this."

"You have to officially deem me alpha bitch of your new crime fighting unit and agree to be my slave. I'll take your advanced years into consideration, don't worry."

He threw his head back and laughed. "Uh, I think this is going to take some heavy negotiating."

"Yes," Reggie bitched, "preferably in a room with a locked door so I don't have to witness it."

Grabbing Jack's hand, I kept my shoulder pressed against his chest as I turned to face the rest of the crew. "What do you say? Freedom and the ability to do what we do best without having to look over our shoulders anymore?"

"And a lower paycheck," Reggie grumbled, then straightened. "Hey, Deputy Director. We *do* get paid for putting our asses on the line, right?"

Aiden raised a blond eyebrow (he had perfected when to break that puppy out). "Yes. You will be compensated. Not in the millions as you've received in the past, but you'll be given a fair wage. It'll be spelled out in the agreement."

Uncle Liam winced as he shifted his heavily beaten body and peered at me. With that look, I saw his answer in his eyes.

"Then..." I turned to Jack. "I guess you've got yourself a fancy promotion and a bunch of misfits for employees. Congrats."

He picked me up and twirled me around as he whooped. Setting me down, he murmured against my ear. "From the first moment I saw you under that streetlamp in Portland, you stole my heart. I pray you never give it back."

I bumped his cheek in my bid to whisper, "I like to think of it as an exchange, since you've captured my heart completely."

"I love the sound of that." A devilish light twinkled in his eyes, and he grinned. "Now about that fantasy involving these cuffs..."

Newsletter and Thank You

Want a free short story? How about a chance to win a $10 digital gift certificate each month? It's easy! Click on Newsletter, add your information, and subscribe! It's that simple. For the Short Story, you'll receive a link from BookFunnel to download the story about the SBG Series's Delta Squad's final test before they became active duty. You don't want to miss it!

THANK YOU FOR READING!!

If you enjoyed *Stealing His Heart*, would you consider leaving a review?

Maybe tell your friends to take a chance on me?

It'd make my day and help other readers find my books drowning in those crazy algorithms

Also by P. A. DePaul

About the author

P. A. DePaul is a Publishers Weekly Bestselling and award-winning author.

Her books are full of action, suspense, and romance.

As a hybrid author, she has books published traditionally and independently. Her traditional publishers include Berkley, a Penguin Random House imprint, and Harlequin Books.

She loves connecting with readers! You can find her on these social media and book sites:

Website, Facebook, Instagram, TikTok, GoodReads, Amazon, BookBub, YouTube.